EDGARTOWN
Free Public Library

THE REFLECTIONS and histories of men and women throughout the world are contained in books. . . . America's greatness is not only recorded in books, but it is also dependent upon each and every citizen being able to utilize public libraries.
— Terence Cooke

Presented by

26 West Tisbury Road
Edgartown, Mass. 02539

D1600639

Anneliese's House

Women and Gender in German Studies

Elisabeth Krimmer, Series Editor
(*University of California, Davis*)

Anneliese's House

A TRANSLATION OF LOU ANDREAS-SALOMÉ'S 1921 NOVEL *DAS HAUS: FAMILIENGESCHICHTE VOM ENDE VORIGEN JAHRHUNDERTS*

TRANSLATED BY FRANK BECK AND RALEIGH WHITINGER

 CAMDEN HOUSE

Rochester, New York

First published 2021 by Camden House

Camden House is an imprint of Boydell & Brewer Inc.
668 Mt. Hope Avenue, Rochester, NY 14620, USA
and of Boydell & Brewer Limited
PO Box 9, Woodbridge, Suffolk IP12 3DF, UK
www.boydellandbrewer.com

Originally published as *Das Haus: Familiengeschichte vom
Ende vorigen Jahrhunderts* (Ullstein: Berlin, 1921)

Cover: *Lady in an Interior*. Oil on canvas, 1924 (detail), by Sergei Arsenevich
Vinogradov (1869–1938). Private collection; photograph courtesy of Sotheby's.

ISBN-13: 978-1-64014-101-8

Library of Congress Cataloging-in-Publication Data

Names: Andreas-Salomé, Lou, 1861–1937, author. | Beck, Frank, 1949– translator. |
    Whitinger, Raleigh, 1944– translator.
Title: Anneliese's house : a translation of Lou Andreas-Salomé's 1921 novel Das Haus:
    Familiengeschichte vom Ende vorigen Jahrhunderts / Lou Andreas-Salomé ;
    translated by Frank Beck and Raleigh Whitinger.
Other titles: Haus. English
Description: Rochester, New York : Camden House, 2021. | Series: Women
    and Gender in German Studies | "Originally published as Das Haus:
    Familiengeschichte vom Ende vorigen Jahrhunderts (Ullstein: Berlin, 1921)" |
    Includes bibliographical references.
Identifiers: LCCN 2020055168 | ISBN 9781640141018 (hardback ; acid-free paper)
Classification: LCC PT2601.N4 H3813 2021 | DDC 833/.8--dc23
LC record available at https://lccn.loc.gov/2020055168

This publication is printed on acid-free paper.
Printed in the United States of America.

*In memory of our friend and colleague
Gisela Brinker-Gabler,
who inspired and guided so many in discovering
Lou Andreas-Salomé*

CONTENTS

INTRODUCTION

Lou Andreas-Salomé rose to prominence in the German-speaking world as a novelist and critic in the decades preceding the First World War. In 1882, at the age of twenty-one, she befriended Friedrich Nietzsche, whose ideas helped inspire her first novel, published in 1885, and in 1894 she wrote the first psychological study of his writings. In 1897 she entered into a close relationship with Rainer Maria Rilke, which, despite a break of several years, continued until the poet's death in 1926. After turning to the study of psychotherapy with Sigmund Freud in 1912, Andreas-Salomé would come to be called "the world's first female psychoanalyst" (Popova).

In each case, Andreas-Salomé met these men before they were widely known and admired. Nietzsche had yet to author his *Also sprach Zarathustra* (Thus Spoke Zarathustra) when they first interacted, and he later commented that he could not have written the work if he had never known her. Rilke was a twenty-one-year-old art student— still with the first name René—when they met, and he would later acknowledge her influence on his ensuing works. She began her studies with Freud only a decade after he had published his ground-breaking book on the interpretation of dreams, drawn to his new ideas by the interest in psychology so evident in her own previously published fiction and criticism.

Nonetheless, critics in the decades after her death tended to view Andreas-Salomé as a mere adjunct to the lives of her illustrious friends, ignoring or even disparaging her own intellectual and literary achievements. Even in the critical discourse, she was often rendered an object of fascinated male desire, whether muse or seductive femme fatale, or deprecated as a dilettantish disciple exploiting those luminary mentors.[1]

In the 1980s, scholarship began to focus on the scope and independent merit of Andreas-Salomé's extensive writings. This first English translation of the last and arguably the most mature of her novels aims to contribute to this ongoing reassessment of the author beyond the German-speaking world, as a writer and thinker whose skillfully crafted and compelling narrative texts made significant literary contributions to modern feminism and to the principles of women's emancipation. The author seems to have written most of the novel in 1904, although it was not published until 1921. Her ability both to explore characters' psychology and to consider social questions of her day shows a kinship with contemporary works across several European languages, including Thomas Mann's *Buddenbrooks* (1901), Anton Chekhov's *The Cherry Orchard* (1904), Edith Wharton's *The House of Mirth* (1905), Romain Rolland's *Jean Christophe* (1904–5), and E. M. Forster's *Howards End* (1910).

Anneliese's House offers general and academic readers alike a presciently modern portrayal of the family and social tensions born of the early stirrings of feminist sensibilities in a still-patriarchal age. (The book's German title and subtitle can be translated as "The House: A Family Story from the End of the Nineteenth Century.") Providing English speakers access to the novel also affords a broader view of the development of Andreas-Salomé's skill in recasting, in poetically adroit narrative form, her own struggle for social and intellectual independence. Her fiction gave a broad audience of her day a range of perspectives on the potential of—and the problems with—women's moves towards autonomy both within the institution of marriage and in the world beyond it.

Biographical Sketch

Louise von Salomé was born on February 12, 1861, in the shadow of St. Petersburg's Winter Palace. Her father was a military advisor to Tsar Alexander II, and Louise grew up in the majestic General Staff Building

---

1   See esp. Kreide, 3–6.

on Palace Square. In summer, her family lived at a leafy country estate in Peterhof, near the Gulf of Finland.

Louise and her family were part of the large German-speaking community in the city that was then Russia's capital. Her father, Gustav Ludwig von Salomé, was born in the Russian Empire's Baltic states. Of French-Huguenot heritage, he came to St. Petersburg as a young boy and had a decorated career in the Russian army.[2] His ancestors can be traced, Stéphane Michaud has shown, to the Huguenot enclave in Magdeburg, in eastern Germany, in the late seventeenth century and, before that, to Provence in the south of France.[3] Louise's mother, Louise Wilm, was born in St. Petersburg, of German and Danish lineage. The young Louise was the last of the couple's six children, four of whom grew to adulthood, and the only girl.

Three languages were spoken in the Salomé household: German, French, and Russian. German was Louise's main language, but she soon acquired a Russian nickname, "Lyolya."[4] She was an imaginative girl, who each night shared her thoughts with God, but respected his omniscience by beginning with "As you know. . . ."[5] Her favorite pastime was

---

2   Andreas-Salomé in her memoirs says only that her father was of "Baltic origin"; his place of birth is unknown. However, she remembered hearing stories, as a child, about the Huguenot enclaves in Matau and Windau, two cities in Courland, one of the three Baltic governorates of the Russian Empire and now part of Latvia. See *Looking Back: Memoirs*, 33. In her memoirs, Andreas-Salomé states that her father was a general. Pechota points out that this title was conferred on Gustav Salomé for his work as a civil servant, not for his military efforts. She twice counters tendencies to take the author at her word on this point — for example by Wiesner-Bangard and Welsch, in their 2008 *Lou Andreas-Salomé: Eine Biographie*, 14–15, and by Schmidt (ed.). She does so, first, in her review of Wieder's 2011 monograph and then in her 2020 article "Lou Andreas-Salomé: Pionierin der Moderne" (48n5). Pechota cites the documents found by Michaud in the Russian national archives (in his *Lou Andreas-Salomé: L'alliée de la vie*, 42n1). She speculates that Andreas-Salomé's statements may have been motivated by the fact that, with the Nazi takeover in Germany, she was in a life-threatening situation, due to her association with Freud; Pechota implies that Andreas-Salomé thought her status as the daughter of a former Russian general might provide her some protection.

3   Stéphane Michaud, *Lou Andreas-Salomé: L'alliée de la vie*, 34–40.

4   Andreas-Salomé, *Looking Back*, 14.

5   Andreas-Salomé, *Looking Back*, 4.

observing people in the street and imagining them at other times in their lives—good training for a fiction writer.[6]

Louise attended an English primary school, and then the *Petrischule*, the Lutheran academy established in St. Petersburg in 1709. At seventeen she turned away from that congregation's conservative pastor and secretly began taking private instruction in philosophy, theology, and literature from the Dutch pastor Hendrik Gillot. He introduced her to the work of Baruch Spinoza (1632–77), the Dutch philosopher whose belief in the unity of God, humankind, and nature would remain important to Louise throughout her life.[7] She had long since lost faith in a personal god, but, as she wrote in her memoirs, that loss led to "a darkly awakening but pervasive, fundamental, and ineradicable *sensation of a community of fate, shared beyond measure, with everything that is*."[8]

This idyll of camaraderie and discovery was shattered by two events: the death of Louise's father in 1879, at the age of seventy-four, just as she turned eighteen, and Gillot's declaration that he planned to leave his wife and teenaged children and marry her. She refused his proposal but remained friends with him; she even convinced him to preside over her confirmation, which she needed to qualify for a Russian passport. At the ceremony, Gillot rechristened her "Lou von Salomé"—the name he called her by, because he had trouble pronouncing "Lyolya."

In the fall of 1880, Lou and her mother traveled to Zürich, where she began attending classes at one of the few universities that then accepted female students. She threw herself headlong into her studies—logic, metaphysics, and the history of religion. But by the end of the first year, overwork had taken its toll. She seemed seriously ill, so in January 1882 Lou and her mother traveled to Rome, hoping warmer weather would help. She carried a letter of introduction from one of her professors, addressed to Malwida von Meysenbug, the German feminist whose literary salon near the Colosseum was a gathering place for free-thinking German-speaking expatriates.

---

6 Andreas-Salomé, *Looking Back*, 6–7.

7 In her *Image in Outline: Reading Lou Andreas-Salomé*, Brinker-Gabler makes frequent note of Andreas-Salomé's enduring interest in Spinoza, and in one section (43–46) she outlines ideas of Spinoza that can be seen to have influenced "Der Mensch als Weib." For an insightful introduction to Spinoza's thought, see Nadler.

8 Andreas-Salomé, *Lebensrückblick*, 24; emphasis in the original; trans. by the authors.

At Meysenbug's home, Lou met Paul Rée, a young writer and scholar. Through him, she made the acquaintance of Friedrich Nietzsche, already the author of *The Birth of Tragedy; Untimely Meditations; Human, All Too Human; Daybreak*; and *The Gay Science*. His study of Greek theater would one day become highly influential, those other titles would also be widely read, and Nietzsche would go on to revolutionize modern philosophy. At the time, however, he was a relatively obscure thirty-seven-year-old professor of philology who had left his post because of poor health.

Rée and Nietzsche were both charmed by this attractive young woman with a brilliant mind, and each proposed to Lou, but she had a different idea. She thought the three of them should live together, as a platonic trinity of scholars: "A simple dream first convinced me of the feasibility of my plan, which flew directly in the face of all social conventions. In it I saw a pleasant study filled with books and flowers, flanked by two bedrooms, and us walking back and forth between them, colleagues, working together in a joyful and earnest bond."[9]

Lou thought the only obstacle to her "simple dream" was her mother. At a Wilm family reunion in Hamburg that spring, she and Lou's brother Yevgeny insisted Lou return home with them to St. Petersburg. Tempers flared, but eventually they agreed that Lou would spend part of that summer at Rée's family's home in Türtz, West Prussia (now Tuczno, Poland), with Rée's mother as chaperone, and then several weeks in Tautenburg, in the Thüringen hills, with Nietzsche and his sister Elisabeth. Between the two visits, Lou would attend the premiere of Richard Wagner's opera *Parsifal* at Bayreuth with Malwida von Meysenbug, who was a friend of the Wagners.

The weeks in Türtz with Rée were mainly a chance to relax, and the Bayreuth Festival was a whirlwind of opera and parties. But Lou's three weeks at Tautenburg were a total immersion in Nietzsche's life, ideas, and writings, which we know from the diary Lou kept during her visit. She and Nietzsche had lost the Protestant faith they were raised in, and both were struggling to find new answers to essential questions—why did the two of them, man and woman, seem to have both masculine and feminine traits? in a life without gods, what should they revere? why do people sometimes desire

---

9   Andreas-Salomé, *Looking Back*, 45.

self-destruction? They were so candid, Lou later wrote, that sometimes it was hard to look each another in the face.[10]

They also talked about books: those they had read and the ones they hoped to write. Nietzsche drafted a list of ten principles of good writing for Lou, which she included in her study of his writings. The list begins: "The first thing that it must do is to live: a style must live." Another principle explained what Nietzsche meant by prose that "lives": "Your style should prove that you believe in your thoughts, and not only think them, but feel them."[11] When her stay was over, Lou and Nietzsche agreed to meet again, along with Rée, in Leipzig that October. In Leipzig, however, jealous feelings between the two men put them all on edge, as Lou feared they would—a thought expressed in an aphorism she had composed in Tautenburg: "Two friends are most easily separated by a third."[12] Lou and Rée departed for Berlin in early November, and neither of them would ever see Nietzsche again.

That autumn Lou and Rée set up their own philosophical salon in a boarding house in Berlin, with participants that included Danish literary critic Georg Brandes, Sanskrit scholar Paul Deussen, and Ferdinand Tönnies, one of the founders of German sociology. Lou soon started work on her first novel, *Im Kampf um Gott* (In the Fight for God), drawing on her Tautenburg diary and on ideas from her youthful poetry. Published in 1884 under the pseudonym "Henri Lou," the story centers on a man named Kuno, whose life brings him into relationships with three women, each of whom he unintentionally destroys through various twists of fate.

The title refers, as Angela Livingstone writes, to "the struggle to find out what to do with overwhelming, onward-driving emotions which once . . . were directed to 'God' but which lost that object when intellect developed."[13] The seams in the book's construction are obvious—not surprising in the work of a twenty-three-year-old author—but "there is something stupendous and elemental about it," says Rudolph Binion, one of Lou's biographers. "Even the most awkward contrivances of plot

10   Mandel, lxi.
11   Andreas-Salomé, *Friedrich Nietzsche in seinen Werken*, 126; quotation translated by the authors.
12   Quoted by Binion, 91.
13   Livingstone, 205.

... have a naïve authenticity to them."[14] Contemporary critics agreed that the book was something unusual, and it sold well. The book's success must have been hard on Paul Rée. He had failed in his second attempt at an examination to become a university lecturer, and in mid-1885 he and Lou separated, thinking the situation would be temporary. He went to Munich to study medicine.

The following year, Friedrich Carl Andreas began tutoring several Turkish army officers who lived in Lou's boarding house.[15] He was fifteen years older than Lou and nearly as extraordinary. Born in the Dutch East Indies, of German, Armenian, and Malaysian heritage, he had been educated in Germany, earned a doctorate in Middle Persian from the Friedrich-Alexander University at Erlangen, fought in the Franco-Prussian War, and then did four years of postgraduate work, to learn Old Persian. In 1876 he accompanied a Prussian expedition to Persia and stayed there for six years, supporting himself in a variety of jobs. He knew Latin and Greek, several dialects of Persian, and nearly a dozen other modern languages, and he was widely read in the literature and history of many of those.[16]

Andreas introduced himself to Lou, and there was a swift and powerful mutual attraction. He proposed to her, and she accepted, feeling, as she wrote in her diary, that they already belonged "... in each other (not only to each other), and this in an almost religious, or at least in a purely ideal, sense of the word."[17] She did, however, have two requirements: their marriage would not be consummated, and she would continue her friendship with Paul Rée. She believed that a married woman was subordinate to her husband and that erotic love could exist only between equals. Andreas agreed to both stipulations.

When Lou explained the situation to Rée, he was shattered. She offered him assurances but did not explain that her relationship with Andreas would be platonic. Rée returned to Munich, leaving behind a note that read, "Have mercy; don't look for me."[18] With that, the central friendship in Lou's life was over. She was still thinking regretfully

---

14   Binion, 125.

15   Wiesner-Bangard and Welsch, *Lou Andreas-Salomé: "Wie ich Dich liebe, Rätselleben,"* 85.

16   Binion, 134 and 562.

17   Andreas-Salomé, *Looking Back*, 213.

18   Andreas-Salomé, *Looking Back*, 55.

about the break with Rée when she wrote an epilogue to her memoirs in 1933; she had omitted the crucial fact about her impending marriage, she said, for her husband's sake.[19]

Lou had one more request for Andreas: she wanted Gillot to officiate at their wedding, so she and Andreas traveled to the Netherlands and were married by him there in June 1887. For the next fifteen years the couple lived in the suburbs of Berlin—first Tempelhof and then Schmargendorf. There Lou began writing seriously again: two of her early pieces, which appeared in Germany's leading newspaper, the *Vossische Zeitung*, were about women novelists who, like her, had published under a male pseudonym: Aloisia Kirschner (Ossip Schubin) and Emilie Mataja (Emil Marriot).[20]

Soon Lou had a more ambitious work in mind: a study of the Norwegian playwright whose popularity in both Europe and North America was near its peak. Her interest in Henrik Ibsen sheds light on her thinking at this time: it makes the terms of her marriage with Andreas more understandable and anticipates problems—and feminist concerns—addressed in her ensuing literary works. A diary entry by the dramatist reveals his unflinching verdict on patriarchal society; in 1878 he writes: "A woman cannot be herself in contemporary society; it is an exclusively male society with laws drafted by men, and with counsel and judges who judge feminine conduct from the male point of view."[21] In her 1892 *Henrik Ibsens Frauengestalten* (Henrik Ibsen's Female Figures, translated in 1985 as *Ibsen's Heroines*), Lou explored the psychology of six female characters from the plays, comparing each one to a wild duck trapped in an attic and examining how each responds to that imprisonment. Fritz Mauthner, editor of the influential *Berliner Tageblatt* wrote: "It is only right and delightful that it is a woman who has so well understood old Henrik's praise of women."[22]

That year saw a crisis in Lou's life. She and Andreas met Georg Ledebour, a charismatic journalist and social activist, and, for the first time, Lou felt a sexual attraction that she wanted to act on, but she knew it would destroy her marriage, as it then was. Andreas saw what was happening and was furious; he threatened suicide, and Lou

---

19   Andreas-Salomé, *Looking Back*, 124.
20   Binion, 146.
21   Quoted in McFarlane, viii; trans. by McFarlane.
22   Quoted in Livingstone, 90.

at first countered by suggesting a double suicide. Then she vowed not to have any contact with Ledebour for a year; by that time, she had decided not to pursue a relationship with him. Her marriage, however, had changed. From then on, she would live a largely independent life, traveling part of each year, yet always returning to Andreas in Berlin, and, later, in Göttingen, when the couple moved there. As Livingstone has written, "She might have gone away into a splendidly normal marriage, one starting from a shared passion, perhaps producing children . . . She rejected all that out of fidelity to the inexplicable kinship with Andreas, and doubtless also for the sake of an unconventionality which guaranteed her independence."[23]

In 1894 Lou published a second book of criticism: *Friedrich Nietzsche in seinen Werken* (Friedrich Nietzsche in his Works, translated in 1988 as *Nietzsche*). Like her Ibsen book, it was well received and remained highly regarded for many years. Writing in 1955, German philosopher Karl Löwith noted that "in the subsequent fifty years there ha[d] not appeared a more central attempt at a presentation" of Nietzsche's personality.[24] Two decades later, Mazzino Montinari, in his 1975 monograph, translated into German in 1991 as *Friedrich Nietzsche: Eine Einführung* (An Introduction), still sees the intensive exchange of thoughts between "young Lou" and Nietzsche as having produced one of the best books ever written about the philosopher.[25]

Lou then returned to fiction. The following year, she published her novel *Ruth*, which was based on her relationship with Gillot. Some critics have disparaged the novel as barely disguised autobiography, but key elements diverge from their sources: Ruth's teacher Erik and his son Jonas are both in love with her; Erik actually divorces his wife (which Gillot never did); and, most important, there is no indication in the novel that Ruth and Erik will remain friends, as Lou and Gillot managed to do. In any case, *Ruth* has always been the most popular of her books.

In a letter to her friend Emma Folke, Lou admitted that Ruth was an idealized version of herself. "In such a case," she said, "the idealization, in view of the imperfections and randomness of human life, is

---

23   Livingstone, 67.
24   Livingstone, 90.
25   See Montinari, 133, and Pechota, "Lou Andreas-Salomé: Pionierin," 50.

sometimes an artistic requirement."[26] This novel marked a shift to what would become the primary theme of her fiction: the struggle of women to find both autonomy and intimacy within the structure of Europe's patriarchal society. Female readers throughout the German-speaking world saw their own concerns reflected in her work, and many wrote to tell her about their lives or even traveled to Berlin to meet her.

German women, like women in other European nations, were organizing to demand full civil rights. In 1894 Der Bund der deutschen Frauenvereine (The Federation of German Women's Associations) was formed, inspired by women activists in the United States and committed to achieving equal access to education, opportunities in the workplace, and the right to vote. Lou was not formally a part of any women's rights organization, but she had friends who were, and as Livingstone says, "she was often regarded as being connected with it—of value for the feminist cause though not one of its fighters." In fact, Lou believed that women had an instinctual knowledge that made them superior to men. As she wrote in an article entitled "Gedanken über das Liebesproblem" (Thoughts on the Love Problem), in 1900, "Always, in the woman's highest hour, the man is only Mary's carpenter beside a God."[27]

In the 1890s Lou formed her two most important female friendships. The first was with Frieda von Bülow, the African explorer and novelist; they met in Berlin in 1892, and Bülow was Lou's closest friend until her death, at the age of forty-two, in 1909. They corresponded regularly, and Lou's letters to Frieda in her final illness are the most comprehensive account we have of her views on mortality.[28]

Lou met Helene von Klot-Heydenfeldt, who also became a dear friend, in 1897. She and her husband Otto Klingenberg had two children, Reinhold and Gerda, and Lou often stayed with them in Munich and then in Berlin, where the family lived later. She admired Helene for her "wonderful blend of two rare qualities: fortitude in dreaming and fortitude in living,"[29] and through the Klingenbergs she came to experience loving and harmonious family life. Lou's 1917 book *Drei Briefe an*

---

26   Welsch and Pfeiffer, loc. 44, translated by the authors.
27   Livingstone, 133.
28   Andreas-Salomé, *Looking Back*, 188–91.
29   Quoted in Binion, 212.

einen Knaben (translated in 2016 as *Three Letters to a Boy*) is addressed to Reinhold Klingenberg.[30] Another relationship that began during these years was more problematic. In 1895 Lou met Friedrich Pineles, a Viennese physician, through her circle of friends in Munich. They may have become lovers then—they certainly did later. In any case, Pineles asked Lou to divorce Andreas and marry him, something she knew Andreas would never agree to. She also feared being unable to be faithful to Pineles. Instead, she entered into a liaison that lasted over much of the next fourteen years. The relationship was primarily an erotic one, but both Lou and Pineles seemed to accept that, and apparently Andreas did, too.

As Lou's books gained popularity, many periodicals asked her for articles, and she wrote about a broad range of topics: poetry, drama, religion, sexuality, and psychology. Her pieces appeared in *Das Literarische Echo* (The Literary Echo), Germany's most respected literary journal, as well as in *Neue Deutsche Rundschau* (The New German Review), *Die Arbeiterinnen-Zeitung* (The Woman Workers' Newspaper), *Die Zukunft* (The Future) in Austria, and St. Petersburg's *Severny Vestik* (The Northern Messenger). She also wrote for *Cosmopolis*, the London-based journal with features in English, French, German, and Russian. Her articles there appeared alongside contributions by Henry James, George Sand, Theodor Fontane, and Ivan Turgenev.

While Lou was visiting Munich with Frieda von Bülow in May 1897, they met a twenty-one-year-old art history student and poet from Prague, whose name was René Maria Rilke. He had been intrigued by Lou's article "Jesus the Jew" and wanted to show her his poetry.[31] Lou was not impressed by Rilke's youthful verses, which she found too effusive. She thought it might help if he had a more masculine name and suggested "Rainer": just as Gillot had rechristened her, she renamed Rilke. She liked the young man, and he was awestruck by this sophisticated woman, fifteen years older than himself. He pursued her with a mixture of diffidence and determination that she found hard to resist, and she and Rilke began a romance that lasted more than three years.

---

30   Translated by Maike Oergel as *Three Letters to a Young Boy* in Andreas-Salomé, *Sex and Religion: Two Texts of Early Feminist Psychoanalysis*.
31   Prater, 36–37.

The most important experience they had together—for both of them—was extended trips to Russia, in 1899 and 1900, during which they met Tolstoy, the writer Sophia Schill, and the painter Leonid Pasternak and his family. The two travelers made such a powerful impression on Pasternak's ten-year-old son, Boris, that he described them, three decades later, on the opening page of his autobiography. He remembered Rilke's black Tyrolean cape and his German: "Although I knew the language thoroughly, I had never heard it spoken as he spoke it." He thought the tall woman with Rilke was either his mother or his older sister.[32]

After a two-year estrangement following their second Russian sojourn—when Lou thought Rilke had become too dependent on her—the two stayed close until Rilke's death in 1926. He was prone to obsessive fears, and Lou's guidance and support were crucial to his completion of the *Duino Elegies* and *The Sonnets to Orpheus*, his crowning works as a poet. Rilke was vitally important in Lou's life, too, providing something that Pineles could not give her. "If I was your wife for years," she later wrote, addressing herself to Rilke's memory, "it was because you were the first *truly real* person in my life, body and man indivisibly one, unquestionably a fact of life."[33]

The years from 1895 to 1902 were Lou's most productive period as a fiction writer; she wrote two novels: *Aus fremder Seele* (From an Alien Soul) and *Ma: Ein Porträt*; two novellas that appeared as a single volume: *Fenitschka/Eine Ausschweifung* (translated in 1990 as *Fenitschka and Deviations: Two Novellas*); a cycle of ten novellas, *Menschenkinder* (Human Children, translated in 2005 as *The Human Family*), and a collection of short stories, *Im Zwischenland* (In the Country Between). She had developed a greater objectivity as a writer, able to portray characters very different from herself and to employ the language of her stories with greater dexterity and control. That paved the way for her sixth novel, *Das Haus*.

When the estrangement from Rilke began in early 1901, Lou resumed her relationship with Pineles, traveling widely with him and often staying with him and his sister in Vienna. That autumn Lou

---

32   Pasternak, 13.
33   Andreas-Salomé, *Looking Back*, 85; emphasis in the original.

apparently had a pregnancy that ended in a miscarriage.[34] No mention is made of Pineles or the pregnancy in Lou's memoirs, but Ernst Pfeiffer, Lou's closest confidante in later years, told British scholar Angela Livingstone that the loss of the fetus may have been caused by a fall from an apple tree.[35]

Late in 1903 Andreas was appointed to a professorship at the University of Göttingen, and he and Lou moved to a large hillside house overlooking the town, which she dubbed "Loufried," which means "Lou-Peace." The name was a nod to Wagner's home in Bayreuth, "Wahnfried"—a compound of "Wahn" (delusion) and "Fried" (peace); the motto above the door there began, "Hier wo mein Wähnen Frieden fand . . ." (Here where my delusions found peace . . .). Early in the new year Lou was ill for several weeks but remained productive. That May she wrote to Rilke: "During the days of my illness I let slip from me a piece of work, a big, cherished work of which the larger half, 300 pages when printed, had fully developed, and it caused me to walk around week after week in a state of heady bliss. One must have patience."[36] Those words were prophetic. For unknown reasons, Lou would not publish her final novel until 1921. Its original title was "Die Ehe" (Marriage), but as the story grew, it focused on the role of its main character, Anneliese, as

34   Wiesner-Bangard and Welsch, *Lou Andreas-Salomé: "Wie ich Dich liebe, Rätselleben,"* 152.

35   Livingstone, 131. The avid interest of some biographers in Andreas-Salomé's sex life fed speculation on various possible pregnancies. Pechota ("Rilke, Lou und die Danziger Schriftstellerin Johanna Niemann," 41) dispatches as fantasy an early favorite, proposed by Binion (*Frau Lou*, 226–27), of a pregnancy and abortion involving Rilke around 1898. Binion's suggestion of a 1901 miscarriage on vacation in Denmark (305) lacks factual verification and seems deduced from the fact that, in the *Haus* novel, Anneliese's pregnancy first becomes evident when she faints after going swimming (chapter XV, 148; see also Vickers, 145). Ernst Pfeiffer's suggestion that the 1902/3 miscarriage of a child by Pineles resulted from an apple-picking accident, as reported by Livingstone, is taken as fact by Pechota Vuilleumier (111), who sees the *Haus* novel's description of the "apple-cheeked" Lotti's fatal "fall from the swing" (chapter 1, 5) as echoing the fall from a ladder that ended the author's pregnancy. The 2017 biography by Wiesner-Bangard and Welsch (*Lou Andreas-Salomé: "Wie ich Dich liebe, Rätselleben"*) also reports the apple-picking accident (296), possibly with the assurance of Dorothee Pfeiffer.

36   Rilke and Andreas-Salomé, 109.

mother and mother-in-law, as well as on her marriage, so Lou changed the title to *Das Haus*.[37]

Like much of Lou's fiction, the new novel was rooted in her observations of friends and acquaintances: "In 1904," she later wrote, "I made our little house the setting for a story, *Das Haus*, in which—with ages, backgrounds and personal relationships altered—I portrayed only people I knew extremely well, even Rainer in the figure of a young boy with happily married parents; and with his permission I also quoted a letter he had written to me."[38] This continued her usual practice, at least since *Ruth*, which largely reenacts her relationship with Gillot. Other examples include *Fenitschka*, which uses an encounter with playwright Frank Wedekind in Paris in 1894 as a springboard, and "One Night," in the *Menschenkinder* cycle, which is based on an all-night visit to a Vienna hospital by Lou and Pineles in 1896.[39]

In the case of *Das Haus*, the portrayal of Anneliese Branhardt may have drawn in part on the personality of Helene Klingenberg (née Klot-Heydenfeldt), who had both a son and a daughter, as Anneliese does in the novel—this according to information that Ernst Pfeiffer provided to Sabine Streiter for her afterword to the 1987 French edition.[40] However, Cornelia Pechota Vuilleumier makes a convincing case for the author herself as the model for essentials of Anneliese, given her own loss of a child and her mother-muse relationship with an initially sickly young poet. Anneliese's husband, Frank, clearly has several of the physical qualities of Andreas, and perhaps some psychological ones, too. Her friend Renate and her son-in-law Markus have traits in common with Frieda von Bülow and Friedrich Pineles, respectively. And her impulsive daughter, Gitta, may give us a glimpse of Lou's view of herself as a young woman. Scenes from life, as well as personalities, are incorporated: the Branhardts' trip to Skagen, on the northern tip of Denmark, uses details from the summer holiday Lou and Andreas enjoyed there in the summer of 1901.

---

37 Pechota Vuilleumier, 92. Exactly when Andreas-Salomé changed the title from "Die Ehe" to "Das Haus" is not known. Binion's undocumented claim that all essential elements of the novel's plot were in place by the end of 1904 (326) would suggest that the change occurred during that time.

38 Andreas-Salomé, *Looking Back*, 108.

39 Binion, 212.

40 Streiter, "Postface" in Andreas-Salomé, *La Maison*, 242.

The years from 1905 to 1911 were a time of transition for Lou. In 1905 their Göttingen housekeeper, Marie Stephan, gave birth to a daughter, also named Marie (referred to by the diminutive "Mariechen"), and it soon became apparent that Andreas was the child's father. Lou accepted Marie, but she began to spend more time in Berlin, where she became active in Max Reinhardt's German Theater company. She helped launch the German premiere of Frank Wedekind's *Spring's Awakening* (1906), which for years had been banned by the censors. And Lou was still writing about the stage. In *Die Schaubühne* (The Theater) in 1908, she observed that theater is "poetry that becomes life," in the sense that it offers the illusion of a new existence.[41]

Lou continued to travel with Pineles nearly every year, including a long trip to Turkey and the Balkans in 1908, but she was questioning that relationship. Those doubts may have prompted her to begin work on her first extended psychological study, *Die Erotik*, published in 1910. She asked fundamental questions with broad implications: how do feminine and masculine sexuality differ? why do both sexes feel an impulse towards infidelity? why do lovers idealize each other—and how does that connect sexuality with religious and social values?

Psychology was hardly a new area for Lou—as Cornelia Pechota notes, she brought considerable "intellectual capital," evident in her earlier writings, to this new book and to her later study of psychoanalysis.[42] A review of her Ibsen study nearly three decades earlier had run under the headline, "Six Chapters of Psychology, According to Ibsen."[43] Her book on Nietzsche looked for the sources of his philosophical ideas in his personality. And, beginning with *Ruth*, Lou's fiction had carefully probed the inner lives of her characters. In the summer of 1910, while in Sweden visiting her friend, the writer and social reformer Ellen Key, she met the psychotherapist Poul Bjerre, who invited her to accompany him to the psychoanalytic conference in Weimar that September. There Bjerre introduced Lou to Sigmund Freud, who had already published *The Interpretation of Dreams* (1899) and was gaining a wider reputation.

---

41   Quoted in Mons, loc. 1254 of 6429, translated by the authors.

42   Pechota, "Kunst als Therapie in Lou Andreas-Salomés Roman 'Das Haus,'" 75.

43   Wiesner-Bangard and Welsch, *Lou Andreas-Salomé: "Wie ich Dich liebe, Rätselleben,"* 94.

In 1912 Lou asked to join Freud's Wednesday evening discussions in Vienna, and she participated in his inner circle from October 1912 to April 1913, learning the new methods of psychoanalysis directly from Freud and other analysts who were employing them.[44] She soon began her own psychoanalytic practice in Göttingen and wrote articles for the psychoanalytic journal *Imago*. In time, she became close friends with both Freud and his daughter Anna.

The following year, life in Europe was upended by the First World War. By November 1914 it was clear that an unprecedented human catastrophe was underway. "I cannot think of any personal fate," Lou wrote to Freud that month, "which could have cost me anything like such anguish. And I don't really believe that after this we shall ever be able to be really happy again."[45] Freud agreed: "It is too hideous. And the saddest thing about it is that it is exactly the way we should have expected people to behave, from our knowledge of psychoanalysis."[46] At the war's end, there was a pressing need for mental health specialists to treat the traumatized survivors. Freud recommended Lou for an assignment at a mental hospital in Königsberg, and she spent six months there analyzing both patients and doctors, one of whom gave H. F. Peters a detailed account of Lou's methods as an analyst.[47]

Two months after the war was over, Lou wrote to Rilke: "All these months you have been so intensely present to me, and in the way you always are: especially as regards my writing, which during the last three years has suddenly become, along with my professional work, as important to me as it was in my early youth. And then came a wish: from among the books (eight by now) that are kept in a safe-deposit box, to send you the one that rightly belongs to you: *Rodinka*, many pages long, admittedly, but at least neatly typewritten."[48] (*Rodinka* is Andreas-Salomé's only novel set entirely in Russia, which might explain why she felt it "belonged" to Rilke.) Another of the works in the bank vault was *Das Haus*. Binion claims, on the basis of entries in Lou's unpublished

---

44 See Andreas-Salomé, *The Freud Journal of Lou Andreas-Salomé*, trans. Stanley A. Leavy.

45 Freud and Andreas-Salomé, 20.

46 Freud and Andreas-Salomé, 21.

47 Peters, 283–84.

48 Rilke and Andreas-Salomé, 285; these were typescripts, or perhaps in some cases, manuscripts.

diaries, that she did further work on the novel after 1904. She apparently returned to it during the summer of 1910[49] and then again in the spring of 1917, when, Binion says, she "put a final storybook luster upon her snug dream house of 1904, in which she felt as fantastically at home as ever."[50] Whether that is a partial quotation, which seems likely, or a paraphrase, Binion fails to say. But how extensive were those revisions? Lou's experience as a psychoanalyst may have sharpened the psychological insights in her 1904 draft, but no draft of the novel has surfaced to prove that. It is also possible that the insights in the published work were there before she studied with Freud, a further development of the astute understanding of hidden desires and motivations seen in her earlier fiction.[51]

The next reference to *Das Haus* comes in a letter to Freud: "I have nothing against the publication of essays, etc. on matters which mean much to me, but I shrink from publishing books which are the product of my imagination . . . and which only the most sordid offer of Mammon is strong enough to conquer."[52] But Mammon's offer would soon be welcome. Germany had borrowed heavily during the war, and the peace brought a sharp drop in the value of the Deutsche Mark, leading to steep inflation. In June 1920, Lou told Freud that she and Andreas could not attend the psychoanalytical conference in the Netherlands that fall because the trip would be too expensive.[53] Five months later, Lou wrote to Ellen Key: "Mammon (though it hardly fetches much these days) is tearing [the eight books in the bank vault] from me after years of quiet hoarding."[54] *Das Haus* was published by Ullstein in 1921.[55]

That same year, Lou published her best-known psychoanalytic article, "Narzissmus als Doppelrichtung" (Narcissism as Double-Direction, translated in 1962 as "The Dual Orientation of Narcissism"), which reinterprets the self-love that Freud saw as regression, if it occurred after infancy. In Lou's view, the self thrives by loving itself, but not itself in isolation—as though Narcissus had become enraptured not just by

49   Binion, *Frau Lou*, 328.
50   Binion, *Frau Lou*, 414.
51   See Erhart, 314n194, and Pechota Vuilleumier, 93.
52   Freud and Andreas-Salomé, 94–95.
53   Freud and Andreas-Salomé, 101.
54   Quoted in Binion, 439.
55   The recurring references, in many critical analyses and biographical sketches, to the publication date 1919 appear to have no basis in fact.

the reflection of his face in the forest pool but by himself in union with the boundless world around him. This experience can restore the feeling of delight and security that we experienced in our mother's womb. As Livingstone expresses it, "We spend our lives actually, elaborately, and admirably remaking that reality."[56]

In 1921 Lou also published her only collection of tales for children, *Die Stunde ohne Gott und andere Kindergeschichten* (The Hour without God and other Children's Stories). The following year, she published a verse play, *Der Teufel und seine Großmutter* (translated in 2016 as *The Devil and His Grandmother*) which had been written in 1913 for Rilke's eleven-year-old daughter, Ruth. Her most experimental work, it draws equally on German classicism and twentieth-century expressionism.[57] And in 1923 *Rodinka*, filled with memories of her Russian childhood, finally appeared in print.

In mid-December 1926, Lou received news that Rilke was gravely ill in France. She began writing him daily letters, all but one of which have been lost, and she received a last letter from him before hearing that he had died on December 27, at the age of fifty-one. In an intimate record of his life and work published in 1928,[58] Lou praised Rilke for grappling with his demons and producing great poetry from that struggle, but she wondered whether his mysticism had, in the end, lost its grounding in human life.

Lou spent six weeks in the hospital in the autumn of 1929, being treated for diabetes. Although Andreas was now eighty-three, he came every afternoon to visit her. "Sitting across from one another," Lou wrote, "was something completely new to us. . . . Each time we saw one another again, it was like a reunion of two people who had returned home from a great distance. . . . When I finally returned home, the 'visiting hours' simply continued."[59] They lived harmoniously together for the year that was left to them; Andreas died in October 1930.

In her final years, Lou was cared for by Andreas's daughter, Mariechen, and her husband, Robert Apel. Confined to the house and

---

56   Livingstone, 188. Pechota ("Lou Andreas-Salomé: Pionierin," 61–63) offers a lucid account of Andreas-Salomé's revisionist view on narcissism.

57   Livingstone, 216.

58   Translated by Angela von der Lippe as *You Alone are Real to Me: Remembering Rainer Maria Rilke*.

59   Andreas-Salomé, *Looking Back*, 129.

garden, she befriended Ernst Pfeiffer and Josef König, local scholars who visited her often and read to her as her eyesight failed. In 1931, she began work on one last book, which she called a "sketch" (*Grundriss*) of memories of her life and work. Pfeiffer reviewed the manuscript with her over a period of several years, and Lou eventually added details about her relationships with Andreas, Rilke, and Freud that she had initially omitted. Mariechen told Binion that "she must have rewritten each chapter twenty times."[60]

After surgery for breast cancer in 1935, Lou was in declining health for many months, suffering from heart disease and diabetes, but was still visited regularly by Pfeiffer and König and was in touch with Anna Freud by mail. She died on February 5, 1937, a week before her seventy-sixth birthday. She had asked that her ashes be scattered in her garden, but German law would not allow that. Her ashes were interred in her husband's grave at the Göttingen city cemetery, with no record of her name and dates underneath his on the headstone. Instead, there were just three letters: "Lou."[61]

Because of her association with Freud, the Nazi authorities immediately confiscated Lou's library, and her memoirs could not be published during the Hitler regime, but Pfeiffer guided the book through its first publication in 1951, under the title *Lebensrückblick* (Life Review). Twenty years later Pfeiffer supervised a second edition, based on a newly discovered manuscript with Lou's numerous emendations; that was the basis for Breon Mitchell's 1991 English translation, entitled *Looking Back: Memoirs*. Pfeiffer also edited the diary Lou kept during her studies with Freud, *In der Schule bei Freud* (In School with Freud, translated in 1964 as *The Freud Journal of Lou Andreas-Salomé*), collections of her correspondence with Rilke and with Sigmund Freud, and, in 1982, a final volume of diary entries from 1934–36, as *Eintragungen: Letzte Jahre* (Entries: The Last Years). Lou's letters to and from Anna Freud, transcribed by Pfeiffer's daughter Dorothee and edited by Daria A. Rothe and Inge Weber, were published as "*. . . als käm ich heim zu Vater und Schwester*" *Lou Andreas-Salomé—Anna Freud, Briefwechsel 1919–1937* (. . . As though coming home to father and sister). Lou left her beloved house, "Loufried," to Mariechen and her husband, but it

---

60 Quoted in Binion, 465, note o.
61 Mons, loc. 4601 of 6429, Kindle.

was expensive to maintain, and in 1974 their heirs had to sell, despite public appeals to save it. An apartment house now stands on the spot.

Readers today know Andreas-Salomé primarily through her letters. Those who love Rilke's poetry find an intimate record of their relationship, from his first infatuated love letter, written the day after they met in Munich, to his final words—in Russian—dispatched from his deathbed in 1926: "Farewell, my dear."[62] Those interested in Freud can discover his paternal side in his letters to and from Lou and her own maternal side in her correspondence with Anna, which in the German edition runs to more than 900 pages.

In three different ways, Andreas-Salomé was extraordinarily fortunate. Unlike many writers, she always had a relatively secure income, first from her family and Rée's, then from her writing. Again and again she encountered people with great minds who were at pivotal points in their own development: Nietzsche on the threshold of his most radical works—he suggested that only knowing Lou made it possible for him to write *Also sprach Zarathustra*;[63] Rilke when he was about to find his voice as a poet; Freud just as his theory and practice of psychoanalysis were maturing. And, finally, those people were able to help her when their assistance was most needed: Nietzsche's advice on style, as she was starting out as a writer; her husband's skills in the Danish language when she wanted to write about Ibsen; Rilke's love when she was finally willing to engage in a romantic relationship; Freud's guidance when she decided to become a psychoanalyst.

Perhaps equally remarkable is that Lou encountered each of these illustrious friends and confidantes on her own terms, never allowing herself to be dominated by them, seemingly confident of her direction and able to pursue her own lines of original thought and creativity. Because of that, her fiction and her criticism still offer fruitful avenues for intellectual, emotional, and spiritual exploration.

Of all the tributes Lou received during her lifetime, one she must have especially cherished came from Freud, who wrote, after nearly two decades of friendship: "I am delighted to observe that nothing has altered in our respective ways of approaching a theme, whatever it may be. I strike up a—mostly very simple—melody; you supply the higher

---

62 Rilke and Andreas-Salomé, 360.
63 Binion, 102, note p.

octaves for it; I separate the one from the other; and you blend what has been separated into a higher unity."[64]

The Critical Fortunes of Andreas-Salomé and *Das Haus*

The 1921 publication of *Das Haus* by Ullstein was well received. Women critics in particular responded positively, and 1927 brought a successful second edition from the Deutsche Buch-Gemeinschaft (The German Book Community), a nationwide book club. Noted Austrian critic and scholar Christine Touaillon and prominent German novelist Gabriele Reuter both praised the story's empathetic portrayal of complex relationships.

Reuter had joined the ranks of best-selling and critically acclaimed German writers in 1895 with her novel *Aus guter Familie* (*From a Good Family*), a sensationally feminist rallying cry, with its realistic depiction of the suffering of middle-class women under the constraints of the Wilhelmine era.[65] That background might awaken expectations that her response to *Das Haus* would align with Hedwig Dohm's often-cited misgivings about Andreas-Salomé's commitment to feminism, as stated—but then qualified—in her 1899 article "Reaktion in der Frauenbewegung" (Reaction in the Women's Movement), when she says: "I found some sentences in Lou's writings to be hair-raising for an emancipated woman, but then again others that could be taken as the strongest argument for women's emancipation."[66] While Reuter

---

64   Freud and Andreas-Salomé, 185.

65   See Tatlock's introduction to her 1999 translation of Reuter's novel. She notes Hedwig Dohm's reception of that work as "a shocking lament, a crushing indictment" (ix).

66   Dohm, "Reaktion in der Frauenbewegung," 280; translated by the authors. See also Dohm's longer 1902 survey, *Die Antifeministen: Ein Buch der Verteidigung*. Kreide takes the quoted passage from the earlier article as a point of departure for her study, as does David Midgley in his 2007 chapter on Andreas-Salomé, both affirming Andreas-Salomé's inclusion among leading feminists of her day. See also Holmes and Wernz, who argue cogently for the feminist spirit of the earlier, short prose works. Pechota, in her 2020 article on Andreas-Salomé as a "Pionierin der Moderne," captures this trend succinctly when she notes the emancipatory thrust of Andreas-Salomé's Ibsen book and the *Fenitschka* duology; she sees the fictional works in general as refuting the notion that Andreas-Salomé did not care about the pro-feminist struggles of

does note the "almost old-fashioned" tenor of the novel's account of domestic harmony sustained in the face of emancipatory change, she nevertheless accords high praise to the psychological perspicacity and realistic acuity with which the novel treats individual struggles relevant to the feminist cause.[67]

A century later, *Das Haus* has begun to assert its appeal to modern readers and to attract the interest and approval of critics in and beyond the German-speaking world. An anonymous review of the 1997 French translation by Nicole Casanova, appearing in the popular weekly *Télérama*, recommended the work warmly as "superbly written, teeming with essential questions about married life, freedom, and the creative vocation" and declared it "one of those books that we can never really close" (rev. of *La Maison*; translated by the authors). In his 2000 biography of Andreas-Salomé, Michaud sees a compelling relevance to the novel's look back to family tensions in the 1890s. He notes how the Branhardt family "breathes life," as its characters' happiness "mingles with the turbulence of existence" (*Lou Andreas-Salomé*, 280 in the 2017 edition; translated by the authors). By that time, critics writing in various languages were already moving—as the ensuing survey shows—to anticipate Walter Erhart's call for a more extensive critical focus on the overlooked complexities of the novel, which make it a revealing contribution to developments in the literature, psychology, and gender theories of its day. Erhart saw that the novel's superficially apparent kinship with contemporary popular romances was belied by the multiperspectival and complex depiction of family tensions; furthermore, he suggested that the book traced essentials of the author's development from her involvement in the emergence of the

---

her "sisters" (51). Renner offers an enlightening explanation of the ca. 1900 debates on the "nature" and role of women as divided into two main streams (36): one adhering to the principle of "Gleichheit" (equality), the other to the principle of "difference." She sees Andreas-Salomé, with her 1900 essay "Der Mensch als Weib," as a leading voice of the latter, arguing not so much for woman's equal access to political and professional roles but rather for the free and full development of the "weibliches Subjekt" (female subject) as mediatrix of a "last harmony of all things" (41).

67   Reuter praises her colleague's veracity ("Wahrheitsmut") and finds the novel's sophisticated psychological depth "wonderful" (she calls it "eine wundervolle Leistung der nichtalltäglichen Psychologie").

"life philosophy" ("Lebensphilosophie") movement around 1900 to her study of psychoanalysis.[68]

In the intervening years, however, the book's critical fortunes had darkened. Critics and biographers focused less on Andreas-Salomé's work than on her life of dramatic, often sensational—and sensational-ized—relationships with "influential persons" (Livingstone, 10). Even while acknowledging the originality and intellectual acumen of her philosophical, religious, and psychological writings—to which, in any case, those male luminaries themselves richly attested[69]—these accounts tended to ignore or even denigrate her literary works. Much was made of their autobiographical elements, often to the point of a misleading overidentification of the literary works with the biographically based events and figures that they evoke.[70] This fostered a tendency to see them as inferior in quality to the theoretical writings and to assign them peripheral importance as biographical source material.[71] Even Livingstone's affirmative study, by relegating the fiction to an appendix of brief summaries, continues a tendency recurring since the 1960s.

Das Haus fell victim to such negative assessments and was found lacking both in literary merit and decisive pro-feminist thrust.[72] Some critics targeted the novel's language and style as forbiddingly affected and convoluted, or maintained that its characters were flat portrayals

---

68   Erhart, 314. Andreas-Salomé's own colleague and mentor Nietzsche was, with his critique of the restrictive effect of modern culture's rational and scientific biases, a major influence on a subsequent generation of writers and thinkers — for example, Wilhelm Dilthey and Georg Simmel — whose "Lebensphilosophie" likewise turned critically away from academic philosophy's enshrinement of rationality and sci-ence, in favor of an approach that also included the intuitive, creative capacities of hu-man nature. Renner offers a concise account of how the ca. 1900 essays "Grundformen der Kunst" and "Der Mensch als Weib," which resonate with the "Lebensphilosophie" writings, remain a foundation for her later ideas on psychoanalysis. On this devel-opment see also Pechota, "Lou Andreas-Salomé: Pionierin," 61, and Weiershausen; Wieder.

69   As emphasized by Cormican (*Women in the Works*, 1). See also Clauss; Del Caro; Ingram; and Wawrytko.

70   Kreide (6) notes Binion's tendency to see every fictional female figure as a more or less varied "self-portrait" of the author, thus "a truest tissue of falsities big and small" (Binion, 475).

71   Cormican, "Authority and Resistance," 140.

72   Cormican, "Authority and Resistance," 128 and 139–40.

of the real figures on whom they were based.[73] Others lamented what they took to be the narrative's ultimate retreat into a "harmonizing" conclusion and thus found it a dated idealization of an idyllic pre-1900 world.[74] Yet, seen in a different light, these negative views invite critical reflections in the novel's favor. For example, it is noteworthy that Binion, one of Andreas-Salomé's most mordant biographers, found the novel's style exemplary (414nf) and saw it as "more fictional" and thus less autobiographical than her previous novels (316). The latter point recalls how the author's writing process echoed her girlhood game of fantasizing about how individuals whose personality traits she knew well would act in fictional situations.[75]

Regarding the novel's supposedly dubious feminist credentials, born of its account of a bygone, pre-1900 idyll of traditional marriage preserved in the face of disruptive change, two points warrant consideration. First, even the most willfully selective interpretation of Anneliese Branhardt's narrative arc as a retreat into the secure confines of her marriage cannot overlook the fact that her development occurs in a context of other female figures—her daughter and her emancipated friend, Renate—who are shown to resist or to alter similar arrangements. Second, we must ask whether a work's failure to depict a fully realized emancipated female heroine automatically bespeaks a non- or anti-feminist stance on the author's part. It is significant that, even on its title page, the novel announces itself to be a look back on an earlier era. In other words, it might be taken to offer readers then and now a distant yet anticipative mirror of still-relevant problems of marriage, family, and women's status. Tellingly, Andreas-Salomé shows the novel's mother

---

73   Especially Schwarz, in his review of the 1987 re-edition of the novel, as noted by Pechota Vuilleumier, 96.

74   Streiter's afterword to the 1987 republication aligns the novel's conclusion with the "ideal of femininity [as] submissive, subservient, and self-dissolving . . . — an image of woman affirmed by the more conservative elements of the German women's movement" (Cormican, "Authority and Resistance," 129). Michaud's review of Nicole Casanova's 1997 French translation sees the novel as a dated idealization of pre-1900 domesticity upheld in the face of all challenges — whereby he appears to follow the assessment of Streiter, who also provided the afterword to Casanova's masterful translation.

75   This is indicated by a note to Anna Freud's letter to Andreas-Salomé of March 26, 1922 (Andreas-Salomé and Anna Freud, 32), citing a 1917 diary entry by the author ("Tagesnotizen 1917, LAS-Archiv") (Andreas-Salomé and Anna Freud, 695).

and daughter responding to patriarchal expectations with increasing degrees of resistance. Rather than offering readers a pleasing portrait of emancipation triumphantly achieved, the novel invites them to reflect on the complex realities through which such liberating change must—and can—evolve.

Such questions have come to the fore as scholarly discourse turns towards a more affirmative focus on Andreas-Salomé's life and begins to emphasize the merits and originality of her theoretical and literary works. This reevaluation can be seen in the biographies appearing since the 1980s—in English and French as well as German[76]—despite a continuing tendency by some to reduce the literary works to the status of biographical source material. The 1980s saw the contributions by Ute Treder and Biddy Martin. They initiated a body of critical dialogue that continues to the present, with a new critical edition now underway, involving international collaboration and the publication of previously unknown or unavailable texts.[77]

This reassessment of Andreas-Salomé's contributions, literary as well as non-literary, is also attested to—and fostered by—the proliferation

---

76　For example, those by Livingstone, Koepcke, Vickers, Michaud, and Mons.

77　The new critical editions of Andreas-Salomé's works are appearing, under the editorship of Ursula Welsch, in MedienEdition Welsch, in collaboration with the Lou Andreas-Salomé Archive in Göttingen. Of the twenty-seven volumes planned, seventeen have appeared to date: nine literary works and eight others. The edition of *Das Haus* is currently still in progress as volume 21. The eighth and ninth volumes of the sequence of literary works (fifteenth and sixteenth of the collected works), *Der heimliche Weg* (ed. by Edith Hanke) and the *Fenitschka* duology (ed. by Iris Schäfer), provide access to previously inaccessible texts of possible pertinence to the genesis of *Das Haus*. *Der heimliche Weg: Drei Scenen aus einem Ehedrama* was written in 1900/1901 and appeared serially in the journal *Über Land und Meer* but was never made available in book form. The volume of the *Fenitschka* novellas includes "Ein überlebter Traum" (A Dream Outlived, 143–218), an early, but narratively quite different, version of *Eine Ausschweifung* that appeared serially in 1897 in *Westermanns Illustrierte Deutsche Monatshefte: Ein Familienbuch für das gesamte geistige Leben der Gegenwart* (Westerman's Illustrated German Monthly Magazine: A Family's Guide to the Entire Cultural Life of the Present; Holmes analyzes the relationship of the two versions). The French and German collaboration *Lou Andreas-Salomé: Zwischenwege in der Moderne/Sur les chemins de traverse de la modernité* (At the Crossroads of Modernity; edited by Britta Benert and Romana Weiershausen), includes the previously unpublished 1934 essay "Mein Bekenntnis zum heutigen Deutschland" (My Commitment to Today's Germany) with a commentary by Weiershausen (see also Mons, loc. 4442–4555).

of translations of Andreas-Salomé into English, some of them of writings pertinent to an understanding of the novel translated here. Of the non-literary texts available to English readers, many address later works that either demonstrate her post-1911 achievements in psychoanalysis or look back at her interactions with Nietzsche, Freud, and Rilke.[78] Especially significant for the background of the novel translated here are Siegfried Mandel's translations of the 1892 book on Ibsen's female figures and the 1894 monograph on Nietzsche (which appeared in 1985 and 1988, respectively).

Both provide a perspective on the author's status as a respected critic during the 1890s, with the former also offering evidence of her emergence as a literary talent. Two German critics have seen the Ibsen study as a revealing forerunner of the ensuing novellas and novels, above all for its grasp of how a literary work can use images and motifs of space—the iconic image of the wild duck trapped in the attic—to portray women's struggles against the confining nature of conventional notions of marriage and how the apparently welcoming haven of marriage can have a fettering effect on women's self-fulfillment. Birgit Wernz's 1997 monograph on Andreas-Salomé's pro-feminist earlier writings sees the Ibsen essays as a "precursor of her own literary treatment of 'women' and 'love,'" showing how women "subvert or otherwise react to being held captive by love and marriage."[79] While Wernz goes on to focus on the *Fenitschka* duology and the stories in *The Human Family*, Chantal Gahlinger builds a bridge from the trapped women described in the Ibsen monograph (363–68) to a discussion of

---

78 The 1960s saw the translation of Andreas-Salomé's 1921 essay on "The Dual Orientation of Narcissism," her correspondence with Sigmund Freud, and her 1912–13 Freud journals. The decades surrounding the millennium brought Breon Mitchell's translation of the posthumously published *Lebensrückblick* (as *Looking Back: Memoirs* in 1991), the Snow and Winkler translation of the correspondence with Rilke (as *Rilke and Andreas-Salomé: A Love Story in Letters* in 1995), and Angela von der Lippe's 2003 translation of the 1928 Rilke monograph. Two projects of the last decade draw attention to her proto-feminist contributions to modern psychoanalysis, namely the 2012 translation of *Die Erotik* (as *The Erotic* by John Crisp) and the 2016 volume *Sex and Religion: Two Texts of Early Feminist Psychoanalysis*, comprising Maike Oergel's translation of the 1912–17 *Drei Briefe an einen Knaben* (as "Three Letters to a Young Boy"), and Kristine Jennings's translation of the 1922 drama *Der Teufel und seine Großmutter* (as "The Devil and his Grandmother").

79 Mary Rhiel, 353.

the sheltered married life with which Anneliese struggles, highlighting how the illusory impression of happy security in fact masks the prison- or cage-like aspects of her life and thwarts women's progress towards autonomy. She notes that Renate's assessment of her friend's world ("Ah, yes, so delightful, this house here! But still a cage!"; chapter VII, 64) resembles later feminist analyses of women and women writers of that era (370) and cites in particular Gilbert and Gubar's description (85) of how women "were trapped in so many ways in the architecture—both the houses and the institutions—of patriarchy."

Two translations of Andreas-Salomé's earlier fiction reveal the accomplished fiction writer she had become while producing the nov- els and novellas preceding *Das Haus*: Dorothee Einstein Krahn's 1990 translation of the 1898 *Fenitschka* duology and Raleigh Whitinger's 2005 translation of the 1899 ten-novella collection, *The Human Family*. These twelve prose pieces offer a perspective both on recurring basics of plot and theme later developed in the novel and on the subsequent growth in the poetic and narrative skills with which the author treats them. The major female figures in *Anneliese's House* echo and vary the earlier examples of women struggling, with different degrees of success, for self-assertion and fulfillment, while, as Wernz has argued, chal- lenging or even unmasking the male guardians of the orders and ste- reotypes with which they contend. Wernz notes that the shorter prose pieces of the late 1890s do not depict fully realized emancipated female protagonists as counter-images, yet subvert male notions of gender, love, and marriage. She mentions *Das Haus* only briefly, but her per- spective is eminently applicable to that novel, whose female protago- nist, while not breaking through to emancipation, nevertheless func- tions as a vehicle for thoughts and statements critical of conventional patriarchy. Much like Wernz, Deborah Holmes, in her analysis of how the novella *Eine Ausschweifung* emerged from its earlier version, "Ein überlebter Traum," defends the emancipatory thrust of the earlier, short prose works, whose "unexpected storylines" she sees leading to "incon- clusive endings" (615). Yet her view that the two novels focus more on the "'ideal,' self-subordinating woman," might be argued to be only *apparently* applicable to the conclusion of *Das Haus*. There, the figures Renate and Gitta can hardly be seen as "self-subordinating," and the main female protagonist's marriage has changed in the wake of moves towards independence that she has thought and even voiced.

Noteworthy, too, is how the shorter works anticipate the later novel in not portraying female-male relationships as conflicts between stereotypical heroines and villains. Rather, they expose how even sympathetically portrayed men are often trapped in their conventional views or retreat into them in panic. Truly despicable males rarely appear, one notable exception being Dr. Otto Griepenkerl in "Unit for 'Men, Internal.'" The more usual pattern, essential to the *Fenitschka* story and concisely evident with Vitali Saitsev in "A Reunion," is to initially favor the perspective and even good intentions of the male protagonist and then proceed to reveal his hypocrisy or blindness—a development that occurs in a complex manner in the case of the novel's Dr. Frank Branhardt.[80]

Also apparent, in the progress from the earlier fiction to *Das Haus*, is the author's increasingly successful integration of dialogue into the narrative interplay of authorial and figural perspectives. This allows opposing positions to be exposed sympathetically; it also sustains an ironic and even self-ironic awareness of how the narrative constructs of the author and characters are related to the context of the text as whole. These multiple perspectives persistently undermine the conclusion's foreground impression of submissive retreat into the inviting security of patriarchal order.

Since the 1990s, an extensive body of criticism on Andreas-Salomé in English has interacted with the expanding German critical discourse to reestablish the literary merit of her novellas and novels. The span from Biddy Martin's 1991 monograph to Gisela Brinker-Gabler's 2012 study embraces a substantial body of article-length discussions and monograph surveys that offer a variety of perspectives on the originality and acuity of Andreas-Salomé's expression of early modernity's

---

80   Andreas-Salomé's portrayal of the physician figure in *Das Haus* expands complexly on that in her earlier prose works — for example of Dr. Benno Frensdorff in *Eine Ausschweifung*, whom Woodford (in "Female Desire") has compared to the critically portrayed physicians in other works of that period by Hedwig Dohm and Gabriele Reuter. For all his appealing qualities and actions, Frank Branhardt appears in a critical light: for example, with his underlying aversion to "feminist" initiatives; his capacity for moments of misogynist ire; his efforts to urge Anneliese toward another, and very risky, pregnancy; and his blind or blinkered view in the closing chapter of his manly triumph in the marital tensions of the previous summer. That — in any case mixed — image of the physician Frank Branhardt is then significantly complemented by the portrayal of Markus Mandelstein as quite a different type of Herr Doktor.

philosophical and literary ferment—often on themes that inform her last novel. Several such contributions examine her critical writings and psychological studies, often revealing positions on women and feminism relevant to the characterization of the novel's female protagonists.[81] Many more short analyses address specific literary works, most often the two *Fenitschka* stories, thus providing a background for grasping how the later novel carries on those earlier reflections on women's struggle for independence against prevailing social constraints.[82]

In those same years, German criticism took the lead in studies devoted to *Das Haus*, with the sequence of monographs since Leonie Müller-Loreck's 1976 study of Andreas-Salomé's narratives offering substantial analyses of the novel—or tracing developments through the other literary works in ways that foster additional insights. The novel is mentioned relatively briefly in monographs by Wernz (1997) and Katrin Schütz (2008), although Wernz lays a valuable foundation for understanding strategies in Andreas-Salomé's earlier writings that are developed with greater complexity in the portrayal of the Branhardts.[83] *Das Haus* is discussed at length in Heidy Margrit Müller's 1991 study

---

81 Some of these focus on a broader range of her non-literary writing, from the "Lebensphilosophie" era to her work in psychology and psychoanalysis (e.g., Borossa/ Rooney; Wawrytko), while most concentrate on a single area — for example, her interaction with Nietzsche (Babich; Del Caro; Diethe, "Lou Salomé's Interpretation of Nietzsche's Religiosity" and *Nietzsche's Women: Beyond the Whip*; Gane; Ingram), the Ibsen essays (Rainwater van Suntum), the theater reviews (Böttger). Particularly pertinent to the genesis and understanding of *Das Haus* are the studies in English on Andreas-Salomé's writings on women and feminism (Brinker-Gabler, "Renaming the Human"; Markotic, "Andreas-Salomé and the Contemporary Essentialism Debate"; Schwartz) and on the later contributions to psychology and psychoanalysis (Matysik; Markotic, "There Where Primary Narcissism Was"; Rothe; Schultz; Wang).

82 Analyses of one or both of the *Fenitschka* stories are offered by Deiulio; Diethe, *Towards Emancipation*; Doll Allen; Haines; Holmes; Ianozi; Markotic, "Art and Intoxicated Desire"; Midgley; Walker; Weedon; Whitinger, "Lou Andreas-Salomé's *Fenitschka* and the Tradition of the *Bildungsroman*"; and Woodford, "Female Desire." Other literary works have been treated by Bidney (on *Der Teufel und seine Großmutter*); Cormican (*Jutta* and *Das Haus*), Ianozi (*Russland mit Rainer* and *Rodinka*), and Woodford (on *Das Haus*).

83 Similarly, Johanna Wybrands, in her analysis of the mother-daughter relationships in Andreas-Salomé's 1901 novel, *Ma: Ein Porträt*, proposes a reading of the insights and losses bound up with a mother's response to her grown children's move towards independence that might be seen to be echoed and developed in Anneliese's struggle with her own progress and anxieties.

of literary mothers and daughters (esp. 128–35), and a chapter on the book concludes Caroline Kreide's 1996 defense of the author's stance as a pro-feminist (105–18). The novel then figures prominently in Erhart's monograph (esp. 314–25) and in Gahlinger's analysis of women's autonomy in Andreas-Salomé's literary works (361–91). Most recently, it has been accorded a detailed analysis in Pechota Vuilleumier's study of the interplay of *Haus* stories by Rilke and Andreas-Salomé (esp. 78–235), which reveals how the mother-son relationship in the novel draws upon the author's relationship to the poet.[84] The relatively few critical discussions of *Das Haus* in English (notably by Cormican and Woodford) combine with these German studies to move towards a grasp of how the work, for all its foregrounded impressions of the female protagonists' resignation and retreat, nevertheless combines a subtle subversion of the patriarchal order with intimations of historical change and liberation.

Grasping the Novel: Interpretive Trends and Points to Ponder

> *No! No! Not one! Never just one! Even the wisest judgment can become unjust, willful, arrogant, when measured against life. And the worst — you see — the worst thing under the sun — is the violation of one person by another.*

— Anneliese to Frank, chapter XII

Essential to an understanding of the novel's subtly subversive feminism is the recognition of the ironic perspectives that it develops about how idealistic visions—of a liberating social movement, for example, or of the literary narrative's intimations of hope and change—relate to the contradictory and constraining complexities of real life. What might appear, for example, to amount to no more than a fictional retreat into the calm domestic circle of a bygone decade, in fact offers a small-scale, familial mirror of the greater context of the Wilhelmine-era "Frauenbewegung" (Women's Movement) and the ideals of emancipation that the author herself lived and, in other literary and non-literary writings, shared with her feminist colleagues and contemporaries.

---

84   Pechota's 2011 article ("Kunst als Therapie") enlarges on her 2011 monograph as Pechota Vuilleumier.

Likewise, the foreground impression of the narrative arc's reactionary retreat into the patriarchal status quo is belied by the varying signs of independence exemplified by all three of its main female protagonists. That vision of emerging change itself is subject to the narrative's ironic awareness of its status as an artistic refashioning of a reality of conflict and constraint, in order to offer appealing intimations of order, sense, and evolution.

The novel's low-key, slowly evolving feminism contrasts sharply, after all, with the more aggressive feminist discourse prominent in Andreas-Salomé's times and among her friends and colleagues, as well as with the unorthodox moves towards autonomy in the author's own life, themselves so often the stuff of creative fiction.[85] Muriel Cormican proposes that this less confrontational stance enhanced the novel's "potential to reach far beyond limited groups of female intellectuals into the homes and lives of women who might be alienated or threatened by the political articulations of champions of the German women's movement, but could still be influenced by feminist notions of emancipation in popular fiction."[86] That strategy may have backfired with some literary critics who saw only the novel's foreground kinship to the sentimental romances in the fashion of Marlitt (Erhart, 314)—as well as

---

85   From early on, Andreas-Salomé's life and personality influenced other writers' fictional figures. One possible example, as Raymond Furness has proposed (loc. 193), is Anna Mahr, the emancipated young Russian studying philosophy at the University of Zürich in Gerhart Hauptmann's 1891 drama *Einsame Menschen* (Lonely Lives). Hauptmann (1862–1945) befriended Lou Salomé in October 1889 in Berlin, where she was involved in the theater and wrote reviews of several naturalist dramas. In recent decades, Andreas-Salomé herself has figured prominently as a named character in a host of works. Her colorful life is central or prominent, for example, in films by Liliana Cavani (1977) and Cordula Kablitz-Post (2016), also in the historical fiction of Angela von der Lippe (her 2008 *The Truth about Lou*) and Irvin D. Yalom (his 1992 *When Nietzsche Wept*, adapted in 2007 as a film directed by Perry Pinchas). Ingram (150n7) has already noted several such works: Giuseppe Sinopoli's 1981 opera, *Lou Salomé*; Roland Jaccard's 1982 novel, *Lou*; Lars Gustaffson's poem "Vor einem Porträt von Lou Andreas-Salomé"; and the dramas *Freud's Birds of Prey* by Robert Langs (2000) and *Lou* by Haley Rice (2017). Andreas-Salomé also plays a role in fictional works by William Bayer (*The Luzern Photograph*, 2015), M. Allen Cunningham (*Lost Son*, 2007), Clare Morgan (*A Book for All and None*, 2011), Lance Olsen (*Nietzsche's Kisses*, 2006), Brenda Webster (*Vienna Triangle*, 2009), and Thérèse Lambert (*Die Rebellin*, forthcoming 2021).

86   Cormican, "Authority and Resistance," 128.

with rigorous feminists who may have seen the novel's conclusion as validating Hedwig Dohm's reservations about Andreas-Salomé's "hair-raising" reactionary tendencies. Nevertheless, the view that the novel subverts patriarchal authority and its instantiation, even in the female protagonist, has been argued in recent critical analyses and is supported by the close reading of the text required of the translator.

The notions of the female figures' capitulation and self-dissolution proposed in Streiter's afterword to her 1987 edition, while upheld in Müller's analysis, are cogently challenged, first by Gahlinger, then by Cormican. Müller notes that Anneliese (in chapter XVIII) sees Markus, with his tolerant love of Gitta, as less possessive than her own husband (129), but then suggests that Gitta gradually becomes more like her mother, giving up her artistic aspirations, turning to her husband with a "profound feeling of belonging" to him (130), and ultimately subjecting herself to his traditional image of women (131). Yet the novel's last two chapters indicate that Gitta's artistic inclinations are not a thing of the past and that Markus has doubts about traditional male notions of women's role in marriage. For all its apparent closure with the patriarchal status quo of the doctor-husbands upheld and validated, *Das Haus* achieves an impression of open-ended, possible progress with its generational relationships of mother-daughter and older vs. younger doctor. Gitta soon disparages her first storytelling efforts (167, 170); yet her creative imagination and the writings alike remain part of her figurative and literal "baggage," and Markus is quick to challenge Anneliese's rejection of such pursuits as foolish (179).

Gahlinger rejects Müller's view that Gitta remains subject to the ideals of woman and motherhood that her mother has adhered to and projected upon her and that Markus allegedly upholds (381–82). She notes instead Markus's approval of Gitta's moves towards autonomy (esp. chapter XVIII, 179–82). While right about Gitta, Gahlinger's reading of Anneliese is less convincing. She proposes that Anneliese remains in her "prison-like marriage" (372), accepting her husband's decisions "unquestioningly" (369), and ever inclined to "deify" both him and his profession (374). That position ignores the instances in which Anneliese thinks and even speaks critically against Frank's ideas and actions— the indications, for example, that Markus's comments in chapter XVIII (esp. 180) foster Anneliese's doubts about how she has tried to live in accordance with Frank's ideal image of a married woman. Above all,

Cormican, with her 1999 article on *Das Haus* and its expansion in her 2009 monograph (*Women in the Works*), sees both Branhardt women involved in a generational process of rethinking conventional expectations of women's roles as wives and mothers and most persuasively reveals a feminist thrust to the way Anneliese challenges and changes her relationship with her husband.

The validity of Cormican's reading becomes compellingly apparent in the novel's nineteenth and concluding chapter. The thoughts and events sharpen the ironic perspective that has been established earlier, so as to subvert the impression that the threats to patriarchal order have been averted and harmony sustained. The last chapter's echoes of the opening chapter at first suggest that the narrative is closing with a felicitous symmetry. The novel ends with signs of growth and conciliation—from the opening chapter's early winter memory of Lotti's death and ruminations on the grim procession of dying Baumüller children to the autumn sunshine in which Anneliese is expecting the child for which Branhardt has so longed. She affirms the mothering role with which, in addition to easing the lives of needy little ones, she has fostered the liberation of her two grown children.

The two older Branhardts have weathered marital tensions born of Anneliese's impulse not to bow unquestioningly to her husband's good-natured and loving, but strongly authoritative, dominance. Frank even happily assures himself that his wife and he have grown—and that he himself has gained in manly strength and control—by enduring the rift that arose from Anneliese's willingness to condone their son Balduin's rebellious move, against his father's advice, to pursue an artistic life in Rome. Meanwhile, daughter Gitta, free-spirited and newly out of school, has, after some minor romantic adventures and a whirlwind courtship, married, then deserted her husband, Markus, yet is now reconciled with him. The young couple plan an extended visit to his family that promises to finalize her migration from one patriarchy to another.

Yet that step by no means sustains the patriarchal status quo: Anneliese, who at first had followed Frank's belief in the need for a man's firm hand in marriage, comes to realize in the penultimate chapter (esp. 179) that the younger Herr Doktor offers Gitta a degree of tolerance and equality considerably greater than that which prevailed in the Branhardt household. This generational contrast is evident when Markus challenges Anneliese's notion that he should take a "firm hand" with Gitta (179). His comment challenges in advance Frank's closing reflection on the "new measure of manliness" he has gained through his summertime crisis (chapter XIX, 196). Markus replies to her: "This know-it-all attitude and drive to control, the 'firm hand' you were talking about—all that arrogance, *especially of the usual, masculine kind*, will go to pieces trying to deal with this!" (179; emphasis added).

Yet even the joy of that young marriage, a beacon of hope and historical progress in the emancipatory cause,[87] falls under a shadow of uncertainty at the final chapter's midpoint, as Anneliese reflects: "The two of them were so delightfully serious and delightfully happy with each other . . . But would it stay so? Gitta herself probably knew least of all" (194). Other minor chords are arrayed around that qualifying mix of delight and foreboding. As Cormican suggests, the sense of a traditional romantic closure is rendered illusory by a number of "negative premonitions or ironic comments that disrupt the idyllic atmosphere."[88]

The chapter's opening episode, with Anneliese reading Balduin's letter from Rome, sets the tone for this subversion. The text of the letter itself is a masterful interplay of ostensible progress and ongoing problems. The Balduin who once wrote while cowering silently next to his father's study (chapter XII, 109) and even tried to incinerate his own manuscripts (111–12) now writes with a poet's voice—namely Rilke's: the letter Anneliese reads is a streamlined quotation of his letter of January 15, 1904, to Andreas-Salomé, used here, with the real poet's implied approval, on the principle that a figure emerging as a poet should speak like one.[89] The anxious "Kaspar Have-Naught," who once limped about on his chilblain-beset feet, now identifies with the heroic wanderer of the fresco he has seen and concocts, from that painting's static dual portrait, a narrative of his own triumphant journey homeward, through the world's strife, to speak calmly to the muse he has made of his mother.

Yet the promising exercise of writing his way to health and equanimity (191) is part of the ongoing secret correspondence between

---

87 See especially Gahlinger, 381–84; also Cormican, *Women in the Works*, 55–61.

88 Cormican, *Women in the Works*, 62.

89 For Rilke's letter see Rilke and Salomé, 94–95. Regarding Andreas-Salomé's use of the letter in her novel and the alterations involved, see Pechota Vuilleumier, 165–78. For more on Rilke's thoughts on the Boscoreale frescoes, see Hewett-Thayer.

mother and son that had caused the rift between Anneliese and her husband. That dissension has ended the happily arrested girlhood of her marriage, creating an independence that is not without dread and that has in fact riven the symbiotic unity of their marriage into a pair of equals moving separately in their own pursuits. As such, the poetry of Balduin's narrative ignores the ongoing reality of its context. It is an Oedipal challenge to the unmentioned father and a willful elevation of Anneliese into a legendary muse-figure, which she tactfully resolves to keep a secret between them, hidden from the astonished or derisive reaction of the outside world (191), its poetic vision thus still underway, an ongoing battle and by no means unthreatening. As Anneliese reflects here, "one way or the other, a son is always at war" (191).

The ambiguity of this episode is part of the pattern of episodes of fictive writing and reading with which the novel invites readers to reflect critically on how the writing and reading of poetic narratives relate to the reality to which a poet and his readers are trying to impart order, sense, and beauty. With repeated instances of a fictive figure reading a poetic creation, the novel offers readers a mirror of their own encounter with Andreas-Salomé's novel that should forestall an uncritical approval of its conclusion's foreground of sunshine and harmony.[90] This is the second time that readers are told of Anneliese's reading her son's artistic efforts. The earlier episode, in which Anneliese rescues her

---

90   There are several instances, in addition to the two episodes discussed here, that refer to the novel's women reading and writing texts of a literary or poetic nature. In chapter I we are made aware of Anneliese's acquaintance with Marlitt's fiction; in chapter II we see her taking up one of Balduin's books of another writer's poems; in chapter IV, there is extensive attention given to how poetic her grandmother's letters became and how Anneliese read them cursorily in the past but with attention to detail now. Gitta, from the outset a weaver of dreams, coiner of nicknames, and agile wordsmith, at this point subjects their foremother's writings to a still closer reading, and later chapters show her creating her own texts, capturing happiness and building imagined realms with words, reading and polishing her own works, and eventually carrying on those texts with her husband's support. It is above all a shared and developing capacity for artistic expression, an interest in reading and even creating imaginative texts — not the prospect of pregnancy (contrast Woodford, "Pregnancy and Ambivalence") — that characterizes this mother-daughter sequence. Thus the novel, in addition to depicting Balduin Branhardt as emerging poet — with his mother's support — seems to be very much in sympathy with women who write and read poetically — and with those men who have an affinity with and sympathy for such activity.

son's manuscript from the flames (chapter XII, 112–13), had withheld Balduin's actual text and offered only how Anneliese had understood it. She saw the gravely fractured father-son relationship idealistically transformed, with the father deified as godlike companion to the man the son will become, as they wander through the world's beauty under his revealing guidance. The absence of the text invites readers to suspect that Anneliese's own fantasy is at work to uphold a reading of how her son poetically mimics the deifying tendencies once part of her own relationship to her husband.[91] Such a suspicion is subtly validated by Anneliese's inability to suppress the thought that the father's revelatory control of the situation might involve "restriction" (114).

The last chapter's reading episode revives those doubts, providing the first disruption of the chapter's apparent "closure." By revealing what the young poet has written, it invites readers, as it does Anneliese, to reflect on the gap between poetry and reality. The benevolently guiding father that she had read into Balduin's poetry in chapter XII is conspicuously absent. The once Oedipus-like limping boy has restyled himself as the wanderer returning home in triumph, the blood still coursing in his feet, while the real father is nearby but unavailable, immersed in his scientific research and entertaining thoughts of his own manly triumph in the conflict over the secret letters.

As for Frank and Anneliese, their respective, sunlit reflections on the year's promising developments are not free of the unease born of her break with her old position of complete dependence. Amusingly gentle here is the ironic portrayal of Frank's reflections on the growth and strength of his marriage through the summertime. He dispels the dark shadow that obscures his sunny vision (196), by adhering, with scientific rigor, to his pleasing results and by promoting what "seems" to be the case into "fact" ("But, in fact, that seemed not to be the case"; 196). He even briefly senses, but then turns away from, what readers already know: his rosy reading of a triumphant reconciliation is an embellishment of the situation in his own favor. The narrator's rare intrusion into

---

91   Gahlinger (374) draws attention to the "deification" evident in what has long been Anneliese's image of her husband, citing her tendency to unite his authority as a husband with his authority as a doctor (chapter II, 12). Anneliese does much the same in her reading of Balduin's poetry (chapter XII, 114). Early on, Gitta seems to reflect her mother's view, imagining her father as the life-giving God depicted in Michelangelo's Sistine Chapel ceiling (chapter IV, 31).

the thoughts or dialogues of the figures at this point could not be more emphatic in revealing his evasion of critical introspection (196: "To the extent that he attained any degree of self-observation at all . . .").

Anneliese may at first appear to have set aside her rebellious responses to her husband's authority, the sorrow she felt at its loss, and the anxiety resulting from the break with the secure, if confining, adolescence of her marriage.[92] Her smiling challenges to Frank's self-centered pomposity are as evident here as in the first chapter.[93] But, unlike Frank, she does not explicitly refer to those past confrontations—for example, to her outbursts against the tendency of his rigid authority to "violate" those who are less submissive (chapter XII, 117) or to her wish for freedom and independence (chapter XVI, 165), which leads to the "death" of their hierarchical marital unity and of the happy adolescence of her marriage to that point (chapter XVI, 166). Yet the complex process of resistance and change in the intervening chapters is recalled when Anneliese, in contrast to Frank, has recurrent moments of shadow and darkness that "unsettle" the chapter's foregrounded impression of happily restored order. These moments involve a sequence of repeated words and gestures that suggest a changed Anneliese, who confronts growth and loss with a resolved faith in the power of her love and emotions to find ways to cope with life's changes.

An arrestingly dark moment occurs when she gazes into Gitta's bedroom, now being refurbished for the new infant's arrival (193). Anneliese reacts not with the expected reflections on the happy transition to come, but with a sense of emptiness and mortality that calls to mind the death of her daughter Lotti and the apprehension, in the second chapter, of the mortal risk involved in the new pregnancy that Frank has urged upon her, despite her silent misgivings. Her mood, with its sense of mortality's "sting of death" (193), refutes the biblical challenge to death that it evokes ("O death, where is thy sting"; I Corinthians 15:55) and plays into the look of worry and sorrow—ostensibly about Gitta's pending departure and future happiness—that she conceals while conversing moments later with Frank (194). His joking response attributes her anxious face to the fact that his new research

---

92   Anneliese's progress illustrates how Andreas-Salomé's works portray the costs or losses involved in progress towards emancipation, as Pechota has noted ("Lou Andreas-Salomé: Pionierin der Moderne," 52).

93   For example, 194; compare chapter I, 4.

project will render her a lonely widow up in the hillside house, thus unwittingly enhancing the undertone of death and loss—and reminding readers of how he and Anneliese, since the end of chapter XVI, have pursued markedly separate interests.

That sequence of death confronted and Anneliese's shielded face misread recurs in the closing episode. There Anneliese views her motherhood as an expression of the omnipresent love that counters the specters of loss, change, and death she has been pondering. This cues readers to note that her affirmation of motherhood, which allows the happiness of her marriage with Frank to evolve, has also fostered the liberating and yet forebodingly uncertain departure of her grown children from the confines of the family home. And it has resulted in her own realization of the anxiety and sorrow caused by that separation. Her association of death's finality with new gateways grasps the promise that the change and loss she endures through these last chapters can open the way to a new life and thus also to her full quotation of the previously evoked Bible passage: "Death, where is thy sting!" As she did after her preceding epiphany of mortality in the new nursery, Anneliese will conceal this surge of emotional "exuberance" when the rest of the family gathers in the garden. Frank will again see her shielding gesture but not its cause or meaning: he sees her but does not see her (199).

The arrival of the family pet in the closing scene enhances the symmetries linking the first and last chapters of the novel, but it also deals a final blow to the impression of restorative closure that they seemed to establish. The first of the house's inhabitants to be described and named, the dog now rushes in to dominate the closing scene, guarding Anneliese in her silent exuberance. The little mongrel has been seen as a domesticated animal, yet "outside culture," its moves between Gitta and Anneliese signaling women's "resistance to total assimilation into the patriarchal order of man" and its arrival here, to guard Anneliese, indicating that she too is beginning to realize her need for independence.[94] The dog's name and ambiguated gender also express the author's approval of the struggle that Frank fails to see. The little dog, as readers learn early on, is a stray female, heavily pregnant upon arrival yet nominally regendered by Gitta—herself strikingly inclined to defy expectations of feminine propriety by appropriating typically

---

94 Cormican, *Women in the Works*, 64.

male prerogatives of projection and gaze—as "Salomo." As Pechota Vuilleumier notes (103–4), this makes "him," on the one hand, the embodiment of patriarchal wisdom and the arbiter of legitimate motherhood; on the other hand, as the male namesake of the author, the Salomo to her Salomé, a vivid and self-ironic self-inscription of the author.

Readers then, as now, could likely see "his" mixed background as a caricature of Andreas-Salomé's diverse ethnic and intellectual heritage—and "his" transformation, from "wayward" female to wise male oracle, as an echo of her image as captivating "femme fatale" who also possessed an acknowledged intellectual acumen. And, as Pechota Vuilleumier proposes (103 and 103n365), with "his" violation of rigidly binary gender roles, the dog is arguably a mirror both of the author's own androgynous self-perception—her own often-remarked combination of "female instincts and masculine intelligence"[95]—and of her identification with the evolution of both Branhardt women away from traditional perceptions of women and marriage.

Playfully highlighted by the rush of the author's alter ego to guard Anneliese's exuberance, the details and context of the final chapter support a reading of the novel that sees, in the mother-daughter sequence, the promise of a move towards liberation from a traditional patriarchy that suppresses both men and women, with even Anneliese following the progressive impulses voiced around her. The interplay of narrative perspectives and dialogue that show her emerging to critical reflection and challenging discussion also ensures the novel's even-handed, sympathetic embrace of all its main figures' thoughts, hopes, and concerns. Expectations of a definitive, radical solution are thus destabilized in favor of an awareness of the possibility of evolution within the ineluctable tensions of modern familial and marital relationships.

With its look back from 1921 to the last years of the previous century, the Branhardts' story invites today's readers to carry on that retrospective process, a century after its publication. In so doing, it challenges us to reconsider gender roles and the opportunities and obstacles they present to us, no less today than when Andreas-Salomé gave the world her novel.

---

95   Pechota Vuilleumier, 108 and 112; compare Klingenberg, 239–40, and Gropp, 49–51.

Works Cited

Andreas-Salomé, Lou. *Aus fremder Seele: Eine Spätherbstgeschichte.* Stuttgart: Cotta, 1896.

———. *The Devil and His Grandmother.* 1922. Translated by Kristine Jennings. In Andreas-Salomé, *Sex and Religion*, 38–89.

———. "The Dual Orientation of Narcissism." 1921. Translated by Stanley A. Leavy. *Psychoanalytic Quarterly* 31, no. 1 (1962): 3–30.

———. *Eintragungen: Letzte Jahre.* Edited and with an afterword by Ernst Pfeiffer. Frankfurt am Main: Insel, 1982.

———. *The Erotic.* 1910. Translated by John Crisp. Foreword by Matthew Del Novo. Introduction by Gary Winship. New Brunswick, NJ: Transaction, 2012.

———. *Fenitschka and Deviations: Two Novellas.* 1898. Translated by Dorothee Einstein Krahn. New York: University Press of America, 1990.

———. *Fenitschka: Eine Ausschweifung; Zwei Erzählungen.* 1898. Edited by Iris Schäfer. Taching am See: MedienEdition Welsch, 2017.

———. *The Freud Journal of Lou Andreas-Salomé.* 1912/13. Translated by Stanley A. Leavy. London: Hogarth, 1964.

———. *Friedrich Nietzsche in seinen Werken.* 1894. Hamburg: Severus, 2013.

———. *Das Haus: Familiengeschichte vom Ende vorigen Jahrhunderts.* Berlin: Ullstein, 1921.

———. *Das Haus: Familiengeschichte vom Ende vorigen Jahrhunderts.* Afterword by Sabine Streiter. Frankfurt am Main: Ullstein, 1987.

———. *Der heimliche Weg: Drei Scenen aus einem Ehedrama.* 1901. Edited by Edith Hanke. Taching am See: MedienEdition Welsch, 2017.

———. *The Human Family: Stories.* 1899. Translated by Raleigh Whitinger. Lincoln: University of Nebraska Press, 2005.

———. *Ibsen's Heroines.* 1892. Translated by Siegfried Mandel. Redding Ridge: Black Swan, 1985.

———. *In der Schule bei Freud: Tagebuch eines Jahres 1912/13.* Edited by Manfred Klemann. Taching am See: MedienEdition Welsch, 2017.

———. "Jesus der Jude." 1894. Edited by Hans-Rüdiger Schwab. Taching am See: MedienEdition Welsch, 2014. Kindl.

———. *Lebensrückblick: Grundriß einiger Lebenserinnerungen.* Edited by Ernst Pfeiffer. Frankfurt am Main: Insel, 1951.

———. *Looking Back: Memoirs.* 1973. Edited by Ernst Pfeiffer. Translated by Breon Mitchell. New York: Paragon, 1991.

———. *La Maison.* 1921. Translated by Nicole Casanova. Afterword by Sabine Streiter. Paris: Des Femmes, 1997.

———. *Nietzsche.* 1894. Translated by Siegfried Mandel. Redding Ridge: Black Swan, 1988.

———. "*Russland mit Rainer*": *Tagebuch der Reise mit Rainer Maria Rilke im Jahre 1900.* Edited by Stéphane Michaud and Dorothee Pfeiffer, with a foreword by Brigitte Kronauer. Marbach: Deutsche Schillergesellschaft, 1999.

———. *Sex and Religion: Two Texts of Early Feminist Psychoanalysis*. 1917 and 1922. Translated by Maike Oergel and Kristine Jennings. Introduction by Matthew Del Novo and Gary Winship. New Brunswick, NJ: Transaction, 2016.

———. *Three Letters to a Young Boy*. 1912–17. Translated by Maike Oergel. In Andreas-Salomé, *Sex and Religion*.

———. *"Von der Bestie bis zum Gott": Aufsätze und Essays. Bd. 1: Religion*. Edited by Hans-Rüdiger Schwab. Taching am See: MedienEdition Welsch, 2011.

———. *You Alone are Real to Me: Remembering Rainer Maria Rilke*. 1928. Translation., introduction, and afterword by Angela von der Lippe. New York: BOA, 2003.

Andreas-Salomé, Lou, and Anna Freud. *"... als käm ich heim zu Vater und Schwester." Lou Andreas-Salomé—Anna Freud, Briefwechsel, 1919–1937*. Edited by Daria A. Rothe and Inge Weber. Vol. 1. Göttingen: Wallstein, 2001.

Babich, Babette. "Nietzsche and Lou, Eros and Art: On Lou's Triangles and the 'Exquisite Dream' of Sacro Monte." In Hummel, *Lou Andreas-Salomé, muse et apôtre*, 175–230.

Bayer, William. *The Luzern Photograph*. London: Severn House, 2015.

Benert, Britta, and Romana Weiershausen, eds. *Lou Andreas-Salomé: Zwischenwege in der Moderne / Sur les chemins de traverse de la modernité*. Taching am See: MedienEdition Welsch, 2019.

Bidney, Martin. "Andreas-Salomé's Devil and Lermontov's Demon." In Whitinger, Special Theme Issue, 141–58.

Binion, Rudolph. *Frau Lou: Nietzsche's Wayward Disciple*. Princeton, NJ: Princeton University Press, 1968.

Böcklin, Arnold. *Das Schweigen des Waldes*. 1885. Muzeum Narodowe. Poznan, Poland. See also https://www.akg-images.de/archive/Das-Schweigen-des-Waldes-2UMDH UN6K38T.html.

Borossa, Julia, and Carolina Rooney. "Suffering, Transience and Immortal Longings: Salomé between Nietzsche and Freud." *Journal of European Studies* 33, nos. 3–4 (2003): 287–304.

Böttger, Claudia. "'... how literature comes to life': The Theatre Reviews." In Whitinger, Special Theme Issue, 97–113.

Brinker-Gabler, Gisela. *Image in Outline: Reading Lou Andreas-Salomé*. New York: Continuum, 2012.

———. "Psychobiography, Mourning and Literature: Lou Andreas-Salomé's 'Rainer Maria Rilke.'" In *Gendered Academia: Wissenschaft und Geschlechtsdifferenz, 1890–1945*, edited by Miriam Kauko, Sylvia Mieszkowski, and Alexandra Tischel, 107–26. Göttingen: Wallstein, 2005.

———. "Renaming the Human: Andreas-Salomé's 'Becoming Human.'" In Whitinger, Special Theme Issue, 22–41.

Bülow, Frieda von. *Die schönsten Novellen über Lou Andreas-Salomé und andere Frauen*, edited by Sabina Streiter. Frankfurt am Main: Ullstein, 1990.

———. "Zwei Menschen." In Bülow, *Die schönsten Novellen über Lou Andreas-Salomé und andere Frauen*, 7–67.

Cavani, Liliana, dir. *Al di là de bene e del male*. 1977. Rome: Rai Cinema, 2013. DVD.

Ciseri Antonio. *Ecce Homo*. 1871. Museo Cantonale d'Arte. Lugano. See also https://commons.wikimedia.org/wiki/File:Antonio_Ciseri_Ecce_homo.png.

Clauss, Elke-Maria. "Die Muse als Autorin: Zur Karriere von Lou Andreas-Salomé." In *Deutschsprachige Schriftstellerinnen des Fin de Siècle*, edited by Karin Tebben, 48–70. Darmstadt: Wissenschaftliche Buchgesellschaft, 1999.

Cormican, Muriel. "Authority and Resistance: Women in Lou Andreas-Salomé's *Das Haus*." *Women in German Yearbook* 14 (1998): 127–42.

———. "Female Sexuality and the Dilemma of Self-Representation in *Jutta*." In Whitinger, Special Theme Issue, 130–40.

———. *Women in the Works of Lou Andreas-Salomé: Negotiating Identity*. Rochester, NY: Camden House, 2009.

Cunningham, M. Allen. *Lost Son*. Lakewood, CO: Unbridled Books, 2007.

Decker, Kerstin. *Lou Andreas-Salomé: Der bittersüße Funke Ich*. Berlin: Propyläen Verlag, 2017.

———. *Meine Farm in Afrika: Das Leben der Frieda von Bülow*. Munich: Piper Verlag, 2015.

Deiulio, Laura. "A Tale of Two Cities: The Metropolis in Lou Andreas-Salomé's *Fenitschka*." *Women in German Yearbook* 23 (2007): 76–101.

Del Caro, Adrian. "Andreas-Salomé and Nietzsche: New Perspectives." In Whitinger, Special Theme Issue, 79–96.

Diethe, Carol. "Lou Salomé's Interpretation of Nietzsche's Religiosity." In "Nietzsche and Religion," special issue of *Journal of Nietzsche Studies* 19, no. 1 (2000): 80–88.

———. *Nietzsche's Women: Beyond the Whip*. New York: de Gruyter, 1996.

———. *Towards Emancipation: German Women Writers of the Nineteenth Century*. New York: Berghahn, 1998.

Dohm, Hedwig. *Die Antifeministen: Ein Buch der Verteidigung*. Berlin: Ferdinand Dümmles, 1902.

———. "Reaktion in der Frauenbewegung." *Die Zukunft* 29 (1899): 279–91.

Doll Allen, Julie. "Male and Female Dialogue in Lou Andreas-Salomé's *Fenitschka*." In *Frauen: Mitsprechen, Mitschreiben; Beiträge zur literatur- und sprachwissenschaftlichen Frauenforschung*, edited by Marianne Henn and Britta Hufeisen, 479–89. Stuttgart: Akademischer Verlag Hans-Dieter Heinz, 1997.

Eberhard Köstler Autographen & Bücher. *"Inniger Schmatz! Deine Lou": Sechs bedeutende Briefe von Lou Andreas-Salomé*. Katalog 151A. May 2016. Tutzing, Germany: Eberhard & Köstler, 2016. Auction Catalogue.

Eilert, Heide. *Das Kunstzitat in der erzählenden Dichtung: Studien zur Literatur um 1900*. Stuttgart: Franz Steiner, 1991.

Erhart, Walter. *Familienmänner: Über den literarischen Ursprung moderner Männlichkeit*. Munich: Fink, 2001.

Freud, Sigmund, and Lou Andreas-Salomé. *Sigmund Freud and Lou Andreas-Salomé: Letters*. Edited by Ernst Pfeiffer. Translated by William and Elaine Robson-Scott. London: Hogarth Press and the Institute of Psycho-Analysis, 1963.

Furness, Raymond. *The Twentieth Century, 1890–1945*. Vol. 8 of *The Literary History of Germany*. 1978. New York: Routledge, 2000. Ebook.

Gahlinger, Chantal. *Der Weg zur weiblichen Autonomie: Zur Psychologie der Selbstwerdung im literarischen Werk Lou Andreas-Salomés*. Bern: Lang, 2001.

Gane, Mike. "In Transcendence: Friedrich Nietzsche and Lou Salomé." In *Harmless Lovers? Gender, Theory and Personal Relationships*, 173–78. London: Routledge, 1993.

Ge, Nikolai Nikolaevich. *"What is truth?" Christ and Pilate*. 1890. The Tretyakov Gallery. Moscow. See also https://commons.wikimedia.org/wiki/File:What_is_truth.jpg.

Gilbert, Sandra M., and Susan Gubar. *The Madwoman in the Attic: The Woman Writer and the Nineteenth-Century Literary Imagination*. New Haven, CT: Yale University Press, 1979.

Gropp, Rose-Maria. "Das Weib existiert nicht." *Blätter der Rilke-Gesellschaft* 11/12 (1984/85): 46–54.

Gustafsson, Lars. "Vor einem Porträt von Lou Andreas-Salomé." In *The Stillness of the World Before Bach: Selected Poems*, edited by Christopher Middleton and translated by Christopher Middleton, Robin Fulton, Harriett Watts, Yvonne L. Sandstroem, and Philip Martin. New York: New Directions, 1982.

Haines, Brigid. "Lou Andreas-Salomé's *Fenitschka*: A Feminist Reading." *German Life and Letters*, no. 5 (1991): 416–25.

Hewett-Thayer, Harvey. "Rilke and the Boscoreale Frescoes." *Germanic Review*, 20, no. 1 (1945): 47–53.

Holmes, Deborah. "The Rewriting of Lou Andreas-Salomé's *Eine Ausschweifung*." *German Life and Letters* 68, no. 4 (2014): 611–25.

Hummel, Pascale, ed. *Lou Andreas-Salomé, muse et apôtre*. Paris: Philologicum, 2011.

Hutchings, Arthur J. *Schubert*. London: J. M. Dent and Sons, 1945.

Ianozi, Regina. "Cultural and Social Border Crossings: Germany and Russia in the Writings of Lou Andreas-Salomé (1861–1937) and Alina Bronsky (1978–)." PhD diss., University of Maryland, 2015.

Ingram, Susan. *Zarathustra's Sisters: Women's Autobiography and the Shaping of Cultural History*. Toronto: University of Toronto Press, 2003.

Jaccard, Roland. *Lou*. Paris: Grasset, 1982.

Kablitz-Post, Cordula, dir. *Lou Andreas-Salomé: The Audacity to Be Free*. 2016. Los Angeles: Cinema Libre Studios, 2018. Blu-ray Disc, 10801 HD.

Karpova, Tatiana, and Svetlana Kapyrina. "Nikolai Ge: A Chronicle of the Artist's Life and Work." *Tretyakov Gallery Magazine* 3 (2011): 32. https://www.tretyakovgallerymagazine.com/articles/3-2011-32/nikolai-ge-chronicle-artist-life-and-work.

Klingenberg, Helene. "Lou Andreas-Salomé." *Deutsche Monatsschrift für Russland*, March 15, 1912, 237–52.

Koepcke, Cordula. *Lou Andreas-Salomé: Ein eigenwilliger Lebensweg*. Freiburg: Herder, 1982.

———. *Lou Andreas-Salomé: Leben, Persönlichkeit, Werk. Eine Biographie*. Frankfurt am Main: Insel, 1986.

Kontje, Todd. "Marlitt's World: Domestic Fiction in the Age of Empire." *German Quarterly* 77, no. 4 (2004): 408–26.

Kreide, Caroline. *Andreas-Salomé: Feministin oder Antifeministin? Eine Standortbestimmung zur wilhelminischen Frauenbewegung*. New York: Lang, 1996.

Lambert, Thérèse. *Die Rebellin*. Berlin: Aufbau Verlag, 2021.

Langs, Robert. *Freud's Birds of Prey: A Play in Two Acts*. New York: Zeig, Tucker, and Theisen, 2000.

Lippe, Angela von der. *The Truth about Lou: A Novel After Salomé*. Berkeley, CA: Counterpoint, 2008.

Livingstone, Angela. *Salomé: Her Life and Work*. Mt. Kisco, NY: Moyer Bell, 1984.

Mandel, Siegfried. "Introduction." In Andreas-Salomé, *Nietzsche*, viii–lxvi.

Markotic, Lorraine. "Andreas-Salomé and the Contemporary Essentialism Debate." In Whitinger, Special Theme Issue, 59–78.

———. "Art and Intoxicated Desire in Andreas-Salomé's 'Deviations' ('Eine Ausschweifung')." In Hummel, *Lou Andreas-Salomé, muse et apôtre*. 155–73.

———. "There Where Primary Narcissism Was, I Must Become: The Inception of the Ego in Andreas-Salomé, Lacan, and Kristeva." *American Imago* 58, no 4 (2001): 813–36.

Marlitt, E[ugenia]. [Eugenie John]. *At the Councillor's; or, A Nameless History*. 1876. Translated by A. L. Wister. Philadelphia: Lippincott, 1876.

———. *Countess Gisela*. 1869. Translated by A. L. Wister. Philadelphia: Lippincott, 1869.

———. *Gold Elsie*. 1866. Translated by A. L. Wister. Philadelphia, Lippincott, 1868.

Martin, Biddy. *Women and Modernity: The (Life)Styles of Lou Andreas-Salomé*. Ithaca, NY: Cornell University Press, 1991.

Matysik, Tracy. "The Interests of Ethics: Andreas-Salomé's Psychoanalytic Critique." In Whitinger, Special Theme Issue, 5–21.

McFarlane, James. "Introduction." In *Henrik Ibsen: Four Major Plays*, translated by McFarlane and Jens Arup. New York: Oxford, 1981.

Mellmann, Katja. "Die Clauren-Marlitt: Rekonstruktion eines Literaturstreits um 1885." *Internationales Archiv für Sozialgeschichte der deutschen Literatur* 39, no. 2 (2014): 285–324.

Michaud, Stéphane. "L'instinct du bonheur: Lou Andreas-Salomé, 'La Maison.'" Review of *La Maison*, by Lou Andreas-Salomé, translated by Nicole Casanova. *La Quinzaine littéraire* 715 (May 1–15, 1997): 12.

———. *Lou Andreas-Salomé—L'alliée de la vie: Biographie*. Paris: Éditions du Seuil, 2017.

————. "Zensur und Selbstzensur in Lou Andreas-Salomés autobiographisch-en Schriften." In *Zensur und Selbstzensur in der Literatur*, edited by Peter Brockmeier and Gerhard R. Kaiser, 157–72. Würzburg: Königshausen & Neumann, 1996.

Midgley, David. "Lou Andreas-Salomé." In *Landmarks in German Women's Writing*, edited by Hilary Brown, 107–22. Oxford: Lang, 2007.

Mons, Isabelle. *Lou Andreas-Salomé*. Paris: Perrin, 2012. Kindle.

————. *Lou Andreas-Salomé: Una mujer libre*. Translated by Juan-Díaz Atauri. Barcelona: Acantilado, 2019.

Montinari, Mazzino. *Friedrich Nietzsche: Eine Einführung*. 1975. Translated from the Italian by Renate Müller-Buck. Berlin: de Gruyter, 1991.

Morgan, Clare. *A Book for All and None*. London: Orion, 2011.

Müller, Heidy Margrit. *Töchter und Mütter in deutschsprachiger Erzählprosa von 1885 bis 1935*. Munich: Iudicum, 1991.

Müller-Loreck, Leonie. *Die erzählende Dichtung Lou Andreas-Salomés: Ihr Zusammenhang mit der Literatur um 1900*. Stuttgart: Akademischer Verlag Hans-Dieter Heinz, 1976.

Nadler, Steven. *Think Least of Death: Spinoza on How to Live and How to Die*. Princeton, NJ: University of Princeton Press, 2020.

Olsen, Lance. *Nietzsche's Kisses*. Tallahassee, FL: Fiction Collective 2, 2006.

Pasternak, Boris. *Safe Conduct: An Autobiography and Other Writings*. Introduction by Bette Deutsch. Translated by Beatrice Scott, Robert Payne, and C. M. Bowra. New York: New Directions, 1958.

Pechota, Cornelia. "Kunst als Therapie in Lou Andreas-Salomés Roman 'Das Haus': Die kreative Heilung im Lichte ihrer Narzissmus-Theorie." In *Ihr zur Feier: Lou Andreas-Salomé (1861–1937): Interdisziplinäres Symposium aus Anlass ihres 150. Geburtstages*, edited by Ursula Welsch, 75–98. Taching am See: MedienEdition, 2011.

————. "Lou Andreas-Salomé: Pionierin der Moderne: Werk und Leben von Rilkes Reisegefährtin." In *Kulturtransfer um 1900: Rilke und Russland*, edited by Dirk Kemper, Ulrich von Bülow, and Jurij Lileev, 47–73. Munich: Fink, 2020.

————. Review of *Die Psychoanalytikerin Lou Andreas-Salomé: Ihr Werk im Spannungsfeld zwischen Sigmund Freud und Rainer Maria Rilke*, by Christiane Wieder. *Blätter der Rilke-Gesellschaft* 31 (2012): 363–65.

————. "Rilke, Lou und die Danziger Schriftstellerin Johanna Niemann." *Blätter der Rilke-Gesellschaft* 34 (2018): 40–57.

Pechota Vuilleumier, Cornelia. *Heim und Unheimlichkeit bei Rainer Maria Rilke und Lou Andreas-Salomé*. Hildesheim: Olms, 2010.

Perry, Pinchas, dir. *When Nietzsche Wept*. Screenplay: Pinchas and Irvin D. Yalom. First Look International. 2007.

Peters, H. F. *My Sister, My Spouse: A Biography of Lou Andreas-Salomé*. New York: Norton, 1962.

Popova, Maria. "Lou Andreas-Salomé, the First Woman Psychoanalyst, on Human Nature in Letters to Freud." In *Brainpickings*, https://www.brainpickings. org/2015/02/12/lou-andreas-salome-sigmund-freud-letters/.

Prater, Donald. *A Ringing Glass: The Life of Rainer Maria Rilke.* Oxford: Clarendon, 1986.

Rainwater van Suntum, Lisa A. "Hiding Behind Literary Analysis: Heinrich Heine's *Shakespeares Mädchen* and Lou Andreas-Salomé's *Ibsens Frauengestalten.*" *Monatshefte* 89, no. 3 (1997): 307–23.

Renner, Ursula. "Lou Andreas-Salomé (1861–1937): 'Nicht nur Wissen, sondern ein Stück Leben.'" In *Frauen in den Kulturwissenschaften von Lou Andreas-Salomé bis Hannah Arendt*, edited by Barbara Hahn, 26–43. Munich: Beck, 1994.

Reuter, Gabriele. *From a Good Family.* 1895. Translated and with an introduction by Lynne Tatlock. Rochester, NY: Camden House, 1999.

———. "Lou Andreas-Salomé. *Das Haus.* Roman. Ullstein-Verlag Berlin." Review of *Das Haus* by Lou Andreas-Salomé (Berlin: Ullstein, 1921). *Deutsche Allgemeine Zeitung.* Supplement. No date. No page. GSA 112/166, Goethe- und Schiller-Archiv, Weimar.

Rhiel, Mary. Review of *Sub-Versionen: Weiblichkeitsentwürfe in den Erzähltexten Lou Andreas-Salomés*, by Birgit Wernz. *German Quarterly* 75, no. 3 (2002): 352–53.

Rice, Haley, playwright. *Lou.* Play directed by Kate Moore Heaney. The Paradise Factory, New York, May 17 to June 3, 2017.

Richter, Adrian Ludwig. *Genoveva in der Waldeinsamkeit (Genoveva in Wooded Seclusion).* 1841. Painting in the Kunsthalle, Hamburg. See also https://www. akg-images.de/archive/Genoveva-in-der-Waldeinsamkeit-UMDHUY5TB0. html.

Rilke, Rainer Maria, and Lou Andreas-Salomé. *Rilke and Andreas-Salomé: A Love Story in Letters.* Translated by Edward Snow and Michael Winkler. New York: Norton, 1995.

Rosenberg, Marvin. *The Masks of Hamlet.* Cranbury, NJ: Associated University Presses, 1992.

Rothe, Daria A. "Letters of Two Remarkable Women: The Anna Freud—Lou Andreas-Salomé Correspondence." *International Forum for Psychoanalysis* 5 (1996): 233–48.

Schmidt, Thomas, ed. *Rilke und Russland.* Catalogue of the exhibition at the Literaturmuseum der Moderne, Marbach am Neckar May 3 to August 6, 2017. Marbach: Deutsche Schillergesellschaft, 2017. Marbacherkatalog, 69.

Schultz, Karla. "In Defense of Narcissus: Lou Andreas-Salomé and Julia Kristeva." *German Quarterly* 67, no. 2 (1994): 185–96.

Schütz, Katrin. *Geschlechterentwürfe im literarischen Werk Lou Andreas-Salomés unter Berücksichtigung ihrer Geschlechtertheorie.* Würzburg: Königshausen & Neumann, 2008.

Schwartz, Agata. "Andreas-Salomé and Mayreder: Femininity and Masculinity." In Whitinger, Special Theme Issue, 42–58.

Schwarz, Egon. "Doppelbett mit Gitta. 'Das Haus': Lou Andreas-Salomés Roman in neuer Ausgabe." Review of *Das Haus* by Lou Andreas-Salomé (Frankfurt am Main: Ullstein, 1987), *Frankfurter Allgemeine Zeitung*, November 19, 1987, 28.

Sinopoli, Giuseppe. *Lou Salomé: Oper in zwei Akten*. Libretto by Karl Dietrich Gräwe. Munich: Bayerische Staatsoper, 1981.

Streiter, Sabine. "Nachwort." In Andreas-Salomé, *Das Haus* (1987), 239–53.

———. "Nachwort." In Bülow, *Die schönsten Novellen über Lou Andreas-Salomé und andere Frauen*, 235–52.

———. "Postface." In Andreas-Salomé, *La Maison*, 319–35.

Tatlock, Lynne. "Introduction." In Reuter, *From a Good Family*, ix–lviii.

Télérama, unsigned review of *La Maison* by Lou Andreas-Salomé, translated into French by Nicole Casanova, August 27, 1997. https://www.desfemmes.fr/litterature/la-maison/.

Touaillon, Christine. "Frauenromane." *Das literarische Echo* 1921/22, column 1495.

Treder, Ute. *Von der Hexe zur Hysterikerin: Zur Verfestigungsgeschichte des Ewig Weiblichen*. Bonn: Bouvier, 1984.

Vickers, Julia. *Lou von Salomé: A Biography of the Woman Who Inspired Freud, Nietzsche and Rilke*. London: McFarland, 2008.

Walker, Joyce S. "Armour and Fetish in *Fenitschka, Eine Ausschweifung*, and *Jutta*." In Whitinger, Special Theme Issue, 114–29.

Wang, Ban. "Memory, Narcissism, and Sublimation: Reading Lou Andreas-Salomé's Freud Journal." *American Imago* 57, no. 2 (2000): 215–34.

Wawrytko, Sandra A. "Lou Salomé (1861–1937)." In *A History of Women Philosophers, Volume IV, Contemporary Women Philosophers, 1900–Today*, edited by Mary Ellen Waithe, 69–102. Dordrecht, Netherlands: Kluwer Academic Publishers, 1995.

Webster, Brenda. *Vienna Triangle*. San Antonio: Wings, 2009.

Weedon, Chris. "The Struggle for Emancipation: German Women Writers of the *Jahrhundertwende*." In *A History of Women's Writing in Germany, Austria, and Switzerland*, edited by Jo Catling, 111–27. Cambridge: Cambridge University Press, 2000.

Weiershausen, Romana. "Entwürfe eines geschlechtsspezifischen Wissens bei Lou Andreas-Salomé: Lebensphilosophie, Dichtung, Psychoanalyse und die Jutta-Trilogie (1921, 1933)." *Zeitschrift für Germanistik* 18, no. 2 (2008): 318–30.

Welsch, Ursula, and Dorothee Pfeiffer. *Lou Andreas-Salomé: Eine Bildbiographie*. Taching am See: MedienEdition Welsch, 2014. Kindle.

Wernz, Birgit. *Sub-Versionen: Weiblichkeitsentwürfe in den Erzähltexten Lou Andreas-Salomés*. Pfaffenweiler: Centaurus-Verlag, 1997.

Whitinger, Raleigh. "Echoes of Lou Andreas-Salomé in Thomas Mann's *Tonio Kröger: Eine Ausschweifung* and its Relationship to the *Bildungsroman* Tradition." *Germanic Review* 75, no.1 (2000): 21–36.

———. "Introduction." In Andreas-Salomé, *The Human Family*, vii–xvii.

———. "Lou Andreas-Salomé's *Fenitschka* and the Tradition of the *Bildungsroman*." *Monatshefte* 91, no. 4 (1999): 464–80.

———, ed. Special Theme Issue on Lou Andreas-Salomé. Special issue, *Seminar* 36, no. 1 (2000).

Wieder, Christiane. *Die Psychoanalytikerin Lou Andreas-Salomé: Ihr Werk im Spannungsfeld zwischen Sigmund Freud und Rainer Maria Rilke*. Göttingen: Vandenhoeck & Ruprecht, 2011.

Wiesner-Bangard, Michaela, and Ursula Welsch. *Lou Andreas-Salomé: Eine Biographie*. Taching am See: MedienEdition Welsch, 2008.

———. *Lou Andreas-Salomé: "Wie ich Dich liebe, Rätselleben"; Eine Biographie*. Stuttgart: Reclam, 2017.

Woodford, Charlotte. "Female Desire and the Mind-Body Binary in *Fin-de-Siècle* Fiction by Hedwig Dohm, Lou Andreas-Salomé and Gabriele Reuter." *German Life and Letters* 69, no. 3 (2016): 336–49.

———. "Pregnancy and Ambivalence in Lou Andreas-Salomé's *Das Haus*." In *Women, Emancipation and the German Novel, 1871–1910*, 106–22. London: Routledge, 2014.

Wybrands, Johanna. *Der weibliche Aufbruch um 1900: Generationalität als Erzählparadigma von Autorinnen der Jahrhunderwende*. Baden-Baden: Tectum, 2020.

Yalom, Irwin D. *When Nietzsche Wept: A Novel of Obsession*. New York: Basic Books, 1992.

Yesterday, Anna. "What is Truth? Christ and Pilate." *Arthive.com*. https://arthive.com/nikolaige/works/14039~What_is_truth_Christ_and_Pilate.

TRANSLATORS' NOTE AND ACKNOWLEDGMENTS

This translation of Lou Andreas-Salomé's final novel aims to preserve both the meaning and character of the author's finely nuanced use of German and her sensitive rendition of the characters' often intense thoughts and dialogues. At the same time, it seeks to offer its readers an English as clear, accessible, and appropriate in tone and register as was the original German to its readers.

On rare occasions this entailed expansions of or even deviations from the exact form or meaning of the original, in order to capture the spirit of the original, to avoid the loss of meanings that would have been clear to the original's reader, or, in only two cases, to alter confusing phrasings by the author.

Foremost among such instances is the expansion of the original title from the literal "The House" to *Anneliese's House*. That change is intended not only to avoid this book's being confused with a host of other novels bearing a similar title, but also to suggest the poetic tone that the main female protagonist, Anneliese Branhardt, imparts to her household, by thought and deed. Her prominence is established in the first chapter and sustained throughout by an imaginative sensitivity whose struggle to assert itself is a major theme of the novel. The few deviations and expansions within the text are explained in the endnotes and, in any case, adhere to four principles that have guided the translation's efforts to minimize, and compensate for, the loss inevitable in the translation process.

A first principle was to ensure readers an experience comparable to that of the original's readers by retaining *important nonverbal features of the original* that contribute to its meaning. These included its paragraph breaks, its emphases—using spaced letters ("Sperrdruck"), the German equivalent, at that time, of italics—and most of its idiosyncrasies of punctuation. On the latter point, the translation made every effort to retain the original's use of quotation marks and spaced em-dashes—the latter being especially prominent in revealing a figure's struggle to formulate and articulate thoughts.

A second principle was to preserve as many elements of the author's language and culture as possible—in other words, to share the basic conviction of the German tradition in translation theory that a translation should bring the intended readers to the foreign text, times, and culture, rather than appropriating and domesticating the foreign text to the target readers' times and culture. For example, the translation retains German titles such as "Herr," "Frau," and, occasionally, "Herr Doktor," and leaves the names of figures in their German form, umlauts and all. Retained as well was the *original German* of Frank Branhardt's nickname for his wife, Anneliese, "Lieselieb" (see the endnote to chapter I, page 3), while Gitta's informal address form for her mother, "Muhme," was translated as "Mama," *with the accent understood to be on the last syllable.*

The resolve to avoid anachronistic word choices or idiomatic English equivalents of German idioms that seemed to lose the original's foreignness and context only occasionally involved difficult decisions. On the one hand, for example, the translation of "Menschlichkeit" as "humanity" seemed preferrable to "mankind" or even "man" in light of the author's pro-feminist stance and writings. On the other hand, the more literal and "foreign" sounding "don't throw your rifle into the barley" seemed preferable to allowing the usual English partial equivalent—"don't throw in the towel"—to force the realm of competitive boxing onto the original's context. Fruitful in such deliberations, as well as in pondering each of the original's use of the ever-vexatious impersonal pronoun "man" (translatable in various contexts as "one," "you," "we," "people," or various passive structures), were consultations with usages in prose works by the author's English-speaking contemporaries, including novels by E. M. Forster, Virginia Woolf, and Edith Wharton.

A third principle was to preserve the apparently intended meaning of a word or phrase whose literal translation might be misinterpreted, through either a "correcting" alteration or a slight expansion of the construction employed by the author. Relatively rare, for an author whose style critics have on occasion found complex, idiosyncratic, or even turgid, were instances of a word choice or phrasing that seemed, in context, to be misleadingly ill chosen. Only in two instances was a word or phrase substituted for the original's English equivalent—as explained in the endnotes to chapter III, page 20 and to chapter IV, page 31.

On two other occasions, linguistic differences or picturesquely invented terms called for clarifying expansion by the translators. This was the case where the absence in modern English of differing—namely formal and informal—forms of the second-person address (in English only you/your) required clarifying expansion of an instance in the novel where a figure's shift from the German formal "you" (Sie/Ihnen/Ihr-) to informal address (du/dir/dich/dein-) signaled a change in a relationship that was immediately apparent to readers in German but lost if the translation remained with "you" and "your" (see endnotes to chapter X, pages 88–90). A second instance was the novel's use of a humorously picturesque term, literally "propriety elephant," for a "chaperone." The translation uses "chaperone," but also includes a translation of the original's metaphor (see endnote to chapter X, page 83).

The fourth and most engaging and challenging principle in this particular novel's translation was to preserve aspects of the language that facilitated and instantiated its theme of the clash between supposedly "objective" analysis and discourse, on the one hand, and poetic and intuitive forms of thought and expression, on the other. With this theme, the novel—which began to take shape in 1904 and was published in 1921—might be seen to bridge and link the full range of Andreas-Salomé's writings, from her early involvement in the late nineteenth century's "Lebensphilosophie" (Life philosophy, see above, page xxv and footnote 67) to her later contributions to psychoanalysis, and it assigns to Anneliese a representative and pivotal role in articulating that theme. On this point, the all-male translating team strove to avoid relating to the author's text in a way analogous to Dr. Branhardt's relationship to his wife's "exuberance." Better, instead, the translators felt, was to remain ever attuned to the author's skilled and subtle shifts, made masterfully evident even in the opening chapter's arc—from the prosaic domestic sphere's mundane concerns to the sensitive phrasing and imagery that conveys Anneliese's struggle with the existential realities of death, grief, and otherness, and the solitary path to happiness she finds on a snowy hillside.

Acknowledgments

Particularly—but by no means solely—in our endeavor to fulfill the last of the above-named principles, the translators were greatly aided by several colleagues. Nicole Casanova's French translation of *Das Haus* was a valuable reference work, enabling us to check the basic accuracy of our translations of some of the complex passages or unusual word choices and facilitating the occasional "Aha" moment in finding the right word. Throughout the translation process, the project also profited greatly from the wise counsel of Barbara Thimm, a writer, translator, and teacher whose sensitive grasp of German grammar, vocabulary, and poetic sense improved several passages of the translation.

As the late drafts proceeded towards submission, the accuracy of the translation and the grammatical and stylistic quality of the English were invaluably aided by the proofing process to which Dr. Rupert Thorough and Annina Brida subjected our text. They combined their perceptive insights into the German text and their skills and knowledge in matters of English punctuation, vocabulary, and historically appropriate style to introduce a wealth of decisively helpful alterations and corrections in the service of the principles outlined above. This was all in addition to the help and encouragement accorded the project by Professor Elisabeth Krimmer of the University of California, Davis, editor of the series Women and Gender in German Studies, in which this translation appears, and by Jim Walker, editorial director of Camden House, with their initial enthusiasm about the manuscript and suggestions about usage and consistency. We are grateful, as well, to the readers they chose to evaluate the text, among them Professor emeritus Dennis Mahoney of the University of Vermont, who, like the other, anonymous, reader, caught overlooked details of the original text's structures and phrases so as to ensure a more faithful translation and a more informative body of endnotes.

The translators also wish to thank Cordula Kablitz-Post, whose 2016 film about the author brought many new readers to her work and who encouraged us to further investigate Andreas-Salomé's fiction. Valuable encouragement and advice were also offered in response to our early plans and chapters by Professor emerita Jeannine Blackwell of the University of Kentucky and by Professor Muriel Cormican of Texas Christian University, who looks forward to using the translated novel in her courses. Carrying out our research in New York and Edmonton required a good deal of assistance from librarians, and we especially appreciate the help we received from Catherine McGowan at The New York Society Library and the staff of the University of Alberta Library, in particular its Inter-Library Loan Department and Humanities and Social Sciences Library.

Last but by no means least, the translators are grateful to their wives, Kathleen Whitinger and Mona Molarsky, and their families, who, through these many months, the later ones so unusual and trying for us all, tolerated the long days of intense focus and frequent bursts of exuberant enthusiasm.

Anneliese's House

PART ONE

CHAPTER I

The house stood on a hillside, overlooking the town in the valley and the long stretch of mountains beyond. From the country road that climbed through the hill's woods in a wide curve, you stepped right into the middle story, as if it were at ground level — so deeply was the little white house nestled into the slope.

But perched up there it had a freer view out over the terraced garden and across the broad expanse below, gazing down with many bright window-eyes and with boldly protruding bays — extensions of original rooms that had been found too confining. This undeniably made for whimsical architecture, but it gave the house an impression of grace and lightness — almost as if it were just resting there.

From the top floor above the central bay, a balcony jutted far out over the tree-planted, wintry garden, enclosed by a stone wall, old and moss-covered. The balcony door stood wide open, despite the early morning hour, and on the threshold, its backside carefully pointed back into the warm room, sat a small, aged, female dog blinking sleepily at the hungry birds that occasionally flitted by, observing them as a spoiled child of the house might look out at begging street folk. Of course, she herself was the result of the widest range of dog breeds treating themselves to nothing less than an aristocratic love-tryst, as evidenced by her dachshund legs, her pug torso, and her terrier head — a diversity capped off by the piglet-style, curly tail at her other end. But by far the most remarkable thing about the little monster was the fact that its name was Salomo. That astonished everyone except the daughter of the family, who had insisted on that name of masculine and royal wisdom, even after Salomo had come straying her way in a highly pregnant state, whereupon he had given birth to four healthy pinschers.

The birds were carrying on with a tremendous racket. Finches and blue tits, robins and linnets, warblers and others flocked together around the suet that had been put out on the balcony — free hanging to discourage the contending field sparrows — along with a bowl of water, set above a few glowing coals on a potsherd to keep it from freezing. In their midst was the housewife, standing at the balcony door, busy and cheerful, and scattering grain for them to eat.

Salomo had his accurate inner timepiece, which told him they should have been at breakfast by now. Fortunately for him, the man of the house was now taking his own timepiece out of his waistcoat pocket and, entering the room, he gave indignant expression to Salomo's silent rebuke.

"Well, Salomo, what do you say to that? For the sake of our daughter's pack of fowl out there, Anneliese is forgetting the two hungry house sparrows that rule the roost here?"

In just an hour he had to be on his way to the gynecological clinic in town. "It's a pedantic quirk for a man to refuse to sit down to breakfast without his wife!" he often said, but he would also say: "Doctors, those overworked souls, should hold onto a few little pedantic quirks; otherwise, before they know it, they'll be bachelors again."

And so he fetched his wife away to go downstairs, putting his arm in hers as he did so. The other way around — once still the fashion, back when they were first acquainted — would have been more awkward, considering how much shorter he was than she.

Salomo followed right on their heels, and once in the dining room, whose windows looked out on tall trees, their branches now heavy with snow, he ascended his throne beside the green tiled stove. It consisted of an upended basket with a cushion strapped on top, and he liked to sit up high and survey the scene, not least of all the dining table, which even in the morning afforded him a pleasing view: breakfast ready and waiting for the man of the house, who on weekdays would not find time for dinner at home until evening.

Anneliese had already sat down, but then she suddenly turned to her husband, still standing beside her. She reached for his arm and pressed her face against it, bowing her head as she did so. Leaning over to raise it, he found her eyes full of tears.

"Lieselieb!" was all he said, but that nickname, the only one he had ever called her by since they were engaged, had a tone at once pleading and admonishing. She said nothing about what was making her weep.

It was a day of remembrance — the birthday of their third child, who had died years ago. He had hoped she would not recall it right away, when he saw her morning-bright face — outside by the birds.

Since she began mourning Lotti's death, she had dressed only in grey or brown. Yet he would most liked to have seen her, so blonde and robust a woman, in cheerful colors.

Beside the two table settings lay the morning mail. He handed her the letter he had read while waiting for his breakfast.

"Read this!" he said, "Nothing but good news. Gitta is already on her way back from her visit, from that trip she took as her 'examination reward,' as she so proudly puts it in her letter. So she'll probably be back home before Balduin. Of course, he should probably leave for a little while again — after Christmas — since this sanatorium seems to have been the right thing for him. No wonder my colleagues spoke so well of its director to me."

Anneliese had perked up and reached out for the letter, saying:

"Yesterday at Professor Läuer's they had such pleasing things to say about our Balder. He really won over the school officials with the tremendous zeal with which he caught up and then completed his school certificate. They realize now that you made it possible — the expensive home tutoring for him, the worst of their pupils! But who's still going to be one of the youngest to go on to university. I sat there with both ears open, relishing every bit of it!"

"Yes, yes. — But now?! Why doesn't *he* relish what he forced himself to go back and finish with such manic energy and all on his own? Why the disgust at his own achievements, in the blink of an eye? — That's not just from overwork. Yes — if only the boy would simply learn to keep marching steadily along, rather than taking flight every now and then."

Clearly the happy news from their daughter had receded for the moment behind worries about their son. The lines deepened in the beardless face, already much furrowed in any case. Even so he seemed, all in all, young. His eyes looked young, and whomever he gazed upon, those eyes seemed to seek out the youthfulness in them.

Anneliese had been completely caught up in Gitta's short letter, but the unexpectedly worried tone had quite affected her; it plainly tore her away from reading on and called forth her own inclination to hope.

"Oh Frank, let it be! Who knows — perhaps many of us learn to walk only late and with difficulty but then are destined to fly high —"

There was a trace of over-ardent exuberance in what she said — evident in the choice and high tone of her words.

And not merely in her words. Her face betrayed her emotion as she drank her tea — that telltale complexion of the reddish blonde, whose surging and ebbing blood is made visible by the most subtle stirrings. This play of colors, seeming to speak through the silence between them, was the object of her husband's gaze. So too the pale, almost violet shadow that the waves of her hair cast over her brow and the nape of her neck — that always pleased him anew. He sometimes thought that was the very first thing about Anneliese that attracted him when they met.

His wife gave the rest of the mail a fleeting look, read a postcard.

"So Helmold is really leaving. — You'll probably miss him down at the clinic. — D'you suppose he'll be gone as long as he thinks? I think he'll be coming back!"

The sly look when she said this, coming after the pathos of her previous statement, made him laugh.

"O ye matchmakers! Even you, Anneliese!" he answered, filling his pipe with Turkish tobacco. "I'll bet, even when you were a young girl, you were all afire for Marlitt-type dashing heroes with gold-blond beards. Maybe that's where this all started."

"There's more to Helmold than a blond beard and long legs. And isn't Dr. Frank Branhardt himself supposed to have taken a liking to him?" she said cheerfully. "Sometimes I think you like him even more than your own children — or at least that he's like a son to you."

Branhardt checked his watch again and stood up.

"Women's logic! That's why! That's why he'd be right to let the wind of freedom blow about his ears, get to know the world before he puts his head in the noose. He'll be a first-class surgeon one day! Nonsense to let himself be tied down so soon."

At that pronouncement, Anneliese laughed, her face all smiles. She stood up, and something of a high-spirited challenge, a tone quite noticeably foreign to her usual way, seemed to color her words as she kissed her husband goodbye.

"Frank, you poor fellow! Having to get tied down so young!"

Her eyes met his in the same recollections and warmth that had welled up so suddenly. Both felt the same proud wish: Of what life has given us, may our children too partake.

They parted reluctantly.

But as Branhardt walked down through the garden he thought to himself: Perhaps his interest in the young and competent Helmold would not be so very fatherly if he could hope his son would prove a better heir to his own competence. Or was he only deceiving himself on that point, after all? So often he had ardently yearned to have students, sons, young men around him whom he could inform, enlist, endow. He lacked time at every turn, couldn't even take on an academic chair. He had to smile: Lieselieb ought to have a hundred sons. —

And still his own son was most important to him — oh, yes, he truly felt that; Balder was his only son and his own flesh and blood. He pictured him as a boy, as clearly as if he were standing right next to him, the snub nose, the freckles. — He had his mother's same delicate coloring, her red-blond hair, too. But it wasn't only those aspects of Anneliese that made his every feature so dear to Branhardt.

As he walked along, he thought of laying his hand on the boy's shoulders, of how he spoke of him and himself as "we."

Meanwhile Anneliese had made her way downstairs to the housekeeping rooms on the house's bottom floor, built right into the hillside. At the small window where the stairway turned, she stopped: looking out past the garden she saw a short, heavy-set figure striding briskly but calmly along the road down to town.

How happily they'd bantered with each other — had not mentioned her at all — Lotti. Only the living have claims on us — it weighed on her heart.

My sweet child, my darling: this is your day! thought Anneliese.

She stood, her brow pressed against the small window pane. Branhardt's figure moved farther away, became less distinct, disappeared behind the bare trees along the road.

Healthy and with apple-red cheeks, Lotti had turned eight years old. Then a fall from the swing; her injured back, pain, traction, and, finally, release in death.

If human strength had helped Anneliese make it through that time, it had been her husband's and the example he set. Even though he suffered as she did, he did not, like her, give himself over to grieving for the dead little girl. The gaze that wanted to fix on his child he instead kept steadily focused on the living who could not do without him, and even today his struggle with the unforgettable was the reason he seemed to forget Lotti's day.

But his day-to-day work was such that it could push many things to the back of his mind. For that to happen, the daily had somehow to become the extraordinary, Anneliese thought to herself.

And she quietly set about her domestic duties.

*   *   *

Next to the kitchen areas on the ground floor, there was a small suite looking out on the terraced garden. It was occupied by a very capable married couple, Herr and Frau Lüdecke — she in charge of the kitchen, he the garden, although he had once, as a professional gardener, seen better days. Frau Lüdecke found their changed circumstances demeaning; oddly enough, she objected mostly to the fact that her husband worked in the same house as she did. She would have found it appealing to come to fetch him away at the end of his workday or bring him a dinner pail for his midday meal, the way other wives did. Herr Lüdecke was good natured; in the summer, on particularly nice days, he would obligingly join her in a rather romantic dinner back in the farthest corner of the garden, where there was a wooden hut with table and chairs. Of an evening, especially when there was moonlight, they would take a short stroll like lovers, and if they encountered others doing the same, Frau Lüdecke would blush, even in the darkness. For ten years of childless marriage had left her young bride's romantic ardor miraculously undiminished, and, whenever Herr Lüdecke chopped wood for the stove or carried the laundry basket, she took it as a gesture of chivalrous love.

The news that "Little Herr Balderkins" would be returning home to start his university studies was most warmly welcomed by Frau Lüdecke, since she was much taken by students in full fraternity dress. Gitta's return, too, she found timely. Who could know how long the girl would still be with them? "Ach, Gittakins wearing her bridal wreath! Herr Lüdecke always looks at the myrtle bush with that in mind —"

Purely from fear that the downturn in her husband's fortunes might cause people to address him simply as "Lüdecke," his wife had become so accustomed to referring to him emphatically as "Herr Lüdecke" that she hardly ever strayed from that usage, even in her inner thoughts.

Perhaps an embarrassing similarity grated on Anneliese's nerves, between Frau Lüdecke's rapturous dreams for the children and what she herself had said over breakfast. Didn't their visions suddenly seem like the pictures on candy boxes: "A Bride in Her Wreath," "A Dapper Student"?

With less attentiveness than usual, she listened to Frau Lüdecke's morning conversation, down in their small quarters with the frilly lace curtains and the canary. Everything there was kept almost unnaturally shiny and new, as if it had just left the shop or as if Herr Lüdecke were made of asbestos. His wife also took it amiss when Anneliese was too quick to turn her attention to Frau Baumüller, Frau Lüdecke's lesser rival in the service of the house, who was outside on a small ladder, wiping the windowpanes.

Frau Baumüller came every morning from the small village of Brixhausen, on the other side of the woods; she would stay through the day and then be given food to take back home for her impoverished family. She had ten surviving children and a body that no longer took the trouble to restrain itself: almost every year she had given birth to — and then buried — a little one, the last one only days ago. Born healthy, it followed its departed predecessors, about whom no one ever really cared.

When Anneliese spoke to her about the infant's funeral, Frau Baumüller dabbed at her eyes with the window cloth but kept silent and carried on with her vigorous rubbing. Weeping? There was no need for that here, where they knew her.

Her philosophy on the matter always ran the same: "With the little ones, it weren't no different, an' it was better for the big kids." And that's how she was: maternally glad at heart, deeply content that no new arrival would be able to take the food out of her children's mouths. She looked down from her stepladder at Anneliese — so imposingly indomitable, even with an aura of womanly dignity — her childbearing prowess a force ever enduring and ever working against her.

Gitta, who could have taken out a patent on dreaming, had once dreamed that the Baumüllers devoured their smallest children, which is what made them all such a robust and sturdy lot. Anneliese was well acquainted with all the sons and daughters; she helped look after the older ones, provide food for the little ones, and bury the dead ones. Her involvement in the lives of her domestic help went considerably beyond what was common among her acquaintances. She lived far away from these acquaintances and, owing to her husband's lack of free time, refrained from socializing with them. Instead she found it worthwhile to learn of many a contact in the surrounding villages through the Baumüllers and Lüdeckes.

Hearing Frau Baumüller's words tugged at Anneliese's heart. She imagined, in her mind's eye, a few of the next youngest ones, with their ashen little faces looking feeble and resigned far beyond their tender years.

She saw the procession of children — countless strangers, loved and forgotten — who, born into poverty, then had to return alone, before their time, into the vast darkness. And all the while Lotti, her image indelible, stood before all her senses.

Anneliese went back inside to the ground floor. There, next to the Lüdeckes' lodgings and underneath a small wooden veranda, was a brightly lit room, the so-called trunk room, containing nothing but cabinets and chests and all the things no longer or not yet in daily use. She took some old things, some new, out of the drawers and put them into a handbasket. And when she added toys to the underthings and warm clothes, then it was old things — that had nevertheless stayed new.

As yet she had not wanted to give them away — but now Lotti was to come with her and give out the presents.

Anneliese had adopted the lovely custom of combining her children's birthdays with giving aid and cheer to the needy. Her children participated in this undertaking with enthusiasm, sometimes with money intended for things on their own birthday wish lists. Why should that stop on Lotti's birthday? Because it can no longer be her parents' expression of gratitude to eternally unknown powers? Didn't that day still hold its eternal gift, inextricably? Always, forever, this day meant possession, not just loss.

Out of that procession of children, marching into the darkness, love saved the most loved of them, so they might stay, not passing on, forever undiminished. The Baumüllers' little ones were dead not only because they had died.

Anneliese set off on the road to Brixhausen, on the other side of the woods, encountering women with their backpacks on the way to their day's work in town.

It began to snow. People from down in the town had gathered to go walking, their faces cheerful, their mood made ecstatic by the long-awaited snow. Full-fledged adults were throwing snowballs at each other; an otherwise quite sensible-looking old gentleman wearing a great high-collared overcoat was singing in full voice: "Tarum, tarum, tarum, winter has begun!" They all felt proud, honored, and uplifted because they had turned white and no one could know if tomorrow they would be black again. It was as if they were all heading for a masquerade, and Anneliese felt as if she were in disguise. A short, steep pathway cut across the walkways that wound their way uphill. Up there it grew quieter. The slopes below lay under deep snow, covered by a gentle fall of flakes, with no wind and almost free of noticeable frost. A ghostly intrusion in the still air, as if on little white wings, bore away everything that was not of the utmost purity. It seemed to her that, if this kept up, the clouds would open, and down from heaven would climb the great and whitest angel of the Lord himself.

Anneliese strode along slowly in her snowflake coat, her basket large and heavy on her arm.

There before her lay the little village, almost erased from sight by the weather.

She would be able to tell her husband about her walk this evening! she thought, as if pondering something beautiful.

Of course, she could hear him admonishing her — mostly by his own example — not to make herself weak with grief, not to follow the dead. And she saw he was right. But wouldn't that be a sad commentary on a life that was *only* brave and not also rich — a life that had to be sparing with its most vital capacity to give? And with its abundance — of which Lotti too had been allowed to partake, as would now the poor, from this basket?

These were Anneliese's thoughts as she walked, her basket on her arm, all alone for the first time, on her way to happiness, along a little path she herself had devised.

And so she descended through the calm winterscape, down into the little village of Brixhausen.

CHAPTER I I

When Branhardt came home in the evening, he could hear music as he approached the house.

He was happy every time he was greeted that way, and for this he knew many a reason. Before they were married, in her eighteenth year, his wife had wanted to study to become a concert pianist, and her husband knew very well that their early marriage had held her back from a brilliant future. Of course, he never asked her to do that. She demanded it of herself, denying her own desires —. Perhaps out of fear her soul might stray too far away — too far from the demands of the very straitened material circumstances to which they were relegated in those early years.

So when Anneliese, hesitantly at first but then ever longer and with greater ardor, turned to the baby grand piano they owned then — when, as the years went by, she would ever more blithely and openly give musical expression to the undercurrent of her inner life — Branhardt took it as a sweet feeling of love, a conclusive affirmation of the bond between them, an expression in sound of all that tied her and Branhardt together. Anneliese's music was once again Anneliese's marriage to him.

Entering the house each evening, he would make his way at once to the still-unlit sitting room; with his ever-quiet tread he would arrive almost unnoticed, and sink deep, barely visible, into one of the armchairs — the most restful place he knew.

Unmusical himself and too pressed for time to attend concerts, he came to know music almost exclusively through Anneliese. That's why, little by little, it seemed to express so much about Anneliese herself.

The fact that music, in a sense, revealed as much about his wife as she revealed about music — that for him was music's true allure.

And Anneliese learned ever more astutely how to use that fact in a way different than he was aware. With her music, she shared with him much that he would have called "exuberance." She drew upon powerful depths of emotion, and, fresh and fair in her deft mastery, she let the piano speak. In her husband's silence, while the piano spoke, she savored her capacity, for all his roguish playfulness, to persuade him without words, to win over his fond embrace.

Then, when Frau Lüdecke ever so cautiously opened the door to call them to dinner and Branhardt gazed upon his wife in the dining room's sudden brightness, her face shone with that heartfelt joy in living that even the most melancholy music would impart.

And to such a face he could all the better recount the trouble and toils of his day.

In her typically absolute fashion, she idolized her husband's profession, even identifying it with him personally in a way. The notion that he might ultimately have taken up something else no longer entered her mind. In addition, his professional life was so bound up with his married life that, in all decisive matters of her role as a wife and mother, his authority as a husband was inseparable from that as a physician. Anneliese liked seeing matters this way, as if, in Branhardt's medical practice, something of the finest and most human quality would redound to him solely as the fruit of their most personal, mutually shared experiences.

Now, in their children's absence, they could converse more freely than before. But, day by day, they missed "their two" as they sat across from each other, just the pair of them, like the young, childless couple they once were.

And so it happened that, one day after dinner as they lingered at the table, Branhardt said:

"They grow up, and they're gone! What we really need is some new blood, Lieselieb! Looking at a woman like you, most people would say: she should be surrounded by a band of sons."

Anneliese fell silent. She had been gratefully happy some years ago to find herself expecting another child. — It was twins, but as a result of unfortunate complications with the birthing position, and after horrendous suffering on the mother's part, they were stillborn.

Even though she was far from what could be called neurasthenic, this one serious illness of her otherwise healthy life had left an indelible impression. Yet that crisis, in one stroke, put her among the ranks of all those to whom Branhardt had devoted his life and, in matters of serious illness, tied her to her husband in a new way.

She suppressed a shudder. "Seeing as how that would no longer be possible, Frank —"

He gave her a quizzical look: "What do you mean, no longer possible?

"Since back then."

"Yes, back then! But since then — you're still young — you just don't believe it because you have grown children! You're young and in thriving good health. There's really no need to give up."

She raised her arms, shielding her face on each side so he couldn't see her, her gaze fixed straight ahead on the white tablecloth. Giving up, he called it! Had he — could he — really have wanted that? — he, who had seen her suffering so horribly, so inhumanly — who as a doctor had made her suffer, of necessity —. Was she a coward — was he being brutal with his wishes? Didn't he love her too much to make her go through that again — didn't it take just a bit, a tiny bit of caring love to make him see that?

Branhardt glanced over at her as she sat in silence, her face still resting on her hands. Perhaps he had some inkling of what was going on in her mind. He said quickly:

"An isolated case, one in ten thousand; there's no way such a thing could be a decisive factor! You mustn't think back on that anymore — only of the future! A woman as brave as you: you'd always be brave again — I know you, after all! You're born to be a mother, Lieselieb: and that's the decisive factor."

She had looked up — but even without looking she saw how he stood there before her — in his tone, his bearing, so free and convinced. It was not the words that were convincing but something more directly persuasive — something almost physical, an assuredness that made him attractive — attractive despite his unimposingly small and compact build.

Even before he had finished talking, even as something in her was rebelling against his words and her soul was trying to hide from him, she knew: she saw he was right — and she was already prepared to wish

with him, to wish fervently for everything from his life that let her own
life take shape.

In a few minutes they were speaking about other things. Branhardt
soon forgot their short conversation. If anything in the following days
could have caught his attention, it would only have been this: that, in
the music from their twilight-dark sitting room, even more music was
speaking to him than usual.

*   *   *

Branhardt usually retreated to his rooms after the evening meal to
work, unless he were called on the telephone — which often happened
— or they had made special plans. The usual custom was that he would
come to the sitting room only briefly for tea with his wife and children.
But much of the time he would get into a hopeless dilemma, inclined in
principle to adhere to his routine of evening work, yet drawn by temperament to participate fully in all the family matters.

It was better with only the two of them: they eased involuntarily
back into the old habit of spending evenings together in the study next
to the library and having tea there. While Anneliese, with her own lamp
and her own work, sat by him, Branhardt could immerse himself until
late at night in the theoretical matters he could not attend to in the
course of each day's practical demands.

Anneliese had laid aside her sewing and brought along a book from
Balduin's shelf in his bedroom upstairs. A poet whom she otherwise
would neither have read nor desired to know; but, with her son far
away, she was sometimes inclined to do something he would do, simply
to feel involved with him.

Some passages afforded her pleasure with their lofty verbal beauty;
many were alien to her — and others reminded her in a particular way
of her Balder, with those eccentric and unrestrained ways that so worried his parents.

Even in childhood, Gitta, ever the master at inventing names, had
never called him anything but Prince Generosity or Kaspar Have-
Naught, so early had Balder's radical mood swings set in, his shifts from
blazing to sputtering, from complete mastery to utter ineptitude.

Where did this morbid tendency come from? She thought of her
family, of Branhardt's. — His father, up there on the North Sea, had died
a very old country doctor; his mother, a dark-haired Swiss girl from

Tessin, had died young giving birth to a stillborn baby. Yet his memories of her were nothing but happy and pleasant.

When the tea had been brought in and Anneliese was serving it, she suddenly said:

"Do you remember those old letters I was sent from the Courland a few years ago, after my mother died? — Some of them mentioned my grandfather's illness — I didn't read them very closely. — You know, he was mentally deranged when he died."

"Right. Caused by a fall down in the cellar while he was fetching wine or some such thing. — A concussion. — Why do you ask?"

Standing up to get his tea, Branhardt saw Balduin's open book and had no trouble guessing what his wife was thinking about.

"You know, Lieselieb, children seldom have healthier parents and forefathers than our two. — And then there's your line, generations living deep in the peaceful countryside, there in your cozy corner of Courland! With those inheritance laws, that primogeniture system that left so many siblings in poverty, you people made a botch of it, but the quiet of the place, that's part of you, my love. And I have precious need of it!"

He spoke cheerfully and made Anneliese feel the same. Leaning her head back against the cushion of her basket chair, she remarked:

"Gitta, she had her small share of that quiet country life — at least to the extent that a suburb of a capital city can be considered 'country.' — But sometimes I wish Balder had been born there as well, out on the edge of the forest, near the pines and heath, instead of in our better, more comfortable apartment! Instead of the middle of the city, among barracks and clinics, noise and dust. If our windows were open to let in a bit of the summer, and the trams went hurtling around the corner, he would give a start in his sleep. I still picture that to myself whenever he's so nervous. Even you were that way then — those were years of hectic overwork; — that's the only reason we moved here. —"

Branhardt ran his hand over his high brow, his close-cropped hair in steady retreat above it, but without allowing any misconceptions about that high forehead, which was so often distinctly prominent, as if trying to uphold its right to be there not simply by the grace of advancing years.

" — A person like you, someone so harmoniously balanced — with a son like Balduin, taken with all his faults and virtues — that *is* hard to explain. Every new person brings so much that is new and foreign that our flesh and blood cannot fathom — and that we nevertheless pass on, blindly, without guilt, ultimately even without being responsible. — That is something incalculable — beyond our grasp. A barrier between the generations. — — In every case and in every sense, children go on to a life of their own, beyond our association with them."

He returned to his work, but merely browsed distractedly. Standing up, he paced back and forth with his light step, as if the conversation would not let him go. That went on for a while before he settled at his desk again.

The question still touched Anneliese's heart.

Children go on? . . . beyond our association with them —? What if you follow them? Would that break or wound a mother's heart? And then why not —?

And her thoughts went on:

Innocent in themselves, and not responsible —? Oh, what good is that, if you love them?!

Hours passed; night approached, but Branhardt stayed at this desk. His powers of concentration, "a gift of excellent nerves," as they said, were often the envy of his colleagues. Once allowed to stick with a topic, he had a hard time stopping.

Anneliese had spent more than a few nights like that at his side, especially in the first decade of their marriage. Those nights were not like being in the company of a bookworm who just buries himself away. No, often they had amounted to a lively struggle, because his nature was to embrace life in its entirety, and he had to force himself to concentrate on one aspect: To turn away from many things that seemed part of that wholeness, in order to be even more fruitful from a new point of view. That process played out before the fine eyes of his wife like a deeply human drama, with its victories and defeats.

That drama's setting, this study, was almost always the same, since they had kept its basic furnishings wherever they went, like a snail its shell. In their very first house, on the city's outskirts by the pine trees, it had constituted almost the entire apartment, with the one bedroom across the hall and the kitchen as the loveliest little dining room, where Anneliese presided over the stove.

When Anneliese thought back to their close quarters as a young couple, they had something of an almost solemn solitude. By day, Branhardt's professional duties bound him to the institutes in the city and far away from her; and for her that was nearly as it should be. The

experience of her love had become so strong she almost needed the solitude. Like a too fiery wine, happiness had intoxicated the barely mature
girl, far from her family — robbed her of her balance. Instinct told her
that he must not observe her in the same way she watched over his
professional struggles and progress. Her many hours alone by herself
in those rooms, whose confines had become a kind of poetry for her,
helped her attain a happily expectant composure through the coarse
and simple work of her hands. Left her space to work on herself, in her
womanly way — in that deep, tremulous earnestness of a woman who,
not just for herself but for the man she loves, adorns her house with all
the most precious things she knows — summoning up and adorning
her soul for him. — No, honeymoon happiness it was not, not for either
of them, this happy weight.

That modest suburban idyll — though perhaps better guarded by a
pair of lions than by turtle doves — gave rise to Gitta.

Anneliese's thoughts, fighting off slumber, dreamed themselves
away. How could it be that this suburban forest was so beautiful, so
vast and silent, despite the trash and paper that littered its needle-car-
peted floor and all the bicycles and people whizzing through? — She
thought she could still sense it all, the warm fragrance of the stand of
pine trees facing their few windows — the twinkling lights of the huge
city in the distance — the muffled hum of its traffic, and the way it was
slowly creeping ever closer, one new house after another — and how the
untrammeled silence was still there, often right nearby, peacefully resting under old trees or on the last bit of meadowland — like unwitting
lambs straight in the path of the approaching, all-devouring wolf —.

When, late in the night, Branhardt went to the bookshelf, he
noticed his wife had dozed off in her basket chair. Her head with its
reddish hair on the leather cushion of the back rest, she was sound
asleep, an expression of sweet delight on her face — dreaming, as she
was, of a forest of fairytale splendor that looked as it sometimes had
back then, in the setting sun of winter, all silver. And she knew it was a
forest without end.

Branhardt set aside the book he had come for. Her face, which was
not beautiful and, through all those years, could have faded into banality
if it hadn't borne the intimate inscription of her soul, spoke eloquently
to him. He loved it as strongly and deeply as he had in his youth. But
differently now, because he too bore, perhaps in harsher letters, what
was also written there: the signature of life itself.

Truly alike in their inmost desire, they had somehow also become siblings.

He stood looking at her for a moment, and, with a deep joy, felt a certainty overcome him: each loss of youthful luster on this face is only like one more veil that falls from a sister's countenance.

Anneliese felt him touch her shoulder.

" — Let me stay in the forest!" she murmured.

"This is no way for you to get a good night's sleep. Get up, Lieselieb. Come, I'll help you upstairs."

Neither came back down. The lamps were left burning on the writing desk and on the sewing table.

In the morning, shortly before dawn, as Frau Lüdecke was getting up, she immediately saw the shimmer of lamplight on the snow-covered garden paths. She gave a disapproving shake to her head, its white bonnet tilted down over her brow. She wore that at night because of Herr Lüdecke's fear of hairs getting into the bedding. Hairs were something Herr Lüdecke was sensitive about.

"Oh God, dear God, he just overdoes it with his studying. Herr Lüdecke, I wouldn't let him do that, wreck himself studying!" she promised herself and hurried upstairs — to knock on the door with a gentle reproach, since she had to heat the rooms. She never dared more than a wordless rebuke, only in the most serious instances driving it home with a gaze and a sigh.

But when she opened the door, the study was empty.

All her life, Frau Lüdecke held to her secret conviction that someone had evaded her reproachful gaze at the last minute.

CHAPTER III

With a red ribbon around his neck, right about where he was no longer a terrier but not yet a pug, Salomo rode along to the station, with people staring in wonder as he went by — which put him in a happy mood. He liked red ribbons; and, besides, Gitta wanted to see him looking festive when she arrived.

At the last minute, Anneliese saw Branhardt coming to the train — even though it was at a time when normally he could hardly get free — and even though Salomo's show of emotion made it seem almost impossible to greet Gitta in human fashion.

She returned home as fashionably svelte as when she had left, but also, despite her slim, still childlike figure, in the same good health, so refreshing to Branhardt's doctorly eye. He had just time enough to wait for the baggage and pack his wife, daughter, and Salomo into a hansom cab — but at the last moment he jumped in with them.

That was ill advised, since every move took him farther away from the clinics. But then — as Anneliese often noted — something about Gitta made people careless.

And she didn't have to say anything of interest to do that. When she was three or four years old, he had listened to her just as tolerantly while she read to him, her tone serious but with the newspaper held upside-down — and later, too, when she would confide in him about truly pointless matters.

Anneliese sometimes said she had not known that dubious side of him until she bore him this daughter.

At home, up in Gitta's room, next to her parents' bedroom, Anneliese noticed the one thing about her daughter that had changed, when she took off her hat to reveal that, yet again — as so many times before — her hair was cut differently. The girl's dark-blonde hair, nothing less than luxuriant and with a slight wave, was remarkably amenable to all experiments.

As she unpacked, Gitta chatted with her "mama" while moving about her room. Its floor was covered with dropcloths, rather unaesthetically, to protect a belatedly applied coat of varnish. Gitta claimed her new coiffure was intended to match that of the girl riding the unicorn in the print of the painting *Silence in the Woods* that had hung on the wall since her childhood, figuring prominently in her dreams and indelibly named "Genoveva" by Frau Lüdecke.

On the table under the picture, there had been a golden alarm clock. "We had to hurry and return it to Helmold," Anneliese commented. "Remember how he lent it to you, joking how it was for 'that dreadful slugabed' because you almost overslept your exam? Now Helmold's moving away for good."

"So?" Gitta said somewhat distractedly, her thoughts already elsewhere, eager as she was to get out of the room, out of the house. She had to go with Salomo to the chicken yard, the one part of the whole household that really interested her. Max, the rooster, recognized her at once; he climbed out of the warm garden peat to greet her, crowing ecstatically. The last of his proud tail feathers that had survived molting season waved about like a wind-skewed weathervane. But two of the hens, Lena and Margareta, were missing! Gitta knew where they had ended up; her face red with anger, she ran in to see Frau Lüdecke.

Yes, Lena and Margareta had become soup hens. She would have to be just as hard-hearted about the countless chickens coming in the spring. If Gittakins didn't travel away occasionally, there would be nothing but elderly hens and young roosters, and that couldn't possibly make for good eggs. It went against the cosmic order of things — and that meant more to Frau Lüdecke than the world order.

Not so for Herr Lüdecke. He improved things quietly. Holding his pruning shears on his way out to trim the hedges, with his reserved bearing and the gold-rimmed spectacles he always wore, he looked like a banker who had taken up gardening in order to lose weight.

From the Lüdeckes', Gitta had to descend to the bottommost cellar room, where fruit was stored on wooden racks. She had someone to visit there, too: a dear little hedgehog, who was there to eat the mice. For that reason, his presence in the house was suffered gladly, though as far as Gitta was concerned he might have just as well been producing mice as eating them. His name was Justus, and sometimes, after dinner, he was admitted to the family circle.

After Justus, she headed for the garden to greet the birds. From those still flitting through the bare branches, one could have imagined they had assembled to honor Gitta, who all winter had made the balcony their paradise. That further bit of birdsong, a faint flapping half lost in the distance, might not belong to the hillside house's own avian population, but Gitta was far from regarding them as foreign; she preferred to extend her garden's boundaries.

So it took a long time for Gitta to perform all her greetings, and it was her secret where the world of her household ended.

Now she stood silently inside, her eyes fixed on the windows. That was for her the nicest feature of the little old white house — the way it gazed out through so many window-eyes.

It looked out now upon nothing but winter. Only on the bushes or the low branches was there still a feeble leaf, trembling in the calm air — as though fearful a wind might come up. But all the towering treetops stood bare — their green mask cast off — etching the rhythm of their branches in austere, pure lines against the bright, daylight sky.

The house had two vistas: one off into the distance, over the descending garden, of the valley and town and faraway hills — and the other up towards the hillside woodlands, blocked in the summer by a wall of treetops. Today that contrast was almost reversed. Often, as now, the valley was shrouded in winter fog veiling the longer view, while the hill's bare trees suddenly revealed tracks in all directions, off into the distance, the path winding its serpentine way upward between the slopes. One could see a long way, even to part of the plateau high above, and then *imagine* what lay beyond —

Gitta knew all this well. It could bear no surprises for her, not in any season. Yet ever anew it struck her as surprising, as if she had yet to fathom it.

*   *   *

Meanwhile, beside the small wooden veranda behind the house and above the "trunk room," Anneliese had been standing with Herr

Baumüller from Brixhausen, who was replacing a few of the rotting steps in the narrow stairway leading down to the garden. They were talking about the Baumüllers' oldest daughter, Therese. Thesi, as she was called, had become a "perfect" cook under Frau Lüdecke's tutelage but couldn't find a job because of her severe stutter.

Baumüller, tall, ungainly, and a worthy counterpart of his wife in strength, had worked, one after another and one on top of the other, as drayman, mason, butcher, joiner, and a few other things too — a jack-of-all-trades, although, as the result of a fall from a scaffold, he dragged one leg and on occasion had been summarily dismissed. Made opportunistic by need, man and wife alike got by without honesty in the strictest sense, and that was not always balanced off by competence. Anneliese was aware of this and believed the best remedy for it to be frequent opportunities for work and earning. And when her close acquaintances shook their heads at the fact that she so often took on the Baumüllers instead of hiring more reliable help, she sometimes thought as her daughter did, in the chicken yard and regarding Frau Lüdecke's "cosmic order of the worlds": "We're ordering our lives much too practically."

She was still talking about Thesi when Branhardt arrived, a little earlier than he had said, and called out for his wife. He was holding a small bouquet of lilies of the valley, likely meant for Gitta, but he looked very annoyed.

Gitta soon heard her father in the house; she ran to greet him and found him in the dining room, where the table was already set, with her mama. But, as soon as she came in, they fell silent, and the looks on their faces brought her to an awkward halt.

Branhardt looked at her. All he said was: "I returned the golden alarm clock Helmold lent you, since he's leaving."

"The alarm clock —?" she stammered, uncomprehendingly. But then suddenly this ill-fated alarm clock loomed large in her memory, where, heaven knows how, it had been hidden, and its alarm — which she had secretly turned off — clanged through her like the trumpet of the Last Judgment.

Branhardt kept his eyes on her face.

"It wasn't simply lent to you, then — as we thought. Helmold said to you: either the day would come when it would show you two the hours together — or, by returning it, you would be saying he had nothing left to hope for. — Is that what he told you?"

Gitta looked miserable. She rubbed her back up against the oven, since there was no way she could simply crawl in, frightened and silent. Her father's lips had gone so tight and pale —.

And now he banged his fist on the table, making the dishes jump. "Is that what he told you?"

"Yes!" she cried out, bitter and remorseful. "That's what he said! In those very words! But to think he remembered it so exactly, word-for-word! I thought of it, too. Very often, in fact. But sometimes not at all. Then I forgot it. And just now was a moment when I had forgotten it. I've just arrived back —"

Frau Lüdecke, cheeks red from the kitchen, brought in the steaming dinner, unaware of how out of place her festive smile was. She was convinced she had prepared a meal that would put any other cook to shame.

They had to fall silent. Branhardt paced back and forth.

Anneliese tried to mediate. Branhardt never became this angry.

"There's a misunderstanding here we must clear up. Helmold unwraps the thing from the paper, stares at it and asks: Was that what she really wanted? to send it back to me? And will —"

Branhardt quickly cut her off: "Leave him out of it!" Gitta looked into his eyes, light brown and so large that they had plenty of room for all his frightening anger. Gitta wished they would get very small.

"That he could take it to heart — him —! That you could use it to do something to him, to a man whom many now see — and many more will see — as capable — a complete man! That you weren't afraid to make a fool of him! For heaven's sake! Have some respect for a man's worth and concerns! Keep your female fingers off them!"

He thought: now we should sit down and dine; the dishes are already getting cold! Everyday life would gloss it all over. But the indignation in him would not stand for that, it wanted to explode first — the indignation of one man for another.

The little bunch of lilies still lay off to the side, thirsting, on the table. They were supposed to be set at Gitta's place. Anneliese filled a small glass from the water carafe and put the dozen blossoming stems into it. Then she thought: better to push it more towards the center of the table.

They sat down and began to eat, but only for appearance's sake. They had to make a more serious show of it when Frau Lüdecke came to exchange the plates, and, with her second appearance, she usually counted on being briefly included in the conversation.

The lovely torte she had made to celebrate the day stood heavily among the dishes. Beside it, the bouquet of lilies, small though it was, now had to be shared by everyone. Salomo, his head sunk down on his red ribbon, his batlike ears pricked up and alert, sat on his throne by the oven and, with his eyes half shut, seemed to ponder how the matter was to be settled.

As soon as propriety allowed, Gitta and Salomo stole away, forced to a quick departure.

But Gitta found no peace in her little room upstairs. To think her parents were angry on her homecoming day! And her father — how touching it was of him, really, that he was not at all angry for his own sake, on account of the comical role he ended up playing, with the alarm clock in his hand — no, it was for Helmold's sake. Oh, how wonderfully convenient it would be if Helmold no longer existed. Her parents would be happy again.

And then: what did they mean when they said the misunderstanding had to be "cleared up"? Gitta sensed darkly it could mean something like a betrothal. Her parents had suddenly come to know how betrothed she basically already was, and now she too was all too clearly aware of that fact.

She could not possibly bear all these uncertainties for long, and so, after about an hour, Salomo and she went back downstairs. Something had to happen!

Even though the angry man was her father, it never occurred to her to first seek a bit of motherly protection for the discussion. The two of them were too much an inseparable whole for that to work, even though they might have differing views. At any time, what one of them was feeling could migrate over to the other, and vice versa.

So she knocked on the door of Branhardt's study and, brave and honest, walked in to her parents and said:

"Dear Father, dear Mama, forgive me; I will certainly never do it again. — — And since it's already a misunderstanding, I think it's best to leave it as such. If we try to clarify it completely, it will only get worse and worse."

It was not clear what she meant by "get worse."

Anneliese went over and put her arm around her.

"Gitta child, it was an unintentional slight. You're so childish that you really don't know how precious gifts from one person to another are and that we must treat them with care."

"Oh, Mama, I know! But it's not as easy as you think! With something so precious, a person doesn't know where it will lead — it always goes amiss — and that only makes you want to just forget about it!"

"You should have confided in *us*, instead of keeping it to yourself. — Are you really so sure there can't come a day when you'll be sorry for what you've lost by being so thoughtless?"

Gitta looked uncertainly over at her father, who did not seem at all concerned. His face turned completely away from her. Looking strangely good natured, he sat over by one of the bookshelves, where he seemed to be looking for something. Gitta held more closely to Anneliese.

"Because I still — I — have —"

Then she faltered, frightened, uncertain if she should go on. Again, she looked over to her father. But he appeared not the least bit curious to hear any more. With great calm, he remarked, only to his wife, as if his daughter were not even there:

"It's Helmold's own fault: how can he feel hurt, even for a moment! We have to pity a man who'd go courting such a capricious thing."

At that, Gitta suddenly broke out sobbing. Much too late now, and to absolutely no purpose. She was sobbing too much to object, but it went through the room like a loud, woeful protest.

There was nothing at all charming about the way Gitta wept; it was always to excess, as little children do, making people smile and think: that will cry away the pain!

But it was good for Branhardt that he had turned his back on her.

CHAPTER IV

The small addition with a wooden veranda, above the "trunk room," was next to Branhardt's study, separated from it by a double door and fitted with large, multi-paned sash windows that let in the sunshine from all sides and afforded a lovely view of the hills across the valley. Plants spent the winter there on boards and benches, and there was a small iron stove for them. Beside it, a door opened out onto the roofed veranda — just big enough for one comfortable armchair — from which a wooden stairway dropped steeply into the garden.

Anneliese thought this should be Balduin's domain during the day, and since they were expecting his return tomorrow, she was getting it ready for him. She had the plants and most of the racks removed and his books placed on the main shelf. She went over the pale-green oil paint of the walls with a moist cloth, covered the old garden table with dark-green baize, drew some polka-dot muslin along the lower windowpanes, and then brought in a few wicker chairs kept on the balcony in the summer. That left no room for a bed.

Yet, as she worked at making the room pleasant and comfortable, she quietly wished this were not necessary. She admitted to herself how much she longed for a son who would stand by her, cheerful and strong, in the bloom of manhood — his father's youthful mirror, and one day, the "support in old age" one routinely wishes for.

Was it natural that she had to be so anxious about shielding him from disturbances? That she was already worried that his bedroom next to theirs was too close to the stairway and all the comings and goings? It was also too close to the guest room, for which a visitor had just announced herself: Renate, a friend of Anneliese since childhood, who was rather lively in manner and generally expected more consideration than she was inclined to show.

As fresh as Anneliese's heart had been when she began her work, such reflections had tired her by the time she went upstairs to dust herself off and remove her apron.

Up in her bedroom was the parents' old bureau, which the children, on account of its cunning array of drawers and compartments, called "the box of secrets." It contained the correspondence of her mother and even older letters, and Anneliese had thought of them again recently, when she commented to Branhardt about the purported mental illness of her maternal grandfather. She turned on her lamp and opened a drawer.

Branhardt, who usually arrived home at about this time, was on his way to a medical consultation in a town two hours away by train and would be staying there overnight. Gitta, after her long time away, was out visiting her "best" friends. So Anneliese pondered her letters at leisure and soon found what she had been looking for: reassuring news in the writings of her grandmother; after the death of her first husband, who indeed had been mentally ill, she had remarried. These writings so captivated Anneliese that she soon forgot her original intention. There were diary pages concerning the deranged man, and the torment his wife suffered because he "no longer understood" resonated through them, as did her passionate struggle to rescue him from the confusion within himself — not to lose the path that led from his happier days — but, with the force of longing and memory to shower her husband with so much beauty that it seemed to dispel the darkness around her image of him.

Anneliese sat and read page after page, ever more deeply moved.

Then came memorial pages with black borders, but their theme was more often reunion than loss, for the widow's pious faith saw the departed rising again, and with mental clarity — he was once more close to the experiences of all her days, which she faithfully laid out before him. The reader of these pages could now picture him free of struggle and pain, free too of the anxiously exaggerated images made of him — could see him conclusively, in the clear, golden outline of his true nature.

The ensuing years brought this woman happiness again — belated, yet abundant. But even then — in fact, on the day she entered into her second marriage — she turned her soul, so full of innocence, to him with whom she shared everything. And no one could laugh at the naivete with which she did so, at the childlike boldness of the beliefs that carried this earthly happiness to heaven in the most matter-of-fact way, without diminishing its warm, earthly power. From then on, it remained so: at every commemoration, anniversary, and child's birthday — she always gave an unstinting account of her heart's experiences to him who gazed down on her. Yet he himself no longer appeared here in the same compellingly clear image as before. — He seemed to have risen in the beam with which he had illuminated her — already extinguished, as it now shone only for her — only as a glow and a blessing over her world: a part of her own beauty.

This dark undertone, working by the light of faith, against the writer's will, had a simplicity and power as though conceived by a great poet. This woman, who wrote to the dead about what she was living, had poetry in her blood.

In Anneliese's mind, no trace remained of those black shadows of heredity she had so anxiously set out to find. She stood in grateful silence in the light that broke from this past — and also came to rest upon her children.

When Gitta returned, she was surprised to find her mama in the bedroom.

"Ah, such old letters — already so yellowed — who're they from?" she asked.

"From your great-grandmother."

"But Mama, you look as if she'd just written them to you. Hadn't you ever read them?"

"Maybe not — or with the careless eyes that beauty shies away from," said Anneliese. She hugged Gitta, who had leaned over to look at them.

"Are they so beautiful? Oh, let me read them, too, dear Mama! I'm her great-granddaughter, after all."

"I should hope you are." — Anneliese had to think how wondrous that was, and how fine that in the tone of these letters there was something whose childlike purity could speak to such a young girl — and also swell the heart of a person who has struggled to come to terms with herself.

She handed her daughter several of the pages.

At once Gitta plunged into reading with a thoroughness far exceeding Anneliese's. She noted every turn of phrase. Many passages she read twice, and Anneliese had to struggle to call up from her memory everything Gitta eagerly wanted to know about the writer. From time to time, she would break off reading and exclaim: "No! What a great-grandmama!" And she would ponder the smallest asides with an intensity that quietly pushed the purely emotional to the background.

Anneliese thought to herself: Anyone seeing this sober, almost austere seriousness, this silent understanding, would have trouble believing Gitta was a thoughtless do-nothing, though she had demonstrated as much only days ago.

Even after reading, Gitta was far from finished; on the contrary, she had just begun. For now she insisted on knowing about her great-grandmama's children, and then about Anneliese's family, in which she had never shown the least bit of interest.

Anneliese's mother, Brigitte, Gitta's namesake, had been a different type than her great-grandmother. She was a proper, simple lady of the house, able and sensible, and secretly animated by the desire to raise her five daughters to be like her — but ever thwarted in that aim by a warm kindness that made her take over the mundane work herself and leave the girls to indulge their intellectual interests, about which she herself did not give a *pfifferling*. With all that, her daughters were never really aware of her plan, which their mother did not know how to explain. So each girl followed her own lights, and joy went before them, at all times, throughout the house.

This practical woman's impractical love proved a great success, with each daughter turning out better than the one before. Although their mother always kept as far as possible from their various intellectual pursuits, each of the hours devoted to them bore the mother's indelible image: a white-haired woman, lovingly bent over some task that was not hers by rights but rather that of the ten young hands and eyes to which she was devoting all her time and energy.

Telling Gitta about all that might no doubt be less edifying than everything she could read from her great-grandmother herself. But Anneliese gave freely from her mother's trove of love, convinced something so beautiful would only help a young life find its own way to beauty. She could not talk about those experiences in a way calculated to educate and impart a lesson; she felt they were too precious for that.

*   *   *

Gitta had attended the girls' academy that had just become affiliated with the local gymnasium while she was still in school. She scraped through in a thoroughly leisurely way and only because even her father thought it would be of benefit. Other than that, no one could accuse her of having "intellectual interests," although she had struck up a friendship with none other than the school's model pupil, a pastor's daughter from nearby Hasling. Gitta insisted she did so purely from selfless joy in that girl's perfection and out of genuine affection for her many virtues. Gitta was just as unflinching in her insistence that she herself was intellectually gifted only at night — which was hard to verify because she always went to bed with the chickens. Yet when she woke up, she always seemed to think she possessed, in addition to her intellect, a truly outstanding talent for drawing; she could see heads and whole figures in outline so tangibly before her. But even a sketch pad of coarse paper and nice, soft pencils — some of them colored, like the ones for little children — produced nothing.

Early the next morning she sat up in bed and quickly turned on the light, resolved that what she could not draw she would express with exceptional vividness in words, on the rough paper, and using the colored pencils. Salomo immediately stood up in his padded basket, yawning — his earnest dog gaze, as bright and dutiful as ever despite his being half-drunk with sleep, was fixed on her like a muse, ready to assist.

The stars still twinkled in through the window, though gazing through the hazy air was like looking through a drawn curtain. Only the many lights of town shimmered up the valley, the impatient day of humanity.

Then a cab came slowly up the road — and stopped. The garden gate creaked.

"It's Father!" Gitta said to Salomo. Branhardt was returning from his medical consultation.

Whenever Gitta thought about her father's professional activities, she summed them all up in the idea that he helped humans into life. She did not ponder the details of how that happened. She merely thought of the outstretched finger of the Lord God on the ceiling of the Sistine Chapel, reaching to touch Adam's hand: "Come alive!"

Dawn's faint light shone through the rising and falling mist.

Poor Father was very likely tired and hungry and in need of warmth, and he had to get back to the clinic so soon.

Gitta had a lively imagination. It helped her to see, just as vividly
as with the faces and figures she wanted to draw, how she would get
up right away to look after her father, to see to it that he had what he
needed — even though Frau Lüdecke knew how to deal with such situations. Besides, a breakfast prepared by his daughter's hands would
taste quite special — so it always said in books. It was time to get up
anyway, Gitta thought, before she sank back into a deep sleep.

Gitta was known to go to bed with the chickens, but by no means
to get up with them.

Upon her typically late arrival at the breakfast table, she was greatly
surprised to find Balduin there. His cab, not Branhardt's, had rolled up
as dawn was breaking. Although he had been only a few hours away by
train and could have conveniently arrived at midday, he had set out in
the foggy gloom of night to surprise them, something he took pleasure
in doing. He always hoped something special might come of it — which
it never did.

But nothing detracted from the happiness of coming home; his
face was aglow with it, as if he had braved a thousand perils all the way
from Australia. Looking at him, you would have thought nothing could
ever dampen his spirits once he was back "at home."

"Now you're Prince Generosity again!" Gitta said with a laugh. But
she was a bit ashamed, too. When she herself was allowed to travel, she
was so boundlessly desirous of change — naturally, it was also nice to
return home, but one took that for granted as a last, added-on happiness. "But, of course, if you're released from such a prison!"

She followed him up to his private domain next to the veranda,
where he was already delighted to put his luggage. He gave a lively
account of the institution, how being there was at once boring and
arduous. Gitta had already come up with the catchwords for his
feelings: "prison!" and "release!" With the astonishing deftness of
a quick-sketch artist treating a set theme, he developed an entire
album of caricatures of the staff, the guests, the doctors — but even
as Gitta's happily applauding laughter drove him to ever more daring attacks, there remained, stemming from the catchwords "prison"
and "release," something almost artistic in his portrayal that was
not mere caricaturing but an anxious yearning for release — and
more unjust than any mere mockery of reality. It was like a sudden
revenge, not really intended, but just from the high spirits of homecoming and improvised by the minute.

It also came from the hope of never going back there. Balduin knew very well he was unlikely to see any of the people there again, who in truth had all been kind to him — and he felt ashamed. A worse shame than if he had behaved improperly right in front of someone and then had to make them forget it by being doubly decent. With this shame, anyone could seize and control him at will, making him vulnerable and helpless, until he talked himself into an exaggerated state of devotion — or perhaps until, in too confidential a moment, he betrayed someone else.

Anneliese, who joined them, had eyes today only for what was fresh and cheerful about Balduin. A healthy young person, that's what he looked like, despite his slim and lanky limbs, which went very well with the boyish outfit he still wore — clothes then thought of mainly as cycling togs, although Balduin had never ridden one of those machines. His hands, however, nobly formed by nature, were marred during winter by chilblains, which nothing could prevent. His feet were similarly afflicted, year after year, and his constant awareness of them impaired his gait and even his facial expression.

"You're doing so well; you should stay here now!" Anneliese said, getting to the heart of Balduin's secret wish, which, in the course of his satiric rant — what one might call his dismantling of the institution — had grown from merely a wish into a desperate determination never to return to that unforeseen scene of destruction.

"Stay here? Well, of course, Mother. I'll tell Father right away — I'll go find him downstairs — I'll start my studies now! I want most of all to jump right into the middle of the semester — history, literature — oh, you'll see, Mother — you'll see!"

"Really, Balder?" she was standing with them in the small corner, where three could barely move, but she couldn't have him near enough. "Of course, I *knew* that! — oh, you, I knew it! That's how he *must* come back to me, happy and healthy — *my own* Balder, his same old self, as he lives and breathes!"

Anyone looking into Anneliese's eyes would think she were standing before a lit-up Christmas tree and reflecting its radiance. But Christmaslike about all this, too, was how the lights were already aglow in her thoughts, one after the other, before they all burned together.

Gitta observed her mama's joy with mixed feelings, seeing her side by side with her brother, discussing the future with him. What happiness Balder had brought with his return home! By contrast, hadn't she made trouble as soon as she arrived, and disappointed the whole world? Now she really had to come up with a brilliant coup of her own.

When Balduin found his own inner assurances directly expressed by his mother's deep faith in him — they were actually anticipated by that faith — he was seized by a peculiar anxiety. Of course, his faith in all this was unshakeable — rock solid, as a matter of fact. He was sure he had never believed in anything so firmly. Yet seeing his own hope mirrored in Anneliese's, he felt the driving lash of his commitment to bring it all to a beautiful completion — as beautiful as it became through her gaze upon it and through her whole being, which took it in.

Of course, his own vision of things was painted up in all the rainbow's colors and exaggerated as much as possible. But that did not bind him. And if, under his mother's tender, earnest eye, he appeared the least bit untrue to his goal — like someone who quails yet brags, dissembles and then fails — how could he live with himself?

Ah, yes, it was splendid to be back home! But for that reason — for just that reason — not for him! What was splendid always moved farther away when he reached for it — so strangely unattainable. Hungry and weary, he came to a table so richly decked out for him and could not partake thereof.

Anneliese could not help but notice how his lively expression changed as they talked, like a fading light. He began to complain about all kinds of things — minor details; a rip in his coat lining; how he felt at the moment, with his one foot beginning to hurt —. Finally, it didn't take much to leave him standing there, a poor man indeed, dressed in rags and smitten with sore boils.

Gitta noticed it, too: Prince Generosity had taken his leave, and there in his place stood Kaspar Have-Naught with his chilblains.

CHAPTER V

Balduin soon found himself on his way down to see Branhardt, who apparently had gone straight to the clinic after his consulting trip and would not come home until evening.

After the conversation with his mother that morning, he felt doubly driven to see his father — who thought so much more soberly than she did — who did not expect that every one of his son's high hopes would be realized but would stand by him until his confidence was justified by the young man's actions. Balduin saw both parents as the embodiment of all he so urgently wished to be! Who else on earth could make that possible for him? After all, their life was in his blood — that was the firm, fixed bedrock of his life, though all else might make him confused and unsure. That calming certainty filled his heart as he walked along.

His good mood diminished as he approached the clinic area. He had always been exceptionally sensitive to certain impressions, and his father's quarters did nothing to help, not only by their close proximity to the clinics themselves, but because they deliberately lacked anything that could have imparted a comforting touch of the personal — intended, perhaps, to express his father's principle that comfort was to await him at home, with his family —?

While Balduin was waiting, they were starting to serve breakfast. Branhardt had indeed gone from the railway station to the clinic, where he was still busy. If only he'd come —!

A son's love, when it involves such need, such dependency, loses all the poetry of free feelings, Balduin thought. How much better it was for Gitta, in the natural simplicity of her child's love.

Already his sense of himself was losing its poetry, like an unwatered flower left too long in the sun. With each passing minute, his mood wilted away, his original impatience now strangely pierced by a stinging fear.

The awareness he had impressed upon himself so forcefully on the way to town — that he depended on his father — suddenly entangled him in the misconception that he was a confined, imprisoned person who clearly would rather be free but was now fidgeting about like a fly caught in the finest of cobwebs.

When Branhardt arrived, his son was about to dash away, simply as proof of his own freedom — he desperately needed the most drastic one he could find.

He struggled to compose himself.

Branhardt, a man schooled in punctuality and the decisive moment, had no idea he was several minutes too late. He welcomed his son with heartfelt joy and quickly learned about his plan to jump straight into the winter semester.

If Balduin had been formulating all this on the spot, it would have come out confused enough, but it was still fresh in his mind just as it had come to him, in oracular form, at that moment of inspiration with Anneliese — and his immediate and anxious craving for freedom only exaggerated the tone.

"I'm pleased that's your own wish! After all, you'd fully earned the right to a breakdown, the way you were pushing yourself," said Branhardt in good humor, as he put his arm around his son's shoulders. He had to raise his arm to do so: "And the boy couldn't resist growing another good bit over my head!"

Then, all business, he turned to the boy's troubles, had him take off his boot to attend to the nasty chilblain on his foot.

"Nothing to worry about," he said cheerily, as they sat down to their delayed breakfast. They were under time pressure now, but there was no mention of a need to hurry. Branhardt ordered some wine for a welcoming toast and played the host for the tall, slim boy — his guest. He served each thing, filled his glass and entertained him with a liveliness that could still create space and calm for every matter.

Balduin observed his father's lively self-assuredness every time as if transfixed — something about it beguiled his senses, his eyes, lulled his willpower. This dominance seemed to emanate from his father's lofty brow, with its sharp, vertical furrow that even happiness could no longer smooth away. It abided behind the man's free and easy gestures, which suggested the capacity of that power for playfulness.

Even the fact that there was nothing imposing about Branhardt's diminutive stature reinforced that feeling for Balduin — as if the man had absolutely no need to strut or make a show of strength, because he could enchant and conjure — it seemed like witchcraft.

As they talked, Branhardt asked about his stay at the sanatorium, with Balduin only seeming to answer, preoccupied as he was with the chilblain and wondering whether his father would want to lance it. To avoid asking that question, he laughed altogether too much, and his face, its freckles still prominent even in winter, blushed right up to the roots of his thick, handsomely wavy hair. In his efforts to buck up his mood, he exaggerated his description of life in the institute in exactly the opposite direction from the one he had taken with Gitta that morning. Once he got going, he raved about how well he had felt there — as his father might have expected and as he must, in any case, have been pleased to hear. Balduin was well aware that Branhardt took an immense, heartfelt joy in his son's willingness to confide, and this drove Balduin deeper and deeper into a current taking him in the wrong direction, away from the point at which he hoped he and his father would agree. He gained nothing by sitting with his father no longer as an afflicted patient but rather as a young but equal friend, with whom Branhardt could get along as if with his own youthful self. His father might have that pleasant illusion, but for Balduin it was merely an aesthetic experience he sustained through his sensitive involvement, and he could only envy his father's pleasure.

Amidst all that was said and unsaid, the joy of his reunion was blown out like a flame without a wind guard.

He returned by cab, ordered by Branhardt on account of his sore foot, and felt more unfortunate than ever, as if he had forever lost a friend he could have had that morning, even an hour ago, but whom he had fobbed off with a false Balduin.

Limping a bit more than absolutely necessary, he walked through the garden to get back to his private domain up the stairs and across the wooden veranda. One of the sash windows was open, and the little iron stove was hissing red-hot to ward off the cold. On the table with the dark-green baize stood a glass with resin-scented spruce branches interspersed with burning-red rose hips, which Gitta had skillfully picked from a wild rose bush. His return was greeted by the gaping yawn of his suitcase, its contents still scattered on the floor.

Balduin's attempt to sort through things was hampered by the inflamed areas of his hands, which burned every time he touched something.

He tired of rummaging and sorting, but then found that sitting still left him beset by a puzzlingly large number of flies. These surviving but doomed swarms were even harder to brush away than in summer. They buzzed about, weak and nervous — sometimes dying unexpectedly in midflight, or creeping around on him with their cool little feet to die. So, there he sat amid their agony — no more than a meeting place for flies.

Eventually, he opened the door onto the veranda. If only the robin were still there, the one Gitta had made so trusting last winter that it lived up here with her. During the day, it would hop and flit through the house, snapping up all the flies and spiders.

Balduin stepped out onto the wooden stairs, into the fresh November air. He heard the call of a bird of prey. The sun hung like a red moon in the slightly hazy sky over the town. It didn't feel like daytime, though it was early afternoon.

The solitude over the small bit of garden made it seem vast — a hermit's kingdom that shunned daylight and human contact —. How sensitive mother had been to give him this one corner for his own — to provide him with this little stairway out into the open — always a way out! Here he could feel content.

But no sooner did Balduin start down the stairs into the garden's wintry silence than he thought, just in time, of Frau Lüdecke, who was sure to see him from her window. She'd be at him right away, as the flies had been — she'd call him "Herr Balderkins" and say a lot of other things, too —. That morning, arriving in the grey dawn, he survived this, because he was hungry and had such need of Frau Lüdecke.

He had no doubt she was watching out the window. She had a regular passion for sitting there by the shiny canary cage, looking out through the well-ironed tulle curtains.

Balduin stayed up on the veranda, looking hopelessly down into the garden, as if into a paradise closed to him, its entrance guarded by Frau Lüdecke holding her little flaming sword.

* * *

Anneliese had not noticed Balduin's return from seeing his father. She had a visitor who laid claim to her attention — too much so, thought Frau Lüdecke, in whose view that guest was being honored as though she had rolled up in her own carriage.

Of course, Anneliese's friend, the old peddler woman — Frau Hutscher by name — did not arrive by private coach. But Frau Lüdecke resented the fact that the Branhardts would dearly have liked to take her into their house. They definitely had a weakness for the likes of her — for the Baumüllers, for the Hutscher woman, and, yes, Frau Lüdecke was honest enough to admit, for the Lüdeckes too — the lot of them half-failed existences, people whom the Branhardts picked up somewhere and who, in their company, retained or acquired what could be deemed independent lives, not as domestic servants or "the under-the-stairs contingent." This relationship in particular eluded Frau Lüdecke's understanding and nearly detracted from the high esteem in which she held the Branhardts.

Anneliese had known Hutscher the peddler woman for many a year, since the day she had found her collapsed at the foot of the woods and then cared for her. Even now she could barely understand why Frau Hutscher didn't faint from hunger or exhaustion more often; nor did she know for whom she kept a stock of those wondrously useless items in her backpack: colored bouquets, silver belts, golden combs, diamond stick pins and the like. Yet perhaps it was thanks to the fresh air — the only place she could thrive in — that, for all her privation, she did not look her seventy years; she had no white hair, and only her eyes were growing weaker, as years went by.

Sitting still indoors was torture for her, so Anneliese's attempts to keep her on, doing worthwhile work, were of no avail — she couldn't stand it for more than a few days, and she didn't do it well, either. Her hands — of remarkably noble form, as seldom found among common folk — had too long suffered her feet to do the day's real work. "If I rest, I rust!" she liked to say, with only her feet in mind and claiming the phrase was from the Bible. The more her bad eyes kept her from reading the Bible, the more confident she became in moving all the sayings she especially liked or was impressed by into the New Testament.

She sat in the warm dining room, blissfully happy at having ended up there once again, spooning in the warm soup prepared for the poor, toothless woman — and brimming with new happenings and new cares. Her son, who worked in a carpet factory, was coughing up blood, while his wife was out gadding about. Things were worse still for her daughter, a servant girl. Frau Hutscher had educated her Grete to be a phenomenon of respectability, with the warning that "the wages of sin is death!" And, right to the end of her youth of toil and hardship, Grete had remained steadfast against all temptation — until an "honest suitor" seduced her, all the way to the registry office. Nobody would think a savings-bank book — the sure sign of a steadfast youth — could be a motive for marriage. Now she was rid of the savings book and of him too, and she lay abandoned, disabled, and pregnant under her ailing brother's roof.

Making her way through this tale of woe, Frau Hutscher consoled herself from time to time with one of her maxims, even if it were no more than "hope never fades" or "learn to suffer without complaint." It was hard to believe she still took heart from these commonplace sayings, and some people were annoyed when she offered too many of them for free, along with her wares. Yet in the old woman's hands even the most withered and dying of this bundle of maxim twigs somehow remained green and alive. They saw another springtime and even grew into trees in whose shade she could lie and from whose fruits she could draw sustenance.

So rich was Frau Hutscher.

This time she did not want to stay overnight, and so she departed at dusk, having received a large assortment of things, the barest necessities, stuffed into her backpack with all the rest. Anneliese worried to see her go, unable to see how her hapless old friend would manage everything: caring for her son and soon the young mother and child, while no longer able to roam the countryside. How could she do all that with her tired hands and dim eyes?

Frau Hutscher, bent under her pack — out of which she had produced ruby earrings for Gitta and diamond cufflinks for Balduin — was aglow with satiety and love.

"What is accomplished comes from God!" she turned back to call out. "For so it is written: Come unto me, all ye that labor and are heavy laden! And it is also written: well begun is half done!"

Anneliese was often teased about her "peddler friend," who, much to her advantage, was known by that title far and wide. But at times, when the old woman trundled off with her gnarled walking stick, it seemed to Anneliese that she had left her with something uplifting, even if it was not always to be found in the New Testament.

When Anneliese went upstairs to look in on Balduin, she could hear her two children having a spirited argument in Gitta's room, and they didn't stop for a moment when she came in.

Gitta was sitting at her desk, agitated. Apparently, she had been telling her brother about their great-grandmother's letters and offering up some comments on them she had made in her sketchpad. Even without knowing what they were talking about, Anneliese could tell from one look at Gitta that she had set out to become her "great-grandmama," with a change in coiffure as her first step. On each side of her head coiled an artful thatchwork of tightly interwoven braids, much as bedecked the ears of the ladies in old family photos.

That wasn't enough to impress Balduin. His criticism poured like a storm of wrath over Gitta's braid-swaddled head. Why was she simply repeating in her notebook what was already in the letters? And how were her silly notes any different from the slavishly imitated braids around her ears?

In his excitement, his voice kept straining and cracking.

As a critic, Gitta was no match for her brother. He alone, not she, could do things that connoisseurs and experts alike would have to accept — and even respect.

But Gitta was still furious. She had just succeeded in feeling almost exactly like her great-grandmama. She wept with indignation and chagrin, and Salomo barked at Balduin.

Salomo was sitting on the hem of Gitta's dress; she had taken care to slide it under him, since he was always bothered when his backside came into unexpected contact with something cold.

Sitting on her chair by the door, still holding the earrings and cufflinks, Anneliese listened and watched in amazement. Did she find it all so strange because the two had been away so long, or were both her children really not quite right in the head?

Balduin paced doggedly back and forth, and from time to time Gitta reminded him sharply about the recently varnished floor. That seemed to get through to him. Despite his excited state and the loose felt slippers he was wearing on account of his chilblains, he was careful to step on the protective cloths that had been laid out. So he took one very long step and then a very small one, which looked funny enough. The sight of his skinny calves and bony ankles between his knee britches and those bulky slippers was grotesque in its own right.

Balduin began to explain how to do it — not from their great-grandmother's point of view, but their great-grandfather's. *His* feelings were what was new, not yet recorded. Once Balduin started offering practical suggestions, Gitta became interested. Yet she did have objections: "Identifying with him is not very pleasant," was her egotistical view.

Balduin stopped in midstride. "But wonderful nonetheless! Imagine this loneliness — and then this woman follows him into everything — into the darkest things that draw him towards the abyss —. Suppose he feels that: how much torment, how much bliss that must be! That must be absolutely tempting, to steal away into ever darker darkness, simply to see how far — how far a person follows. This solitude and this rapture — they put him in heaven and in hell at the same time — not just later, after death — no, already rewarded for everything, punished for everything —!"

Balduin broke off. "If you can't imagine that, then you're a camel!"

"Yes, yes, marvelous, very good!" Gitta said excitely. Her anger had subsided. She didn't protest about being called a camel. The last of her forgotten tears still on her eyelashes, she gazed expectantly and obediently at her brother.

He had stopped pacing. The lamplight fell on his handsome brow, its skin so delicate a contrast to his reddish hair and ennobling his freckled face, whose features, like Anneliese's, were somewhat undefined.

His voice high and clear, he spoke of these eerie matters as he stood there, his feet in their felt slippers and planted together on one of the dropcloths, as if on a pedestal.

Serious and composed, he spoke almost without interrupting himself; and Gitta wrote.

Her eyes were wide and frightened. Unselfconsciously and with pencil flying, she made all the required changes to her brief notes. She'd chosen a pale violet pencil for the task.

Anneliese sat motionless.

How Balder spoke of such things — not in the nervously exaggerated way he talked about everyday matters, not excitedly uncertain as usual — but with calm conviction, like a person who finds joy in standing by his own words. Yes — standing by them!

As if, for the very first time, she were hearing him speak of a reality, instead of the fantasies he was grappling with.

A clue came to her about what that reality was, where he was at home — and why he couldn't be quite at home anywhere else, not even with her — and what it was for him "to create poetry." As he was now, before her own eyes, so he was in reality: not a Prince Generosity, nor a Kasper Have-Naught — but himself, Balder.

She didn't move as she sat there — she watched, she listened. — And her children just let themselves go on in front of her, as if it were all as familiar as the rocking horse and dolls of their childhood.

And it did not occur to either of them that, in play or in earnest, their mama could learn anything about them that she did not know already.

CHAPTER VI

For eight days the upstairs guest room had been harboring a guest. Renate, Anneliese's friend since girlhood — her parents' country estate had neighbored Anneliese's family home — was on her way from her residence in the capital to the southern part of the country, where she was to give some public lectures. She had studied library science and was often engaged by private archives or libraries in need of order. She was also responsible for several specialized studies in history, which had helped her earn a doctorate with a notable dissertation. Despite that, she was less a scholar than an expert in organization, and her talents were not restricted to putting wayward books back in order. Just as she had been able, even as a young woman, to sustain a charitable society on the international stage, she was later skilled at bringing an idea persuasively to bear among the most diverse groups of people and eliciting their support, and her public lectures, happily aided by her aristocratic bearing, often created a sensation.

Branhardt, who approved of all that was clever and competent, also marveled at the vitality of this almost morbidly delicate woman — on whom, as he put it, "a husband would be wasted." But Anneliese was aware of how remarkable all this truly was, for she alone knew of Renate's tired nerves, her legacy from an ancient, dying lineage — knew her struggle against herself with "what remained of that squandered strength." She alone could see Renate's "manliness," which earned her both friends and enemies, as her heroism.

Sometimes they enjoyed music together. As little girls, they had begun piano lessons with the same teacher. Although lacking any notable talent for playing, Renate understood and loved music above all else, and never did she visit, even for a single day, without Anneliese's having to offer up a treasure.

Then Renate would stretch her diminutive figure out in one of the armchairs, with a second one pushed under her feet and her hands clasped behind her head, which, since a bout of typhus, was adorned by a short, sparse crop of ash-blonde curls. A wonderful nonchalance seemed to be one of her essential requirements for listening to music, and often for life itself.

Even the most thrilling concerts had been spoiled for her by an uncomfortable seat — and also, when they were schoolgirls, by Anneliese's sitting next to her, because Anneliese so seldom shared her emotion, her struggle to hold back tears. Anneliese would often laugh openly about all the beauty and splendor she heard, and the two of them would then reproach each other, one for weeping, the other for laughing. The grand, serious music to which Renate was drawn became something she allowed herself only as a rare luxury and from which she had to recover each time as if from a quivering wound.

That is how it was this time, too, after she had called again and again for Beethoven.

"Oh, stop — do stop!" she murmured helplessly throughout the *Appassionata.*

"You feel set upon because you demand too much of yourself!" said Anneliese with concern.

"Set upon?" Renate fell silent. Then, struggling, her words harsh, she went on: "Whoever listens to that suddenly wants the impossible — cannot bear that her youthful self, that arrogant lady, once liked being humiliated."

"Reni —!" Anneliese jumped up from the piano. "You! Think of what you are: strong, proud! How dare you speak of yourself like that! — Why is he so important?" — she asked breathlessly.

Renate raised her head. "Oh Liese, you dear thing! But no, one shouldn't delude oneself." And she said calmly, firmly: "I've seen him again."

With that, Anneliese returned to the piano and sat at the keys, hunched forward. Saw him again! So it was the same as always. — Yes, it was, even though she's encountered better, more honest friends, even though she had tried anew to forget.

Anneliese's hands lay heavy on the keyboard. They would have liked to plunge in, to drown out and dispel the words she had heard. That one could be so suicidal in one's love. Her Renate — raised by her countess mother to be proud of her class and her presumptions and now a thousand times more noble, by virtue of her own achievements — and he a man whose wife she never could have endured being — something of a horseman in spirit, skilled only with the whip.

Renate roused herself and walked over to the piano, giving her frame, less statuesque than her friend's, a spontaneous stretch. But her face, its features finely cut and beautiful though now nearly free of youthful charm, looked deeply weary, and her eyes brimmed with tears.

"It's always as if I were the only one — and yet it's in all of us — the strongest thing in all of us: this insane attraction to subordination!" she said hopelessly.

And, all at once, she was crouching on the carpet by Anneliese. She embraced her, firmly and passionately, and said:

"When you think about it — very, very honestly and deeply: when you think about the most rapturous experiences between you and Frank, of such moments — even if they were only moments! — wasn't something like that the strongest in you, too?"

She almost whispered her question, their heads nestled close, touching, as they often did as young girls. Anneliese lifted her tightly clasped hands to her lips, searching within herself with the deepest honesty — searching for what could make them, as two women, into sisters.

"When I think back," she said slowly, "yes, there were such moments: when something was very difficult for me but I felt I should do it and had to do it, it was helpful when a will came from him, compelling, inspiring! Yes, compelling, but at the same time encouraging me. It never would have been possible, if it were not for my — no, our — benefit — because for mine alone — —"

Renate sprang to her feet as Anneliese trailed off. She walked around the room, her hands clasped behind her back. She walked slowly and deliberately across the bright flower pattern bordering the carpet at the center of the floor, and with such willfully heavy tread that it seemed as though the carpet flowers were being trampled.

A trace of annoyance in her voice, she went on: "Are you really so incorrigibly considerate, Liese, that you accept me just as I am — you, whose thoughts are so well-behaved — so tied to your family — or do you occasionally appreciate, but only for my sake, a few weeds amid your tidy rows of grain?"

That made Anneliese laugh, which was like a release.

"It's not at all so simple with the grain, Reni. A person must embrace both weeds and grain, and each in good measure! We know how weeds are often sown in entire fields, to rejuvenate them, because the weeds have more root value than the useful crop and they reach deeper into the soil to loosen it up. — Don't you know that as a country girl? Long after all the lovely blooms have wilted, only then do the weeds do their work; deep down in the ground their little roots prepare new soil for the grain. — 'What are weeds?' — as Pilate says — 'to me.'"

"Oh Liese, how absolutely beautiful!"

Renate was back in her armchair, her head tilted back, her eyes closed. "I thank you! Now play — play, you dear, wise girl, whatever comes to you! Now I can listen!"

*　*　*

Back in their schooldays, "Reni" had looked down on "Liese" a bit cavalierly because she took her music so seriously that she wanted to live only *for* music — and even *from* music! Then, after Renate herself had become a "striver," she reproached Anneliese for marrying so young, for abandoning her chosen profession. Thus, during and after their close childhood friendship, they really did not come to know each other fully — but they did that while living far apart. It was Anneliese's good fortune that Renate herself, through the years, remained visible in the distance, as a steady light is to the boat out on the sea, a guiding beacon.

They saw each other only occasionally, wrote each other ever more rarely, and neither desired more from the other.

Once Renate arrived, however, she made all the greater demands on her friend. It was good that Anneliese, simply on account of Branhardt's tight schedule, had already refrained from social commitments. These days, invitations came only for the children, sometimes to dances, which Gitta declined, since Balduin could not accompany her, at first because he was laid up with his bandaged foot and now because he was still limping about. One day, the afternoon post brought a formal, printed ball invitation. Anneliese searched the house in vain for her daughter, who had been invited out for that evening. She found her at last in Balduin's private domain on the veranda. Gitta was wearing his big, soft felt slippers and about to uncork a bottle of the kirsch cider he was so wild about. The small room with its many windows had been decked out even more with books and pictures, and Balduin was keeping it in rather pedantic order, all of which made an unusually cozy impression.

"A ball invitation for Sunday!" Anneliese said. "What are you up to here? You're going to drink up Balder's whole bottle?"

"Just one sip, Mama. He doesn't begrudge me that much, and if he has to unseal and uncork it himself, then he agonizes too long about whether he really wants to, or whether he should bring the bottle to the corkscrew or the corkscrew to the bottle. As for his felt slippers — well yes, I'm happy to keep them warm for him. That's good for his sore foot, our limping Kaspar Have-Naught."

Anneliese kissed her. As sudden as that, Gitta could be like a proper little wife, caring. But then again, the two had precious little to do with each other, unless it was in a way that made them go berserk over the least provocation.

Gitta read the invitation.

"You don't have to go if you don't want to," her mother said.

Gitta appeared deep in thought.

"This time I'd like to, Mama. The white gown would be just right — Frau Lüdecke can iron it for me. — With a larger gathering like this, Mama, there might well be someone there whom I'm not likely to meet again."

"Someone? Who would that be?"

"I haven't seen him often. Twice in his evening attire, once in his street clothes — in them he looked quite different: almost like nothing at all. — But the last time, at the costume ball, you know — as an Arab."

"Yes, but who is he, anyway, Gitta?"

"His name is Markus. His first name, I mean. His last name" — she sighed — "is Mandelstein. I wish he had a Romanian name — he's from somewhere there. How beautiful his name could have been! — By profession he's a physician, or some such."

"A physician? — Yes, Father mentioned him to me once. I believe he wants to work towards his professorship here. But why is his name so important? It makes no difference for dancing," Anneliese said.

"Yes, dear Mama, probably not for dancing. — But I'd rather marry him."

"What are you saying —?!"

Anneliese had been bent over the little stove, which tended to go out if not carefully watched. She started up, as if sparks had flown in her face.

"Have you completely lost your mind, Gitta?! I hope this Herr Mandelstein hasn't been courting you behind our backs."

"No, Mama."

Anneliese breathed a sigh of relief. What was she shocked about? Gitta was always having these amazing whims that never went anywhere.

"Well, with your one-sided adoration you can give him the most beautiful of names in your own mind — that's always been a passion of yours," she joked, trying to dispel her shocked tone as she ran her hand over Gitta's hair.

She could see the young woman was at odds with herself.

"You see, Mama — that's the way courting is — not everyone's way. — But that's not to say —. Actually, I even believe that —. Letting it be noticed, talking about it, that's often the very last thing, dear Mama. Don't be angry with me, but it seems to me — I think — everything may very well be there already — just thinly veiled, you know — and often that causes unbearable pain, because it can't get out yet. It's the same with a boil that eventually bursts," Gitta concluded thoughtfully, and she seemed moved.

Her mother stood before her, silent. Despite the comparison Gitta had used — ghastly even from a doctor's daughter — Anneliese could not laugh or make it into a joke; she was struggling for words. She commented, with forced matter-of-factness:

"I'd like more facts, Gitta! It must be something, beyond the usual flirting, that's led you to such idle assumptions. Somehow this gentleman must have behaved in such a way that —"

"It's not how he behaves, Mama, that's just it!" exclaimed Gitta, and now her face was aglow with enthusiasm. "There are people you can see everything about merely by looking, you can see it all there, and maybe even why it's there — and I mean everything — like Helmold —" she hesitated a bit to say his name. "But then there are people like this man — you see nothing. Sometimes you rub your eyes and think: So where is it? But still, it's there! Something festive and powerful, something whose love comes upon you like great bells ringing, like a storm or a song. — You feel it — you feel it!" she repeated, and her small face with her father's features looked completely enchanted.

Anneliese took her daughter in her arms, her own heart beating with a strange anxiety. She went on, somewhat abruptly:

"Gitta — don't go — to this dance — child, don't go. You know how only a short time ago you played with such things — you did wrong, you hurt someone. — You start playing again — and you'll hurt someone else — you'll get in over your head." Anneliese didn't know exactly what she was afraid of, but she refrained from considering that more closely. Under no circumstances did she want Gitta to be involved in this new affair. — And so, since her daughter remained silent, she made the decision for her:

"You'll be my good child and not go!" she concluded and kissed her on the forehead.

A strange thing about those kisses: only rarely did Anneliese demand or prohibit anything, except in questions of a purely practical, everyday nature. But when it did happen, then the decision was final and sealed with a kiss. Against the authority of this kiss, there was even less chance of appeal than against one of Father's sternest looks.

They exchanged a few more words on routine matters, about coming home that evening. They heard Branhardt arrive. He was in the next room, and Anneliese was about to go see him, when, right at the door to his study, Gitta ran up and threw her arms around her neck.

"Mama, dearest Mama, let me go to Hasling for Sunday and Monday, to visit Gertrud at the parsonage —"

"Naturally, why not? But why does it have to be Sunday, when Father's at home with us?"

"It's just — on account of the dance. — Oh, don't let me be here at all, if he — I mean, if there's this dance."

She had gone pale.

Anneliese felt all her limbs go heavy. — She acted as if she didn't notice anything else about Gitta; she was unconsciously trying not to notice her own feelings. But the look on Gitta's face, suddenly so pale and with trembling lips — it was all so touching that later she couldn't get it out of her mind, no matter what she was doing.

At dinner everyone noticed that Anneliese seemed unusually distracted and not her usual self, not fully engaged in what she was saying.

After Gitta had left, she was alone with Renate in the lamplit sitting room. Her friend could not help observing:

"Raising children, that must be an unholy misery — well, yes, a joy, too, of course. — Yes, if you could just be a piece of nature: creative, profligate, without pain, without scruple! Or, if you like, the Lord God himself, who guides his children's hearts 'as he does the rivers of water.' — But to be caught in the space between the two —. Good parents are tragic people."

Anneliese, uncustomarily quiet at the moment, looked up, all alert, and said, in a low voice:

"Yes — conflicted creatures, that's what we are — we give birth, without knowing to what; we educate, without knowing whom; we must answer for it, without knowing how; and we can give up neither our power nor our fear."

She noticed Renate's astonished gaze, so astonished it made her smile. She corrected herself quickly, her eyes lighting up: "But then again, that's the most marvelous thing — all this contradiction from out of the depths — and that we are an active part of all this riddlework! — Who would wish to renounce life when it's most alive?"

"No, at least you wouldn't — good heavens!" Renate laughed. "And we're still surprised that such a woman gets on so well in life."

She was stretched out in her armchair again and even smoking — an actual cigar, since she claimed she couldn't smoke cigarettes. In any case, she hardly ever did that, and then only on special occasions known only to her.

She fell silent and thought to herself:

How true! Theory and practice, philosophy and religion, and heaven knows what, how little all that means compared to this one simple thing: the desire for life of a completely healthy, physically harmonious person — and I'm not one of them. — Only such a person knows what life really is. Life can be trusted — if Liese trusts it.

Anneliese too was silently pursuing her thoughts: Renate certainly sounded "childless," although she was so maternal! All those young people who thronged to her, seeking advice and help, which often included the most essential material care. Perhaps only Anneliese knew why her friend was sometimes so very short of cash, even though being without money was something she found inordinately hard to endure.

Renate watched her cigar smoke for a while and then remarked:

"It seemed to me your children were giving you headaches today."

Anneliese admitted as much. It did her good to talk about Gitta, who was occupying her every thought. She confided some things about her: the Helmold episode, noting how long ago that all seemed. Then about Gitta and the old letters from her grandmother. She didn't mention the latest worries.

This awakened Renate's interest. "Yet you always treat Balduin as the 'problem'? How old-fashioned! Surely you couldn't be so prejudiced as to think of Gitta as 'only a girl'? For God's sake, leave her freedom to try her wings!" She told Anneliese Gitta should not be allowed to marry too early.

That was especially clear to Anneliese this evening.

"She should be allowed to pursue her fantasies as much as she wants!" Anneliese assured her, having become much happier. Her wishes were transforming Markus Mandelstein from an imminent danger into a mere image, like that of Gitta's great-grandmother in her notebook, whose torn-out pages had long since been swept up and thrown out. "I really do want her to find expression for all that weighs on her heart — to be able to say more about it than something like 'Oh, Frank!' Unfortunately, I've never gotten past that one exclamation."

They laughed about that.

"To be you and still be able to take this different view, that would truly be more happiness than one person deserves," Renate said, "and who knows whether a happiness as great as yours might already be well on its way to the Kingdom of Art — perhaps one station before that. With your dreadfully good instinct, you will probably get off the train at just the right time, since otherwise it will pass Women's Happiness right on by — if it doesn't go off the rails completely."

But Anneliese was not at all interested in such railway mishaps, and the two of them had quite an argument about the exact geographical location of happiness.

They sat up late into the night talking excitedly, almost like when they were young girls.

Anneliese went to bed shortly before Branhardt, who once again had been called out late in the evening. She would have liked to share with him all the demands this day had made on her motherhood. The children had pressed so intensely upon her heart that she had lost the realistic grasp that Branhardt always achieved.

But sometimes it was hard to express everything the way she felt about it. Even recently, when she told him about the impression Balder made upon her as he was arguing with Gitta about their great-grandmother, she felt it couldn't be accurately reproduced with mere words.

For the children alone, we must have a God-given talent for eloquence in all tongues. Being a mother: that really means crying out for a talent for many things — for everything! she thought to herself — and she would have liked not to have bypassed the Kingdom of Art.

But this evening Branhardt seemed preoccupied with other matters; he was taciturn and lay awake for some time. She knew that when a stressful day robbed him of sleep, it often meant a difficult case had followed him home. Later, when that matter of life and death had turned out well, he could fall into an almost unrousable sleep, even in the middle of the day.

As she lay listening whether he had fallen asleep, her own cares quietly faded away, no longer standing out so urgently, compared to those many worries of strangers, along with which her own family and their concerns counted among the uncountable.

Although she had not spoken out to him, she drew near to this silent, watchful man who struggled with the unknown and to that place where, seen from below, one looks very small but can see very far.

CHAPTER VII

Then came the last Sunday of Renate's stay at the hillside house. The midday meal was early, in good bourgeois fashion, and the restful holiday atmosphere allowed them so much time together that Renate finally had to smoke her after-dinner cigar in front of everyone.

Branhardt assured her she needn't feel bad on his account, since there was no way a harmless cigar could make her appear more emancipated to him than she already did. She protested in vain: her bit of independent living an emancipation! It was merely a much-needed way of restoring her will. That was like branding someone a mermaid for taking a cold-water cure. It was the same with her short hair, a result not of her convictions about women's rights but of her stay at the hospital.

With feigned melancholy, Branhardt reminisced about the long braids and ladylike flowing skirts of her first visits. He also mentioned the domestic skills she had revealed when she arrived unexpectedly at the crucial moment before Balduin's birth. Renate found she looked splendid in Anneliese's long housecoats and even claimed she could cook, if need be. Oddly enough, everything turned out to be beefsteak, nearly raw in the English style, with an egg. Those middays together — with little Gitta in her wicker pram next to the table and all their thoughts with Anneliese and the newborn — brought Branhardt and Renate very close.

She was aware that, since then, he had acquired a bit of prejudice against her, perhaps because he tacitly believed her "emancipation" entailed certain female issues, rumors of which had occasionally reached him. He struck Renate as one of those men who are far more tolerant in theory than in practice and who become less so if such a person comes closer to them or theirs. She had to content herself with his very indirect flattery. In any case, she had no doubt that, in the majority of cases, Branhardt would have a very energetic response to the gentle Liese-question, "What are weeds?"

After dinner Gitta hurried into town to catch her train to Hasling, planning to stop first to pick up Anna Leutwein, the pharmacist's daughter, a school friend of hers and Gertrud's. Balduin thought it polite to stay home a while before making a few collegial visits to professors in town.

Renate had enjoyed his company during these days. Early on, when he had to stay seated, his leg propped up on account of his bandaged foot, he found it embarrassing to see her stand or have to fetch something. Later, he would blush like a little boy about his felt slippers. She saw no vanity in that — but rather a fine chivalry, a sensitive taste like her own — except for the cigar. For someone who remained a stranger to Balduin — he had never behaved otherwise towards her — the propriety of his behavior completely concealed his morbid irritability, so that Renate was always somewhat amazed when the others mentioned it. Clearly, this was a form of self-control he did not accord his family.

The weather outside was not exactly inviting. With galoshes pulled over his dress boots, Balduin went stomping ponderously through the muck, at times slipping and grumbling on icy patches. The several indifferent visits he had to make included one he would have liked to avoid. That was the young historian, a Dr. Sänftgen — the only truly young teacher among the pedagogues who had tutored him for his final exams — how ardently those two had worked on their studies together! They made what was to be taught and learned into a kind of intellectual ramble that unleashed Balduin's talents and ignited his character — resulting not in mere camaraderie, but in ecstasy. Then, after Balduin had passed the test and, overworked, exhausted, and disgusted, cast all those concerns aside, he was shocked to realize that his most intimate friendship, his most trusting confessions, his most secret spiritual life had become caught up in it all — and he was ashamed, like someone who was supposed to go out with nothing to cover his nakedness.

The young historian, recently promoted to senior teacher, although some years older than Balduin, was awkward and inexperienced in life. He could hardly wait to see his young friend again — had invited him to visit. In his dry scholarly life, which he never would have dared to enliven on his own, the contact with Balduin had summoned up previously untapped wellsprings — and he thirsted for more. He did not know — and never would have understood — how routine, even monotonous, it had become for Balduin to fake his way up the illusory sprouts of intellect to the loftiest feelings — only to reach a point from which he couldn't get down, except by a daring leap.

Balduin postponed the visit to Dr. Sänftgen to the very last — but then it had to be, if only to dispel the unrelenting fear of encountering him unexpectedly, like a ghost. Balduin would be in town every day now, for he had managed to get his studies off to a serious start. How had he ever agreed to plunge into this hurried course of study, right now?

He thought back: it didn't happen until he returned home — actually, his mother had said it — that is, suggested the possibility — and then he had gone to his father —. Oh, this persistent past that a person can feel holding tight, like some sticky stuff that can't be brushed off! So now he had to perform great feats, just because he'd been a bit diligent — and then he had to be an eternal friend, just because he'd been a bit friendly. He would study history — he who couldn't bear a trace of history or recollection in himself — who hated it in fact! He who would so like to start anew, brand-new, reminded of nothing, a beginner every day.

A person should be able to change any time, giving everything its due and bound to no one — free, utterly free! Yes, sometimes the horrible thought came to him: everything, even his own parents, those in whose blood he seemed forged within unbreakable boundaries — he had to be able to change them, exchange them, do away with them — reject them as though they were strangers to him, and he a stranger to them —.

This was the highpoint of his thoughts and of his third visit. Then just as in a dream the climactic event suddenly awakens us before it unfolds, Balduin started up, out of his megalomania and back in his own skin. He didn't even regret he had thought it; it no longer belonged to him.

He walked mechanically down some stairs and found himself standing again on the wet, foggy street. And he found himself caught up in a very different feeling — although almost the same one, really: a very quiet feeling, as if he were taking part in all things and all things in him — as if he were the child of everything and everything a mother to him — as if he were becoming quite small and at peace, willing and trusting — a little thing among things and at one with the creator of it all.

Wonderful images went through his mind and then passed on — rhythms sang. —

Amid the sleet-like December rain and gusts of wind that seemed bent on playing catch with his hat, Balduin experienced moments of the deepest happiness.

Then, waving from afar and almost at a run, a young woman approached him — an acquaintance of Gitta named Ida Mittenwald. She and some of Gitta's other girlfriends had a strangely intimate relationship with Balduin, one almost free of that half antagonistic, half coquettish inhibition with which they usually regarded young men and even adolescent boys. They were coquettish with him, but in a slightly different way. They knew he was able to write poems to girls, and that was more desirable than cotillion medals. Ida Mittenwald knew herself quite rightly to be the prettiest of these girls, even though she had "jumped the rails" and not finished gymnasium.

She called out to him:

"So, have you heard?! — And here you are, walking around as calm as can be — no, I believe I saw you simply standing still! — And it concerns you most of all!"

To the sensitive Balduin, the world seemed to burst apart in front of him. In this moment, he came back from so far away that it seemed to him the humanly impossible might have happened in the meantime.

"What is it? What should I know?"

Ida Mittenwald gasped for breath to tell him the news.

"Gitta has run off with a Greek man."

"Gitta? I beg your pardon, she left for Hasling a few hours ago."

"Yes, but with a Greek."

Balduin stared at her. He was relieved that Gitta was concerned; she would quickly put the issue to rest.

"Yes, go ask the Leutweins; they know all about it! — That's where Gitta met the Greek man. — Anna couldn't go along to Hasling because he was visiting them."

As anxiously as Balduin listened, he kept watching the rapid way she spoke, straining to show distress, even though she was about to burst with childish delight about the scandal. With his wide, golden-brown Branhardt eyes resting on her so calmly, Ida Mittenwald's report made the facts more confused than they already were. She felt the most urgent desire to appear beautiful to him in some way, although not as she did for other men at a ball, in ribbons and flowers, but more poetically ideal. When he continued to look at her as not at all a subject for any poem, an unreasonable anger at Gitta arose in her.

"Well, anyway, I don't have time for standing around on street corners," she announced brusquely and turned to go.

"Yes, but how did you learn about this, Fräulein Ida?" he asked.

"How did I learn about it?! The whole town knows! Because the young wife — the Greek man has a wife! — had a crying fit — naturally! He's her husband after all! Why should she spare Gitta? — So Gitta's going to get it now! He'll drop her! A man like that, who'd leave his angel of a wife."

Having played that trump card, she strode off.

Balduin went straight to the Leutwein pharmacy.

Going to see his historian, Dr. Sänftgen, was now out of the question, he thought to himself with relief — his sister's affair now took precedence.

The pharmacy "The Dove," where as children they had been given licorice and peppermint wafers, stood in the shadow of the Church of the Holy Spirit. The proprietor was not down in the shop on Sundays, so Balduin, who had hoped to deal with the matter with him alone, had to go upstairs to the family residence. To Anna, whom Balduin called "Annine," he had once written a poem referring darkly to a great mission that prevented him from courting her — with the epigram "Ophelia, get thee to a nunnery!" He thought she would help him stand up for Gitta now, and if need be, he would write another poem to her.

Upstairs, parents and daughter were gathered around the lamp on the family table, "Annine" busy embroidering handkerchiefs.

Balduin's arrival caused quite a stir. He was awkwardly urged to take off his overcoat and have a glass of liqueur, but he kept his coat on and came right out with his request for an explanation.

"Annine" let out a huff of laughter, although she herself found that improper and in Balduin's presence otherwise never forgot what she owed him as his erstwhile muse. She was so at pains not to embroider past the red "L" on the handkerchief that she was almost going cross-eyed.

Pharmacist Leutwein put great stock in keeping the sociability in his house at the same level as in "professorial circles," and he insisted repeatedly that not a word had been spoken, no word whatever, that was not of the "most cultivated level." — It was a harmless visit from a young botanist, the son of an old university friend — "a Greek, to be sure, but only on his mother's side" — traveling through on his honeymoon.

The pharmacist's wife, a tall, gaunt figure, her gaze stern and refined behind her spectacles, did not care at all for his obsequious tone. "Leutwein," she cut him off, "you know she was looking at him! In all truth: Fräulein Gitta looked at him! What's more, I think she kept doing it!"

"Gitta does not know any Greek man!" Balduin interrupted her, trembling with rancor. He was beginning to sweat in his overcoat, but he was not about to take it off. "What I want to know, only Fräulein Anna can tell me — I'm told she went along to the railway station."

Anna let out a huff again, making her florid face, which in any case was more colorful than pretty, turn crimson under her dark hair. It was especially this florid, almost Mediterranean grandeur that had seduced Balduin into casting her in Ophelia's wreath of straw.

She replied in a rush: "What you're all making of it! Father, why are you so apologetic? — Mother, why the accusations? — there's nothing to the whole affair! I know Gitta! The newlyweds went along, and we were all chatting. We got to the station too early, and so we all took platform tickets, and then — just when the train was pulling out — well, then the 'Greek' simply jumped in with Gitta. — Why did he do such a thing, if his wife has such delicate nerves? Gitta? She's now safe and sound at the parsonage. He'll have to see how he can get back to his wife — there are no more trains back, but if he jumps like a rabbit, he can probably be with her by tomorrow morning!"

With that performance over, she burst out laughing, a liberation after all her huffing and puffing.

Balduin stood up — he was so grateful for her honest words — liking her more than when he had written that poem to her, which he simply could not understand doing. She noticed his grateful gaze, saying to herself: He's as much in love as he was then — and she pondered whether some day she might be embroidering an A.B. on her handkerchief.

Her father accompanied Balduin out, with many bows, suggestions, and assurances. No sooner had the door closed behind him than Annine hurried out of the kitchen, which led directly to the stairs. She let play, in somewhat more sentimental terms, the helpful kindheartedness she had expressed moments before with such spontaneous honesty. This repetition of what had touched him no longer had the same effect on Balduin, but, at this second farewell, to respond to her and thank her, he tried to kiss her hand — but then her mouth came surprisingly close — so he kissed it.

His Annine fled with a short, sighing cry — but Balduin went clomping down the stairs and past the brightly lit pharmacy, thinking to himself: Stupid! That's the result of Gitta's taking off with a Greek. — Stupid to imitate that.

He knew much prettier girls than Anna. Yet this little "deviation" was enough for him suddenly to find it far more possible than he had half an hour ago that Gitta really had gone off on some crazy escapade. He was the one who knew so well how to recognize, in the oddest moods, in the seemingly strange, some perfectly natural occurrence, while, on the other hand, natural occurrences often appeared to him in all their strangeness, with all their wonder.

The whole atmosphere, now overcharged by his own and other peoples' romantic affairs, was affecting him — a mass suggestion arising spontaneously from the town gossip he now felt humming about his ears in the night wind. — And so, as Balduin arrived back at the hillside house, almost at a trot and bathed in sweat, he nearly burst into the room with the exclamation:

"Gitta ran off with a Greek!"

*　*　*

In fact, however, Balduin's comportment was quite different and in fact impeccable. He deliberately offered his portrayal of events — reserved and tinged with a pleasant humor — in Renate's presence, as she sat with his parents in the living room. She noticed at once how considerately and properly he had handled matters and once again thought to herself: they're completely misjudging this fellow.

Balduin closed with the reassuring words that there was absolutely nothing to the whole matter, since he knew "Gitta would not bite off more than she could chew." Those who knew him heard the unstinting tribute behind his brotherly frankness.

The news caused less of a stir among those at the hillside house than it had in town. Or so it seemed. Branhardt expressed no emphatic opinion in Renate's presence, but was content to telephone down to the telegraph office to inform Gitta they were expecting her to return on the early train from Hasling, rather than in the evening, as originally planned.

Nevertheless Renate, as she looked at his calm, determined expression, imagined it would be quite unpleasant to chalk up offences beyond the limits of this father's indulgence. Anneliese struck her as nothing less than admirable: she could see no trace of suspicion, anger, or fear of her fellow man — there was nothing to do but face the results of the gossip.

Yet Anneliese did not entirely deserve such admiration. It was not from subtle tactfulness towards her son or her friend that her bearing remained so unmoved by something that only a short time ago might have deeply disturbed her. But recently she had sensed — and the more she observed Gitta's character, the more acutely she felt it — that the period of dallying escapades was past and all that was to be feared now was a very different crisis.

No sooner had Renate retreated, not coincidentally, to the guest room, than Anneliese went to her husband in his study.

He was sitting, apparently unoccupied, in the wicker chair where she usually sat with her sewing. She knew he would be quite averse to speculating about what had happened. If that were no more than a groping in the dark, he found it hard on the nerves, childish and pointless.

But Anneliese said something quite different from what Branhardt was reluctantly expecting:

"Frank — who is Markus Mandelstein?"

He turned to face her.

"What's this now? — Why are you asking about him?"

"You mentioned him to me once — do you remember?"

"An exceptional mind!" said Branhardt. "A neurologist, more a theoretician. Did quite a bit of work in physiology — in our institute he's spending a lot of money on animal experiments — testing English compounds. Very able. Very Oriental father. — Why are you interested in him?"

"No particular reason. — You mention his Judaism. Are you against it then? — I mean, for example, would you think a mixing with Jewish blood would always, in every case, be undesirable?"

Branhardt didn't seem to need much time to think it over:

"Yes!" he said.

"And why, Frank? Do they have to be inferior —"

"Inferior? Who says that? But in any case — different. Whether that's just basically so or whether it's come about through the complicity of us all — it's all the same. The 'difference' is there. And it would cause a variety of other difficulties, too, but the essential thing is that difference."

Anneliese was sitting off in a corner, out of the lamplight. He could not see that she looked too distressed to be suddenly asking about Judaism out of abstract interest. Now she said, lighting up with hope:

"If that's so — then things so different from each other can hardly attract each other intensely."

But Branhardt, unaware, dispelled this small hope.

"Oh, but they can! Why not? On the contrary! The most foreign, even contradictory things are known to awaken the wildest passions. But — the question remains: can that difference result in a close and lasting relationship? You could almost say, the problem of all marriage is the extent to which the old saying can become a reality: 'Ah, in times past, long since lived out, you were my *sister* or my wife.' For that to happen, the roots reaching back into the past must not be too far apart, even if passion doesn't care about that."

He stood up and was adjusting his lamp, a genuine, old oil lamp with its shiny brass double bowls, which he preferred to any other light when he was working.

He was pleased Anneliese had not gone into speculations about "the Greek adventure," but her silence at his lovely quotation, a clear allusion to her and himself, surprised him. He turned from the lamp and looked at her.

"Well, Lieselieb — but what a look? — Surely you haven't got a case of the nerves from all this silly gossip. — No, you know — anything, but please, not that!" said Branhardt, and he leaned over her with his assuring gaze.

Anneliese raised her face, laughing, trying to match his tone — and began to weep.

And only now did Branhardt learn what was actually happening with Markus Mandelstein.

*   *   *

Above them they heard Renate pacing back and forth.

Her room was located over part of Branhardt's study and did not provide much space for walking. Her increasingly emphatic footsteps were likely driving Balduin to despair, as he tried to sleep in the adjoining room.

Renate smiled when she thought of Gitta. At the bottom of her heart, she let herself have faith in this foolhardy trick she'd pulled.

Why was that? Even with Anneliese's fine and undivided care, these two children of hers, thought of as mere continuations, might become mere imitations and dilutions, banal versions of something uniquely harmonious: their mother. Then again, that perfect circle breaks — and all the prospects and possibilities start swirling anew.

Of course, such heresies could not console their parents.

She imagined Gitta among the young creatures of whom she knew so many and some of whom she had guided. She saw her in hundreds of relationships and situations and marveled at why they all came out so well.

She assumed they were deliberating quite the opposite downstairs: namely, how their little hatchling could better be kept under their wing. Or rather: Liese was letting Branhardt tell her how to do it.

Renate suddenly stretched her arms up — her hands closed high over her head:

"Ah, yes, so delightful, this house here! But still a cage! And tomorrow or the next day it will go on — forward into life again — into everything that so gloriously destroys — us! But not itself! — Amen."

She stayed at the window and gazed down at the light Branhardt's study cast into the garden. She recalled how she and Branhardt had joked that day about the time she had suddenly descended upon them, when Balduin was about to be born.

Back then, all this did not seem like a "cage" to her.

With marvelous clarity she recalled many of the details: how Anneliese, her contractions already begun, still came out, rejoicing, to greet her. How Anneliese sat with them for a while or walked back and forth. Her hands, which seemed hard at work, held some fine, small piece of knitting, but her face was like that of a woman who had set aside all work and was composed and aglow, as if before a grand party.

It was not Anneliese's physical courage that touched Renate; she had that herself. It was the power of the soul, which this day — despite everything and unconditionally — had to render up — and did render up — its entire, solemn being, into the cry of the last — and the first — minute.

Later, she would often think: what she had experienced there was not simply the birth of one child, poor and mortal — not one more among the little oxen and donkeys of nature — it was the son of man.

To an open soul it was all clear again — like a gospel of joy, proclaimed to all that lives: in the endless repetition of everyday things, it is not the banal that prevails as life's inmost law, but the eternally new, the divinely inexhaustible, out of which comes each springtime, each rising of the sun, each genius.

Renate was still standing at the window when she heard Anneliese come upstairs to bed. Anneliese hesitated a moment at her door, yet all remained silent. Her arms at her sides, her curly head leaning against the windowpane, Renate looked out into the quiet night, where many stars were shining.

CHAPTER VIII

Early the next morning, Balduin met his sister at the station. He felt it was up to him to enlighten her about the situation, and also that they, the younger generation, should look at the episode from their perspective on the way home, before facing the judgment of the adults — for he considered himself to be her first and most natural protector. Throughout this matter, because it did not plunge him into nervous confusion, Balduin acted admirably.

Yet what he was firmly counting on — Gitta's mischievous face — was disappointingly missing. Alighting from the train, she bore a gruesomely serious, even gloomy expression. As they headed home, she listened silently to his comments and was far more monosyllabic and morose than he thought she ought to have been. The closer they came to the hillside house, huddled under Balduin's large umbrella in the pelting rain, the more oppressive he found her guilty-looking, hangdog face. He had rarely seen Gitta plagued by such a bad conscience — and certainly none so patently bad as this. The vice of laughter was actually her strong suit.

In the entryway, Anneliese greeted them, helped her daughter out of her wet coat, and said: "Good morning, Gitta child, good to have you back!"

Yet that was meant as a public greeting for all eyes and ears, which now had to be followed by the agonizing embarrassment of an interrogation in Father's private chambers. Balduin, because of his extensive knowledge of the matter, was willingly admitted into the room, a gesture of trust that struck him as very fine. Standing by the doorway, not without a feeling of trepidation, he waited to hear what Gitta would reveal.

"How in the world did this impudent person come to jump into your compartment?" Branhardt asked, without any introduction.

"The poor fellow! He was quite dreadfully shocked himself, you can be sure. I've never seen anyone look so bewildered." She faltered. How should she go on now? "We were both terribly shocked. He would have loved to jump back out the window! — God, he was in love with his wife and on his honeymoon. And there really was no wagon coming back from Hasling — except one carrying pigs. Although the pastor helped look for one."

"That's all quite interesting!" Branhardt said, calmly checking his watch to see if he had to set off for the clinic. "But — what made him get up to such mischief — how and why? You haven't told us that yet. Frau Leutwein claims you were staring at him the whole time — and we'll hope that's just nonsense."

Gitta turned to Salomo, who had excitedly come waggling up to her. He had been whining and scratching at the door until Balduin admitted him to the family council. Salomo clambered up on Gitta's lap as she sat uncomfortably on the edge of a chair; he commented briefly on her unseemly nocturnal absence and curled himself up.

That took a few minutes, and then Gitta answered, her gaze fixed on Salomo's pug part:

"Certainly not the whole time — that's nonsense — but did I stare at him? Yes! But I wasn't even aware I was doing it — not until later — I didn't know anything about it. — And then — he started in on it, too — I don't know how — but he couldn't do anything about it — and I, I was so glad — whenever I looked at him — so wildly glad —"

At this, Anneliese, as she sat in her armchair by the sewing table, moved as if about to speak, but before she could get a word out, Branhardt asked calmly:

"Glad! — Good heavens, this 'Greek' is such an attraction?"

"He wasn't. But he reminded me of something," Gitta replied cryptically, her eyes still fixed seriously and with a strained expression on Salomo's stout back. "Later not at all — but in the beginning so very much."

"Whom did he remind you of — Gitta?" Anneliese asked, somewhat stiffly, her voice low.

"Of Markus."

She spoke of a stranger as "Markus." — A silence followed.

Balduin gazed at his sister, wide-eyed, as if at a baffling new creature.

Salomo, who might have taken a slight trembling in Gitta to mean she was being threatened — and who in any case was quite uncomfortable lying there wedged in her arms — slowly raised his head with its large, alert bat ears, carefully scrutinized the others and started a growl on general principle. The entire state and truth of things still eluded even his wisdom; they did seem very tangled up indeed.

Gitta dropped the perplexed animal from her lap. She folded her hands — and suddenly had a very miserable little face.

"Father! Mama! think of what else I'm bound to do for Markus! — Give him to me, I beg you! — Give me to Markus!"

Balduin felt as if every hair on his head were standing on end. So, that's how it looks, he thought, if a person suddenly goes crazy; and that person was Gitta.

When Gitta did not immediately get an answer, she slid to her knees, threw her face and arms across her chair, and broke into a crying fit.

"Because I wasn't supposed to see him again, Mama! — But if I don't see him again, I'd be better off dead, Mama! — I love him! I love him! I love him!" she stammered, convulsively sobbing in the most horrible manner.

Salomo barked. Anneliese tried to console Gitta. Branhardt lifted her up off her knees. Balduin was no longer watching. His hands over his ears, he had fled the room.

He didn't go far. Outside on the stairs, he stopped, his knees trembling too much to go on. Gitta, in over her head. Gitta, abandoned to God knew what terrible forces — to someone about whom all they knew was that his name was Markus, the poor fellow!

But Gitta was so strong! Why couldn't she just be stronger and cast off this frenzy? He couldn't forgive her for that. It plunged him into an anxiety that made him feel as if the walls of the house were not protection enough to ward off an attack by diabolical powers.

Fists pressed to his head, his eyes angry, he leaned against the study door, whose thin, flimsy wood was all that stood between him and the horrible scene behind it.

And he, who loved Gitta, he, who hated even the slightest coercion more than anything else on earth, thought only one thing:

Just don't give up! Better the straitjacket!

*   *   *

Aside from Balduin, no one learned about the episode. It didn't get out of Branhardt's study.

Only later in the afternoon, after she had run some errands in town, did Frau Lüdecke end a long report to Herr Lüdecke by saying: Greece, there's always been something offensive about it, and on top of that the heat made people there go around naked; we know that from the statues. Gittakins shouldn't have anything to do with that.

And the very next day another lightning-fast effect of the small-town scandal occurred, when Markus Mandelstein sought permission to court Gitta. He approached Branhardt in writing and with all the proper formality. What he might have heard and how these events were related were not explained.

Gitta was not at once made aware of the honor accorded her, but she did become her happy self again. After she had trustingly burdened her parents with her load of worries, she showed not the least signs of the hysterical excitability that might have been feared after her outburst. With the most carefree delight in being alive, she went walking with Salomo in the hillside woodlands, which were snow-covered one day, mud-covered the next.

So life appeared to be back on the old tracks. Renate had left; Branhardt was completely taken up with his work. Yet, amidst it all, a strange mood wove its way into the hillside house: one full of imperceptible secrets in a way that seemed to fit in with this month of Christmas preparations — yet was quite at odds with the giving of gifts. Anneliese could unexpectedly become tearful; she was tender with her two children, even more affectionate than usual. Branhardt was reflective; sometimes he would pace back and forth in his study for hours, and the fact that it wasn't always a medical case was evident from the presence of his wife, with whom he would talk things over.

One day, when Balduin came home from a lecture, Markus Mandelstein had just made his first official visit. Balduin learned about it out in the garden, where Gitta greeted him with snowballs, her face and eyes radiant with happy high spirits. Markus, she reported, was about to travel off for a few weeks to deal with family matters; but then he would be coming to visit them quite often.

From the window, Anneliese observed her daughter's unbride-like behavior with the snowballs. She too was thinking that Herr Mandelstein would soon be visiting more often, and she heard in her mind the town gossip that would soon result from this turn of events: "Gitta ran away with a 'Greek'? No, she's only gotten engaged to a Jew."

Those were unfounded notions, nothing more: the free play of fantasy and false rumors — no one would speak about Markus Mandelstein that way! "So petty, so foolish; like Balder, I'm exaggerating things irrationally!" she thought, annoyed with herself. She wrestled and fought honestly with her heart and its prejudices.

She called to mind everything Markus had said, how he'd looked. — Her heart searched for him; it accepted him, this stranger, and wanted to love him. — She tried to relate the future to her present, to make it part of her life — from within herself she *had to* reach out to him with another name: "My son."

That same evening, Anneliese said to her husband: "Oh, Frank, I am sure I shall love him! All we've heard about him is good, but most beautiful of all is the way he speaks of his family. Such a good son and brother, that makes a good husband."

"That's one way of seeing it!" Branhardt answered. "Do you think we would have become so devoted to each other if marriage had not taken you so far away from your parents — and I hadn't lost mine so early? — Ultimately, we pour ourselves into our most devoted relationship and satisfy our souls — so, let's wait and see."

Just as he had judged Markus Mandelstein with more impartial objectivity than Anneliese, despite his prejudice, he was now less likely to overestimate him. He was well-disposed towards him — and that was quite enough for a start.

These days no one was paying much attention to Balduin, though he himself would have much preferred anything but that, thinking instead he should be looking after the others. For it was clear to him that no one was doing anything to rescue Gitta from her situation.

Balduin became morbidly sensitive to disappointments and dangers that could threaten Gitta — and to what in her nature was related to him and which he alone, perhaps, could have sensed.. Did none of them know how to look after her when she went splashing into the water, from sheer foolishness, right where it was deepest? — Didn't he have to look after her himself? Once she was in the water, his meager powers would not save her from drowning. Brooding darkly, Balduin cowered in his private realm, despairing at the magnitude of this task, which called upon him to set the world to rights again for Gitta.

He suddenly felt his brotherly tie more acutely than ever, because it touched a sore point in himself. If this stronger component of the brother-sister pair, Gitta, could not find happiness — then what was in store for him? His anxiety made him feel far more like a Siamese twin than merely a brother.

Balduin lost weight. Branhardt began to take notice, asked him about it one day, and took him seriously to task: all this might seem tender and touching, but in fact it was a morbid condition, nothing grander. Balduin, he urged, had to look to overcoming his own difficulties, instead of setting aside his own small burden to shoulder the greater one of someone who alone had to bear it to the end. The healthy outlook was: let charity begin at home — in the sense that only he whose own life was whole could devote himself to another.

Balduin decided his father was right. He was giving Gitta nothing at all — but he was losing himself. At times he was exasperated beyond measure at suffering on her account, while she played with Salomo.

He hadn't the least objection to the Jewishness of Gitta's chosen one, but ultimately, he resorted to using it to influence her.

"Your name will suddenly be Brigitte Mandelstein instead of Branhardt," he said angrily. "Is that what you want? Remember those two girls back in your school — with their horse-tail braids and the hips — you never liked them at all."

For a moment Gitta seemed confused. "No — that's true! Especially from behind!" — And she was lost in thought. But it was not long at all before she was clear on the matter, and her face lit up, radiant with the bliss of seventh heaven.

"If I had known Markus existed, I would have loved them, too, and even from behind!" she resolved.

"But do you have any idea at all whether you suit each other?" Balduin asked, still probing, "whether he loves the same things as you, the same people — or also, like you, animals?"

"Animals by all means. Only in quite a different way than I do. He says he could spend a fortune on them. — But then, of course, he cuts them up."

Gitta looked glum as she said that.

No doubt about it, she's crazy! thought poor Balduin — and gave up the fight.

They had these brother-sister conversations up in the woodlands, where, after the recent freeze and snowfall, they went sliding down the slope on an old sled from their childhood. Sometimes Balduin was embarrassed when children in the street looked at him. Sometimes he groaned as he pulled the sled back up the steep hill. But he was caught up again and again by the slide back down.

And still it was the downhill rush that most reminded him of the fate awaiting Gitta on her life's journey. But then the transformation of this frightening experience into something he could repeat at will, and then get up from in one piece each time, made him feel good.

Markus was invited to dinner immediately after his return from Romania. Balduin worked himself into an incredibly agitated state, which resulted in a minor conflict with Anneliese, since he would have most preferred to stay away. At the last minute, Branhardt unexpectedly took his side and gave him permission to get himself invited out to visit a friend. Clearly, he wished not to let Markus's first visit be made still more complicated by Balduin's unpredictable behavior; so he told him he could take part only if he were sure he could conduct himself like a reasonable person.

It was nearly pitch-dark when Balduin came back home. The gloomy weather made it feel like deep in the night, although it wasn't late yet, and he could still see the lamplight shining in the bay window that faced the road.

He hurried quietly up the stairs to his bedroom. For a moment he had the reckless notion of going back downstairs and looked in the mirror to put his hair and clothes in order with trembling hands.

But he stopped at the top of the stairs, listening to the indistinct voices from below — and then, as he hesitated, the sitting-room door opened, and Markus Mandelstein, followed by Branhardt, stepped out into the hallway.

Leaning over the bannister, very much from on high, yet feeling quite small from anxiety and fright, Balduin tried to get a look at what form of destiny had entered their house.

Balduin had been told Markus Mandelstein was thirty, but he would have guessed older. He was rather tall, more lean than the opposite, but not slim in the hips, as Balduin could clearly see when the man turned around.

With spiteful pleasure, Balduin decided: "She can't like him from behind either!"

As Markus Mandelstein put on his coat, still speaking with his father, Balduin could easily study his face in the bright light of the staircase. It was light in shade, typically Mediterranean. His brow and gaze struck him as handsome, intelligent — an impression to which the nose contributed; at its base there was a boldness to it that gave him an engaging expression — but then, after beginning so well, the nose went on a bit too long. And that had the remarkable effect of countering the face's boldness, giving it instead something of a worried look. The mouth was delicate, while the lines around it were covered by a dark, dense, but close-cropped beard.

Now his father was expressing his regret that the winter weather had rendered the shorter footpath down to the street lights a danger to life and limb.

At this moment, Balduin joined them. Blindly, almost without knowing what he was doing and even less for whose sake, he found himself drawn down the stairs and into the jaws of "fate."

"I've got my hand lantern," he said.

Branhardt seemed very pleased as he introduced them to each other. He had waited impatiently to see if Balduin wouldn't overcome his worries and come after all. He felt badly that, in giving Balduin his fatherly permission to be absent, he had acted out of practical rather than pedagogical intentions.

Markus Mandelstein gave Balduin a look of complete, open sympathy — a look that said: "Gitta's brother!" — but not without a fleeting trace of a physician's interest, awakened by the fact that, against all expectations, he was confronted by such a doddering creature.

They set off silently side by side, watching their step on the uneven, icy path. Balduin's lantern cast only a small patch of light on the snow ahead, as they walked on in the darkness behind it.

Just as before he could hardly endure knowing this stranger was in the house, come unbidden to take possession of it, Balduin suddenly had to deal with the fear of simply letting him go now — now, as he was carrying away all kinds of things of theirs. He felt he mustn't let him get away completely yet — let him run free, so to speak. Markus Mandelstein's power and danger to the community grew next to him in the darkness, step by step, as they walked along together in the gloomy silence.

This made Balduin lapse into a loquaciousness whose tone seemed almost to flatter this man of mysterious power. From all he offered up, something could be heard of the fearful self-exposure of children and the weak: "Don't hurt us! Be nice to us!"

Markus Mandelstein's voice had a warm, deep tone that was curiously calming, insisting on nothing, unlike Branhardt's curt forcefulness. What's more, in the dark, one hardly knew whom one was walking beside, to whom one might have called, "Who's there, friend or foe?" All around, on the wooded slopes, there was nothing but the play of light from the lantern in the almost absolute black of night. Little by little and ever more unhesitatingly, Balduin poured out to his companion all his anxieties — happy at last to be rid of them that way. — It seemed as if, to no longer feel threatened from behind, he had turned and run into the arms of the enemy.

Eventually Markus even learned much about Balduin's fear of him — and it would not have taken much for Balduin to ask his advice about what he could do about it.

The family had taken in Gitta's suitor with all the friendliness with which people use conventional formalities to conceal more complex relationships. But Balduin was the first to make clear to him — albeit in such unthinking and childish fashion — the undisguised fact that he was truly one of them, which warmed his heart and seemed to liberate him. He would never forget it. The family visit, with all its inevitable uncertainties that could make even the smallest misstep ominously important, had been a gruesome ordeal for him that, in his heart of hearts, had made him no less anxious than the young man at his side.

But Markus told himself that Balduin's hasty open-heartedness would likely be followed the next day by a hangover, and since he had no headache remedy to prescribe, nor any way to put a stop to the outpourings, he sensitively tried to create a balance by sharing more of his own intimacies.

He talked about his family. His mother was dead. His father, though a well-off Romanian Jew, rarely strayed from the narrow circle of family, which he loved above all else. Markus portrayed him as still reigning over them as patriarch, unshaken in his faith by the fates of his people, naïve and pious, holding fast to the articles of faith in "Israel's Destiny." Markus said it was a basic fact that, by leaving his family, by going out into the world, an individual Jew experienced for himself the entire tragedy of the past — the dispersion of the "chosen ones" in the lands of foreign rulers. For, in the loving circle of his family, he would still grow up as though in his own land and in the dream of his people. As if, at such a final, narrow point, everything still gathered together, indestructible, unperturbed by its surroundings — much as the Israelites had once hidden their god in the Ark of the Covenant so he might guide them through nations whose local gods ruled the primordial soil.

Balduin's interest was at once drawn to this people, who had wandered through the millennia, clinging to an ever-refuted dream. Nothing, nothing in the whole world, could so quickly build a bridge between him and Markus. Only a nation of poets could do such a thing! He asked Markus whether that did not make him proud.

"Of a self-deception? — In the old Ark of the Covenant, there might have been only a stone!" he answered. That sounded sober and faithless enough, and it was spoken with a smile. Yet it sounded — in the night and in the dark tones of his voice — as if someone were claiming to have only a pebble in his hand so as not to reveal that what he was holding shimmered and flashed with jewels. Balduin felt that, and it took no more to ignite his fantasy and make him set himself up as a savior of Judaism. Why merely relegate it to a past? Why not help the dream into the present, if it defines itself as indestructible?

Markus replied, his voice melancholy: "The dream still exists, yet does not exist — like places buried by a catastrophe, in the midst of a living, breathing life. The most eternal, the most transient — whichever you like. Whoever brings them to light, up from the depths, sees them return to dust, ripe for the grave. — You can call these things your homeland, but you can no longer live in them."

Markus's companion did not realize how much of himself Markus was giving him, as he spoke softly in his dark, calm voice of his things and his people. It was a gift offered spontaneously, out of gratitude and kindness. Markus knew he could do so — after all, the young man at his side was Gitta's brother! And since, in a moment of surprise, he had nothing conventional to offer, he resorted to what he most seldom shared.

Caught up in their conversation, Balduin didn't notice they were now walking in the bright, gaslit streets of the town, where his unquenched lantern was out of place. For some time now he had not thought about returning home. He was burning to say hundreds of things, and he couldn't understand why he had not included at least something about the Old Testament in his study plans. It would be wonderful to know Hebrew! — to exchange with his newest friend words not meant for the ears of others.

As luck would have it, Markus Mandelstein lived far away, at the other end of town. At last, they arrived at his door and said goodbye to each other. Balduin now suddenly found himself alone on the street, holding his little lantern; he felt confused. Of course: go in, stay there, just sleep at Markus's — that didn't work, it would sound the alarm back home. But still it was basically the only thing that would have best suited the stormy tempo of this friendship.

It seemed to Balduin they had set off together from the hillside house a long time ago, as if he had run away from his family and gone after Markus like a lapdog without a master.

From far, far above, the few lighted windows of the hillside house twinkled down at him through the bare winter woods. He still had such a long way to hike back! Simply because they didn't live down here, in what now seemed to him to be the hundred-times-more-comfortable part of town. The walk down had gone quickly — much too quickly. Of course, he should have turned back; his sensitive feet had developed some ominous spots over the last few days — they had just been waiting for this walk to flare up into new chilblains — and on top of that, he'd come limping home on tired feet only a few hours before.

Balduin set off in a bad mood. He felt only the distance, which wasn't getting any shorter, and he looked like an old and ailing night-watchman, because he was carefully protecting the ominous spots on his feet.

In his vexed state, he could no longer think about the events of the evening, or about a person's or a nation's dream of being chosen that was contradicted by reality. At every step, he felt one thing with pressing clarity: that it must be quite different to go through life without chilblains than *with*.

CHAPTER IX

Branhardt and Markus Mandelstein first became acquainted through female monkeys. Some results Markus Mandelstein had achieved with his six monkeys were of direct scientific interest to Branhardt and led to several discussions. Only once had a medical case brought the two together — a very sad one involving a lawyer's family in whose home Markus was also a frequent guest. The wife, no longer young, was facing her first confinement under dangerous conditions that appeared to confront those involved with the necessity of giving up the child to save the mother. At any rate, so it seemed to the non-specialist Markus. But Branhardt believed they did not have to give up hope of the mother's survival if she carried the child — desired for years and surely her last — to term.

If there were anything at all in the world for which Markus might have envied Branhardt, it was the confident resolve with which he spoke of the case — not only to the anxious woman and her worried husband, but even to himself — and in that way instilled so much faith. Markus took great pains not to lack this tone, even though as a physician he had practiced it for some time, and with his exceptional self-control he often succeeded with a sufficiently virtuosic performance. Yet, in response to this situation, he forced himself to come up with such masterfully subtle nuances of the assuring tone as eluded even Branhardt.

The outcome proved Branhardt right. But a few days later, quite unforeseen complications arose from something else entirely, and, after a true masterpiece of surgical intervention on Branhardt's part, incomparable treatment marked by the greatest medical devotion, the suffering new mother died a gentle and painless death. That day, Markus saw tears in Branhardt's eyes, which were surely not given to shedding them — he saw him sharing the pain of the others with a tenderness that came upon those poor people like the most human form of consolation — and made Markus appear wooden and lifeless in comparison, unable to give expression to the empathy that crippled and inhibited him. When, in his helplessness, he came to the funeral with an almost artlessly beautiful wreath, he envied Branhardt again and more profoundly than before. While Markus could not match Branhardt's confidence, in the end he surpassed him through the probing subtlety of his mind; yet the sympathy he truly felt only made him foolish.

Some weeks later, shortly before his first visit to the hillside house, he heard Branhardt discuss the fatal case with other physicians and sensed the new understanding and valuable insights his colleague had gained from the matter, setting aside personal matters and drawing attention to the scientific results that would benefit similar cases — much to the appreciation and approval of the other doctors.

With what logic the gears of his soul's clockwork meshed so flawlessly! Markus admitted to himself that he had observed this. Here was someone who, first with a physician's acumen, then with such fine human warmth, had given his will and his soul, as naturally as he now breathed a sigh of relief, as the man of knowledge he was — one now inclined to hold fast to what he had gained from the experience.

With the same logic, this man, who compelled himself to pretend and to act instead of letting the case awaken doubts, must have been burdened with an ever more general sense of sorrow. Thus, on this third point Markus Mandelstein begrudged Branhardt nothing. — But every time he looked at Gitta, he was happy her father was such a man.

It seemed to Markus as though Branhardt felt very little like his future father-in-law. Yet they shared more and more scientific interests and understood each other very well in those matters. Branhardt allowed himself to devote time to these discussions only to the degree that it suited him practically, but he always tried to find a bit of time, in a way only Branhardt's nerves could manage. He often brought Markus home with him from town — with no thought at all of Gitta, but simply for his own sake. They could be seen coming up the road, deep in conversation, with the shorter, older man tucking his hand under the younger man's arm or stopping repeatedly to make an important point.

But Branhardt did not let his collegial relationship prevail over that as his future father-in-law because he had any objection to the young man's becoming part of the family. Rather, it was because he did not care to be reminded that his daughter was of marriageable age. So, even after they arrived home, he let his uninhibited egotism keep Markus to himself for hours in his study, enjoying — in Gitta's place, as it were — the company of this rising young talent.

When this happened, Gitta's behavior was always the same. She would indulge her father and lend him her Markus for a long time. But when she thought they had gone on long enough, she would come to them, bringing something she felt Markus ought to know about. She insisted he be made acquainted with all that was hers, and that amounted to an astonishing array of things. When it was Justus the hedgehog's turn, everyone was happy the introduction went well; Justus even showed Markus his bright, little face. Of course, only for a moment, and then he took hold of a sheet of the evening newspaper that had fallen off the table and went rattling off to bury himself in it. But it was made clear to Markus he shouldn't take that as an insult; it was one of Gitta's daily joys, referred to in the house as "Justus reading the late edition."

In the difficult transition period of Markus's initiation into the family, Justus's role was as important as it was beneficial.

Some evenings Markus would bring his violin, and he and Anneliese would play together.

There, by the piano, she and Markus became better acquainted. They discovered shared tastes in music and confessed, mutually and with laughter, that both their lives had jumped the tracks, since she should have become a concert pianist and he a conductor. But that was only joking. Anneliese did not find the moment in which she could have grasped and understood him — and only when she saw him with his violin did she occasionally sense: this man is not of such a measured heartbeat as his stiff ways and bearing might suggest, but perhaps a little immoderate and in need of his passionate love of music to speak for him and give his feelings the form to set them free.

Markus suffered no illusions. It seemed to him that, even with respect to music, the similarity of taste was a result merely of a dissimilarity: Anneliese was most strongly attracted by what was akin to her, whereas he was attracted more by his opposite. That aspect of their relationship was of no less interest to him than their supposed concurrence was to Anneliese. More perceptive than she, he felt there was something that likely would remain unshakeable between them, despite their mutual good will, and that perhaps was more deeply rooted than prejudice.

Although piano and violin created a way for Anneliese to approach Markus that was as neutral as Branhardt's shared medical interests, she, unlike her husband, could not forget for a moment *why* their mutual understanding was so necessary. Everything that bound her to Markus secretly wove and spun the threads of her maternal tie to her future son.

Just once, a brief moment seemed to favor, unexpectedly, their sense of a connection involving more than the two of them.

In the sitting room, on a receding wall created by one of the quaint bay windows and slightly out of view, yet close to those who were there on a daily basis, hung a chalk sketch, white on grey, which had often attracted Markus's gaze. One day, as he stood alone, waiting by the open door, he reached out for the picture and took it down from the wall.

It portrayed a child's face, life-size, with a firm chin and lovely, lovely eyes. He found it poignantly beautiful — and guessed who it was —. And a wish as deep as a spell took hold of him — a power so urgent, so compelling, that impulses both imperious and imploring, both humble and demanding, became indistinguishable, as if shaping destiny. In those minutes, the unshakeable thing standing between him and Anneliese no longer existed. She was bound up in what made Gitta his — in what fulfilled the wish: "So may it be — Gitta's child, and mine."

Anneliese was just passing the doorway as he stood there, enthralled, captivated by the lovely picture. She came in slowly, inwardly trembling, and, as he looked up to meet her eyes, he saw them fixed on him with a radiance so open, so strong, that it went straight through his heart.

It was joyous, yet confusing — so abruptly confusing he could not withstand this first, full look of love.

He might well have let her look into the depths of his soul — into his last wish. Yet he blocked that view, so firmly. Anneliese saw that. She lowered her eyes; a shyness came into her face.

The unrepeatable minute went by unused.

* * *

Amid all these moments of understanding between the family and their future son-in-law, Balduin was quite content to play the observer, interceding with a certain affability only when he felt things weren't going fast enough. His own worries about the matter struck him now as a mere bygone whimsy. Yet he was frightened to think how easy it could have been for Gitta to pass by Markus on her way through life.

But he was still in a good enough mood to venture a short poem about how Markus and Gitta go completely to ruin as a result of their union.

He had had the idea for it before. Those unsettling feelings somehow took poetic form — and it was simply wonderful for Balduin to rediscover them again and savor those shivers of apprehension artistically.

He also went along on walks with Markus and Gitta through the woodlands, taking on the role of chaperone — or "propriety elephant," as they called it. But Balduin always wanted to discuss so many things man-to-man with Markus that, when they were out on these peculiar walks, he would actually snap at Gitta if she thwarted those intentions. Some might have found that astonishing if they weren't aware of the resolve with which Gitta controlled matters so they were the way she wanted them. It wasn't clear whether that was equally agreeable to Markus. But he felt so uncertain about everything that he simply got stuck in his rigid compliance, like a sword in its sheath. Only his relationship to Balduin developed freely and unimpeded, since the young man's devotion to him was without complications.

Markus possessed to a high degree the ability to carry on soliloquies with himself when he felt the need, even while engaged in conversation with others. It was not noticeable that he was doing it, except for a slight distraction in his gaze, lending it a sympathetic expression — which the speaker might well attribute, in all sincerity, to his own effect on him.

In any case, Balduin did this in the most credulous way.

He would self-indulgently give himself over to the exquisite pleasure of unburdening himself before his new friend, in fresh air and the best of moods, of everything he felt oppressing him, things he revealed to his parents only in his weaker moments — since he preferred to appear before them as they most wanted to see him. He found an almost perverse joy in seeing through himself before Markus's sharp eyes, which could not harm him in the least — that is, without the consequences of his parents' pedagogical reaction.

In addition, Markus always understood exactly how he had to answer so as to contradict Balduin gently and, with utmost skill, catch all the cues the young man threw his way.

Once Markus failed miserably.

Balduin had been telling him about the anxieties that thwarted all aspects of his life and ended self-mockingly by saying: "No sooner is there *nothing at all* to worry about or fear, than, sure as death, the proverbial falling roof tile comes to mind — and actually lands right on your head."

It was not hard to guess that the one fitting response to this cue was to say: what you've heard about those dreaded roof tiles is slander; they're rock solid.

But just then Markus might have been peering through the bare branches, looking for a light-colored jacket; Gitta and Salomo had gone off again, who knows where. — Or maybe it was simply distraction that made him respond, amicably:

"Yes, those damned roof tiles! They're loose wherever you go."

Balduin gave him an uneasy look.

"Do you really believe that? I always hoped: the brave person knows better, and only my cowardice makes me afraid."

Markus stopped on the spot, only now shaken out of his distraction. Now he finally understood. His gaze was no longer sentimental — but fanatical. His eyes flashed with something that nearly made Balduin flinch — almost as if this were no longer Markus at all.

"Cowardly? — no! What does that mean? Courage — or at least three-fourths of it? Often, it's nothing but a kind of idiocy — a failure to take rapid note of all the possibilities — a mental deficiency. Or a rush of mere animal brawn, a misperception of relative strength, thus again an error in judgment. — But whoever *lives* with an awareness of all dangers — including the possibilities he *feels* most keenly — is he a coward? No! *That* courage the others don't have on us!"

Balduin too had stopped and stood as if rooted to the spot. He bored through his future brother-in-law with his eyes. Then he burst out:

"So you too are —" he almost let slip the word "cowardly" but then gave his sentence a jubilant finish: "You're that way, too! Oh, I always knew it, always. We didn't need Gitta to bring us together. We're a pair — wholly and completely!"

No, not a stranger, this man with the fanatical gaze — that was the real Markus, who brandished like a club what Balduin lamented as making him defenseless. The last barrier fell! And Balduin embraced him ecstatically.

When Gitta and Salomo turned up among the tree trunks, they saw the last moments of this tender scene. Gitta was about to whistle, as they had agreed to do if they were ever out of sight of each other for too long. But, tactfully, she didn't.

"Now they'll probably kiss, these two," she said to Salomo, and waited for it, holding the half-frozen elderberries, which were hard to find, but which Max, the rooster, always wanted.

The kiss didn't happen. But Gitta thought Markus appeared strangely delighted.

Anyway, he is already considerably more married to Balder than to me! she thought, laughing to herself.

And so it was: the way home that the three took from this questionable walk in the forest led to a walk into town for just two of them, with Balduin accompanying Markus. Leaving Gitta and her parents, the groom-to-be took, if possible, a still more formal and restrained leave than usual.

For he was seized by a raging desire to go with Gitta instead, to take her in his arms, carry her home, and put an end to all the walks up the hill, by staying down in town — just the two of them.

Only Anneliese took note of Markus's all-too-formal behavior.

Having initially resisted Gitta's choice more than Branhardt did, she had made the decision part of her own will, as strong-natured persons sometimes do, and imbued it with her own reserves of feeling, until her affirmation of the fact became almost too forceful.

She wouldn't have been Anneliese if, in these days before the official betrothal, she did not recall a wealth of those blissful occurrences, the ones that never recur. It seemed to her that, even awakened out of a sound sleep, she would be able to recite a list of them without a pause or omission.

She didn't dare mention that, lest she be accused of being "sentimental." "Exuberance" was Branhardt's word for it.

Call it what one would, her own memories weighed on her heavily, lowering their wings because her daughter's way of living didn't let them soar.

She remembered so well the secrecies of the days before their wedding, the stolen kisses, the glowing cheeks, the moonlight irresistibly tempting them to find clandestine romantic moments. Was that all out-of-date now? Didn't it mean anything to today's young people?

Two days ago the moon had shone down from the wooded hillside with such fairytale beauty that even she and Branhardt opened the window and leaned out, as if enchanted. Markus didn't seem to realize there was nothing to prevent a stroll through the garden, and Gitta didn't seem to think of it at all.

Only Balduin went spooking around out there like a ghost, ardently declaiming his poems to the moon.

CHAPTER X

The Christmas tree still stood in the sitting room, stretching out its richly decked branches. Because the Baumüller children and other little folk from the surrounding area were given Christmas presents, the tree still received its childhood ornaments each year, including chocolate figures and rock-hard marzipan sausages that, a decade ago, had so charmed the hearts of Gitta and Balduin that they survived their greedy stomachs.

Gitta and Markus found themselves alone for once in the cozy room, made bright by the winter sun and smelling of sweets and dried-out pine needles. It may have been white and cold outside, but sunlight warmed the room, as if the December frost, awakening from its frozen state, had been given the gift of speech and called out: "It's springtime!"

Gitta sat studying several photographs. Her elbows propped on the table, she looked like a schoolgirl doing her homework — women's faces, portraits of men, one old man with a long-flowing, white beard, bearing a distinct resemblance to one of the prophets — though she couldn't say which, since after her schooldays she'd never thought of any of them. But now, in a sense, they were to be her relatives.

Markus was waiting silently to hear what she would say, but she was silent. Only her earlobes, one of which he could see, turned red. Then she gave an odd shrug to her shoulders, made a move like a shying horse, and broke into tears.

Markus stood there, utterly taken aback, but didn't move.

"You don't like them!" was all he said.

That struck her to the heart; she pulled out of her childish outburst:

"No — it's not that — why wouldn't I like them? — I like them very much — it's just that they're even there — I mean, all at once facing the whole lot, and you merely one of them — nothing incomparable, just someone with all these people behind you."

Her struggle to make herself understood had calmed her down right away. She was so caught up she forgot to dry her tears — she almost laughed:

"It's stupid of me — but I wish you would remain as if you'd just dropped in from nowhere — not one of several versions — no, just uniquely you — for me alone. — It's stupid, I know —"

These strange words — clearly not the kind usually used to greet future in-laws — Markus had followed with intense interest. He kept chained up within himself every rising feeling of offence that would prevent his fully understanding. There seemed to be nothing this young woman could not reveal to him without holding back — and her look confidently confirmed that she knew that.

This dangerous exchange had only brought them closer in their trust.

Markus said:

"Not stupid — no — but unfortunate. Since there's so much in me to which my family is the key. — And a Jew, the way he is, his whole, uninhibited self, is revealed only through his family."

He looked calm and thoughtful. His family, too, had not been at all enthusiastic about the pending matrimonial alliance — it was a blow to Markus's father. — First, they had to learn to love Gitta and, through Gitta, Markus's own freedom. Gitta's love for them could come only as a late — and perhaps the last — fruit of her love for Markus. — Would that fruit ripen for him at all? It had to! — He would take on any task to make it so; long — long content with incomplete love, before this wondrous one fell to him — courting Leah for seven years, before Rachel gave herself to him — but it had to happen eventually! — and, in happening, give him back his "homeland"!

Their conversation faltered. Anneliese would have thought: they're hardly speaking to each other, as so often. But what might have surprised her was that, even when alone together, they still were not using the informal address with each other. People become accustomed to the formal "Sie" when addressing someone, just as they do to the informal "du" in their thoughts. Markus himself was used to that, and he also thought using "du" between them would at once turn the painful, embarrassing barriers — all of them — into mere chalk lines.

While he silently gathered up the photos, Gitta blushed at the way she had behaved, and, at once shamefaced and defiant, she said:

"You bring me these pictures — and just now you were very nice to me — but there's one thing you have never actually said to me."

Markus cast her an inquiring look.

"That you care for me at all!" she murmured defiantly.

He paused. "No! — you're right. — In fact — I just forgot to."

"Then why don't you say: I love you?" she asked expectantly.

"I love you," said Markus.

"And I you," she declared.

"I thank you very much!" Markus answered.

They spoke stiffly, seriously, and still addressing each other formally, without finding the least bit of humor in it.

Markus was taken aback. He reached for Gitta's hands, which she had folded on the table, and clasped them awkwardly in his own, lowering his brow down to them, and Gitta felt the coldness of his hands and their helplessness.

As he did so, he said softly: "It was more beautiful — then — before! — More beautiful — before we carried on and talked to each other this way."

She kept silent, still puzzled. What he was saying seemed extraordinarily strange to her — and especially that he was saying it! That he preferred the uncertainty, the mere longing for each other, to what now was so real and secure. But it had been beautiful, he was right about that — so beautiful, this world of wonder that still promised everything, unspoken, unmeasured, unknown — this seen but unseen wonder world roaring around them like a storm or a song.

They had to make it so again! Gitta was seized by the most urgent desire to act.

"We're doing it all wrong! — we must change, we must move ahead — now! — these trials must end — we've been testing each other this whole time." And she thought: and what for? I would love him even if he were seven times a murdering thief!

Markus looked up, excited: "Yes!"

"We must make our engagement official, now!"

Official! How good that would be. It made Markus's skin shiver. Yet it had to happen. They had to stand firm. This was the crisis, and their recovery could begin only after the crisis had passed.

"Do you think so, too, Markus?"

"Oh yes!" he said, his voice a bit weak, and right away he stood up — the air felt stuffy in the morning sun gazing in on them, outdoing the heat from the oven.

Gitta too jumped up from the table and went right up to him, wanting to give vent to the joy in her heart.

Standing before him, eye to eye, she paused — she saw how rigid he stood, his nostrils flaring in his unmoving face, his jaw set.

She looked at him — and suddenly it flared up around her! — Storm and song — roaring around her, like before.

"To be *your* wife!" — And she said "deine" for "your"; that endearing word came to her breathlessly, there at his neck.

Like an iron ring, his arms closed around her.

*　*　*

On the morning of Saint Sylvester's Day, Anneliese and Gitta went into town to take care of some errands for the first days of the new year. Also, the shop on the marketplace finally had the grey fabrics from which Mama was to choose for her new winter coat, which could not happen without Gitta's having the last word.

They took the long way through the open fields, now white with frost, that ran alongside the road to town. With the mild temperature and calm wind, they hardly felt the winter, although it seemed to flaunt its splendor before their eyes. "Like in the confectioner's shop window: with the glint of red sun and the twinkle of frost — and all edible," said Gitta, who was talking all the while; "or like winter on greeting cards — with snow-white and sunrise-red, my first official well-wisher."

Anneliese hardly answered. Suddenly she was thinking of the engagement — which Gitta hadn't cared about at all since her crying fit, but which had now been so hastily made. Did that mean she really wasn't mature enough for the seriousness of marriage?

Anneliese couldn't help but start in on the matter. At first, Gitta merely lent her a friendly ear, but then she became intensely interested. When her mama talked about "marriage," she could think only of her own. Gitta knew what was coming: it all sounded like nothing but fairytales, and then her mama would carry on like the princess whose every word, once out of her mouth, turned into flowers and jewels.

In fact, what Anneliese wanted to admonish Gitta about, to the best of her knowledge and belief — about the effort and earnestness of life — was all imperceptibly transformed in her memory into something very joyous, even magnificent. As if, in what we call marriage, the everyday and the festive were no longer distinguishable from each another — much as in nature the restless work in the innermost part of a plant is festively revealed to the eye as blossom and color and scent.

In the draper's shop, Anneliese looked happier and younger than an hour before. She felt in a lighter mood and able to have renewed faith in the grand occasion — the literal *Hochzeit*, the "high time" — that her daughter was so eager to experience. Distractedly, she ran her hand over the grey and brown samples laid out before her and then reached over cautiously to touch some nearby fabric of a deep, delicate violet. She blushed slightly as the alert shop assistant quickly moved it closer.

"I think — I'll take this one," she said.

"Oh, Mama!" Gitta exclaimed, and, as the startled young man looked on, she leaned over and, for all to see, kissed the hand that, for the first time in years, had grasped a colorful fabric.

For Gitta's sake, to celebrate her betrothal, Anneliese ended her long period of mourning for Lotti.

With that, Gitta, after the host of good intentions and silent vows already piled up within her in response to her mother's words, felt like she would explode. But Mama need not have worried. If it were necessary to be proper, able, happy, and wise for marriage, then that's what Gitta would be! Clearly, marriage was a lot like those magic yarn balls you had to knit away at. If you were honest and diligent, then you ended up with more than just a sock or a sash, since the more you knitted, the faster the tiny treats hidden there would tumble, bit by bit, into your lap. Of course, Gitta had usually cheated on her magic yarn balls.

Back home, Gitta retreated to her room. She used the last day of the year to make a list of all the faults she would have to overcome. Having resolved not to leave her childhood room for married life until she was free of fault, she had to make fast work of it. To get a grip on the task, she wrote each fault on a separate sheet of her notebook and stuck them to her tabletop, using long pins with green-glass heads, like butterflies. That resulted in an unbelievably large number of fault-sheets. The penultimate was number 47: "That I need eleven hours of sleep," and the last one she ruefully pinned in place read: "That I am more loyal to animals than to people."

Next door in her parents' bedroom, Anneliese was taking a short nap — an hour all to herself before evening. Excited and emotional, all her thoughts focused at first on the immediate present. But gradually, in the calm and deepening twilight, the world around her receded more and more. Before her soul stood Lotti.

She thought of the little girl who no longer came running to her with her joys and fears like her other children — who stood mutely apart from them, finished with all of life and strangely completed by death, now an artwork of God that her mother carried within her soul and where, oh so often, she found peace and became still — recovering a share of eternity for herself. So Lotti would remain unchanged with time, while her sister grew up to be a bride, a wife, a mother herself, she would remain in her child's clothes — always close to all innocence and remembrance — born anew, again and again, with every child Anneliese would see playing about her, bound up with her most tender feelings — a comrade, even to her grandchildren.

And in the stillness of dusk, Anneliese stretched out her arms to Lotti with a smile, embracing her with the quiet, tender thoughts the day does not hear —

Then Branhardt came to her, full of the living, full of joy even in Balduin, after seeing him so obviously interested in the studies he had chosen — but admitting with a laugh that the Old Testament now played an unforeseen role, though fortunately it did not alter his plans to the point of changing his calling and creed.

Markus was expected that evening. After their New Year's punch, they set off, as they did every year, to the hillside woodlands to hear the New Year's bells ringing down in town.

The calendar promised a full moon, but wind-blown clouds allowed only brief glimpses of it. It was colder than it had been in the morning, and when they reached the heights — Salomo snuffling along in the lead — it blew mightily out of the east, from the woods.

Branhardt strode along with Markus, a good distance behind the others, his arm thrust under the younger man's, the two of them deep in a discussion — but this time not of a professional nature.

Balduin was the first to reach the top of the slope and, not wanting the bells to take him by surprise, stood looking eagerly down on the town, now aglow with light, where the bells were about to start ringing.

Even the moon was curious and suddenly came out from behind the clouds, punctual to the minute, as in the theater. All five pocket watches announced in its kind light that the moment had come to say "Happy New Year!" but the town below was silent. The wind still swept in from the east, its soft drone drowning out all other sound, explaining to the moon that it had made its appearance too soon.

Then, as they all argued lightheartedly whether the wind or the moon knew better, their laughter was interrupted by the tolling of a lone, loud bell, echoing from the deep woods at their backs. — It was so loud and penetrating that they felt as if there were an invisible little church behind them, blown there by the same wind that made inaudible the New Year's hubbub down below, blowing it away, sweeping it up and carrying it off — into the distance. It seemed strange: to behold the town so silent below, as if struggling in vain with its sea of light and noisy festivities — and, from out of the darkness, as if granted dominion over everything, near and far, the one resonating, solemn bell.

After the merriment he'd joined in himself, Balduin felt the bell's ringing cut through him with a nervous shudder, nameless and surprising, surging too loudly and suddenly filling the universe for him. Since he could not simply stand there in the moon's bright spotlight and cover his ears in front of everyone, he felt caught in a terrifying struggle with himself, staring with feigned indifference at a point in the clouds and hoping the voice of the ghost bell would turn back into the simple village bell of Brixhausen, once it had realized it was not affecting him at all.

His hands clenched at his sides, he had a wild thought: just to be able to do *that* — master the things that spoke most violently and loudest to him. For he felt it was precisely those things that wanted him, and they were precisely what he wanted! If that could be! Just as with the New Year's bells, each thing would ring in for him an unbelievably great life.

Markus stood by Gitta, quite unmoved by what was going on around him and without empathy for bells that reminded him of nothing at all. What lingered compellingly in his mind was his conversation with Branhardt. — Deeply moved, he wondered whether he would make Gitta as happy a wife as Anneliese had become. While he feverishly asked himself that, fear and doubt crowded cunningly around his feelings as though around a well that, all too deep, concealed its own waters.

How had Branhardt achieved such a happy marriage? Above all, he'd had faith — in all matters, a rock-solid faith in his success — but if something did not completely succeed, then he'd learned to hold back from making immoderate demands, for all in life is a concession, and whoever understands that, without letting it make him a coward, is life's master.

But then Markus's timidity grew into a vaunting arrogance: not happy like Anneliese! — Gitta must become even happier! He could not find happiness in the way Branhardt had. He couldn't believe without seeing, but he couldn't let up, let go — never! — never stop life from lowering its scooping buckets to the very bottom of his well to fetch up his waters — no, not satisfied with what was attainable, possible — even if the golden buckets never came back up — —

Markus barely noticed the others were heading back home. Even Gitta, around whom his thoughts were circling, he had watched half-distractedly in these past moments. But then, all at once, he had to smile. She'd bent down to Salomo — who'd clearly been deeply unhappy about having to sit on the cold ground because it was New Year's Eve — and took him in her arms. Markus's imagination made a strange jump in another direction, and something in him brightened with hope for the future. The darkness out here, now with no moon, made him forget that the small creature Gitta was picking up and holding in her arms with maternal care was only Salomo.

As they approached the hillside house, things swung into action. Frau Lüdecke had been sitting with Herr Lüdecke beside the New Year's punch, floating nutshells in dishes of water and pouring the Saint Sylvester's Day lead. But she heard them coming just in time. Even though her lead pouring was approaching its fateful moment, she dropped everything and ran up to the sitting room to light the candles on the Christmas tree. This was why she had asked them not to "plunder" the tree. It really made itself very pretty when all its splendor suddenly radiated and glittered out into the winter night, so welcoming — with its golden nuts, red apples, stars, little sausages, angels, and marzipan figures.

Frau Lüdecke was first in the house to call out "Happy New Year!" — standing in the doorway, full of great anticipation, eager to drink the toast. Branhardt raised his glass and said:

"To a good new year for our little bride! And to the wedding of our dear children come springtime!"

With that, Gitta, as if on cue, embraced Markus, and Frau Lüdecke began to weep out loud.

So, she was the first to know! And now she also knew the clump of lead — still uncertain whether it was to be a dog or a ship — could be nothing other than a strangely shaped myrtle wreath.

Dabbing her eyes with her handkerchief, Frau Lüdecke flew down the stairs to give Herr Lüdecke the news.

PART TWO

CHAPTER XI

The fruit trees bloomed late that year.

For Gitta almost too late. On her wedding day, most of the blossoms were still buds. She had to make do with the cherry trees, and they hurried along to flower on schedule.

But then came a blossoming more lavish than ever — a true legacy of a wedding feast — that's how the garden looked — a belated celebration that did not want to end and still could not get enough of its own abundance, strewing blossoms on the paths wherever people went, and lifting shimmering crowns above their heads.

Frau Lüdecke said something sentimental about it every day, Herr Lüdecke something philosophical. Even Branhardt, despite the increased workload caused by the time-consuming wedding days, seldom went down to the clinic in the morning without making a few rounds through his unnaturally beautiful garden — about which he commented, rather unpoetically, that its glory now tasted cursedly of leftovers after the main meal. He felt that something about this blossoming was lacking — and that was Gitta, with her passionate delight in it, and, simply, Gitta herself.

Balduin often accompanied Branhardt through the garden, walking beside him in taciturn near silence. A better reader of souls could not help but notice that, all the while, Balduin was mentally circling his father as if he were a house, uncertain whether to try entering by the front door or perhaps going around the back instead. Branhardt naively attributed his son's reserve to the beauty of the fruit trees. But one morning, when the blossoms were already starting to go brown and fall in the warm, sunny air, Balduin fired off the following pistol shot of an announcement:

"It would be good to travel south. The farther the better. Best of all, perhaps, as far as Egypt."

"*Just Egypt*?!" Branhardt asked, laughing. He didn't seem very surprised. "I'd like to follow Gitta to Venice, too. And Egypt? Didn't she say she'd like to go to the desert on her honeymoon and see Arabs dancing in their white robes? You know, we all still feel some of the elation from the festivities — I do, too! But that feeling flies away from us like the blossoms of a tree when its time is up."

Balduin was certain it wouldn't fly away, it didn't come from Gitta, and it wasn't "elation."

But now he said something else, his voice neither very loud nor particularly clear:

"Father, the thing is this: instead of studying — it's for a big piece of work that I'd like to go away."

His hands clasped behind his back, his head slightly raised, Branhardt had stopped and was silently gazing up into the trees — as if he were listening intently to the barely comprehensible statement. In fact, he was thinking intently of his own response, even after Balduin had fallen silent. Then he remarked, as if faulting himself:

"Yes — no doubt that was a mistake, a serious mistake. I should have held my ground, sent you back when you came home for Christmas — when you wanted to stay here and plunge, head over heels, into your studies."

"No, no! It wasn't a mistake!" Balduin broke in, almost touched, as if eager to spare him his paternal self-reproach. "It was good — everything's good, everything's in order. And now it unveils its meaning so wonderfully! It was good! One lecture, for example — without it, I'd —"

Branhardt was following his own line of thought.

"If all this were only about your studies!" he said. "But the fact is, you simply don't know how to follow through on what you yourself wanted at all costs, what you struggled for — and not for even half a year! Look — this makes all the hopes that have emerged lately nothing but the most harmful possible distractions of an irresolute will."

"Father!" Balduin exclaimed, now desperate. His resolute will was exactly what he wanted to talk about — and that he only seemed to be abandoning something from lack of will — on the contrary, he was now living as if under a law — *his own* law — otherwise he would not feel driven into foreign lands, alone — him, so indecisive.

He hurried to explain everything thoroughly and precisely.

It was also amazingly accurate, reasoned down to the last detail. As rushed and excited as he was, he still wove together all he said so logically. He began with his urgent desire, explained the necessity of his work, and ended with something about how all would be lost if he couldn't make it to Egypt.

Under the spreading apple trees, the last to retain their rosy-white finery undiminished, Branhardt walked beside his son towards the house — going slowly, in thought, with the result that he carelessly broke off the blossoms of some low hanging branches. It was time for him to go down to the clinic, but he ignored that, too, without his almost instinctive glance at his watch.

At the garden gate, he said:

"You should distrust yourself in such cases — precisely on account of your flawless arguments — yes, those especially!" And, thinking of his son's long speech, he smiled slightly, as serious as he was. "What grows normally never has such a surprising grasp of its own hidden roots. It's when we're seized by some impulse that's not really an organic part of us that we're inclined to cobble together something so artfully, just to feel we're on solid ground."

Branhardt stopped; he'd run out of time. He gazed at his boy, so tall he had to look up at him! So quiet and pale, and the size of his light brown eyes made his expression nakedly obvious — his sadness gave them a nearly empty look. Branhardt forgot his hurry again.

He would have liked to reach out and stroke the boy's cheek, as if Balduin were a child in physical distress. For he felt his son's concern was like such distress; there was no objective way to approach it.

But all the more objectively his whole will collected itself, wanting to help and advise and not to be influenced or misled by plaintive wishes.

He put his hands on Balduin's shoulders.

"Don't toss your rifle into the barley, son! Don't give up the first time things go bad. Try this instead: don't think about whether something is pleasant or unpleasant. Start by setting aside everything that distracts you from what you've begun — your studies. Let's say: go half a year without looking left or right. Then we'll talk again."

A derisive answer occurred to Balduin: "Thanks for the diagnosis and prescription!" But he couldn't open his dry, cracked lips.

Glum and angry, he watched his father walk away, leaving the garden and turning down the long road to town, now stepping along quickly to make up lost time. Balduin's eyes were fixed on his father's walk. It didn't look at all rushed, just as a bird's calm flight gives no sign of urgency. He was convinced his father was taking his time to ponder what would happen next and what was to be done, and how to face it with full presence of mind when the time came.

But here was Balduin, even now, in the morning, tired. After all the weeks of work, his hopes soaring, perhaps too much of an exertion.

How feebly it had all come to nothing, the great, carefully prepared discussion, and how uplifting Balduin had actually imagined it would be. Full of a compelling pathos that — like the trees in the garden — spoke with blossoms and by fruits convinced! How often he had played out every single statement in his mind, said them aloud to himself, and even — but more often, far more often — whispered them, yes, almost prayed them, to him, his father here on earth, so good, so intelligent —.

Balduin leaned against the garden wall, behind whose budding shrubbery he could look up to the wooded hills and see some people from town out for their stately morning walk, and farther off a troupe of singing students coming his way.

He stood there unmoving, defiant and despondent. Embittered by the cheerful voices as they moved on, as well as by the dismal silence they left behind. Incapable of doing the assigned work of preparing for the morning's lecture or his own writing either — an outcast between the two.

The house stood silent and mute behind the blossoming trees. Not even Anneliese looked out at him: she was busy in town, helping to organize Gitta's new home.

*   *   *

Balduin thought Gitta's return from her honeymoon would be tremendously unsettling, and he was already anxious about it. Yet so glum was his present mood that even this great event struck him as hardly different from the everyday. One of the cabs coming up to the woodlands in nice weather would now happen to contain Markus and Gitta instead of other people, that's all. Because they arrived a day early and unannounced, all kinds of preparations to greet them were incomplete, which gave Gitta the chance to joke about having to stay up in the hillside house to help weave the half-finished welcome wreath of dark-red climbing roses for her front door — much to the superstitious horror of Herr and Frau Lüdecke.

Despite his low spirits, Balduin took a close look at Gitta. But the only new thing he noticed about her was yet another changed hairstyle: this time with a deep center part, as in many Madonna paintings, the humility of which was so at odds with her face that he decided neither the humility nor the coiffure would last.

Italy hadn't impressed Gitta at all. Springtime back home was a thousand times more beautiful! The colors and people there screamed, Venice was a theater, and the lagoons smelled dreadfully. She hadn't rested until they went to the seashore. But Markus praised the somber splendor of the old palaces, that dream of the past in the south's eternal present. — "Which shows how little suited we are to each other!" he added. Then he told how Gitta, lacking the least sense of direction, had gotten hopelessly lost two steps away from their hotel and desperately wanted to swim back across the lagoon. He seemed pleased she had been so woefully lost without him.

Twice they had made new acquaintances. First there was a young nun whose beauty had so captivated Gitta that for a while she spoke only, with some bitterness, about why she herself hadn't been packed off to a convent. Then there was a melancholy youth who confided in Gitta the many calamities that had assailed him. She thought herself into these manifold misfortunes with such compassion that she discovered several disturbing aspects he had, fortunately, overlooked, and she was hardly able to stop herself from informing him how much more unfortunate he was than he knew.

Markus related this in a humorous tone, creating the cheeriest mood imaginable as they drank their tea. Anneliese was the only one who thought for a moment that it was too cheery.

When her daughter arrived, her feelings had been so happy and profound that she didn't know how to contain them, like someone who has both hands full of gifts and doesn't know whom to share them with. As Markus left with Gitta that evening, she stayed at the garden gate, even stood outside it. Did she want to follow along for a way —? See for herself what they were like now, when they were alone together? A crazy idea! But didn't she feel some disappointment? Or was that simply her "exuberance" again?

Branhardt too stood by the garden gate, holding it open for his wife. He felt content beyond all expectations. At least Gitta hadn't looked like some young wives returning from their honeymoon, with faces ravaged by emotion, with shadows under their eyes as if they'd been chased through every excitement. Something girlish had clung to Gitta unperturbed. Shouldn't that make him feel happy, as a father and a physician? He felt how he loved her.

When Anneliese joined him back in the garden, he joked:

"Not so simple, being promoted to mother-in-law — something of a superhumanly higher rank, wouldn't you say?"

Hearing no joking response, he went on in his emphatic way, ever so sure of its effect:

"Lieselieb, don't wish for *more* than the two young people wish for themselves."

She heard in his words only his superiority in practical matters and pulled herself together, admiring him, as always, but remaining silent.

So they stood at the gate, side by side, silent, neither knowing what the other was being silent about.

* * *

In the new villa district at the end of the parklands leading down from the hill, Markus had rented a small, two-story house, set in a modest garden, with a kitchen on the bottom floor and all the modern comforts the hillside house lacked. When Anneliese arrived the next morning, she found him still busy setting up house, their brand-new furniture and the long-serving items he didn't want to part with standing awkwardly about, as if they hadn't been properly introduced. Gitta went around, her hands clasped behind her back, somewhat curious to see how "such a married home" was created. The last room in the back, looking out into the greenery, was still empty. It was supposed to be her private room, but she wouldn't hear of it. The idea of "marriage" was that you didn't have anything private — just as Mama had nothing all her own, other than her old bureau, that "box of secrets" in their bedroom, and the even more secret-filled piano in the sitting room: two possessions all the richer in content.

"I shall lock this room as a symbol of the girlhood room I have sacrificed. One must adapt to a female's conditions of existence!" Gitta eloquently put it.

Markus urged her to retain that lofty language. He was standing on a small stepladder, sorting his books, and he added that for the empty room he would have a golden key made, as Bluebeard had done, allowing his wife inside only after she had found a *practical* solution to the riddle about who would live there: "she does not live in it, he does not live in it, and yet she and he live in it."

Anneliese was pleased this morning by his humorously calm bearing. Freed from the former conflict of engagement's half-measures, he seemed more natural, also more in command. And — wasn't his humor perhaps one last way to keep his feelings in bridle and reins, just as his stiff reserve had been?

In the bedroom, a pretty semicircle between the bathroom and a dressing room, both in white, Gitta was unpacking her things, and Salomo had curled up on some of her dresses, clearly assuming they'd been provided as his bed there. But Gitta had decided Salomo would not be moving to Villenstraße. It was horribly difficult for her, almost like having to sacrifice twelve children from a previous marriage, yet some fine feeling made her sense that a pet dog Salomo would not fit into the Mandelstein household. In fact, she left behind far more than just twelve children dear to her heart, up in the hillside house, its garden, and the forest.

So her first intimate conversation with her mother centered exclusively on Salomo.

But then, with the open-heartedness she was used to showing her mama, Gitta turned to more confidential revelations — noting how she had thought so little of Italy because she had eagerly expected it would be something special. Of course, she'd often thought to herself that there was not much to a honeymoon. — But so little? She wouldn't have thought that.

Anneliese asked if she'd told Markus.

That gave Gitta a fit of laughter. Of course not! How could she possibly tell him "there was not much to it"?!

But then — one time it was almost beautiful. When they came back to Venice from the Lido, before they left. She had felt something in those nights like never before — an intimacy and a storm of happiness like never before. And weren't those feelings really for Markus? That's why she would have liked to tell him about it — at night, in the dark. But they lay there, their beds close, each draped with a large mosquito net, and every time she reached out her hand to him, it always ended somewhere other than in the opening of his net. Besides, the opening was so devilishly hard to figure out, and all Markus was expecting was mosquitos. So she watched him in the half-darkness, sleeping under his muslin netting, observed him devotedly, and that was all. — "On the other hand, of course, we weren't bitten or stung!" Gitta concluded, "but those were still the most beautiful nights."

Anneliese tried to join in her laughter; they were cheerful together, affectionate and happy in each other's company. "Don't wish for *more* than the two young people wish for themselves!" she resolutely repeated her husband's words to herself. She also admitted — thinking of her own fortunate happiness in love — that disappointments might have had a destructive effect. Yet Gitta seemed to shake off such things, like a poodle does rain. And wasn't it better that way?

In courageous desperation, Anneliese turned a deaf ear to the voice trying to whisper to her heart: from complete happiness to unhappiness is only one stop — you get there right away! But, starting from half-happiness, there are many stops and stays — always another one —. You still end up at unhappiness, only much wearier.

Balduin arrived later, with an expression in which indifference and boredom were battling for supremacy. From the day they arrived back home, Markus had noticed that his brother-in-law looked worse than usual, even more dispirited in bearing and attitude. Sometimes he quietly doubted whether Branhardt was dealing with his son in the right way, for in his opinion Branhardt's educational effect, as powerful as it was, stemmed far more from his own strength, poise, and abundance than from any probing consideration of the spiritual needs of those less blessed with such gifts.

With the two women busy together, Markus asked Balduin how he was feeling. Balduin did not find that pleasant — an irritating reminder of the "medical professional," of his father. No, and Markus in general, now so comfortably secure within his four walls, a married man, had long since ceased to be the same person with whom he had gotten along so well out in the hillside woods, the man to whom he confided almost more feelings than he actually had.

So Balduin wandered around like a stranger within these four walls, now and then looking at an object in the well-ordered study, which smelled of turpentine and wallpaper paste.

"My God! Someone who hasn't been in conflict with his family — oh, of course, yes, you went through all that once, and even ran away from them — but that's all so long ago. You're done with that kind of feeling."

"Done with it? How so? I still have two brothers. I have to go through it twice yet," said Markus. He was sitting there smoking, something Balduin found disgusting.

"Oh, for the others! But is there any comparison? Even if we're the most selfless people in the world, we can't summon up so much anger and longing," Balduin countered.

"No. You're right," Markus admitted, and thought to himself: may you never experience how terrible it is — to know full well you must hurt someone.

They didn't know what to say to each other.

Then Branhardt came in, and, with him, life.

At dinner, Markus's young servant waited on them, a slim, dark-haired Romanian, whom he'd brought along much as he had the furniture that didn't fit in, and who was basically as adept as he was unreliable. Branhardt found the situation quite amusing, especially for the neurasthenic patients to be expected there, since Thesi could make herself understood only by stuttering and the Romanian only in highly exotic fashion. But Gitta wanted to break him of the habit of speaking Romanian, and Markus wanted to cure Thesi of her stutter. The fact that Markus found Thesi's stutter so interesting had probably already filled Frau Baumüller with the most far-reaching hopes of other peculiar judgments by the young Mandelsteins.

After dinner Branhardt had to depart. Hardly anyone noticed when Balduin, after having sat through the entire meal as if he had taken Trappist vows, quietly took his leave as well.

That evening Anneliese let the children walk her and Salomo home.

It was a hot, humid evening that seemed to promise a thunderstorm. When Markus and Gitta arrived back home they found the smell from the bouquets decorating their entryway hanging almost oppressively in all the rooms.

"We should just throw them all away," Gitta commented, ungratefully. She leaned far out one of the windows. "There's a time when people bring springtime inside, to save it, preserve it — where inside there's more spring than outside in the wild, changing weather. But there comes a time when you don't like it anymore, when there's too much spring for the room. To lock up summer in vases — that's more what Frau Lüdecke does."

Markus kept silent and smoked. Her rather unkind rant could likely have sprung from a sudden, nervous excess of emotion — her mama's first departure perhaps? — or maybe even Salomo's?! — On their honeymoon he'd noticed she was mostly homesick for Salomo. Gitta could sometimes be put off by the most imperceptible things, like a horse that unexpectedly starts, rears up, and runs off, heaven knows where to. With her heartiest approval, he'd called it her "horse sickness": *equus morbus*. Gitta always seemed to him so surprisingly sensitive, yet, at the same time, full of unbridled, raw energy.

There was no storm. At bedtime they left the door to the small balcony over the back garden wide open. They chatted about the more severe heat they'd become accustomed to in Italy and thought of new travel plans. That was one of Markus's favorite things. Remarkably, since he'd fallen in love with Gitta, he dreamed much less of their future home together than of trips they would take — of wondrous foreign landscapes they would see, landscapes that would have to tell them what they had never told anyone else.

Then all was quiet. But as Gitta was about to fall asleep, she called to mind a memory from their trip:

"Remember those two old English ladies in Venice? They thought you were an Italian, I think, who was enjoying showing his wife his homeland! But — you didn't show me your homeland at all."

"No," Markus said. He lay motionless, not even opening his eyes.

"So, when then?" Gitta asked, with a big yawn. But he didn't respond, so she gave him a bit of a shove to get his attention. "So, when?"

"On our honeymoon, I guess."

"When?!" — Gitta laughed and marveled at how a person half-asleep could talk like that.

She couldn't fall asleep as quickly. The humid night air wafted in through the door. The tall maple trees whispered. Were their tops dense enough to block the view of the ugly walls of the houses across the way —? She'd completely forgotten to check during the day, and finally she was so curious she slipped quietly out of bed and tiptoed out onto the balcony.

There was some light in the sky, but she couldn't be sure about the other houses. The back garden went right up to their neighbors', and she could imagine she was looking into a whole world of trees.

A deep silence prevailed outside; the nightingales had ceased their singing; the birds now sat with their brood. Back at the hillside house, she knew the sounds of the night, the cry of the owl that nested in the old stone wall and was feared by the brooding birds, as was the weasel on its nightly hunts. So much peace and peril filled that garden amid the woodlands at this time of year — the acacias smelled so sweetly then; the linden trees were just budding.

Gitta suddenly understood why she had complained about the flowers in their entryway. Because she herself wanted to be thrown out of the stifling indoor air!

All around her was the June night, the familiar night of home, which she had longed for in the south. Yet it didn't seem to be the same one she had thought of. She didn't know what it was, but something enclosed her night like a barrier — the same as those invisible back walls.

Then, as if she were still in Italy, not at home, she began to recall "the" night, "her" night, out of which flowed dreams and memories, not like *one* life but like thousands, in which she lived a thousandfold.

Gitta was so intensely and intimately caught up in these bygone dreams and nights that when she went back inside, she felt almost astonished for a moment. There in the dusky semicircle of the bedroom was a wide double bed, with someone already sleeping in it.

And Markus in his night clothes looked more than ever as he had at the costume ball: as an Arab.

CHAPTER XII

In the days that followed, Anneliese was often at the small house in Villenstraße — on the flimsy pretense of "showing her daughter the ropes," although Gitta quite unexpectedly revealed talents for domestic organization that neither Markus nor her mother would ever have expected. It went little noticed that Balduin had "gone private" more than ever, almost always leaving or returning to his secluded quarters by the back stairs. He truly enjoyed the stillness of the house as never before, its emptiness all around him. He was separated from the only sounds, a short distance away, by the padded double door of his father's study. Yet when he knew Branhardt was at home, that's where his attention was strangely drawn. As Balduin sat writing, he listened intently, straining to hear his father's familiar tread next door — the usual scraping of his chair — the dry cough after all his smoking that seemed to say to his pipe: "Now that's enough of you!" It seemed as though these things that caught his ear created an atmosphere around him, into which he bent deep, as though into a second room. He wrote more quickly and more animatedly — with an expression as if he were not only listening but also watching: as if, like theater curtains, the double door parted, until before him — on a stage before him, as it were — the entire interior of a human solitude were revealed, unnoticed by the person himself.

From day to day, however, Balduin tended to avoid his father, and so it was already high summer when Branhardt, encountering his son one day under the fruit trees, the scene of their great discussion, stopped beside him with one short question:

"You're not going down to your lectures anymore, then?"

Balduin had been expecting that question for so long, working out the tone of voice he would answer in — perhaps too long, so he had lost some of the natural satisfaction with which he might have spontaneously exclaimed: "If you knew where I was coming from — and *how* I'm coming, how rich, how successful I've been, you wouldn't even ask whether I go down there!"

Without hesitation, he replied:

"No. Because now I know what I *may* choose. What I may trust myself to do. What I may do, with my own strength."

But something arrogant, though not intended, slipped into his tone. The impossibility of offering evidence of what he was claiming tried to overcome, to overtake what he was saying. Ultimately it sounded like one last, desperate piece of proof for something utterly unproved.

"May do? The strong man may do anything; the man who is weak or threatened thinks he may do anything, because no sense of well-being makes him cautious or because he has no well-being to lose," Branhardt said calmly. "My boy, don't deceive yourself with fake cures."

Then, after a pause, standing close to his son, he went on: "Perhaps you didn't understand why I recommended — prescribed — that you first spend this half year of self-discipline engaged in your studies. This was done on behalf of what is equally true for all of us, without exception — for stonebreakers and poets alike: we must acquire competence so we *may believe* in ourselves."

Balduin barely waited for him to finish, overcome with the urge to answer, almost breathless:

"Put me to the test! Set me a task — but with what is really mine! Then, not just myself — but others — all others — I'll make them believe."

"What I have in mind cannot be learned from something at the mercy of creativity," Branhardt interrupted. "Only from human necessity. Done on command? How soon would the mere idea of that put a hex on the white paper in front of you and make it stay white?"

Balduin went pale. That was no way to treat his dreams! Don't tell him beforehand they'll fail — don't hypnotize him with blank paper. Then his dreams will stay blank, too. He felt with dread that his father could refute him at any time. He was refuting him now, conjuring up his insecurity out of the darkest corners — he felt as if bats were stirring and darting where only moments ago all had been bright and sunny, with birds fluttering and singing.

As if from afar, he heard his father go on:

"It's possible you could find something more fruitful than what you had planned to do here. There are always countless possibilities. But to go running after them blindly could mean you never learn how to realize them."

Balduin heard that, too. But he no longer heard any kindness or concern — no effort to cast a protective shield around him. It seemed instead to beat him down, subjugate him. Nor did he hear any such concern in what Branhardt went on to say:

"Not that I disparage the plans for your work. But I want to protect them for you — protect them from you yourself."

As far away as that voice came from, Balduin still felt the overwhelming closeness of the man speaking beside him — a physical sensation of oppression, of binding, almost of assault, no, even more: as if the space he occupied were abolished — as if his one foot-breadth of earth were taken from him — until suddenly he was hurled out of his father's looming power — thrust away, thrown away, fading into an almost powerless state that was about to become thoughtless action —

How he got back to his private quarters he himself later could no longer recall. He must have simply gone chasing off.

When Anneliese came back from Gitta's a few hours later, she saw, as soon as she entered the garden, that the slide windows of Balduin's room were open and smoke was pouring out.

The little iron stove there had its hitches and twitches throughout the seasons, whether from the winter wind blowing down the chimney or the summer sun shining in. She also knew how Balduin burned huge amounts of paper when he was working. If he made the slightest mistake or wanted to make an improvement, he had to begin all over again, a "brand-new start," with no "past" watching him from the paper. Hence the little iron stove's frequent sacrificial fires.

Anneliese climbed the wooden stairway from the garden and came in through the veranda. "I'll get the damper, Balder," she said, reaching for the sooty stove lid, but she stopped at the sight of her son.

His eyes were reddened, his face flushed. The table swept clear, its drawers empty, the handwritten sheets they had contained strewn on the floor, some books fallen or thrown down from the shelf — his room looked like a wild departure was underway. And there he stood in the middle of the room.

His mother's expression, as she looked at him in silence, made him blush even more. He grimaced impulsively, but offered a dogged apology:

"Those damned scraps get stuck in the stove door. The trash smokes."

Anneliese picked up the papers at her feet.

"Why burn everything, for heaven's sake?"

Why? — The simple directness of the question struck him as puzzling. Why? — Wasn't he carrying out an order? — That is, the opposite of an order — the opposite of his father's wishes and words, which had run on ahead — leading him here from the garden. Now he knew it. He'd been in a rush to obliterate, to burn. He made flames out of the words — scorn and hatred: "I want to protect your works for you."

Or was he burning them only out of fear? So the white paper behind the written sentences could not be lurking — to give the lie to every sentence, to wipe away each one, as if it were only defiling its whiteness —.

Anneliese asked no more questions. She grasped at the papers fluttering around her, blown about by the evening wind from the window. She saved what was lying nearest the stove and brought it all together on the table. It wasn't hard to put them in order. Sometimes the size of the paper changed according to the content, sometimes even the paper itself — there was smooth paper and ribbed, coarse paper and the finest. It was laid out every Christmas with the other gifts in assorted stacks, and then it had been amusing to see how Balder, delighted, would go and touch it with his sensitive fingertips, as if it were cloth for a garment.

Anneliese sat at the table and sorted and smoothed and read. Balduin looked on sheepishly. He'd withdrawn as far as his lair allowed, sitting on the windowsill of the open window. She was so silent, didn't scold him — but read. Yes, that too was a silently imposed punishment — did she know that?! No one had ever been allowed to look into his workshop — to see unfinished things. That was dreadfully difficult to bear: eyes looking at all these most secret thoughts — a hundred times worse than their death by fire.

Perched on his windowsill, his legs drawn up, hugging his knees — in an almost contorted position — Balduin stared at the papers he'd written over and over with so much artistic feeling, as if they were meant to speak even before they were read. Not out of self-satisfied trifling, but because in the over-intense excitement of the inner work he found something calming about seeing the words become, even outwardly, so completely his own work — the work of the whole man, even of his hands. Not some provisional scrap of paper with a chance of finding its way into print — which Balduin was not yet thinking about when he was writing.

His gaze turned to Anneliese, in search of help. Not a stranger — it was only his mother, whose eyes were seeing all this — she, the mother of all he was struggling to create, because he was just the way she had created him. "My dear mother!" he said to himself, simply as sounds, until that word seized him, deepening to an infinite sweetness and meaning — until, like rushing poetry he had never fully expressed, it came to him again and again: "My dear mother!"

Then suddenly he could no longer stand it. He had no idea that what made him bolt now, out of his unnatural position on the window-sill, was mainly his contorted limbs. In the honest belief that his soul, not his body, was driving him away, Balduin went stiff-legged down the wooden stairway and into the garden.

*   *   *

Anneliese hadn't even noticed his departure. It was late when she looked up from the gathered pages. Such joy had captivated her that only slowly did she recall the scene that had led to her reading.

Right in front of her, taking up the breadth of the window, was the sunset. Under it, sharply drawn, as if with a ruler, lay a haze that hid the distant hills and took church tops and a few towers from the town's profile. The view did not extend beyond that. Whatever lay farther down the valley could be a human settlement, meadow ground, or nothing at all.

Anneliese looked out at it dreamily, as though she were still reading.

She had read only one piece all the way through; it was still incomplete but gave the impression of a whole. It was the most recent work of these weeks or days, as evident from the handwriting, whose ink had not yet had time to darken.

Obviously, a previous work had been broken off for this one. The impression was as if Balduin had jumped up from his work, intent on satisfying for himself the desire whose fulfillment his father had denied him and wandering out into the world. But more than this desire was realized; its fulfillment was, too. Here his father took him by the hand

and went with him as his traveling companion, calling upon all the beauty around him to reveal itself — offering the world as a gift. Each of these verses was a cry of thanks from the one who was being so richly endowed, who received it all like a child, so that he became a man, a mature person, a sage. Each of the verses somehow managed to unite them, so that the world looked like a garden through which a god walks, taking a man by the hand. Often the abundance of worldly things stood there almost as clearly formed as reality itself, but the features of the father were present as in a picture-puzzle, partly visible, partly invisible. He was recognizable to *this* reader. To a stranger, he might be like a sky that lights a landscape without restricting it.

Balduin did not return to his room.

But was it Balduin she should speak to? Anneliese quickly roused herself from her reverie. She reached for the pages — as though she knew exactly what she should do with them — but suddenly stopped, as if the flames meant to burn them up were bursting out of them. No, it was clear to her: this was so much his father's story — the boy would forbid him to read them.

So she headed empty-handed for Branhardt's study, pushed back the bolt of the padded door and was about to knock on the inner door.

Someone inside had already jumped up — and opened it.

"You, Lieselieb? You're coming to me *from there?*"

She didn't know where to begin. Without the pages, she felt so exposed, so dispossessed — the word "disarmed" came involuntarily to mind. Her husband's eyes looked at her so searchingly — they saw that her hair had become a little tousled, her hands blackened by coal. There was even a spot of soot right across her chin.

"You look almost like Cinderella at the hearth — but no, quite different: like Cinderella after she's danced with the prince and is missing nothing but a slipper," Branhardt said, becoming cheerful.

"Listen, Frank — I'm here because of Balder — did anything happen between you two today?"

"What do you mean? Well, yes, a brief exchange of words. The boy was acting a bit nervous."

Anneliese sat down on a chair beside the door. "We may be dealing with him in the wrong way," she said. Branhardt seemed rather astonished.

"There was nothing more to our exchange of words than what you and I have often discussed and about which we think the same way."

"Yes, Frank, I know! And that Balder is to become competent only for the sake of his own life's desires. But — what if our way might be the wrong way for him? — I was just sitting at his table, looking at his work — and surely it knows the most about him — more than we do."

"And?" Branhardt asked.

She felt she could sum up what filled her heart in two words — in one phrase, that is: it truly was "a king's son" from whose room she had just come. All at once she understood the struggle the boy was having, trying to explain what was so important to him.

"The fact that he often appears inept, Balder — you see, it's because things reveal so much beauty to him — too much to realize in everyday life. We can't do that either, but we're satisfied with piecework — half-blind people who don't realize what he's looking at and what makes him dissatisfied and helpless."

Branhardt stood still before her.

"A long speech, Lieselieb. But — you seemed even more frightened by Balduin's morbid nature than I was."

"And I am!" she cried. "But this is so absolutely clear to me now. For him, things must be realized poetically. Then he can work more harmoniously — and cope with everything in his life a little better. Not the other way around! *That* way is blocked for him — and with *the other* you and I chase him into dead ends."

"Well, then, out with it — what evidence do you have? Why doesn't he give me these things to read? I know he doesn't like sharing them. But eventually he'll have to come out and face the world."

Anneliese was suffering. She sensed how impossible it would now be for the boy to let Branhardt see what she had read. But there was more to it — he needed them to insist on seeing his work.

"You're in a sensitive mood now because Gitta's out of the house and your only son is here," Branhardt said, pacing back and forth. "I'm ready for any confrontation with Balduin, but it seems to me your motherly tenderness should be more wary of itself. It's better that he gets a bit melancholy or defiant than that we endanger him with false assurances."

Anneliese leaned her head back against the chair. "Oh, Frank!" she said sadly. "We let his melancholy pass in silence as if it had to be that way, and, in our infinite wisdom, we shield him from dangers that perhaps he ought to face. — I wish I could wrap my tenderness around his gaiety — only that! — and *then* see him become a man, choosing and chancing *his* dangers — in spite of us, Frank!"

Her words sounded so heartfelt that Branhardt gave heed. Something spontaneously poetic and beautiful in the way she spoke touched him in a strange way.

"To hear you talk like that, Lieselieb — well, the boy's to be envied for having such an understanding mother — but it really sounds like you've been fighting the same battles yourself. — Be that as it may: believe me, children can't be brought up in such poetic, fatalistic fashion. The fact that I, as a man and a physician, think more soberly about such matters shouldn't surprise you."

She did not relent: "Frank, I could be right, even if my status as a lay person leaves you in the right. There are things we understand only when we look at them from several sides. Isn't it possible that what makes the boy ill is also what makes him healthy — his self-healing, his renewal? And, even if that made him a bit more of a problem for us than before, what difference does *that* make? As long as it brings him to himself — that *always* means: back to health."

Yet, as she spoke, she felt her heart constrict to think it might *not* be so. If what he wanted to create were to completely ruin him — wouldn't she then, though with trembling heart, surrender him to Branhardt's stronger view, as if to his fate?

For some minutes Branhardt stood silent, looking down. The resentment at having to confront his wife about this matter showed on his brow. He approached her.

"You're under his spell," he said emphatically. "The same dreamers — the two of you. I already admitted: that's enviable — a precious gift for the boy, a security like no other. But that's why you're taking his side. You're standing up for him, not over him at the same time. — A little exuberance — Lieselieb, that was nice! — but, at the same time, that was always your mistake."

That didn't sound at all like a reproach, but almost tender — perhaps he was recalling pleasure-filled hours.

But in Anneliese it aroused opposition — resistance. — The fact that a mother acted exuberantly shouldn't be an excuse for being strict with her son; no matter what she might feel and do — it should find *justification* in him, not help to *oppress* him! Yet she was secretly frightened that she might have been driven to say these things because of that exuberance of hers, for, in all other matters, she still believed in her husband's superiority.

She bowed her head and fervently clasped her hands. With the peculiar gesture she made whenever strong excitement was hard to put into words, she raised her folded hands to her lips. Out of the conflicts, the helplessness of her soul there suddenly arose, in quickly chosen words, a strange, almost arbitrary feeling of defiance, hostile to Branhardt.

"No, not like that," she murmured, "you don't have the right to simply go ahead and decide."

If there was one thing Branhardt found laughable it was authoritative posing. He often intentionally avoided situations that would make domestic conflicts of will inevitable. But, if there were a conflict, then what would prevail, always without a fight, was, as a matter of course, *his* will.

Now he went on, pondering and posing a question:

"I don't understand. — You will probably serve the boy best if you help him to be more obedient. But in the end, one person has to decide."

But Anneliese had already jumped up; she was responding more to the question posed by her own defiant hostility than to what he had said, although she directed her answer to him:

"No! No! Not one! Never just one! Even the wisest judgment can become unjust, willful, arrogant, when measured against life. And the worst — you see — the worst thing under the sun — is the violation of one person by another."

Rapidly — more rapidly, it seemed, than he had ever heard her speak — the words came rushing and tumbling out, as if suddenly and violently set free from some place where they had been forgotten, forgotten by Anneliese herself, but where they had been secretly talking, still stammering, babbling. — —

How would he even have thought that! Shocked, Branhardt pulled away from Anneliese — shocked by her, by himself.

In hot waves, the blood surged and ebbed in her face.

Wasn't this the first time he had ever seen her like this? Wasn't he, in fact, seeing her for the first time? He also saw that she was beautiful, the way she stood there, between outrage and rapture and somehow clad in an armor covering her woman's clothes — exotically beautiful.

Then a recollection came to life in him, as if there were a beauty like that about her when they first met: her weapons at the ready — her sights set. — As if she were decades younger.

Didn't she look to him then like a wonderful youth, before he thought of her as a woman?

Branhardt had to force his mind back into the present.

Were they still even discussing their son?

As far as Balduin was concerned, they had left their quarrel hanging, rather than reaching a conclusion about the facts, about the works at hand. But, of course, they were no longer dealing with such individual cases.

Anneliese gazed at him head on — that is, she looked down a little. That was something that used to make him physically uneasy. He had long since overcome it as childish, but in this moment, a trace of it made itself felt again, and his anger at himself because of it influenced his attitude, as he repeated with rather too much calm:

"Someone has to decide. You say no. Because it seems we are no longer a unit as father and mother on this issue. And your 'no' affects us not only as father and mother, but also as man and wife, Anneliese — and as two."

At first, only one unfamiliar note in his words caught her ear: he hadn't said "Lieselieb" — but "Anneliese." The pet name bestowed upon her long ago was stripped away like a gem she'd worn as jewelry over her everyday clothes — scarcely noticed, because she'd always worn it — and yet only to be lost, as part of herself.

Branhardt had gone over to his standing desk. He propped his arm on it and absent-mindedly compared some tables he'd likely been working on when Anneliese came in.

She looked over to him from far away, as if she had awakened and suddenly found herself alone somewhere. Again, the blood came and went in her cheeks, but this time it was from shame and displeasure at herself. Oh, how badly, how foolishly she had fought for her Balder's good cause! She had only needed to carry on, to continue what the boy had so convincingly created for her — there in the next room: the companionship of father and son.

Yet no one could have shown the boy his father as a fellow traveler the way she might have done — not as poetry, no, but in life itself, as attested to by his father's own youth.

If only she had told Balder what had made Branhardt a doctor! As a small boy, after his father recovered from a serious illness, they rode out together, and he saw their little buggy surrounded by people who had missed him, had longed for him, like their savior on earth — saw the happiness in their eyes and faces and outstretched hands. Later, in his own student days, he was just as seized by the desire to devote himself to scientific research, casting aside everything else for it. Until the born surgeon in him renewed the struggle — and ultimately the stormy rebellion of his youth confronted one last rampart: meeting the demands of everyday life and the need to support a wife and child.

But with all the ups and downs, even in the face of the most intense experiences, one thing remained strongest in him: the image of the simple country doctor that had left its mark on the little boy's heart. The unheralded "doctor for all work," off in some lost corner of the world, remained for him the noblest ideal. Despite his own rank and distinction and even after the most successful efforts, it was the model against which, in all humility, he measured himself.

Anneliese stood motionless where she was, apart from her husband, with only him in her gaze. Yet she gave no thought to that distance, nor to the missing Lieselieb, which, in the space between them, had dropped away and was no longer an obstacle to the short step back to each other.

She stood and watched, and experienced her son in her husband and her husband in her son, so that again she inwardly rejoiced — between them now, she became anonymous but without any loss, dissolving into the two people she loved.

Branhardt did not look up. He thumbed through his lists, making notes.

The yellowish beam of the brass-mounted oil lamp, turned up to full brightness, illumined his features, which might better have been left out of the bright light. Deep furrows around his beardless mouth and the expression of his tightly pressed lips revealed a still lingering agitation.

Anneliese was touched that he had to reveal his inner self to her that way — naked, against his will. In all the harshness of his words, she saw the resurgence of his own youth, even as he reacted so harshly to the youthfulness of his son. His own struggles, his precious willpower, his hard-won experiences — that's what he wanted to impart to his boy — yes, and force them on him if need be, before they were lost to him. For even now it would destroy him, should his son not continue his life-sustaining work.

Branhardt had sat down at the table beside his desk to write something down; he wrote rapidly, without a break, no longer merely putting on a show of being busy.

Then she was at his side, very near, very close, with both arms around him.

Strong as death, the warmth of her arms embraced him.

"Oh, Frank — not as two —"

CHAPTER XIII

On her way home, Renate passed through the area again and stayed for several weeks, not in the hillside house this time, but at a nearby summer resort, to which friends had invited her.

Only now did she get to know Markus, and she stressed how glad she was to have caught him before he left for the Dutch congress for natural scientists, at which he was offering a paper. She soon drew him into ever longer conversations about his female monkeys, whom he had to thank for his presentation and who, as she saw at once, were quite close to his heart. Another thing she noticed at once: Anneliese knew a great deal about these monkeys, Gitta hardly anything at all. In fact, Gitta would stick her fingers in her ears as soon as the conversation turned to animal experiments and warily check the expressions of those present to see whether they had finally exhausted the topic before she took her fingers out again.

That's why she wasn't going along to the conference, where everyone would be looking at her ears. She much preferred to sit out those brief straw-widow days in her girlhood snuggery up in the woodlands. Renate joked that a second divorce was now unfolding in the hillside house. The first involved the Lüdeckes. Herr Lüdecke, it seems, was refusing to go walking with Frau Lüdecke, even in the loveliest moonlight. Instead, he had recently taken to keeping steady company with a few simple friends in a tavern in town. Of course, he'd done that in the past, but never so regularly and never during a full moon.

"Herr Lüdecke no longer loves me!" Frau Lüdecke declared with calm resignation. Renate was amazed to see how Frau Lüdecke's bridal airs, indestructible through ten years of marriage, fell from her nicely dressed frame and withered into an implacable spinsterhood.

Everyone had an occasional laugh at the expense of Frau Lüdecke and her romantic ways. But Markus felt Renate's interest in the matter — which, though excessive, revealed the comical side of the situation — made the Lüdeckes look like something the hillside house was in fact wonderfully lacking, namely "the under-the-stairs contingent" — "domestic servants."

To be sure, Markus was very uncertain in his impression of Renate. He said to himself: a Dr. Phil. and, on top of that, a "scholarly old librarian," as she liked to call herself, and ultimately nothing and nowhere anything other than the great lady. On the other hand, with her stature more modest than imposing and her delicate proportions, with her gracefully formed head and its delightful, natural curls of light blonde, she somehow, but palpably, gave the impression one could converse with her in a quite unscholarly — and anything but ladylike — manner.

What were the essences here, what mere appearance? That confused him, because he sensed in her an approach to appearance that had made it something essential.

The day before he left, on the way home with Gitta from stimulating hours at the hillside house, Markus asked himself what Renate, all joking aside, would say about the fact that his wife was neither "interested in his monkeys" nor inclined to accompany him to Holland. What would she — a Countess So-and-So on her maternal side — be saying to Anneliese right now about him, whom she'd treated so charmingly? Well, perhaps something diplomatic, because she never erred when it came to tact. Yet this is what he imagined her to be thinking to herself:

This eternally wandering Jew boy — why doesn't he die out! Must he make trouble in every country — and now inflict an annoying copy of himself on us?

Markus felt as if he were gasping for air.

Entering his house, he stopped in the entryway, as if he couldn't go on.

Gitta had seen him like this before: the way he would walk along not only in silence but also ahead of her one moment, then lagging behind, and twiddling the fingers of his one hand as if in his sleep. Then you couldn't see much more of his inner self than you could with Justus, the hedgehog. But in such moments, she lay in wait for his true hedge-hog face, which she secretly suspected she had never seen.

Markus turned, awoke from his brooding, and looked at Gitta — and saw dear, loving eyes, incomprehensibly understanding eyes, fixed on him.

He let out a cry of joy. Everything suddenly scattered, like thick fog that clears to reveal a mountain peak that was not at all unattainable but close, close, right at the climber's feet.

He took hold of his wife and lifted her up in the air.

"Well!" said Gitta. "What's gotten into you today?"

"The idea we should go to the mountains for the autumn holidays!" he answered.

"But you always say the best part is being up there *all alone.*"

"That's true. But just as a test, I want to take you along."

All the while his heart yodeled with joy and jubilation, as if he'd already taken the mountaintop. And as if, from up there, he were correcting what he thought Renate had been thinking:

"No! With the eternal Jew it's something quite different. What keeps him from dying off is not his endless begging for alms in country after country. If that were so, he would indeed be dead and buried, as dearly as he's been treated. Instead, he goes on searching, always searching for a place where he can give away what he possesses, his most prized possessions — where he can give away his best, so it lives on when he dies."

In reality, nothing was further from Renate's mind than ethnographic comparisons, and even her participation in the Lüdeckes' miniature tragedy involved far more objective irony than empathy, since she was wholly occupied by the personal affairs of her own that had brought her to the nearby summer resort — and they were affairs of the heart.

No sooner had Markus and Gitta left and Branhardt gone to his study than the two friends found themselves together in the adjoining sitting room, alone and confidingly close, Renate deep in one of the armchairs and Anneliese crouching beside it, to catch Renate's every word. That wasn't really necessary in the hillside house, but they followed their youthful habit — and even now it awakened in them something of bygone times when they had secrets to whisper about.

"I like him, even now — even without knowing him!" Anneliese said. "He'll bring you happiness — after all you've suffered. I'm also pleased you two are being so honest with each other — and that he understands all that has happened — and that you could let him know that."

"Understands it? Let him know? Oh, yes. Something like the fact that I liked a man who was not always worthy of such a great honor — which can happen to any poor Grete. — Good God, Liese, do you think that's true?!"

She bolted impetuously out of the armchair. But just as quickly she pulled herself together, a fine arrogance on her face, its features nearly free of youthful allure, yet beautiful.

"You just said I've suffered. No, Liese, I've *enjoyed* — that's much closer to the truth. Even being walked on: when we *love* the man who does it, that's what we *wish* he'd do. He only appears to be the enslaving master, but in truth he's our tool — the tool of a most hidden desire — the servant of a desire — for all I know!"

Anneliese too had jumped up.

"I'm closing my ears, Reni! Never, ever can we love like that — with such crucified human pride! To love, you must have full command of yourself — with every fiber of your being — in order to love another, to understand him, often better than he understands himself. Perhaps in the past there were women who *endured* such men — confusing man with God —"

They stood close to each other, face-to-face — almost closer than before, but no longer like the two who once whispered girlish secrets. The women's glances they exchanged spoke of these latest findings.

"O Liese, Liese, how easily your frightful rationality sweeps things away!" Renate said, shaking her head. She sat down, deep into the arm-chair, yielding a bit. "We can get through this sitting down; don't stand there so rigidly, like a cliff amid the surge of life. Crouch down by me again, and listen carefully this time. I want to tell you something: it might indeed be pride that finds pleasure in being crucified, that sees such treatment as something *it* alone would find exceptional, never before experienced. — What did you say about poor little women, past and present? Of course, they would nurture the opposite dream — the dream of breaking their chains — having a bit of dominance of their own, at least while a man was in love with them. That's all quite logical. But, believe me, the intoxication of happiness begins only with fanatical irrationality — and I believe that to look for heaven with any success, you must search in hell."

* * *

Gitta's move back to the hillside house did not have the disruptive effect one might naturally have expected. In fact, Gitta seemed bent on nothing but sleep. She could yawn at any moment and, on one occasion, fell asleep in broad daylight while sitting with the others. Whenever she awakened, she performed prodigious feats of absentmindedness.

Renate smiled knowingly at these symptoms. They all teased Gitta, except for Anneliese, who didn't ask about it, since she had a tender shyness about giving someone cause to tell untruths and felt it wasn't always so easy to tell everybody everything.

Nevertheless, on the morning when Gitta was supposed to return to Villenstraße to watch over Thesi's "great housecleaning project" and especially Mother Baumüller's tendency to take certain liberties, Anneliese suddenly said to the young straw-widow:

"You're going back home — don't take anything from here you don't need. Don't forget, girl, there are all manner of beautiful and tempting things that in themselves are not in the least bit wrong but that can interfere in the life of a couple. They can make you linger in anticipation of all that should be achieved and affirmed in the course of your life together."

Gitta looked uncomprehending and frightened under the gaze of her mother's clear grey eyes — almost like a criminal caught red-handed. But, instead of answering, she hastily asked a question; without knowing why or wanting to do so, she did it — looking straight into the eyes of her mama:

"Tell me — if you hadn't married —"

Anneliese answered just as quickly, perhaps too quickly:

"I would have given up music anyway. Then, for my father's sake, I would have become a nurse in the hospital where he was a medical consultant."

Astonished, Gitta saw how even now — with this simple admission — a blush of happiness and youth came over her mother. Gitta was taken aback. She merely said to herself, in silence:

"But then — well, she doesn't know how beautiful — — the 'other' is!"

Gitta hadn't actually done anything wrong up in her girlhood bedroom. Of course, she'd found a few things that hadn't made their way down to Villenstraße. In the old room, she stepped so deeply, so curiously back into the old times, without wanting or expecting it. At least, into the nighttimes. Did that come from Frau Lüdecke's "Genoveva," which still watched over her nightly from the wall above her bed — from the unicorn peering into her dreams? Or perhaps from the colored pencils, forgotten in her desk drawer? Not that she had used them. Yet, as if on their own, they went drawing in front of her as soon as she awoke in the night. Their colors were somehow all around her, giving life to strangely invisible realities. Wouldn't it have been a shame to sleep through that?

Regardless, Gitta had donned a new personality, armored with heroic intentions, as she walked down to Villenstraße that evening — accompanied by the whole family and by Salomo, whom she'd taken along "for protection," since the Romanian servant was also away.

But all the way she had the strange feeling that the wild waters that had carried her off to unknown shores had suddenly frozen under her feet, at her mama's bidding, so she really couldn't go anywhere but straight into the Villenstraße and on to the Mandelsteins'. Yet all the while, she enjoyed the tingling sensation of very, very thin ice over deep, deep water — in any case, no one would have been allowed to skate on it.

Once at home, she sat in the mild evening air in her favorite place — the narrow balcony off the bedroom. Her fantasies — which, unlike her brother's, would not let their pleasures be disturbed — no longer bumped up against the back walls of the garden, which even the lushest summer could not hide. From her house to the one opposite, it was as she wished: nearby or worlds away.

Then Gitta went inside, bedded Salomo down, and undressed. As she turned on the shiny taps in the adjoining bath and stretched out blissfully in the porcelain tub, she made the most prosaic observations about the benefits of abundant hot water, which the hillside house could not provide, and she was very much looking forward to getting a good night's sleep without the disruptive influences of the last few nights.

But something peculiar happened: she felt as if those temptations and disturbances no longer existed, as if she could no longer recall them.

Gitta leapt out of the tub and sat down, wet and expectant. Had it been that way only in the water —? No, on dry land as well. It struck her as almost comical. Should something so certain — almost more certain to her than the blood in her veins — simply be gone, as if it had never existed?

But then the comedy ceased. Only the certainty remained: it *had been* certain, like nothing else, like nothing else in the world. Crouching on the edge of the bed, she faced it now, as if it were a door that had fallen shut of its own accord and locked her out. A never known, never suspected feeling took hold of her — of insecurity, helplessness, even homelessness. What was she to do, where would she be herself now? It was Markus's own house in which she had been so slyly trapped as soon as she left her girlhood room today. And at the door of that room of old promises her own mother now sat, barring the way, like the Hound of Hell incarnate.

So Gitta thought, and in that hour she knew nothing of the fact that Markus was her husband or even that her mother was her mama.

*   *   *

But when Thesi finally knocked timidly, rather late the next morning, Gitta looked at her as if dawn itself had stepped into the room, and Thesi in her modesty could hardly believe that look was meant for her. — What did Thesi want?! Oh, yes, Thesi was there on account of Mother Baumüller, who had been called in for the big housecleaning.

Although she herself had planned it, the situation left Gitta at a loss.

Perhaps they should go to the market first? Thesi asked, proud to be making suggestions. Gitta nodded, beaming with happiness: yes, oh yes, they should go at once!

Frau Baumüller laughed when she heard the report from her baffled daughter, left so suddenly in the lurch by Gitta's housewifely virtues. She checked her purse for "market money," seemed satisfied and not the least at a loss for a suitable way to spend the day. After breakfast had been set out in the dining room and Salomo's bowl by the oven, and Salomo himself had given the courtyard a look, mother and daughter trundled off.

Gitta pondered quickly: she wasn't expected at the hillside house today, fortunately. There was an incredibly delightful silence in the empty house! Almost like in the night itself — a night with sun in the sky. — *Here*, now, even day would be night.

Until a shrill ringing destroyed the calm. The telephone —? No, the front doorbell. Delivery men rang the bell downstairs by the kitchen, but you couldn't hear it upstairs. Gitta jumped up; Salomo, lying in the sun by the balcony door, started barking. Gitta's eyes searched for her pocket watch — where was it? — and then the town bells began ringing, striking again and again, more times than Gitta thought possible — it still seemed quite early. Thesi wasn't back yet.

Then the doorbell rang again; Salomo started to whine. He pushed his way through the parlor door, ran out into the hallway and, sniffing and wagging, scratched at the door to the short, wide doorstep. That could only be Mama!

Gitta stepped out of her slippers and, half dressed as she was, crept over to the round peep hole, looked out — and saw her mama.

Gitta stood stock-still. Suddenly she felt her arms, her shoulders naked; she felt shy — with an embarrassment that didn't know quite what it was embarrassed about — everything was so closely connected; since now Gitta would be sitting properly in her little dress, if she hadn't — and Thesi would be there, too — where was she? —

The dog was still scratching and whining woefully. Then, a dear, cheerful voice outside called out: "Salomo, my pet, open the door!"

That made him jump up at his mistress as if he'd gone crazy — wagging, howling, as he only did when he bayed at the moon on spring nights. Salomo — interceding for Mama!

How then — why then — wouldn't she open the door for her mother?!

No! open the door, open up! Gitta thought — urgent and convinced as if she were already doing so, although she kept standing stock-still, her gaze fixed on the handbills and letters that had come through the slot on the door from the midday post. She didn't even realize how far apart thought and action still were — or how surely Mama must have guessed she was home and was speaking to *her*, not Salomo.

But while she was still standing there, feeling oddly stuck to the floor, it suddenly became quiet, strangely quiet — as if no one were standing outside the door anymore — or as if someone were listening intently and hardly daring to breathe, like her.

Then — things changed — the faint rustle of clothes, footsteps going down the stairs.

Suddenly Gitta realized she'd done something hurtful to her mama — and realized something else as well: that in this moment she hadn't been at all like her mama — because the violence of last night had still been in her — muffled and misunderstood, but lingering like a coal-black, nocturnal dream — and keeping her mama away from her and all that was hers — —

Gitta heard the door of the front entranceway open and close down-stairs. She rushed into the nearby front room, Markus's unused waiting room, and went to the window.

Yes, she saw her mother down on the street — walking slowly, not even looking back.

Inadvertently, Gitta turned her face away. From the mirror on the opposite wall, mounted there so worried patients could check how they looked, her face stared back at her as if it were a stranger's — in fact, quite a dissolute, remorseful face — —

The one Gitta studied the other with a disapproving gaze.

But not for long: her happiness was too great. The joy of regaining, so wonderfully, the stolen happiness from yesterday. Now she knew what had to be done to be free of her little girlhood room, where happiness would come to visit. Before it stole away, you had to capture every piece of it you could in words, each like a tiny, theft-proof coffer, which would then yield it back up again unharmed. You couldn't simply lie there, dreaming about it; you had to work at it.

*   *   *

Gitta brought the mail from the door. There was a letter from Markus. Also, various things addressed to him that he didn't want forwarded. Would he be coming back so soon?

She felt a faint stirring of regret: where in the world had Markus wandered off to, thinking he was coming home? Oh, he'd gone far, far away! When she looked for him, he seemed quite small, quite thin, almost a mere dot. Like an aged widow who had long since overcome her loss — that's about how she felt.

His letter said nothing about returning. He was brief, even briefer than usual. Markus didn't understand that sort of thing. Even with his research manuscripts, he was hampered by his difficulty in finding the right word — and then he often consulted his clever wife.

Gitta walked with her letter from the entryway to the dining room and back: his closing words made her laugh out loud. He'd written: "best kissing, your Markus."

She never called him "Markus." And now this strange Markus, accustomed to sending people "best greetings," had obviously not found a more suitable phrase for sending her his kisses.

When she saw this monstrosity of a complimentary close, Gitta was standing by the dinner table. At the sight of her uneaten breakfast, she suddenly sensed her voracious hunger and stood there gulping down whatever came to hand in the way of cold tea, zwieback, and buttered bread. Still chewing, she looked closely at the letter's rather bulky handwriting, each written character flowing out of the one before, and studied it as long and intently as an examining magistrate — and she saw the writing coming adrift and multiplying, and another letter all of a sudden growing out of it — one that made her heart beat more intensely — and what was there was Markus. — But he would probably never learn to compose such a letter — oh, if she could do it, instead of him, now that she had learned how to "work." — — She left the rest of the breakfast and went back into the small waiting room, where there was a little table with writing implements and paper for taking consultation notes, and began to write. It wasn't so easy at first; she had to cross things out. But then she smiled, satisfied. There was even something of Markus in the handwriting, and the words read as if she had drawn his soul right out of his body.

But finishing the letter didn't take her much longer: it offered only a brief respite — there was still too much to do, breathtakingly much.

The sun, which came in here only from the west, finally began to fill the room, casting broad, dazzling beams across the table. Frau Baumüller and Thesi had come, left again, and returned. Now they were rattling about in the kitchen. Gitta looked up. There was nothing but sun all around her. That's how it had been in the morning on the other side of the house — as if there were nothing but sun. Aside from that she hadn't really noticed anything.

Gitta went to where she heard the clattering.

Frau Baumüller, who was just laying out an astonishing array of cold cuts on the kitchen table, hid her initial anxiety behind talkative dexterity. Thesi disapproved of their buying the cold cuts, but also of Gitta's most recent behavior, of which her mother was taking advantage. But she disapproved most of all of herself, with her spineless wavering between her mother and her "mistress." This threefold disapproval made her look quite glum. These subtleties of the situation eluded Gitta. With a radiant expression she spoke to the two as good, dear people whom she was sincerely pleased to see again. She had nothing against sausages — on the contrary, the sight of them seemed to enhance her good mood. The same hunger as at midday, when the breakfast tea caught her eye, now focused, full strength, on the sausages, and, perched on the edge of the kitchen stool and chatting happily away, Gitta helped herself to slice after slice from the greasy paper with a blissful delight in the rich plenty before her, which finally, however, dwindled alarmingly. At any rate, when the lady of the house finally left, sated and grateful, Frau Baumüller looked far more serious than before, but Thesi was smiling.

The electric lights stayed on through the night, not only the little shaded bulbs in the bedside lamps but the large ceiling light, too. Thesi saw that, because her window on the ground floor looked into the back. Gitta was intent on staying awake and finishing her work before sleep drove away her new sense of security — drove away all the words — and caused her to lose her bearings. Of course, it seemed to her there weren't enough such words in the language, and it was dirty work in any case, like having to build a city of palaces from a heap of paving stones. But she would trouble and toil — make an honest effort, so that one thing or another was built that she could always know again.

She must have fallen asleep instead. It was almost day. It was hard to tell in the glare of the artificial light, but a little bird high up in the maple tree let out an audible "peep!"

All it said was "peep!" — it sounded like much more.

Gitta awoke with the feeling that it was confiding in her.

About what? she thought and opened her eyes wide.

Daybreak — summer morning — had it all been there before? It seemed inconceivably new to her — never touched, never experienced: as though just composed by God.

Yesterday was not yet quite gone within her — it lay, still visible, on the horizon; a city from which she had departed when sleep overtook her.

Though half-veiled now, it looked much more finished from a distance than when she was trying to build it; almost completed, with towers and walls — a city, built by day and night.

Gitta gazed at it as if from some forest edge of summer-warmed moss. She was aware it only *seemed* complete and still awaited her work. Yet, too blissfully drowsy even to stir hand or foot, she yielded to what was lightening all her limbs so wonderfully. Perhaps she was simply too expectant for any action of her own. The "peep" of the little bird had sounded to her like a promising prelude.

Someone was snoring loudly in the next room. But it was only Salomo.

Then the snoring suddenly stopped. Warily, Salomo raised his head, his brow deeply furrowed in thought, and straightened up in his padded corner.

What was he waiting for?

There — a noise on the stairs — the door.

"A thief!" Gitta said to Salomo. But the word did not make a deep enough impression on her, as if it were one of the leftover, indifferent words in her heap that she hadn't been able to find a use for.

What would he steal? Let him! As long as he let her live, she thought, God-fearing and gentle.

Then it occurred to her: hadn't she only recently been robbed and then had everything restored to her, more beautiful and complete? But when — and where?

Now there was a creaking — a tentative footfall in the hallway: he was actually coming closer — right up to the bedroom door — and now, as Gitta was about to jump out of bed, the door swung open.

But Salomo didn't bark; he merely let out some sweet, grunting sounds. Markus's black-bearded face peered through the opened door — looking a bit worried, but more pleased by far.

A cry of delight — all at once smothered by the intruder's kisses, raining down passionately wherever they landed, with no apparent end in sight, insatiable until nearly breathless.

"Why are you half dressed, Gittl?"

She struggled to gather her wits. "How did you get here — you'd just written —"

"To surprise you, and now you surprise me: as soon as I arrived, I looked over the gateway from the cab and saw light in the garden — a bit disturbing, of course, but nice, too! So full of life, as if you were waiting — as if you had called out to me: come here!"

Gitta lay dazed and still. — Hadn't she been awake already? Hadn't she been talking to Salomo and to herself? Yet Markus's kisses broke over her like a tempest moving through her sleep. Hadn't he ever kissed her before?

"As if you called out to me: come here!" she still heard his words. She wanted to correct them: she wasn't "here" at all, no, she was far from here. But the kisses stayed on her lips, as if keeping them closed, on guard so they didn't say anything foolish.

Markus had already gone back into the outer hallway to take off his topcoat. As he picked up his valise, he encountered Thesi, who was hurrying up the stairs, the dress she had hastily thrown on sitting a bit crooked. Her long braid was hanging down her back. But she had put the kettle on for several cups of strong coffee — she knew Markus's weaknesses. "Co-co-ha-ff-ee" — she hissed out her promise, letting slide all her painstakingly learned speech in the joy of her "do-ho-doctor's" homecoming.

Despite her rush, she also stuttered out complaints about the little Romanian, who wouldn't be coming back in time and whom Thesi couldn't stand. Less on account of his undeniable unreliability than because Markus communicated with him in phrases unknown to Thesi and even to the rest of the world, while it was almost impossible to understand Thesi even in German. Green with envy, she couldn't see that these were little more than a few Romanian scraps of home, always the same ones — "to give vent to their nostalgia," as Markus put it.

Through the half-open door, Gitta could hear their conversation, as well as Markus's unfeigned enthusiasm for the prospects of coffee, and his jokes. Then she could hear chairs being moved into place in the adjoining dining room and the clinking of crockery. It was only when she heard this bit of domestic back-and-forth from a distance that Markus's presence became fully real to Gitta. Yes, far more real than what was actually happening.

A reality entirely different from any she had ever experienced came flooding over her. On the beautiful nights in her girlhood room she'd pictured such a thing — she had dreamed it. Among the faces that hovered before her then — so alive she could grasp them, draw them — Markus had been there, his shape, his presence.

Perhaps *that* was why she had left her own room, that narrow space with room enough only for unborn visions. Only now did she know it again. Yes, actually only now, in this moment, when reality suddenly became complete. A reality that you didn't first have to create in poetry, much less express in words — always so difficult to find — one that is complete on its own: a life that can take care of itself.

The light shone down festively in the semicircle of the room, where there was almost nothing but the big double bed with Gitta in it. Had the light known, better than she did, why it had to shine through the whole night and far and wide, letting her sleep, as if under wedding lights?

Had her wedding already taken place? Oh — why had it already happened!

She felt as if she hadn't been there before. As an observer, the way one reads, that's how she'd been going through her marriage — not yet the way one writes: with an unconscious wish of devotion — a wish to create what one received.

Gitta could still smell Markus's ever-present cigarettes; his cap lay on her bed, it had fallen off while he was kissing her.

Now he himself came back into the room and turned off the light.

"It's daytime, you know!" he said.

They could hear the twittering, frolicking birds.

The room filled with a tentative brightness that nevertheless struck Gitta as brighter than the glaring ceiling light had been. The day gazed in through the balcony door so knowingly, so revealingly — almost as if all the words she'd just been thinking to herself were suddenly heard aloud through the air.

Instinctively her arm went up, shielding her from the brightness pouring in from outside — or as if it could turn day back into night.

With the change of light, Markus, too, sensed something had altered — he looked more closely at Gitta's face.

And he quickly stepped forward and bent over her. Then it was as if unuttered words were speaking audibly to him out of thin air; the silent mouth spoke, its lips trembling so like a child's, and the eyes confessed what Gitta had never admitted to him.

Lightning flashed through Markus's gaze and through all his features, so that, for Gitta, they suddenly changed — back to how they looked at the great costume ball — when, there among all the strange and disguised people, for the very first time, he became sure of her love.

And at that moment he received Gitta as a gift, as he had dreamed of doing back then — the only time when Markus, too, had been a poet.

CHAPTER XIV

Everything at the Mandelsteins' was topsy-turvy, or so it seemed to Thesi. The bells that summoned her didn't start as early in the morning anymore. Holidays had begun, but nowhere to such an extent as at the Mandelsteins'.

The father-in-law complained about his son-in-law. Branhardt was sorry Markus now had little to contribute to their professional interests and discussions. "Which shows again why doctors shouldn't marry!" Branhardt concluded, with a favorite maxim he used only when he was most convinced of the opposite. Anneliese was pleased, too, since she had always hoped Gitta might have some real newlywed bliss. But then one day she found her daughter weeping more bitterly than ever before — and was relieved to learn that her tears were the result of childish grief. Bending her head over the flame of the gas stove, Gitta had come within a hair's breadth of going completely up in flames. Only the crown of her Madonna-like hairstyle was burned, on the right side — down to the skin. The young girl of before would have endured the loss with better humor than the young woman did now, thought Anneliese, watching Gitta's stunned misery. She wrapped the poor victim in her peignoir, sat her down at the vanity table, and contrived clever ways of at least concealing the worst damage. Markus wouldn't look so closely, she consoled her daughter — men were happy to be deceived about that sort of thing in their own best interests, and that cheered Gitta up again. Unfortunately, things took a different turn. While Anneliese was called away to do something downstairs for her tearful, singed daughter,

Markus came home. Returning, Anneliese saw the two of them standing face-to-face — and *both in tears.* Markus was stamping almost rhythmically on the floor. Gitta had squinted her eyes tight, as if otherwise she'd be looking at her own head, for she saw herself in his face!

Anneliese froze. Was that a man? Or was it a boy crying over a broken toy? Didn't it occur to him at all that his wife had escaped a terrible fate? Didn't it occur to him that the first thing to do was to help *her* get over it?

No, nothing occurred to him but the misery of his own boundless disappointment. Gitta and her hair were so strangely bound together for him. Not that there was anything special about her hair itself; it was more the way it did what she wanted it to do. Her changing hairstyles were always a mystery to him: the way she could have a little hair or a lot, as she wished. But now, so entirely against her wishes, she would have no hair at all on one side of her head and bear this for all to see, like a placard announcing her utter powerlessness.

Anneliese let out a cry. Markus had seized her daughter with both hands, dragged her back to the chair by the mirror, taken hold of one of the shears lying there, and was running them over Gitta's innocent head. A butcher with his knife — no, Anneliese thought it was worse than that — he was acting almost like an executioner. His face showed clearly — clearly and crudely, it seemed to her — that the fire had taken something that was rightly his — his property.

He sheared her right down to the scalp.

"Off with it all!" he said, his voice terse, harsh, stunned. And more and more soft, dark-blonde hair fell victim to Gitta's trimming scissors.

Branhardt accustomed those around him to rash behavior that was not always considerate of others. But Anneliese felt one thing for sure and certain: he would never have laid a hand on her physically, as if she were his personal property. Anneliese was ashamed to admit that the term "harem-like" occurred to her — an old prejudice welling up in her against Markus. How could Gitta let that happen — her head shaved bare, like that of a slave? she thought, inordinately upset now herself.

But Gitta had other concerns. When Markus was finished, she opened the means of sight she had squeezed shut — not to look in the mirror, but instead, as she swung wildly around, to look Markus straight in the eye.

"Tell me — and don't lie: like a scarecrow?"

He actually nodded! Vigorous, unequivocal nodding.

"Why, no! Not one trace! Not a bit! None at all, for me!" Anneliese cried indignantly. "Hair is nothing! A vestige of animal fur! It's nothing to do with being human! What's so important about hair?"

"And remember: it grows back!" said Markus. "You're so kind, dear Mama! Gitta, perhaps you'd better return to the hillside house for a while, until you've regained a bit of hair!"

At last, a touch of humor. Gitta leaned her shorn head back into Markus's open hands, nestled it into them, and murmured:

"You! — how warm — I've never felt you that way."

"I can believe it. After all, it's brand-new territory. Until now it's always been buried under some coiffure that had to be treated with respect and about which I wish to say no ill, since one must always speak well of the dead — but that hair was driving me to an early grave."

But Gitta seemed to be finding more consolation in the warmth of his hands than in the humor of his words.

"It's lovely — this feeling, so lovely! I think I prefer your hand to my hair. You — don't have eyes anymore, only hands — oh, have a thousand, thousand hands, then I won't be ugly anymore!"

Markus stood and looked down at her silently, at her trembling, childlike mouth, and his eyelids were lowered, so Anneliese couldn't see the expression behind them.

She didn't want to see anything, either.

*   *   *

No one was more horrified by Gitta's "baldness" than Balduin. It made him see the heads of the prettiest girls he encountered as billiard balls and feel that the decision to remain celibate had ripened in him. Of course, Gitta soon thought nothing of her tragic fate anymore, and even a blind man could see that Markus remained enamored of his bald-headed girl, in spite of Balduin's tireless comments on the aesthetic impropriety of this state under such circumstances.

Balduin, it seems, was once again on good terms with Markus, having lately been descending from his veranda in a more cheerful and sociable mood — which everyone noticed without knowing what caused the change. But, on closer inspection, one of the main threads tying Balduin and Markus in particular seemed extremely thin: it was based almost solely on the fact that Balduin, seizing upon Markus's habit of addressing his young mother-in-law as "Anneliese," simply took to imitating him, making it his own and ultimately his favorite word.

He proposed to visit his sister and brother-in-law during their holiday trip to the Tirol, since to his family's surprise he had accepted an invitation to the Dolomites from a former schoolmate — one with whom he hadn't been especially friendly.

The Branhardts planned to go to the seaside, up at the northern tip of Denmark, where years ago they had enjoyed a very pleasant time. But Renate would not let Anneliese go without her coming to the summer resort first. When Anneliese came back home after a few days, it was only to pack up Balduin's things.

That was always a great event, even if it involved only the smallest valise, and this time he insisted on an unneeded second one. It was so hard to predict what he would require from time to time. Besides, while he kept his drawers and closets in a state of meticulous fastidiousness, the way young girls do, he damaged and wore out his things too quickly. By contrast, Gitta, who was far less orderly, would just keep wearing something to the point of exhaustion, until it had to be given away just to be rid of it.

Balduin "helped" his mother by dragging more and more things into his bedroom for her to pack.

"Don't leave any of that out! Think of all the possibilities — a person never knows how far he'll go," he urged cheerfully.

She'd been pleased to see him in a good mood for some time now. Balder's eyes narrowed roguishly that way only when there were happy thoughts behind them. She was cautious about asking probing questions. On the one occasion — after her discussion with Branhardt — when she had asked whether he didn't want to give his father something to read — Balduin had responded with pointed silence — and gestures that might most delicately be compared to a mocking death spasm. So, with a sigh, Anneliese confined herself to purely practical matters.

"Very well, you should have no lack of what you need! So you can have a nice holiday with that boy!" she said, bending over the open suitcases.

"What? — That boy? I could imagine something much nicer," he countered, his expression too clever by far.

"What are you thinking?!" Anneliese looked up, with a worried look. "You want to see him, don't you?"

"Listen, what I'd like, most of all, is to be a beetle with the sun shining on its wings as it climbs one moment, tumbles the next. But you would have to be the sun. — You can't ask more of me than to raise you to the heavens, Anneliese."

She counted out a dozen new handkerchiefs for him, commenting as she did so: "The sun shines on it mainly so that it climbs better and better and tumbles less and less."

But that remark did not go down well. "That's what Father would say about the sun," Balduin let slip, and when she started up angrily, he took her by both arms and kissed her face. "No, no, I won't say it again — don't be angry. The sun's not that way at all, Anneliese — it doesn't really shine to do that!"

His mother shook him off: "Stop talking nonsense! Otherwise I'll never get to the end of this!"

At the same time, she felt shocked: that foolish boy is making me repeat Frank's words — and Frank claims I speak for the boy — where do I stand in all this?

He let her rummage around in silence. He was sitting on his bed, beside the two suitcases laid out on chairs. Then he said slowly, and with no trace of trying to be clever:

"Listen! I must be able to write to you. To *you*. If I write now, will father read every letter, as he usually does when it's addressed to the two of you?"

"Of course. That's not only his duty and his right; it's his whole love for you that makes him want to do it."

"I know!" Her son looked at her, his eyes now wide and serious. "Why assure me of that now? I know it perfectly well. — But I must be able to write to *you*, Anneliese, just as I'm speaking to you now. I could do that only if it were just the two of us — isn't that so?"

Anneliese straightened up and sat down beside the bed. She looked worried and shook her head. "That won't work, Balder. How would that happen? When we see so much of each other, that's what we do, sometimes two of us, sometimes three. But, when we're only in touch by letter, you can't decide to visit your parents separately."

But she understood him, and she couldn't help admitting that at some point such a wish would not have been impossible. His parents would have laughed at this odd fellow who preferred the half to the whole — that might have been possible at some point, but not anymore.

Lost in thought, she hadn't noticed they'd fallen silent. Then all of a sudden, she heard Balduin speaking — and wondered if she were hearing him correctly:

"I'll send it to a post-office box. You can ask at the counter about letters from B.B."

It grew even quieter in the little room, eerily quiet.

Balduin, his head bowed, looked up with glistening eyes, straight into his mother's gaze, which pierced him like steel.

Anneliese held her hands together in her lap, forcefully, as if she had to feel them there to come to her senses.

"What did I do — my child, my boy? — what did I do wrong — that you could believe — that you felt permitted to say — — —"

Her voice was lifeless, strangely flat.

Balduin couldn't stand it. He put his hands over his eyes.

"Forgive me — forgive me, now you think ill of me. You think: that's betrayal. And I, who wanted to be loved by you — loved to the point of depravity — completely! It's insane, and I know it — demanding, I'm always demanding — and my own accomplishments: zero! It's insane — you ought to stop loving me."

Anneliese kept silent. He was beating himself; she couldn't beat him any more. Deep within her a strangely sharp feeling awakened for what was drawing her child into dishonesty. Not being free — not free! Even at the last limit of loving and trusting, still some "you must!"

Even as a tiny tot of barely two, Balder hadn't wanted to play with anyone but her. Everything he found or possessed he brought her for their play: tufts of grass, toy soldiers, pebbles, his jumping-jack puppet. She had to be everything he needed: the greengrocer woman, chimney sweep, or empress. She didn't need to do much, just keep still.

Was the big boy now any different from that little lad? Wasn't it now the same immaturity and helplessness, which he was growing out of on his own — so that, more mature and complete, he *could* grow towards his parents?

And by preserving this possibility for her son, wasn't she acting in the spirit of Branhardt's own youth, holding true to his spirit of independence, which he suppressed only in these moments of worry about the boy?

Anneliese sat quietly for some time. Then she looked up.

"In your hour of need — when you simply can't go on without it — then do so. You yourself will judge whether you should. If a letter comes addressed to me alone, then I alone shall read it."

Balduin lowered his hands and looked up, his face radiant — incredulous and delighted. In the utterly childlike glow that suddenly poured across it, as though from another life, he reminded her of Gitta.

He jumped from the bed. Like a gust of wind, he rushed to embrace his mother, but the sight of her stopped him. She was sitting there so still.

It was impossible to thank her with words or kisses. He would have to take the thanks with him. Keep it with him. *Hold it* until it took root inside him like a kernel of grain — his planted seed of life from which everything new would grow.

As Anneliese went down the stairs into the sitting room, she met Renate, bounding up them. She had come to see her once more before going home.

Still catching her breath, she reached out to her on the stairs:

"What's happened, Liese?"

Startled, Anneliese overreacted: "Happened? Did something happen?"

"No, I meant: why do you look like that? Did you end up sleeping up there? A powerful dream must have visited you. It's just leaving your face and coming down the stairs ahead of you."

But Renate had been eager to ask an entirely different question ever since Anneliese's visit to the resort: "I haven't had a minute to talk to you, just the two of us! And I so wanted to hear your impression — right away."

She put her arm around her friend's waist as they went down the stairs.

Anneliese answered with a smile:

"My impression? Absolutely splendid! And I noticed something remarkable about him: with his blond hair and Junker features — he reminded me of someone — or maybe only of a type."

Renate let out a rather dry laugh.

"That's all I wanted to hear! — How couldn't he remind you of someone? In particular, a few of my previous 'attempts at rescuing myself' whom we've met together."

"But Reni! How can you talk about him like that?" Anneliese pushed Renate's arm away, genuinely angry.

"Quiet, Liese! Now don't deceive yourself. Doesn't he look like my own family couldn't have chosen better for me — or might even have chosen him for themselves? You see, in such cases it's obvious something downright typical has triumphed over the individual Renate."

"Now stop it! Enough!" Anneliese said briskly and pushed her through the door into the dining room. "It's good Frank and Balder will be here soon."

"Hear me out — about the individual Renate and her poor taste. What we see triumphing here is an older, worn-out version of myself — a hand-me-down from Mama. Don't be angry. It's a far, far better 'me'!"

Even if no one in the house knew "officially" about the change in Renate's life, she was still the recipient of what might be termed their silent best wishes, which they expressed with a bit of champagne — Anneliese clinking glasses with her and whispering: "Here's to home and peace, Reni." Branhardt was more than well pleased with the turn of events, and their half-open, half-secret status enhanced the mood, making it bubble a little, like the champagne. Balduin may have contributed most to the effervescent good cheer — and for similar reasons, since he too was so tingling with happy expectations that he could hardly bear it. What Renate had noticed before was even more obvious this evening: Balduin did not seem the least bit troubled; his face could become expressive; and, on the whole, his open features and slim build made him inexplicably handsome. Was it his trip to the Alps that so delighted him? she wondered. He looked more like someone already firmly settled in the wonderland of his deepest longing — and at home for good. She became caught up in such a serious discussion with him, about the difference between literature's value and the way it is valued in the marketplace, that she noticed neither that Branhardt had been called down into town by telephone nor that Anneliese had not returned. Only when the cab drove up to take her down to the station in the rain, on her way back to the resort, did she jump up to look for Anneliese.

She found Anneliese in the twilit sitting room, seated at the piano. An almost irresistible desire had drawn her there to release in music what she had been pushing away all those hours. But if she touched the keys, then everything — even the most secret things — would resound through the house, like rejoicing or weeping.

This magnificent piano had been a gift from Branhardt when they moved into the house — to "give it a soul." The place had been bare and empty then, the furniture had still not arrived, the two small children staying with friends. When Anneliese came in and saw the piano, she embraced her husband with a happy cry and swung around with him in a whirling dance. Since not a soul was watching, they danced on, caught up in gay abandon, to an old waltz melody Anneliese sang. Until they stopped in the middle of it, breathless, and kissed, telling one another their old love would stay true, even in their new home.

That had been beautiful and fun.

Hands in her lap, head lowered, Anneliese sat at the keyboard. Her thoughts drifted from the old waltz melody further back into the past, to her girlhood home, where she first heard it, where she had danced to it with her sisters whenever her mother played it for them — the old waltz was all her mother could play, and then only half of it. But they all wanted to dance, and so she had to play. All the freedom of girlhood, all the joy of childhood arose with this memory. To have her old mother back again, who couldn't grasp in the least the ideas her five girls got into their heads, yet whose goodness alone made every wish possible for them — who, with little to work from, created a marvelous zest for life, as she did with the waltz. To have a mother —

Renate came to the sitting-room door and opened it. Just as quickly she let it close — puzzled. Was it possible?! A full hour Anneliese had been sitting at the piano, and it remained silent?

Here I've been struggling with the complexities of my own life and not thinking of what's happening to her! she thought, angry at herself, but fearful at the same time. Suspicion and doubt gripped her heart: Wasn't everything as it should be? Was Liese, too, with all her talent for living, sometimes just another creature bearing its burden?

Bright and cheerful, the old-fashioned waltz melody sounded a response.

∗   ∗   ∗

Balduin was first to depart, and the Branhardts left the next morning, accompanied to the station by their daughter and son-in-law. As Gitta was leaving the station with Markus, a fierce thunderstorm began, so she stepped into a cab. Markus did not ride home with her, since he was worried about two of his female monkeys that had become seriously ill the day before. He was constantly looking after his precious animals, and now Gitta was most deeply involved. It made no difference that she "loved them in an entirely different way." However different the causes, their feelings for the monkeys were as alike as two eggs, and they talked to each other about them like worried parents, except, in this case, the man acted as nurse and guardian.

All day long, Gitta was alone. A few people asked for Markus; the telephone rang. Then all noise ceased, save for the rain, which drummed and dripped. Waiting emptied the time. Then Gitta turned to organizing things for their holiday journey, which had been delayed by the trouble with the two ailing favorites. While doing so, she came upon some papers whose contents stared out at her as if from another world, densely written papers on a doctor's stationery. This still existed, with no regard for her at all! — this had not suddenly stopped *being*, weeks ago! No — it did exist. But now, as she read it again, she could see that, basically, it didn't really exist at all, because so little of it had been realized and shaped. Wasn't it strange how much clearer the ideas seemed to her when she read them over, now? They could not possibly have continued taking shape in her since then; there hadn't been the least bit of room for that, not the briefest fragment of time within her. But, still, it was a fact.

Some of those earlier difficulties had since been resolved with playful ease. Others had not, or at least not yet — but, in those cases, the difficulties in the initial work were gladdening signs of progress.

Gitta walked back and forth in the dining room, the longest room in the house. From time to time, she stopped at the table and scribbled something in pencil on the large pages of stationery.

As she paced the room, her face remained serious, her brow furrowed, as if she were struggling with small children. But it was only the words that gave her trouble.

Once she was interrupted by Thesi. She had taken Markus's hiking clothes out of his leather travel bag, intending to air them and check them over, and was much dismayed to find two moth holes in his knee socks.

Gitta went with her to look for matching darning wool, always with the same severe, almost threatening face. Thesi thought it was because of the moths.

She came back only one more time, to bring the tea things and take dinner out of the dumbwaiter.

After nine o'clock, Markus's latchkey was heard in the front door. He was astonished and pleased to find his wife sitting before the untouched things, waiting to have dinner with him. She must be simply starving! And he was hungry as a bear.

Gitta listened gravely as he explained the current condition of the monkeys. Her expression touched him, so full of inner calm, all for the sake of the suffering creatures. But today, for the first time, monkeys were not her main concern.

Instead she was looking at Markus's mouth, attentively, as if reading his words from his lips. But she wasn't hearing words at all; with an intensity she herself found incomprehensible and hateful, she simply watched how he chewed while he spoke — for, in spite of his hunger, he wanted to tell her all about the situation.

Gitta knew how such things could quite suddenly awaken in her a kind of malicious interest. She'd once said with a laugh that it struck her as an all-too-human aspect of human beings, this visible but, at best, inaudible process of chewing. With Markus, though, she had never found fault with this or anything else. She felt a deep, childish, unspeakable heartache when she caught herself observing him through such eyes.

I simply can't forgive him for gulping when he drinks his tea! She thought hard and recalled that she'd claimed to love him even if he were seven times a murdering thief.

Without taking her eyes off him, she pondered briefly whether she could shift her gaze to another part of his body — and shuddered in fear that it would be the same, part-by-part.

Gitta was still sitting stiffly at the table. Markus must have eventually found that peculiar. Gently, he took her chin in his hand:

"Sleepy — Gittl?"

She jerked her chin away. Her ability to dissemble was not phenomenal. Markus's eyes widened with fear:

"Gittl — what is it?"

She tried to say very calmly: "Not sleepy" — but then it burst out of her, her voice hoarse and trembling with suppressed fury:

"No, just alone — just alone at last — and sleep!"

Markus jumped up. He stared at her. She saw that and tried to make herself understood, but then gave up, lowering her face to the table and burying it in her arms.

"I know — that's no way to talk — or behave — why, for God's sake, why did you all let me get married? — me — at least the nights — just leave me alone at night."

She burst out with it — distraught, incoherent, broken up by her sobs.

Motionless — without the least gesture — Markus stayed rooted to the spot. His face was motionless too; only his eyes, tremendously alive, spoke.

Over and over he was thinking: now this — after *these* weeks — —

Minutes passed — like hours, it seemed to him.

It once crossed his mind that he had never really "fought" for Gitta — she had seemed unswayable to him. She could come to him only of her own accord — not by conquest, but peacefully — and only from depths that lay beneath all differences, all banality, status, race. He thought to himself: was it already too much that we broke the silence between us back then? Today had happened because we broke it. Our unity was a reality. Now life is saying the opposite, and life is in the right against us.

Markus stood almost woodenly in the middle of the room; his face set, he seemed to be gazing far off, beyond Gitta, and wondering where all this would lead.

Not a word was said.

C H A P T E R   X V

Once past the last train station, where the Branhardts had stayed overnight, the landscape became as desolate as the sea. All the changes of time and man receded before the reign of what forever resists them. As before, scrubby flatlands stretched out on all sides, covered with sedge, so that the narrow canals set in dead-straight lines were lost to sight and only a few deep-blue gentians, growing here and there on their edges, imparted a touch of beauty. Little brown goats, also scrubby as ever, were grazing. They looked wooden in outline, as though carved by a clumsy hand, and even their jumping and bleating were so automaton-like that they scarcely seemed separate from the landscape itself.

Farther still, over the dune ridges, green shimmered, narrow strips of beach grass, planted year after year and stalk by stalk into the rippling ground in the hope their tiny blades would hold back the still tinier grains of drifting sand. And, at last, beyond the lifeboat station, whose foghorn, now as ever, blared out its warning over the deceptively gentle shoreline — beyond which terraced reefs lay in wait for ships, the Branhardts arrived at the farthest point of land, the last barrier that stands between the North Sea and the Baltic. That spectacle seemed to have lost some of its grandeur, much as, in the eyes of adults, childhood scenes appear smaller. For back in those stormy days of early spring, the two seas had thundered together with far greater force than now in high summer. It had been breathtaking to stand before them — clothes fluttering in the wind, and holding fast to each other's hands, as if they might fly off into infinity. It roared into their blood, and it roared through their days and nights, until their two lives embraced each other and flowed into each another as never before, freed of all human barriers.

They encountered a second change where they had stayed — in this case the opposite: a giant hotel, no less, was under construction where their small cottage had been, with a restaurant already set up next door. But on the beach was a fisherman's bright stone cottage they found inviting. The fisherman's wife, whose husband in this season rarely put into the remote little harbor to come home, moved with her still-nursing infant into the garret room, and the Branhardts at once occupied the bedroom and parlor.

It was a magnificent day, the sea a pure enticement to plunge in. But such paradisaical behavior, while urgently invited by the deep dune crater near the house, seemed to be discouraged by the look of propriety introduced by some newly erected cabanas — advanced posts, it would appear, of the hotel-to-be. They bowed to the progressive outlook of the times, which Branhardt soon regretted: right after her first swim, Anneliese, to his great surprise, fainted in her cabana.

So, right at the start he had to care for his wife, which this healthy, robust woman seldom enough required but which he could provide better than anyone else. Anneliese tried to laugh off having to be carried piggyback like a child, although she liked the close mutual devotion of their lives that it expressed so clearly. In the next few days, she was astonished at how her longing for news from her children was quietly fading, and once again she noticed how happiness really is something whose capacity to grow and multiply sets it apart from all else. In years gone by, of course, the letters from her children had played an important role, for only with a heavy heart had Anneliese left her school-age children in someone else's care. Every day they would take the long walk over the sand to the little post office, to get the letters a bit earlier: Gitta's, so hastily daubed and delicately blotted; Balder's, so amazingly vivid and stimulating; and then the third, drawn up with such reverent care in large letters, more calligraphy than content — Lotti's first and last letters.

They recalled those walks but did not repeat them, and in all the things they did, memories of the past spoke to them in the present and, beautiful in themselves, enhanced the beauty of these rich new days and made the two doubly at home in them.

Amid all the foreign folk they lived alone, as if on an island. They watched as the woman, with whom they could communicate only by way of gestures and broken phrases, went about her work, knitting, mending nets, and tending to child, kitchen, and the demanding but meager strip of field nearby — or turning an ear to the weather, her husband's fate and her own. Indeed, the lifeless sea, when the breeze blew off the land, was the most lively thing, staying quiet for no one, as fields do for the farmer — heaving up the fate of each and all, unpredictably, one moment treacherous, another beneficent, like the utterances of a primitive monster.

When the husband returned home, driven into the harbor by adverse northeast winds, he found rest in what his wife had created, and this division of inside and outside life expressed the contrast of the sexes with the compelling certainty of a natural occurrence.

Some nights, when a storm came up or when the infant in the garret room cried and the fisherman's wife sang it to sleep — thinking perhaps of her husband, in his storm-tossed boat — Anneliese felt very strongly the stark reality around her. Then the two small downstairs rooms with their seashells and their strange beds seemed a mere borrowed happiness — a fortunate haven for these few, very few holiday weeks.

On one such night, she awoke from troubling dreams and struggled to come to her senses. She had dreamed that Lotti had come — over the sea at its wildest — while the people on shore crowded around, curious, for Lotti had grown up, fully matured, as if she had gone on living. Or wasn't it Lotti? "Are you Lotti?" her mother asked, trembling with longing, although in Lotti's inexpressible human magnificence she had recognized, feature by feature, her child from before, and the people on the shore were all astonished, for none had ever seen anything so beautiful.

On that morning, Anneliese arose very pale and feeling dizzy.

When Branhardt noticed this, he recalled Anneliese's fainting spell after she had gone swimming, which she hadn't been allowed to do again. A thought flew through him — and he suspected the same thought might already have occurred to Anneliese.

They did not mention it to each other right away. But all at once the intimacy of their togetherness was suffused by something strangely new. What each of them felt privately, without guessing the other's thoughts, was like a fine, warm joy of expectation, almost as when they were about to be married.

If those feelings seemed only to delve deep into their shared memories, they were not experienced as a remembrance, for they no longer thought about the past. They no longer compared their stay with previous experiences, as they had been doing. For them, time's wheel suddenly rolled on its own, and these brief days of holiday no longer rolled with it: they fell into eternity.

But at last letters did arrive. The first was from Renate and was anything but long and detailed. She wrote:

Dear Liese!

All that "home and peace" (remember our champagne toast!) has come to naught. My previous experiences could have taught me you can't drive out the Devil with Beelzebub. The problem is this: my Beelzebubs come and go, but the Devil stays. But be that as it may! And who needs peace? No! The battle goes on!

Renate

This letter would have called forth much more excitement and worry had it not been followed by one from Gitta the next day. Even the postmark puzzled Anneliese; the content stunned her. Gitta wrote from a town in the heath that she had visited with them one Easter and to whose "memorable solitude" she had retreated "simply to be alone for once." But then she had come to feel homesick for her mama, for her father, and was writing to tell them she was heading their way.

Of Markus not a word. Not a word, Anneliese asked herself, to explain this mystical "need to be alone"? Why weren't they still in the mountains, and why wasn't Markus coming with her?

Branhardt's sole need seemed to be to vent his anger in a thundering storm, the like of which had never rained down on Gitta's head. But when he took a closer look at Anneliese, he struck gentler chords and preached calm. They had no idea what was going on, and there was nothing they could do at the moment, since it looked like Gitta was already on the way. So it was best to rein in their imaginations and wait.

That was hard for Anneliese. The more the matter appeared to fluctuate between harmless and ominous, between bagatelle and catastrophe, the more upsetting it seemed. Above all, his inability to spare Anneliese these unexpected anxieties made Branhardt angry at his daughter. Yet this time of painful waiting contained a strange sweetness for him, because of one particular factor: he saw how Anneliese, at his mere behest, at his wish, at his will, really did regain her inner calm. He sensed, as never before, his full power to guard and protect her — in other words, as never before, he sensed her love for him.

* * *

Gitta's next message was a telegram from the Danish border, its content even more astonishing than that of her letter. "Stuck here. Salomo barred by Denmark. Appealing to minister. Won't leave Salomo. Gitta."

Fortunately, the minister responded chivalrously to Salomo's plight, and after a day and a night of delay, Gitta was allowed to travel on, even if she arrived unannounced and could not find a ride. She made it to a beach resort along the way on its omnibus, left her luggage there, and covered the rest on foot. As she walked, she was taken by the head coverings the female resort guests were wearing — artfully knotted, brightly colored kerchiefs — and since her still sparse hair left her hat turning in the wind like a weathervane, she purchased one like theirs and arrived, her headscarf's tail fluttering, Salomo on a leash, looking as at home as a long-time guest.

Of course, the face peering out from under the jaunty headgear was at odds with this casual overall impression. Gitta looked embarrassed to be arriving at the fisherman's cottage having lost Markus — along the way, so to speak — while bringing along the less indispensable Salomo. But the reunion's conversation so spontaneously focused on the anxieties he had caused at the border that a bystander wondering why Gitta was here at all might have concluded she'd been sent to a seaside resort for Salomo's sake.

At any rate, she talked about him very animatedly, as her curious gaze was drawn to the array of giant clam shells on the chest of drawers, the dried-out starfish on the sideboard, and the coral-like sponges in vases.

"Who could have thought this inconceivable country would forbid bringing dogs in — allegedly because a foreign dog with rabies bit one of their local dogs. They had to send for a veterinarian from God knows where — to test Salomo's mental state! — and he laughed and said that his name alone vouched for his mental state. Fortunately, he spoke French. — — Oh, so many clam shells, Mama! And such a rosy-red one."

"You could at least have left the little beast behind," Branhardt commented.

"I already had him with me on the heath. He's all I have left," Gitta explained, with an admirable transition from the shell of the matter to its core.

"But child, what's this all supposed to mean? What's happened that you're not with Markus?" Anneliese asked anxiously.

Gitta gave a tug on Salomo's leash, but he quite rightly took it to be a mere expression of embarrassment, since he just sat there quietly, his brow furrowed.

"Mama, I think Markus and I have separated."

"You just *think* so?"

But Branhardt interrupted Anneliese. "You are here with us and in our care. My dear child, if Markus has done something to you, what —"

"Markus? No!" Gitta cut him off. She seemed quite horrified they would think Markus could do something awful.

"Then you'll be kind enough to explain your actions to us."

Gitta gave a sheepish, but dramatically accurate account of what happened that last evening, at half past nine, in their house on Villenstraße.

The thunderstorm Branhardt had so considerately broken off when Gitta's grim letter arrived now broke out in its fullest imaginable force, made even more powerful and unrestrained by the lull in the emotional weather. Thunderclap followed lightning bolt, and Gitta at once provided abundant water. It seemed to her that her father had only once before given her such a scolding — even in almost the same tone — although, strangely enough, she couldn't remember when. If nothing else, wasn't it certain that this was the first time she'd run away from a husband?

Anneliese kept silent — even after Gitta had left the little room, sobbing loudly and followed by a terrified Salomo. Branhardt was more upset than he wished to admit to himself, and not entirely without some pangs of conscience. He was angry at himself for not having raised a better kind of wife for Markus, because Gitta's good-for-nothing tendencies he had mostly seen as charming rather than being angered by them. This inner bind tore him between "husband" and "father," making him react vehemently in favor of Markus and increasing his anger at Gitta.

He had already sat down to write to the offended husband, when Anneliese came up behind him and laid her hands on his shoulders, pleading.

"Frank — these last days you taught me patience with the words: we don't know anything yet. Frank: we don't know anything now, either — too little to judge or intercede or decide."

He interrupted her:

"Yesterday and today, that's two different cases, Lieselieb. Today we share responsibility for Gitta's actions. Markus must be given his due; that's clear enough. That's why it's up to us to act."

"Not yet, I beg you: let things be clarified, decided by themselves for the time being."

Branhardt threw down his pen and turned to her: "I simply don't understand you! Especially with your silence while Gitta was standing here — I thought you agreed with me! But that's nothing but the passivity you're stuck in right now. A bad thing if I let myself catch it, instead of —"

Anneliese replied cautiously, so as not to intensify his irritability, the source of which she sensed very well:

"You want to act for Markus, Frank — but we don't know Markus well enough. Would he act this way?"

Branhardt stood up with such an angry show of indignation as to put the rose-red giant clam nearby in danger.

"Could there possibly be any doubt about that?"

"We don't know him," Anneliese repeated in the same gentle way. "We're making an arbitrary assumption. At least promise me one thing: we'll wait for some comment from Markus himself — against Gitta or us."

At the most inopportune moment the fisherman's wife came in with a load of bed linens, to help prepare a place for Gitta on the wide, hard sofa. It was bedtime for her. Her presence stopped Branhardt from answering, and, when he saw Anneliese busy helping her, he left.

Anneliese leaned far out the window to look for her daughter. The beach lay in darkness, but from near the cabanas she could hear Salomo's perky yapping.

Indeed, Gitta was lying in the sand with him. She had really been quite seriously desperate, almost to the point of "taking to the water." But then she had decided to use the sea to bathe in. And now, having reemerged after an extended stay, she felt nothing less than newborn!

Such a real sea shower, that was priceless! She had simply washed herself clean of all regret and dejection. They were replaced by other bolder, more contentious convictions, and it would have struck Gitta as only natural to heroically forsake everything for them — to renounce completely not only her husband, but also her parents, her happiness, and her well-being.

Despite all that, she and Salomo felt pleasantly touched when Anneliese called out from the window. Gitta gave the artful arrangement of the sofa bed an approving look, finding it set up like "the real thing." For her physical self was well and truly tired, and that meant her more immortal self had to fight off yawns to tell Mama the essentials of the revolution after her swim.

"One thing is clear to me: marriages must be abolished," she said, hurriedly undressing, "for, if it should happen that a person suddenly no longer likes being in love —"

Anneliese did not go any further into that.

"You think that's so because you left Markus wholly in the dark about why you've run off," she said, helping her daughter out of her clothes.

But Gitta kept on about abolishing the institution of marriage. "Ah, no, Mama — even if he had known everything — that doesn't help! The one thing, the terrible thing, remains: the fact that two people suddenly no longer like each other at all — not at all. The fact that I simply could no longer stand him — I almost hated him. But it was still Markus!" she added, and she trembled slightly around the mouth, which, like a child's, so easily looked hurt or on the verge of tears.

Anneliese, as she gathered up her daughter's scattered clothes, told her she might better be quiet and go to sleep.

But in Gitta, now lying in her sofa bed, the revolutionary spirit was still awake — despite a few tears in her eyes, although it was uncertain whether they were tears of sorrow or from yawning.

"And I'm still clear about one thing! Even if Father should prove right when he says I'm a good-for-nothing — just think, as terrible as that is: for me it's much more important that other people are, if at all possible, more perfect than I am. If I can find them to be delightful and enchanting, then I'm happy! But, if they have imperfections, that makes me suffer — even if they are only small ones. It breaks my heart. I suffer much less from my own imperfection. To sit enthroned amidst so many imperfections — that's my idea of hell; the opposite would be not nearly so bad; I think I'd burn away with gratitude and delight!" Such a notion made her small face, so full of character, simply radiant.

She had reached out with both arms to pull her mama down to her, but as she spoke, her eyelids grew more and more heavy. Perfection and imperfection got confused on her tongue, and, practically in the midst of her chatter — the further overthrow of social order still on her lips — Gitta suddenly fell asleep.

Anneliese looked down at her daughter as she lay there, so vital and full of life — now as if taken captive by sleep.

"What are we to do with you, child?" she thought, with a smile.

She was surprised herself at the serenity of her soul. Although she had not forgotten the real causes of her worries, she could no longer understand the fantastic anxieties that had magnified and darkened everything.

Branhardt, returning from a long walk on the dunes, was more than a little surprised to find Anneliese asleep.

After their dialogue had been interrupted, he was eager to continue discussing the situation with her. And how much more, he had thought, she with him!

But Anneliese was already far from him. With an expression of deep content, she lay asleep in bed by the open window in the light of the ascending moon. She looked as though she were wandering in her dreams over the shimmering silver sea, certain of not going down.

So Branhardt left her in peace. He was as quiet as possible and, lying awake at her side, made his decisions alone.

CHAPTER XVI

After a long sleep and a hearty breakfast at her parents' seaside cottage, Gitta awakened with a burning interest in everything around her. Skirts tucked up and barefoot, she ranged through the water, searching diligently for starfish, crabs, mussels — even simple pebbles, wondrously shimmering in the brine, attracted her like jewelry — until the next morning had transformed her treasures, as if they were still mysteriously bound to the sea, into something quite unsightly — which only made her more eager for the magic of the sea. Most magical of all for her was the marvel of the jellyfish, which seemed to reflect the lovely lines and colors of heaven and earth in their infinite intricacies of light blue, crimson, pale green, deep violet, or sun-bright hues. Like someone who goes to the theater or learns of tragic turns of fate, Gitta was caught up in the dramatic fortunes of the seaside jellyfish. There was a day for each kind of sea dweller. Depending on the weather, the starfish, the jellyfish, or even blue mussels lay on the beach. Then, suddenly, giant colonies of jellyfish would cover the sand, by the hundreds of thousands — and, while in the infinite waves they had all lived the same existence, it was only in this close community that they met the most varied range of fates: some drawn mercifully back to the bosom of the sea; some broken up under human tread; others slowly sucked down into the sand, leaving only a rune-like imprint as a mysterious inscription. Gitta could devote hours on end to these creatures marked by fate.

Sometimes, she would lie face down, somewhere by the water, intent upon thinking through her "marriage mistake," as she called her complex situation. But, after a while, she would find herself propped up on her hands, fascinated by the remarkable leaps of the sand fleas or, at most, baking the finest little cakes out of the moist sand — identical copies of Frau Lüdecke's.

At the outset, Anneliese had thought it was partly Gitta's heartache that made her turn to these childish pursuits and speak less and less of her marital situation. But, in the end, she had to admit with some concern that this young woman was simply too captivated by earth, air, and water. The only thing she confided to Anneliese was rather symbolic: it consisted solely in observing how strangely the jellyfish — one moment so wondrously aglow with color, the next just as wondrously quick to evaporate into nothing — resembled the fate of human love.

Still no word from Markus — neither a wish nor a command. Branhardt, who had decided to leave the matter to his son-in-law, was hard put to rein in his impatience. Come what may, he thought, if someone took his child away from him, he had to keep her from being ruined by her own bad habits. If his hand were not sure enough, he should have kept his hands off.

After so vigorously taking his son-in-law's side against Gitta, he underwent a change of attitude, one not exactly in Markus's favor, and the word "milksop" cropped up.

Nor were there any letters from Balduin. Picture postcards were the limits of his efforts — always involving more picture than news, the latter merely verifying the beauty of the Dolomite cliffs, the most beautiful of which, posed against unnaturally blue skies, were already staring back at the recipient from the view on the card.

Yet Balduin's blue skies, both literal and figurative, were clearly in evidence, even from his handwriting, if one knew it as well as Anneliese did. She was happy for her son — and for herself. She could not easily return to the state of mind in which she had given him permission, without her husband's consent, to write "secret letters" to her.

By now she would have sought to arrange such consent after the fact, if her son's so uninformative yet so revealing postcards had not made this seem unnecessary. In any case, that spared her a difficult task, inasmuch as — basically — it would require the one Anneliese to speak for quite a different Anneliese. These two Annelieses were still not fully in touch with each other — as if only the second of them were away on holiday.

But then there came a morning when the mail for Branhardt contained a letter from Balduin to his mother. She was clearing the breakfast dishes from the single, overloaded table. As Branhardt, standing beside her, made a swift move to take it, she laid her hand gently on his.

"Frank — have a care now, this letter from Balder is for me alone."

"Oh, ho!" he said. Not so much Anneliese's words, as her expression, took him aback. She looked so amazingly earnest. "You haven't even looked at it yourself," he said.

"No, but I know it anyway. That was the plan for letters during this trip, if he were to address them only to me."

"You know, Lieselieb, your present condition excuses many a whim," he said with a laugh, "that's the way it is." She understood him to be saying: the easiest way is to call everything a whim. But that wouldn't work for Anneliese: even the fact that he had it wrong for a few minutes seemed too long to her.

"Forgive me, that was rash — and unfair to you. For Balder's sake — in the event he would find it necessary — I promised he could do that. Without arranging it with you."

"You promised him?"

He sounded astonished and hurt, but more astonished. Anneliese sat at the table, which had to serve for mealtimes, for the writing case, for her knitting things, as well as for Gitta's sea treasures, and mechanically moved the objects on it into their complicated order. Her expression as she did so was so composed and thoughtful that Branhardt all at once reached out, taking her face in his hands and lifting it up to him:

"No longer all mine — Lieselieb?"

With that, she threw her arms around the man beside her and murmured passionately:

"Oh — to do thy will! — Frank, I am, truly, only you! I am nothing apart from you."

He didn't want her to become excited. So he made light of it, as he brushed her heavy hair back from her brow:

"Of course, you have to keep your word. Whatever trouble you two miscreants have gotten yourselves into, I'll let you work out the consequences on your own. There won't be much in it for your motherly appetite, since the boy, in his Dolomite rapture, isn't exactly offering lavish epistles, and the time is near when we'll all be together again. — So, go ahead and read; who knows what subtleties, which he takes for mystical secrets, he has transcribed from the landscape and wants to reveal to you. Gitta and I, we'll humbly limit ourselves to the profane."

But Anneliese did not read the letter until some time later, as she sat alone on the ridge of the dune crater. That was good. For what Balder had written confused her. For one thing: he did not want to come back home at all for the time being; he felt too keenly that if everything were to be right again, as it had been, he had to stay away from the house, and especially from Father. Second: he had entered negotiations with a publisher Markus had recommended — or, to be exact, by way of that academic publisher with a more literary one. Through them, he had placed some of his earlier works in journals; now it was a question of a favorable arrangement regarding advances and guarantees for publishing new works. If those negotiations were successful, then he would write Father, whom he didn't want to rely on financially, and he hoped Anneliese would intercede for him. But, third and most important, as an unconditional provision in all these matters, he must be *allowed to write to Anneliese*, and not only in "emergencies" — no, always. Being away, for him that meant to be near her, always — to be at *home*, wherever he was.

Regarding the manuscripts on which everything now depended, his comments were rather strange, almost as if he were talking about things he was taking to a pawn shop and, for that reason, was most inclined to part with those he loved least — not with those for which he would prefer to endure deprivation rather than do without them.

Anneliese was very confused. The publisher — that could only be Markus himself. And she was sad and joyful all in one breath — scolding her son yet hugging him.

*   *   *

Yet before Anneliese had pondered how to prepare Branhardt for Balduin's next message, it arrived unexpectedly early.

Mother and daughter had been sitting out on the spit of land where the two seas lay calmly under a mild wind. Almost in quadrille tempo, as Gitta put it, the Skagerrak and the Kattegat were splashing towards each other. Only far, far out, almost imperceptibly, was their restless struggle rising again, urged on constantly, as if by a lurking villain, by the underwater reefs that tripped up the two tranquil seas, even in their most peaceful mood.

Anneliese thought they'd been talking a long time about the reefs; Branhardt still hadn't come. At last, she left Gitta there and, with a restlessness even she found surprising, headed back to the cottage, looking for Branhardt.

He was sitting at the table with its many things — Gitta had called it "the display table" —, bent over a book and smoking up a storm. He seemed not to notice Anneliese's arrival, and, as she approached him, all he did was turn his head slowly in her direction. There was something so strange and cool in his eyes, so shocking, that her question died on her lips.

But Branhardt answered without waiting for the question, with an affirmative nod.

"Yes, indeed — the letter, it came — the one to me, I mean, since we certainly mustn't go on confusing what's mine and what's yours. — It was mailed express — that's why it arrived at this unusual hour. Oh, yes, he's in some hurry — he probably would have preferred to send a telegram. But why am I telling you all that? You're much better informed than I am."

"I didn't know, Frank," Anneliese replied, fumbling with weary fingers to take off her sun hat.

"No? That he wasn't coming back home? — Look, you must have known, or at least expected it. — This wild notion — this whole plan, as carefully as the two of you have orchestrated it, still raises exactly the same misgivings as before. To do this, Balduin has sold off all sorts of works — perhaps prematurely, hastily, without thinking, the way he does things — and that might jeopardize what he most wants to do, rather than help. And I say 'might' — because, the way you two have done things, I can no longer judge or grasp the entire situation — now you must do that, Anneliese. You're the one who *knows*."

He went on talking in the hushed tone of someone who wished not to be heard beyond the room he was in — and in long, finely honed sentences whose level-headed deliberation tortured Anneliese. Yet his emotions were betrayed by the hand in which he held the letter, rhythmically rapping it against the table's edge — creating the impression he was holding some object he would love to smash to pieces.

Anneliese reached out imploringly, grasping his arm: "Frank — oh, not like this. Listen to me — try to understand."

"I've understood perfectly — namely, that this episode with the mother-son letters was not merely some frivolous holiday whim — it was well thought out and planned to accomplish something I wasn't supposed to hinder — and, what's more, a vital matter."

Anneliese summoned up all her ardor and conviction:

"I had such a strong impression he needed that — that he had to have it: being so unusual, having such difficulty finding his way in life. Otherwise, if I had ever — it was only for now — oh, Frank, it won't always be —"

"No, always would be a bit much," he interrupted her calmly, closing his book and standing up. "But it seems to me, even the way it is now is a good deal too much. You know it knocks my judgment, my whole grasp of the boy's situation, right out of the saddle, and that relieves me of any further responsibility. That falls to you now. At any rate that's more proper than doing it behind my back — so underhanded —"

Anneliese would have thought not a minute — not a second — could pass after these words, without his taking them back.

But he had closed the door behind him. Gitta came and went. The close quarters that had to accommodate them, so near the stone-floor kitchen they shared with the fisherman's wife, made any intimate discussion impossible.

Branhardt walked around in the dune crater, quickly striding up, then down.

Mama's boy! he thought angrily. Not mine. Then, after a while: When she says "Balder" it's as if she means "Baldur," the god of springtime, and she treats him with reverence. That's why she liked the name, of course.

As he said that, he recalled with a strange, almost insistent, almost excessive clarity the time last winter when Balduin had returned home and came to greet him in the clinic. He remembered how they sat at breakfast and drank to each other's health. He could still see the boy's freckled face, which he loved so much and not just because it resembled his mother's — how it became lively, flushed; how Balduin opened up to him, speaking like one friend to another. It seemed Balduin had needed his father, a man — that he had run to him impatiently, on his limping foot, away from his mother and sister.

It should have been possible to grasp him then, to hold him. Branhardt caught himself trying desperately — as if that would help — to relive that moment again, hoping to make it turn out differently.

But that made him stop and ponder what he was thinking. He stopped brooding and imagining. What did that mean — could childish, injured vanity on his part — or a deep hurt — be the cause of all his childish efforts to explain the situation?

No. He needed only to recall how it had been with Gitta. He didn't like it then, either, when he had to give her up — in other words, he was intensely aware Markus had fallen in love with her. This bit of rivaling love for his daughter, which everyone saw as a typical reaction, had made him smile and actually only pleased him. A healthy person is quite right in living as lovingly as possible, embracing the world he possesses in every direction and without anxiety or stint. Nothing else can so safely protect him from coveting the possessions of others, from missteps and transgressions, as this cheerful and full-blooded possessiveness.

Suddenly, Branhardt dug his feet into the tumbling sand on the dune. If that were so, then why was he reproaching his wife for her rather over-reaching, nearly exclusive love for her son? She, who poured so much more emotion into the matter? No — she should be allowed to act that way. He had to let her carry on as she wished to do and had to do.

In fact, his ignoble anger about it all had nearly disappeared, and he wasn't deceiving himself about that. He was almost proud of his honest forbearance.

Another entirely different question remained: What was *Balduin's* attitude towards him?

And again, he turned his thoughts to his son, and the pain came back. He carried it like a crying child he wanted to rock to sleep. So he paced back and forth in the rippling sand until he was no longer carrying the pain, until he was really carrying only the child himself — the boy, as he once sat on his arm; he had made him very small again — but very great, too, and his best friend for life.

Shortly before dinner, which they usually had in the rather sparse little arbor behind the cottage and which Gitta had already gone ahead to prepare, Branhardt went into the bedroom to talk to his wife.

"I let myself be foolishly carried away with my feelings, forgive me! We're probably both at fault — and not only now, no: through all these last weeks."

Anneliese nearly knocked him over. She rushed towards him and, feeling nearly beside herself, took hold of his shoulders.

Branhardt looked at her, astonished. He waited a few seconds and then gently lifted her hands from his shoulders.

"Yes, yes, child."

"Frank!" she said, deeply shocked.

She recalled in brilliant clarity the recent moment after Balduin's letter, when she had thrown her arms around Branhardt — and his question — and her answer, her impassioned answer.

Speaking kindly, he said: "We became too exuberant — we were carried away. That made us presume too much of each other — and expect nothing but sweet kindness. I was wrong about that — but you were too. Less might have been more in this case — better."

She stared at him. How did he mean that? She was struggling to understand him. He spoke so calmly and seriously, with no undertone of irony. There was no trace of intensity in his words.

"But Frank! Frank! What frightening things you're saying! More frightening — than before. How am I to bear that?"

"Why? It's not unbearable. The years alone teach us this lesson, as they do so many things. They also teach us to be considerate of each other and accepting, to be kind to each other and less demanding."

His face was serious; but it didn't look hard at all, it looked friendly. Yet it still made her so nightmarishly frightened, that face. This expression, infinitely busy with something, as if each word meant more to him than to her, and he were heeding them.

Only now did he seem to become fully aware of Anneliese's distraught expression, and he went on:

"So you be quiet now, too. Every insight costs something — costs a lot. But we can still remain fair and well meaning towards each other." Then he gazed — searchingly, much as a doctor would — into her face, which, although she hadn't wept, was flecked with red, as though she had. She struggled to shake her head, fighting against his words.

Only then was he right by her side. He held her wrist for a few minutes, gripping it tight. "Pull yourself together — better, better! Don't let the child see you lose composure, not for a minute."

And only when he felt she was in control of herself, did he let her go and avert his gaze. As she moved towards the door, he opened it for her. Anneliese walked over the stone floor of the entryway and stepped just outside the house, where she stopped.

She heard Gitta come running into the parlor from back in the kitchen, calling for her mama and her father. She heard him answer jokingly, and the two of them go back outside, to the arbor, where now, on these early, longer evenings, the lamp was burning.

Anneliese was still standing outside the doorway. What had happened to her? A stranger, an observer, might have thought: an argument — a passing mood! She knew that wasn't it — from the cool shiver that went down her neck, paralyzing her, like lead falling into every limb.

It wasn't merely a mood — it was a change. She had known others in his life. As nothing else, they had taught her what he was like.

She never forgot how she had once watched that young man — storming ahead, wanting to drink in all of life and starting by taking her by storm — become a purposeful human being. So suddenly and unswervingly. An experience in his professional life had taught him why even the greatest man would remain fragmented if he did not become whole, expressly through the power of restraint.

Years had passed, but this new view remained the root of all his decisions. Even his influence on Balduin grew from the same soil, out of that one inner action that remained as a final, external fact and lasting influence.

And now, again, he was presenting her with just such an irreversible decision: "Take it as it is!"

Anneliese, fearing Gitta would call her, had walked slowly down to the beach.

She tried to compose herself, to ponder Branhardt's words. Didn't they say essentially what she herself had wished for and tried to achieve — the month before, in their argument about Balder? A bit of freedom of action — some personal latitude — a letting be — some self-determination. She struggled to understand. What she had wanted, he had now made a reality. Didn't she want it anymore?

Black and calm, the sea lay before her in the darkness, its cool, autumnal breath wafting towards her.

Hadn't Branhardt tried to be kind and just — more just than when they had argued about Balduin — and this time without resentment or anger?

Yes: by taking her hands from his shoulders. Again and again, she felt that one thing: the way he took her hands from his shoulders.

That awakened a misery within her — irrational, senseless — the misery of yearning for his injustice, his rashness, even his anger — for the anger he had overcome so completely, so quickly.

She could still see his hand, the way it rapped Balduin's letter on the edge of the table — and all at once she knew she would rather let

him knock her down with his fist than to see him before her forever so
coldly indifferent — so dead — as if he were long dead to her.

Her thoughts made her shudder all over. Her head in her hands, she
sat on the shore, her gaze on the dark surface before her, which did not
resemble a sea at all.

From time to time, a gust of wind off the land would snap like a
whip at the beach towels drying on the line by the two cabanas, making
them flap and flutter in a noisy tangle. Then it grew oppressively still
again in the autumn night, as can only occur by the sea, when the water
slumbers.

Renate crept into Anneliese's turbulent thoughts, above all her
claims about the happiness of "crucified pride" — the happiness that,
for the most liberated person, is the sweetest exception. For the first
time, she thought she understood Renate. And the futility of fighting
against what Renate had always understood to be her own downfall.

The woman who wanted to be free, like any human being, as a person, as a mother — did she know nothing of that struggle as a woman?

Had she herself never looked down to her roots?

Was it the germ of this inherent sin in her, too, that did not let her
find happiness in the freedom she strove for and hoped for, that did not
let her enter freely into the new common life that they wanted to adopt
from now on, towards each other and towards their children?

If that were so, she wanted to tear it from her garden, like a choking
weed, so that her autumn would be bright and bear fruit, not merely
withered blossoms.

Thus spoke Anneliese bravely to her trembling heart, for in this
hour she emerged from her youth and departed from it in tears.

CHAPTER XVII

And now the last weeks of the holidays approached, and they were different from the bright beginning. In the narrow space of the fisherman's cottage, each lived through them, but so entirely alone.

Only for Gitta did those days, right to the end, reveal a life of splendor of which she had never dared dream.

She had no doubts at all: even the stupor of the first days at the shore could mean nothing less than that her whole soul had escaped into the sea, and her poor body had to stand by and watch, as it moved farther from her with each wave. Yet that didn't matter, for it was as if the sea knew everything that had ever lived within her. As if it returned to her, in enhanced form, what she had lost to it — particle by particle, her soul was coming back to her from the infinity into which it had disappeared. — "Are you singing for me? Are you singing *me*?" she asked, astonished and timid, as the waves, hastening to the shore out of the vast boundlessness, came roiling and foaming round her feet. But whatever they said to her, she could never hold fast to its song; it surged back into the tide — it remained the sea's. When Gitta recalled how only a short time ago she had been so caught up with invented tales and even created the worst scandal over them, all that seemed far away and ludicrous. A thing of ink and paper, completed out on the heath, that now lay buried in her suitcase. It seemed to her like some fossilized thing in the ocean, ancient and quite unremarkable. Never could she forget how, sand-grain small, it had sunk into the immeasurable vastness.

In comparison, wasn't something else sand-grain small, namely what had driven her *into* love — and *away* from it? She did not know. Only that she was no longer carrying any of that around with her, not even in her suitcase. So perhaps it was not the same soul that had disappeared into the sea and now returned to her.

Now and then, when Gitta lay most blissfully silent under scudding clouds, and dark and light passed over the sea, she suddenly realized she had never yet stood with Markus under such a breadth of sky and wondered how that would have been. And then what happened was that she would draw his image into this elemental landscape — but, again and again, it faded away in her wandering thoughts, into a strip of mist that bore not the slightest resemblance to Markus.

In any case, when parents and daughter returned to the hillside house, no one quite knew how it would go with Gitta — unless it was Salomo. For when Gitta departed almost immediately after they arrived home, she said goodbye to Salomo, letting him know in dog language that she was going to her master. In her elevated state of mind, she had come to think it was time to have a discussion with Markus that was worthy of her.

Salomo, even though he did not delve into the depths of her reasoning, was quite hurt by this, since he understood without a doubt that she wanted to leave him. It was clear from the look on his face, when he followed her out to the gate and, ordered to stay home, watched her go, with worried, almost angry wrinkles on his brow, behind which his threefold brain — pug, terrier, and dachshund — was feverishly at work.

Gitta left at midday, reckoning that, if Markus were to throw her out, she could still be back in time for dinner, or, if he didn't, it would be easy to have her luggage brought around. On the way, she didn't think about herself and Markus, but about her parents, who worried her. For she clearly saw something was wrong between them, and, though she was surprised how they tended to trouble themselves with small, worldly battles of the heart, her own struggles had provided her with ample understanding and forbearance in such matters. Ah yes, the poor people who are not yet past that, she thought, as she approached Markus's door.

In the door leading to their suite was the housekey. Proof that the master of the house was there. Gitta turned the key in its lock as quietly as she could; instinctively she went on tiptoe as she entered the half-darkened vestibule. But this likely alerted the man who was sitting in the dining room with the door open.

"Thesi?" Markus called out.

Then — and her whole life long she could not say how it happened — she couldn't resist stammering:

"He–he–rrr — Dh–do-hoktor!"

Someone jumped up. A chair fell over. A seconds-long silence. Gitta's playfulness vanished — for she really hadn't been in a joking mood at all.

Markus came to the doorway, his hand outstretched — but only to turn on the light — and the entryway lit up — incredibly bright for Gitta, brighter than all the seaside sunshine. She saw Markus's face, a bit pale, a bit stern, and looking into his face made her feel a great surge of joy — but stronger was her shock at what she had done, at her stupid joke, and, appalled, she moved off to the farthest corner.

The next moment, Markus reached out his hand to her, as if she had just returned from a short walk. "I'm having my afternoon tea — come in and have a cup. And your luggage?"

She told him it was still at the hillside house. Since he had invited her in for tea, he obviously did not want to throw her out. So she took off her hat, having become so unaccustomed to hats.

"Thesi will be here any minute now, and she can send for your things."

They sat down at the dining room table, and Markus brought a second cup. He poured her some tea and saw to it that she had everything, as if she were an honored guest. She was very touched, but, like a guest, she hardly dared to serve herself.

They heard Thesi arriving, and Markus went out to take care of matters. When he came back, he asked about details, and Gitta answered, but he learned only the most superficial things. She wanted to tell him about her inmost experiences and of the grand impressions that had completely changed her. But she could not see how to do that. She was about to start telling of the seashore and the wondrously colored jellyfish, but then held back when she recalled that they resembled fading, dying love. Then she went on and told him a bit about them anyway.

Perhaps Markus, too, had been through something just as grand? She asked if he had been in the mountains. He often said a person should go into the mountains *alone*.

No, he hadn't been there, but he had been away a lot — to medical consultations with colleagues, in Vienna, Munich, Strasbourg. Each time for only a day.

He didn't say he'd kept his visits short so as not to miss her return, and Gitta was not so impertinent as to think such a thing.

She became more taciturn. The tea, which was such a pleasant diversion, she had drained to the last drop. Markus watched Gitta carefully, as she sat there in her grey-green traveling clothes with the belted jacket, arranging breadcrumbs to look like starfish. Her hair was noticeably longer; it wasn't curled, but still lay, blonde, appealing and soft, around her head.

Unexpectedly, Gitta lowered her head over her teacup and began to weep.

Markus stood up; he didn't go to her but paced back and forth.

He seemed pleased she was weeping like that.

Then she said with a terrible sob: "I bolted — you know, like a horse."

He nodded, trying to calm her. "*Equus morbus.* You're simply that way; I can't find the right word for how you are."

"Skittish!" Through her flowing tears, she helped him, trying to track down the word.

"Right! But it will pass."

"But how will you win me back, if I just bolt like that?" she asked, suddenly fearful.

"You're only hiding behind a few trees!" he consoled her with a smile. But, from the tone of his voice, she felt he too was afraid it might be a very large forest.

Of course, he could not judge until she had revealed to him her new-found insights and why she was now sitting here with him so serenely, with all her selfishness, her desire to write, now so foreign to her. But that could not really please him, for it meant she was also suddenly free of her love for him.

"I always told you I was untrue — at least towards people: only good with animals!" she confessed, tearing her heart to pieces.

Markus paused. "Ah yes, you're right: Salomo. Well, a dog is something at least: more than a jellyfish. Just don't go backwards now, Gittl."

"Don't joke!" she cried, fearing he had not understood her confession. "To a nothing, to a sparrow, I could be true! Not that I could find a sparrow fulfilling — all I mean is that sometimes a bird is something grand — everything that lives is suddenly in him — do you understand? Without a doubt. it's unjust and terrible."

"How so, terrible? But perhaps it is amateurish. You're still learning the a-b-c's. Your animals, I think they're like guinea pigs — although a bit different than for me at the physiological institute — used for some wondrous benefit to mankind." He was standing behind her chair, his hands on the backrest. "Animals are more easily replaced because they're more generic to us — yet that happens between people, too. But the more individually we love, the more faithfully we love the unique, the absolutely irreplaceable. Perhaps you'll figure it out someday! It does bring problems, but it's still very nice."

Gitta half turned towards him to see if he was joking. Then her gaze wandered back to her empty teacup, and she remarked, hesitantly:

"You're being so — you're not being reproachful at all."

"Reproachful? To whom?" Markus's fingers had touched her hair, and he ran them over a few small tufts sticking up at the top of her head, still undecided as to what side they should lie on. "In my view, existence is a rather imperfect affair, so harmoniously embracing all our mistakes and weaknesses. — Would you reproach your sparrow?"

Now she turned full around, almost shocked, to see whether he meant that very kindly or very crudely.

In fact, she did not think existing was such a bad thing. Yet she found Markus's practical application of his view to the present situation extraordinarily appealing. Only now did she begin to lose her one-sided interest in the crumbed starfish beside her cup.

*   *   *

The following afternoon, Markus went to see his father-in-law at the clinic. He acted a bit unsure, since he did not know how his parents-in-law saw "Gitta's flight."

But Branhardt's splendid mood helped put him at ease. As men tend to do after a holiday trip, he said: "The best part of all is returning to work!" But he did not merely *say* it; he seemed to exude a holiday-restored strength from every pore. In fact, a new plan had come to him, an excellent way to combine his time-consuming practice with some research that Markus was familiar with. There were still obstacles, especially regarding his use of time, but, for Branhardt's temperament, such matters merely stimulated his youthful faith in the future. Markus could see the proof of that in his new ideas, as well as in his gaze and gestures.

Branhardt was not so full of himself that he failed to show the liveliest interest in the publication that had resulted from Markus's presentation at the congress; it seemed to him to be of incalculable importance. The way Branhardt could share in the joy about something and make it part of his own experience never failed to electrify Markus, enhancing his courage and drive. Branhardt had hardly ever been ambitious in the usual sense. But, from the joy he took in working and achieving something, he had a good understanding of any kind of ambition; and he credited the younger man, whom he had seen caught up in intense competition, with a high degree of it, even though he did not think very much of his resolve.

Markus was perfectly content to keep his father-in-law thinking that way — if only to avoid the puzzled question: "Why slave away so much just to stay, at best, one step ahead of the other fellow?" The answer he gave himself, in melancholy silence, was: "Why? Because our kind must work to clear the path for all our brothers; because, when one of our kind fails, then all must pay for it; because, for a Jew, no endeavor is entirely private."

Branhardt never did get around to mentioning the most personal topic: the confusion Gitta had caused with the holiday plans, which he really did not want to discuss. Now that the whole matter seemed so obviously to be mere caprice, Markus's approach seemed intentional — not at all incorrect but correct in an almost ingenious way. Yet Branhardt was far more irritated than pleased by having to admit to himself that his colleague and son-in-law could manage Gitta's weaknesses with such superior aplomb.

Not without humor, Markus could sense how his papa-in-law, still little acquainted with his personality, was at once over- and under-estimating him, and he sensed that this created a subtle barrier between them. Despite all the friendly words the two men exchanged, despite their high professional regard for each other, it was no longer quite what it had been. At one point, their relationship had seemed to entail all possibilities, and now this unimpeded prospect, which Markus had especially valued, was no longer there. A reserved tone prevailed.

On the other hand, since their first day back, Branhardt came to see his daughter much more often than before. With a certain annoyance, he made up for the tender enjoyment that he felt he had to deny himself at the seaside resort, for pedagogical reasons, on behalf of Markus. The house in Villenstraße came to rival the house on the hill. Anneliese encouraged that wholeheartedly, since she knew how much time Branhardt could save by having a home at Gitta's, close by, instead of the one so far away.

Once, when she was waiting for Branhardt at the clinic, she discovered an array of nice, convenient things that Gitta, in her sly, clever manner, had smuggled in to him. This made Anneliese happy with Gitta and happy for Branhardt. It had been such a silly prejudice on his part to deny himself anything in the way of pleasantries and comfort down here! Almost the only thing that lent his private, inner office a personal touch was a large portrait of Lotti — a considerably enlarged and hence very coarse-grained photo: Lotti, holding her doll and with a ball in her lap, turning to laugh at the camera. This was the one picture — of the several taken shortly before Lotti's accident — that Anneliese had not kept. It showed life and death too unsettlingly close to each other.

When Branhardt entered his office, he surprised her with the picture in her hand.

His long, alert doctor's gaze took in his wife, as, a bit too hastily, she put the picture back on his desk. Had she been thinking about death, or about life? He often would have liked to read her thoughts, for he wanted them to be joyful now. But, in many matters, she had become shy, like a girl.

All he said was: "I hope you've not had too much trouble with the workers up there!" and they discussed the domestic matters that had occasioned Anneliese's visit. There were repairs and renovations going on up at their house: Gitta's old room was being renovated, with a door linking it to the parents' room, since, come spring, it was to be a snow-white room for the baby.

Anneliese didn't let her consultation with Branhardt take up more time than necessary, assuming he had things to do. Then the two of them fell silent for a moment. Sitting here was always a bit like being a mere visitor.

When she fastened the veil back on her hat, he acted as though she were leaving too early.

"Are you in a hurry?" he asked.

"A tremendous rush!" she retorted, smiling at his question, the way one does at the politeness of someone overtaxed with work. "And you're not? I think I might drop by and see Gitta."

"I don't see enough of you!" said Branhardt, who knew she was suffering more, physically, than in her previous pregnancies. "But tell the truth now: you always behave as if I were invisibly keeping an eye on you. — Like the Good Lord watching the evildoer!" he concluded humorously. "Let us rejoice in our child, Lieselieb!"

Behind the veil her face darkened. Trying to strike a harmlessly jovial note, she responded:

"Naturally you want it to be a boy!"

"A boy!" he agreed with a smile. "You mean for a start. *One* boy? Perhaps a second one as well! And then — and then — well, of course a little woman, too!"

He hadn't meant to sound as if he were merely joking; he sounded truly glad of heart. And, all at once, this man with the furrowed face and high brow appeared quite childlike.

With one of his quick movements, he pushed back his wife's veil and kissed her on the mouth. He felt her inner tremor.

But, as he had to lift his head up to her, the taller of the two, the expression on his face made her think: anyone might imagine he's still growing, simply starting anew — a lad.

"Wouldn't you like to stay a little while? See, I can make you wonderfully comfortable here. Before you know it, I'll be back from my rounds," he assured her, his eyes still cheerful and boyish.

But Anneliese shook her head.

"The fresh air will do me good."

With that, he stopped insisting and walked her down to the door.

But, after her rapid departure, he could not stop thinking of her as he crossed over to the clinic.

For example: why hadn't he told her — especially with their conversation faltering so often in that silly fashion of married couples — about the two young friends whom he was giving his free half- or whole or quarter-hours these days? Perhaps, not long ago, he had made mention of one of them, for it seemed to him the one boy — a craftsman's son struggling free of an unhappy domestic situation — had been seeking him out for some time, until he realized this was someone who needed him as something more than merely a doctor or advisor. The other boy he had come to know by chance as a patient in the neighboring clinic, recovering from a fractured leg — a student in his early semesters, blessed with all the assets of real talent. Just thinking of him, of his keen, clear, boyish face, made Branhardt's heart come happily alive.

Perhaps there would be more than these two.

Not that he was seeking substitutes for his son or that he had forgotten his son. But what pleased him was learning that, from the pain he had felt and still felt, a remarkable eagerness to act could grow — could reach out to the young with open hands, to have some effect on youth, to seize it, to guide and enrich it.

Was that why he hadn't shared any essentials of these new relationships with Anneliese? Because this new wealth grew out of the impoverishment of his relationship to his son? Because this strength sprang from a wound whose nature even she did not fully understand?

If their hillside house were not so far away, everything would have played out before her eyes.

When Branhardt returned to his offices in the clinic, it struck him that, through the years, there was a trace of intention, some conscious effort, in the way he left everything here so bare and cold. It was merely his office quarters, between two rows of patients' rooms leading to the women's wards. In any case, the intention was well-meant and well-executed: the hillside house alone was to be home to each and all. But now he wanted to take the liberty of extending some of his domestic coziness to the clinic here — as if one of the house's illogical bays had gone wandering off with him to become a temporary home for one or the other members of young humanity.

"At any rate, a little hominess — homishness." He groped for a better expression, as if he were his own daughter Gitta and could put things in order only by naming them — "Or at least a homey outpatient clinic."

CHAPTER XVIII

Once again Anneliese found herself on her way to see her husband. But the walk to the clinics was a long one, and she felt weary. As she approached the parklands that ran from the hillside woods into the city, she told herself it would be more sensible to stop at Gitta's first.

She went slowly, lost in thought. These days she often recalled how it had been carrying the other children. What a powerful experience she had with Gitta! Still nearly a child herself, devoting all her strength to her future in music, then suddenly torn from that path by love, she found the desire for a child something foreign to her. Then, one mild summer night, a few months before her delivery, the holiest of insights dawned upon her: he who is sleeping beside you is your husband, but also your child — you are his wife, but also his mother. A rush of music went through her soul like the sound of eternity, wedding it to the eternal.

Then Balder came along — with what jubilant readiness, almost overconfidence, they greeted his arrival! Even though they were living hand-to-mouth, it still seemed he had landed in a veritable fairytale cradle of gold brocade and jewels, with all the good fairies invited as guests and no evil ones abroad in the world. Of course, the young parents soon gained more prudence and experience, and their store of the world's good bounty grew — but it always seemed to Anneliese that, without a little of the blessed, otherworldly abundance that embraced her children like the music of the spheres, like fairy magic, a new little creature was bereft of the barest necessities — a child of poor folk.

Coming from the bright, autumn coolness under the bare trees of Villenstraße into the Mandelsteins', she felt dizzy and was seeing stars and sunbursts. A child of poor folk, she thought, and felt lightheaded, just as a startled Markus realized what was happening and caught her, before she fainted. She recovered on the divan in his study, and he insisted she stay and rest.

Gitta was not at home. Markus was sitting at his chess board, playing against himself.

"Just lazing about in my time off," he explained, embarrassed — "a weakness of mine when I can't work."

"I assumed you'd be playing your violin," said Anneliese.

"At the moment, I really couldn't bear it." — Then he bent over the board, trying to look as lost in thought as possible, so Anneliese could get a bit of rest.

She summoned all her willpower to shake off the dizzy spell that had so unexpectedly weakened her physically and emotionally. Here she was lying in Markus's house, before his very eyes, and the thought that she might reveal to him what no one else knew made her blush. She liked him very much — but in this moment she could not endure so much closeness.

She thought Markus was a sorry sight, sitting there like that — so glum, at least in comparison to his effervescent mood that summer.

So, he didn't like music and not even his work. A maternal warmth of feeling for him welled up in Anneliese.

She tried to cheer him up. "You should get out, Markus — you can treat yourself to some time off without worrying about it! Even with the semester still on and your practice. Head for the mountains you love so much. I think you feel best when you're mountain climbing."

"That's it!" he admitted. "Of course, it's not out of a mountain climber's usual competitiveness — and perhaps not even from the love of nature, even though you can have extraordinary experiences up there. But it's the situation itself — going at full steam, swinging into action with all your strength — even reserves of strength you're normally not aware of. That's unbelievably reinvigorating; it brings calm. A person can convince himself that life, too, can be conquered — just like a mountain."

Frank could talk about life much the same way! thought Anneliese, and she was surprised, seeing the two men, as she did, as so inexpressibly different, and knowing that Branhardt thought Markus was "passive."

Another rather long pause. Markus stood up and moved the low stool from the piano close to Anneliese. But, even then, he could not say anything more substantial than:

"Gitta hasn't come home yet."

"I don't mind that." Anneliese sat up a bit straighter. "In any case, I like to talk to you alone. — You know, Gitta told me everything she confessed to you, about what a useless thing she feels she is. She really should have done that right off, instead of acting so senselessly." Anneliese stopped. She thought she needed to bring up Gitta's "flight" back to them, but at the same time she was afraid of doing so.

Markus was completely at ease about it.

"That probably wouldn't have changed anything," he remarked. "The conflict essentially was all inside her. And, for a creature like Gittl, it really doesn't make much difference whether a few other people fault or condone what she's doing."

"Well, the North Sea disabused her of such stupid delusions of grandeur. She was overwhelmed by it. Take my word: nothing will come of her foolish storytelling," Anneliese said with satisfaction.

Markus suppressed a smile.

"What she experienced *there* — that she *was able* to have such a feeling, that seems like it nearly proves the opposite."

"But Markus! You don't have to put up with that! It's up to you! She must finally outgrow her half-measures and childishness — she must learn to make sacrifices for real happiness and real duty," Anneliese exclaimed excitedly. Branhardt was right after all: Markus was "passive."

"So, you equate happiness with duty and sacrifice?" He laughed out loud. "Are you really so cruel a mama that you wish to see your Gittl crowned as a sacrificial lamb?"

Anneliese was serious; uneasy, she asked:

"What do you imagine will actually happen? God knows what Gitta might have in store in the way of unpleasant surprises. You must act to protect her from herself, Markus — with a firm hand — oh, most likely a firmer hand than we had with that do-nothing."

"What she might do neither you nor I can tell. But whatever it is, it should simply unfold. Perhaps as a surprise even to her," Markus answered. Anneliese looked at him.

"Markus — that's playing with danger!" she said quietly.

"Playing? Good God, no!" He jumped up and tossed the chair aside onto the carpet.

"But this danger you mention?" he went on. "Tell me, where is there beauty that isn't at the same time in danger — and when wasn't the greatest beauty also the greatest danger! — And mind you: this know-it-all attitude and drive to control, the 'firm hand' you were taking about — all that arrogance, especially of the usual, masculine kind, will go to pieces trying to deal with this! That approach is only best right from the outset and with women who are no threat to anyone! But — please tell me — what's so great about a manly stance that has to look out for itself, that's so anxiously self-defensive? Is it worth making such a sacrifice — and, by God, making the one irredeemable, unbearable sacrifice of failing to strive for the greatest beauty one knows? Of course, that's a form of arrogance too — and of course it's the better of the two."

He broke off, his voice growing quieter.

Anneliese was silent, taken aback, uncertain if she had understood him. At last she said: "But *marriage*, Markus — *a coming together*, in a union for ever indissoluble — that's the goal. And of course," she went on, "a union in all respects, even in all spiritual matters. But, of those in particular, Gitta does not have enough in common with you."

Markus shook his head.

"No, that's not how it is, Anneliese. All that about spirit and unions and so on, those things emerge in time — like those grandly painted notions in the foreground of some paintings — but *they* are still outside the frame. A coming together — yes! But that means coming together each time from a long way off — emerging each time from a retreat into oneself. Otherwise, it seems to me, we poor human creatures would never have to lose that earliest homeland of mother and father in the first place. And, otherwise, that home would not become a ghostly specter haunting our development: a house without windows — a grave before the grave."

Anneliese could not answer. She was astonished. Recently, before their journey, Markus's behavior with Gitta had struck her as so erotically overheated — too much, for her own taste. And now — wasn't he moving just as far, *too far*, in the other direction? That would be like building a house without walls. Was there a greater illusion than wanting to love without illusion? If she looked at it honestly, she herself had, on the whole, lived in accord with the image her husband had made of her. It was only from the finest of all flatteries inherent in such an ideal that she had drawn her own most inspired strength. In doing so, had she perhaps also elevated her husband, and at a similar cost? — Help and fetters became almost indistinguishable.

Markus was not accustomed to confiding in Anneliese about anything more personal than monkeys, but in this case his powers of communication — which she had so tenderly nurtured in him — went, unchecked, beyond the most private aspects of his life. It made no difference that he was speaking of them in increasingly general terms. It was easy to sense that he was caught up in his own fears and hopes, how he was giving vent to his most profound worries and wishes — how he was trying to *convince himself* of something.

Anneliese did not take her eyes off him as he stood over her, speaking so intensely, his gaze and gestures coming alive to aid his words. She sensed sparks of new insights in what he said — were those brighter stars than she had seen before? Had she been blind to that light? Had the sun, mist, and clouds of her own world made it invisible to her? To those who soared like that, was love still the same breath of life — sometimes blinding but all-sustaining? Was it still what the atmosphere is to the dark Earth, that alone by which it lives and blooms and grows?

Or was Markus someone who, like the child reaching for the stars, was lost in the icy-dark void between them?

Anneliese thought in silence: *That's* why Gitta had to choose him, because she wants to climb around, unhindered, in the firmament. Shouldn't she have a companion who would save her from that? But, if that were her fate, then it was good Markus was with her — with a love that did not let up and remain below if she climbed too high, a love that would not let her tumble alone into the void.

She felt herself caught up in a wild fantasy and tried to hold back.

Only when Anneliese fell silent did Markus realize how he was rattling on. He knew or had guessed that Branhardt had views quite at odds with his own, so he was belatedly seized by the fear that he had been tactlessly tossing delicate topics about like so many raw eggs.

Before Anneliese was ready to leave, he was trying awkwardly to get her a cab and had gone to the speaking tube to call his servant. But she did not want to ride — the walk would do her good: movement and air, she explained, amused by his overzealousness and reaching for her coat.

Markus, sensing how he was rushing things, gave no thought to helping her into her coat. Befuddled by embarrassment, he said:

"You sat here for so long now! — I mean, waited! And, after all that, Gitta will miss seeing you."

Anneliese answered quickly: "But to make up for it, I've had this hour with my son."

And quickly and warmly she took his face in her hands and kissed him.

Since the formal embraces at the betrothal and the wedding, that was the first time Anneliese had kissed Markus, and never before had she called him "my son."

Whatever Anneliese said or did had such emotional power that this one word fell into his heart like affirmation, certainty, and proof — glad tidings of everything he had tried to persuade himself and her about: namely, the reality of his union with Gitta.

After he had seen her out to the cab, something happened, and Markus's behavior was even more immoderate than at those times when Anneliese suspected that he longed to let himself go. He stretched out on the divan where she had been lying and broke into tears.

Only one person had ever seen Markus do such a thing. That was after he had run away from his family and was allowed for the first time to meet with his father again — and that one person was the little Romanian.

*   *   *

They would have had to wait a long time for Gitta. These days, whenever Gitta left the house, she made a thorough job of it. She would go roving through the brisk, bright October weather, as alone and eager as when she was a young girl. This time she was in a critical mood about nature. Everything was still green-gold-red, and even the poppies were still blooming on meadows that had started to grow luxuriantly again, but now with that earthy, woody, second flowering that comes after the last harvest. Dark everywhere, too, were the turned-up clods of the ploughed fields, giving the landscape a grey-brown hue. That was the one thing Gitta could not love about autumn: the mark of man was so visible upon it. Of course, man did create the field, the waving sea of grain; but those same living ears of grain concealed his intervention. Only now did the farms lie so willingly under his hand, combed and groomed and neatly tidied, like a child ready for school.

Markus was good natured about letting Gitta run off alone but seemed oblivious to the possibility that such appraisals of the autumn fields might be more enjoyable if done together. In general, the conclusion Gitta arrived at was that, even if her whole love life and all it entailed had evaporated into nothingness like a jellyfish during those divine seaside weeks, there was no need for Markus, who hadn't even been there, to be equally enlightened. One might almost have thought he too had cooled off at some northern sea.

At other times, when Gitta was curled up on his wide divan, she would let her book fall, instinctively raise her arms a bit and cross them in the air, creating a portal to love through which Markus had often thrust his black-bearded face. Once, in the middle of one of those few office hours in which someone wanted to speak to him, he had even stolen away to her, because what is stolen is most attractive. Yet now no one looked through that portal: a long, empty street, as it were, stretched out beyond.

At home Gitta found herself with no real purpose. Why trot out her housekeeping talents anew after Thesi had proved unsurpassable in caring for her straw-widower of a husband? Now the girl could even face down her rapacious mother, who had always made her cower, and go through hell and high water for her Herr Doktor, watching over him right down to his last shirt button. Frau Baumüller grumbled that the girl had no such feelings for her siblings, "those poor little worms back in Brixhausen," and she joked, in vain, that Thesi was really in "luh-luh-love" with her "duh-duh-dohocter." Thesi never would have thought of something so outrageous on her own. Not so long as she saw "her doctor" as he walked about on the house's main floor before her very eyes. But, at times, she would involuntarily imagine a little masquerade with him in which he became a completely different person. Then she would see him in his mountain-climbing suit — with all its pointless vents and padding — which made him, in knee breeches and raincoat, merely another strange wanderer, who came to her down in the kitchen asking for a drink, something to eat, and to whom, without the slightest stutter, she could pour out her heart.

In this costume, which she had never actually seen him wear, Markus seized Thesi's fantasy much as he had Gitta's in his white Arab garb.

But recently Markus seemed a man unsuited for either mountain climbing or festive occasions. He looked so weary that Gitta began to feel a nagging little notion she might be partly to blame.

Once, he did not get home until late in the night. Gitta had repeatedly gone out on the vine-entangled balcony of his room to see if he were coming, with the night wind blowing the long red and yellow leaves down on her like rain. Just a few weeks before, what had her wakeful devotion in those silent, nighttime hours called forth! Now she merely waited, and Markus didn't even thank her for it.

"Don't wait up on my account, Gittl!" was all he said when he found her in the room, and he sat down on the divan between the cushions, wearily stretching out his arms along the backrest. "I couldn't get away earlier. A patient."

"Was it something serious?" Gitta asked. She was still sitting by the door out to the balcony, perched on the edge of a chair. Markus hardly ever had patients.

"Serious? Not in the usual sense. A very old man, dying — who'd already had many foretastes of death, out of fear of death. I'm not even his regular doctor."

"You look so weary and pale. You have for a while now."

Markus did not answer right away.

Then all he said was: "My father is old now, too."

"Your father!" — That was it! Gitta stood up and went over to him. "Is your father like that old man, thinking ahead about death?"

"No, oh no!" Markus looked up with a gleam in his eye. "No, that's something he forgot to learn: to believe anything bad can happen. My father thinks there will always be a remedy for him, even a remedy for death or for any misfortune that afflicts his tribe. Wait and endure! A few millennia have tried to convince him of the opposite — offering good evidence, believe me! — But he brushes it aside. What are millennia to a Jew, who reckons with eternity!"

Caught up by the warmth of Markus's description, Gitta said: "That's how your father is!" She recalled the small picture Markus had shown her before their betrothal, along with pictures of his other relatives. It always struck her as the picture of an Old Testament prophet — not in the moment of calling to atonement but when proclaiming the Messiah.

Markus echoed her: "Yes, that's how he is. Serious — and yet his heart laughs along with his god of death and of evil, which put on such a grand show. And he has bright eyes — bright like a child's, actually, and when he laughs, they reveal something deep inside."

"And still, that old man reminded you —"

"Because I *do* know. Because *I* don't laugh."

Gitta sat down close to him. "Your father, I'd like to meet him! Tell me about him."

Markus told her. And she saw what lay so deep, this trembling before his father's death: a battle in which the son stole from the father, taking part of his life from him — tearing it away, as if beating him, slaying him, with his different convictions. First for his own sake, but now for his next-of-kin, his two younger brothers, whom he wanted to save — a battle in which Markus was the victor, but also the most severely wounded. She saw what made death what it was: a life full of conflict and devotion at the same time — the kind Markus always carried with him, everywhere, driving it forward in all his considerations.

Gitta listened to him with indescribable attentiveness. All these people, still strangers to her, suddenly seemed deeply close and bound to her, so powerfully did Markus grasp each fate as if it were his own. It was not at all as if he were telling of only one person — life itself was speaking. The force of his feelings burst the particular case apart — and then the whole, vast thing was standing there, everything that ever lived, suffered, died — yes, died.

It must have grown very late. Markus himself called a halt. He wanted Gitta to get some rest. But she didn't do so. To make herself more comfortable, she drew her feet up on the divan and stretched out on the pillows and cushions, and that worked quite well if she made Markus's arm the last cushion.

She hardly looked up — just listened. She felt breathlessly tense, hearing how Markus, as he described the others, seemed to emerge more clearly than ever before — he, himself, in the more hidden part of his being. She had always known there was another Markus — no: an entire world — for which he was merely a symbol — a world beyond Markus, transcending him as a single person — or simply his person disguised, as he had been in his white, exotic, festive garb.

But instead it was now someone who went darkly clad, bent under the discord of many and for many: a more knowing man who bore the cross for those who lived on blindly, who felt their living and dying more deeply, more bitterly than they did themselves. And yet, the white festiveness of Gitta's dream proved right. For that very reason, he called out all the more unceasingly for redemption, for the most beautiful, the highest, the most exceptional kind of life. That made his call, even in his love, resound with something akin to storm, to great bells and singing.

Markus's voice had grown ever softer, gradually giving out; he leaned over Gitta, uncertain whether she were still awake. But then she hugged him more closely.

Each time he leaned over her, she opened her eyes, as if to see if it were he who walked before her, in flesh and blood, or the poetry of his words coming to life within her reach. Both lived *and* written poetry, only thus did she possess Markus. She had not understood that before. She had only written up some version of him on her own.

Gitta did not want to lose herself in the sleep already gently lulling her consciousness. She felt it would tear her away from something wonderful. Long after Markus had fallen silent, she still heard it talking to her of some happiness, some wonderful happiness.

Then she was awakened by a cockcrow coming from the backyards.

She found herself with her knees drawn up, nestled in Markus's lap, and at once she knew again: something had happened — a happiness — hadn't he come home with happy news?

Happiness! No, there had only been an old man who was dying.

She raised her head and sat up, Markus's arms around her.

He sat leaning back against the wall and looked down on her, pondering all the while the things he had told her. But he was no longer thinking about death when he thought of his father. He thought only of how Gitta would come to meet that old man, for whom the worldly was so eternal and the eternal so worldly, and of how he would hear the two of them laugh.

He thought: *she* would slay death for me! Her presence would bring back his homeland, the eternal life.

The most beautiful thing a person could dream of seemed to stand there, right before his eyes. Perhaps it was still far, far away. But he sat there as deeply rested as if he had reached his goal.

Gitta gazed up as she stirred — bright, bright — a happiness she couldn't even think of was shining so brightly around her.

Like sunshine, Markus saw it before him, too — in her face as she raised her arms, still stiff and sore, stretching them and then wrapping them so firmly and confidently around his neck. Now, she thought, surely this is what they had stayed up so late for.

Once again, the dutiful rooster's crow proclaimed that day had come, though the street still lay dark and silent.

Gitta, who put so much stock in names and nights, would later call this her wedding night.

CHAPTER XIX

Already now the days were dawning red through the mist. Invisible hands veiled the valley, which was open to the house's gaze. And, where the hillside woods had closed off a vista all summer, those hands again revealed mysterious paths and wide spaces among the falling leaves.

While many treetops still wore their autumn colors, those higher up the hill and more shaken by the brisk east wind stood bare, with the medlars clinging to their branches like abandoned nests.

The birds had yet to land on the balcony of the house, their old feeding station, and instead were reaping a late harvest in the orchard meadow and stubble field — they merely flitted by, only more and more often, as if guided by memories of past winters. On the dew-covered outer walls, ladybugs crept busily along, tiny polkadots of summer color, marching on in the wake of the receding warmth. Late-season butterflies tumbled in through open windows as if, in dying, they were searching for the vanished flowerbeds. But, among the trees in the garden, no matter how often people walked there, the spiders were secretly spinning their solitudes anew from trunk to trunk — delicate webworks full of silver dew and always fresh, intact, and untouched: the mysteries and miracles of an autumn celebrating for itself the rites of its own return.

Out among the fruit trees, Anneliese strolled slowly back and forth in the Sunday morning light. Taking more time than an entire letter might require, she read the last page of what Balder had written from Rome:

As I stood before this exhibition of frescoes from a villa near Boscoreale (the best classical paintings I have seen, and people say even the museum in Naples has none better), I saw one I must tell you about. Of all the fragments, it alone was almost fully preserved. It depicts a woman sitting quietly and listening with rapt intensity as a man speaks to her, his hands resting on a staff he may have carried on his way through far-off lands. He still has the look of a man driven urgently towards his destination, the harrying haste of his journey not yet fully abated, the blood still surging in his feet. But whatever adventures and dangers he has to tell about, their sense could be none other than that they drove him onward to be with this woman now sitting before him, imposing in all her calm, complete composure — to be with her, drawn homeward to the soothing summer-night quiet of her presence, away from the world's hazards and chaos and noise. Stillness and motion, the two together in this picture, and the effect all the more powerful because the two figures are of such completeness, such a gravitas in themselves and bound to each other by an overwhelming need.

But no, not what this picture says, but how my own life will tell you — namely, that this is how I stand before you. This alone is the ideal by which I measure my life, my choices, and my conscience, in what I embrace or reject. From whatever springs and streams of mine the waters may yet flow, they must find their way homeward, back to your sea. My life will be only what I can carry back to you, and one day, Anneliese, it will have been as you now receive it.

Balder

The boy was poetically recasting her as the living embodiment of a legendary woman, and, in motherly fashion, she kept that to herself, protecting their shared secret from the mockery or astonishment of others. Branhardt no longer begrudged her receiving these letters, so many of them and so rich in content, and she felt sure he did so with good will and without rancor. So good, so just, he conceded, after the detailed reports from his son, that the boy now made a more pleasing impression on him, in spite of the admittedly superfluous insistence on "going south." To make up for that, Balduin had published a work he called "The Prize of Rome," all the while being supported mainly by his father. He was always reasserting that he had to stay there, in the outside world, even if he had to fight it out alone, beset by all kinds of obstacles. That's what he needed; that alone would improve him.

Yes, he would fight his way free of the enemies that threatened him from within! — that was Anneliese's cheering thought. Of course, it couldn't be a total victory; he was still in constant danger. She had to keep that in mind: one way or the other, a son is always at war.

Anneliese suddenly noticed how this armor-clad metaphor, at least in its figurative sense, gladdened her heart, although it couldn't be less suited to Balder. He'd have given her a censorious look. Something was still definitely missing from the ideal image she drew from his letters.

So it was good he was not there with her. The impractical man was acting in a practical way: creating poetry. He could do that — and in turn, perhaps, fashion himself healthy enough for life.

And yet — if she had him with her now! — Now, with such abundant life flowing to her from him, sweeping her up, bearing her away, and reuniting them.

She cast a longing gaze down through the garden, through which he no longer came.

Back by the apple trees, Herr Lüdecke, despite the early Sunday hour, had quickly set up the ladder to take advantage of the excellent weather and get the last yellow Richards into the cellar. An old woman was hobbling towards him through the garden on her cane, and he reached down, greeting her affably and handing her one of the fruits to marvel at.

Anneliese hurried in her direction, as quickly as her burdened body could, for the old woman was none other than her old peddler friend, Frau Hutscher, now changed almost beyond recognition.

More than half a year ago, Anneliese had heard about all the misfortunes that had assailed her: her ailing son who died, vomiting blood, and poor Grete, her daughter, deserted by her husband and then dying after giving birth. In the same factory town where her son had once worked, she and the infant had found cellar-room lodgings with a widowed coal merchant.

Anneliese saw clearly how hard the last months had been on her old traveling friend, whose hair had turned white and who, now heavier, rather than gaunt, was aged in looks and bearing, and lame of gait. And she complained bitterly: she had to fetch the coal! and scrub and wash — in bad air, without a glimpse of the sky! and nothing to see from the cellar window but people's feet! "As if they had no figures or faces." Strange though it was to hear these small miseries of life lamented while those of death were so great — *they* no doubt weighed the heaviest, with a sorrow that gave her heart no chance to grieve for the departed.

But she could bear it all, if only little Gretelein would not have to grow up beside the rubbish heap! She clung to the child with an idolizing tenderness — to this, her last bit of "the dear Lord's nature," her "pastureland" and "rose bush." Frau Hutscher outdid herself poetically in finding words to describe little Gretelein. Oh, why couldn't she put her in a backpack and go peddling again? Defy the rheumatism from living in that cellar and head out over the hills and meadows of which she sang to Gretelein with all her old hiking songs?

Anneliese nodded sympathetically. Every mother dreams of the most beautiful things for her little child and hopes that it not be like a child of poor folk — yet that was the best the old woman had known. Anneliese thought of the moment when the phrase "child of poor folk" had first weighed upon her heart. And she saw two little children right beside each other.

Caught up in delight over her grandchild, Frau Hutscher had regained her ever-resilient confidence.

"Things will get better!" she consoled herself. "For it is written: Commit thy way unto the Lord, and that's what I do, and who knows what He commands his angels to do for little Gretelein and me? For it is written: expect the unexpected."

Life in the cellar had not made Frau Hutscher any better-versed in the Bible.

While Anneliese was seeing to the old woman's needs and letting her pour out her heart, she was contemplating this: downstairs, next to the Lüdecke's, below the little wooden veranda, was that bright room — the "trunk room," as it was called, because there was nothing in it but cabinets and chests. Wouldn't there be enough room, upstairs in their now-empty house, for a few of those things? Such a room would more than suffice for a grandmother and her grandchild. The main thing was: woods, meadows, air, and light.

Later, Anneliese made her way upstairs, thinking all the while where the cabinets could go. But once she arrived there, she had to consider what she actually wanted to do. The door to Gitta's old room was wide open, and the craftsmen were not working there today. She looked at the snow-white baby room they were making out of it and thought:

Little Gretelein *would* have what she needed there. They could plant her grandmother's paradise all round with some trees, and the summer would fill it with flowers — from the paradise that had surrounded *her* grown children, the little one she was carrying beneath her heart seemed banished.

She leaned heavily in the open doorway. At one spot, where the workers had peeled off the wallpaper, an older bit was peeking through. The room was now undergoing its third renovation, having started out as the parents' bedroom, before the children moved from the larger bedroom, which the parents now occupied, into rooms of their own.

This old bit of wallpaper still showed the original pattern, just as they found it when they moved into the house: all bright little wreaths, each one with a smug little rose in the middle.

Its color a bit too vivid, highlighted anew from wreath to wreath, the little rose recurred, the reveling center of attention, as if it could not get enough of itself.

Anneliese stood staring at it, seeing nothing else. Oh, how long had it been since she saw that old-fashioned pattern, not replaced when they moved in. A whole rose garden, it blossomed before her eyes, capturing all her senses as it bloomed, a big, big garden to lose herself in — not any garden: *her* paradise.

"This! This! To live again! To live! To *live* it! Not just remember it!"

Her lips moved. She wanted to shout it. No one would hear.

Bare and indifferent, the empty room stood before her like a deserted house, like an existence drained of life. Plaster lay at her feet. She breathed in grey dust.

And mortality touched her with the sting of death.

* * *

Balduin's private realm behind the small wooden veranda was serving once again as the winter refuge for the plants, stored on their simple racks. It was also Branhardt's most convenient passageway from his study down into the garden.

Anneliese passed the stairs on her way to the Lüdeckes', where they were celebrating a birthday, and saw her husband sitting on the veranda, amid his books. The deceptively summery weather was an irresistible lure out into the open air.

Anneliese called up to him:

"We'll be having a midday visit from Markus and Gitta! They just walked past the garden, taking Salomo up to the woods, and they wanted to stop in on their way back."

"I'll be packing my stuff away in a bit," Branhardt answered, "and I know what they want to tell us about. They're going on quite a trip — to Markus's hometown. He hinted they were planning that."

Annaliese had stopped. She went on:

"A big trip — and a long one! They might be away until after Christmas, Gitta just told me. They're looking forward to it like children do to Christmas."

She ran her hand over her face, not wanting to look worried. The two of them were so delightfully serious and delightfully happy with each other. She could never see enough of them that way — but would it stay so? Gitta herself probably knew least of all.

Branhardt misunderstood her gesture — or the expression on her face. He leaned out a bit over the wooden railing.

"More lonely, more quiet for you than it already was, Lieselieb. Even now, the only thing different for you about Sunday is that I sit alone up here instead of down in town."

Anneliese looked up at him warmly.

"Oh, no! I really don't see it that way at all. Doing that *is* your 'Sunday rest'! I know full well. On all your days off, we always said they were precious if they were full of effort and work. Doubly so now!"

"Yes, now I'm facing a double load of work, if I'm to succeed with this — and unfortunately work that ties me down, there at the institutes. But it's twice as bad of me to leave you living here in the woods like a widow, Lieselieb."

She laughed him off.

"Oh, don't act so important!" she warned. "On the contrary, it's good the grown children don't miss you — and as for the teeny-tiny one in its special little villa, it's taken no notice at all of your existence. It has no idea that, out in the world, when it moves from its little house into our house, it could encounter anything but its mother from the outside, rather than from the inside. Who knows? maybe I'll keep its father's existence a secret."

With that, she tossed him a challenging look, her face bright and friendly as she continued on her way.

A pleasant smile played about Branhardt's lips, as he turned back to his books. The house did seem lonely now. But soon it would be full of life again, and of everything that is woman's and brings wives to the fore as natural rulers.

He really would not have it any other way. A whole house full of children! Full of sons and little Lieselieb daughters: there could never be enough of them for him.

What a splendid fellow she is! he thought. So splendidly intense, the power of her feelings, the verve of them — her exuberance even; it was always a part of her, but as a brimming over of the noblest kind. No different, he thought, from the music with which she had welcomed him on so many evenings.

That made Branhardt stop and think. How long had it actually been? Had she stopped opening her piano at all — spreading her wings — or did she now do that only when he wasn't there?

But then, that question was pushed aside by the cheerful thoughts his wife called to mind.

Truly, it was no small thing to have had this person at all times and in all things completely to himself! Always and completely? His eyes narrowed a bit as he gazed, squinting into the sun. Something appeared before him, as if painted in the middle of the sun, from the darkness of memory. An hour just recently — a moment when he believed he saw his wife standing before him — and against him — in a strange beauty, a beauty in which, as it were, she had never become his own.

And suddenly, like an apparition before all his senses, the original Anneliese was there.

Anneliese young — as young as could be. A woman? Hardly a woman back then, so slender, in spite of her height — more like a precocious boy going through a surge of growth.

Of course, that wasn't what he wanted from her, and that's not what she became. She grew into a woman — entirely a woman, and his. But, in his first enchantment with her, there was at the same time an enchanted sympathy with her enthusiastic directness and youthful eagerness, qualities that had always attracted him to his peers. For him, Anneliese seemed to contain both.

That's how we too often weigh down what we most love with the most disparate contradictions. Until the wild concoction is dispelled by the reality of life, at once too rich and too simple for such effusions and bestowing its gifts more wisely than our fancies would have.

Branhardt turned his thoughts to all those riches of life that had arrayed themselves, left and right around him, in his Lieselieb domain, which, because it had achieved such a unity, made space for everything that was not already resolved within it.

Then he was once again deep in the scientific deliberations and books he had been working on.

But vaguely, darkly, he sensed a feeling overtaking him — almost a physical sensation — as if something somewhere were not quite right, although, from a scientific standpoint, his results were so pleasing. Wasn't that just a minor aftereffect of a couple of incidents on their trip? Still, he freely admitted he'd been thrown back on himself unexpectedly at the time, but that had made a useful contribution to his thinking and working — indeed, perhaps a much-needed boost of strength to them — and a new measure of manliness.

Those incidents had made him all the more aware of his compatibility with his wife. For, despite their disappointment in each other, which marred the trip, those things showed that the two of them had the most profoundly similar way of coming to terms with such an experience on their own. The same way of coping with life.

To the extent that he attained any degree of self-observation at all, Branhardt in all honesty asked himself if, in saying that, he wasn't artfully embellishing the situation in his own favor. But, in fact, that seemed not to be the case. This affinity of character, this kinship of spirit, was there. It was vividly evident even in these mutual contradictions and conflicts, an expression of harmony that would live on in their children.

The most vibrant myrtle must bloom and fade, its green turning to silver. That's the natural course of events, not a pathological one — and only when it turns silver does it become immortal — no longer a flower, but a radiance.

That is what Branhardt was thinking, and he did so reverently, as he looked back with a grateful heart on his long marriage, gazing into the sun that held sway, far and wide, around him.

* * *

All this while Anneliese was sitting with Herr and Frau Lüdecke, offering her official congratulations on his birthday.

In the room with its tulle curtains and canary, the celebration was clearly in full swing. The center table was adorned with vases of hyacinth — they always had to be pure white and only the "Norma" variety.

A birthday cake stood on display before them, and, because it would not have held the right number of candles, a few dozen more were set up beside it on a flowered plate — to give an indication of Herr Lüdecke's age. This made the table look not unlike an altar, and all the more so because Frau Lüdecke had removed the more trivial presents — the socks she had knitted, the Sunday neckties — leaving only the most impressive items.

Year in, year out, Anneliese had known the altar-like table in the overly tidy little room with meticulously well-preserved things that were never allowed to wear with age — almost like the couple's stubbornly enduring idyll of happiness, the little solar — or, more correctly, lunar — eclipses now long ago dispelled. Here nothing changed. Anneliese might have asked them for their marital recipe, as she had already done years ago for the cake's.

But now she had to talk to them about a change that was needed, if anything were to come of Frau Hutscher's move. As Anneliese had the obligatory taste of the birthday wine she herself had brought, she informed them about the neighbors soon expected there on the ground floor. The news of little Gretelein's pending arrival aroused considerable disapproval. A small child would stomp Herr Lüdecke's lawn flat in the summer, and they'd hear it crying. All the more so since the room in question was right next to the Lüdeckes'. On top of that, they themselves had a small chest stored there, which made the Hutscher intrusion something more akin to an invasion. Herr Lüdecke made no bones about his objections, and Frau Lüdecke also expressed her most serious misgivings. But, while doing so she blushed deeply, since the whole matter touched a wound. If a little Herr Lüdecke were coming along, fine! But she had resigned herself to remaining childless, and now some little, perfect stranger would be allowed to lay claim to her heart?

Anneliese tried to calm the disgruntled couple, and, as she spoke on behalf of little Gretelein, she was, with sly playfulness, securing quarters for the second little trouble-maker in the Lüdeckes' tenaciously self-satisfied world, where evidently not even the tiniest child could intrude without disturbing their happiness. For soon there would not be just two little feet trampling Herr Lüdecke's well-groomed lawn and not just one child's voice laughing and screaming through the house!

Imagining that scenario, she caught her heart taking flight: as if only with these thoughts could she feel the gift of the new life expectant in her. As if that child she had never met were becoming hers, while her own child, though coming from far away, from somewhere much more remote, were a mere personal memory of happiness.

Startled, she searched her thoughts. What new losses was she about to suffer? Was she thoughtlessly letting what was most personally hers, her very own, slip through her disillusioned hands — almost indifferently, carelessly letting it fall away and mix indistinguishably with strangers?

Yet, along with this fruit of her own womb, she was also embracing everything foreign to her — the unknown, the unimagined, every remotest possibility — she opened herself up to love it. Within this seed, weren't all living things given a secret claim to her motherliness? "Motherhood" — that's what the word meant. They were not strangers at all, but one flesh and blood. In that primal, crimson source, didn't the little human creature rest among treasures more limitless than even love's most fervent passion could provide?

Did existence always begin there so namelessly, so nameless in the literal sense — new — that the tiny personal element — blissfully unaware of its own goal — drifted along like pollen on the life-bearing spring winds? Did woman always stand there, as on the first day of creation, free of every restricting, narrowing experience — renewed and young, a girl before God?

Was she only now giving life to two children at once? Were her two last-born, the twins, somehow restored to her in what she was doing?

With that, her thoughts turned to Lotti. It seemed as though Lotti were approaching her life — her mother's life that reached out so far beyond itself. Yet no matter what births would come now, no matter how many more she were granted — none of that would bring Lotti back. Only *those* arms, released from the narrowness of her desire for happiness, of her yearning for happiness — those arms alone now embraced Lotti too, deep within themselves.

Past and future tumbled into each another. As if what is called foreign were extinguished and what is called dead extinguished by the breath of the same ever-present power of love.

A profound new feeling overwhelmed Anneliese.

The Lüdeckes, entirely concerned with themselves and the ominous little cloud threatening the blue skies of their future, had no idea that there, in their tidy, little parlor, someone was quietly experiencing something so good, so grand, as if the festive table were set for her alone, with its fragrance of cake, wine, and blossoming flowers.

Annaliese stood up and left. Deep down into the garden she walked, all the way to the stone walls beyond the fruit trees. She gazed across the sunlit valley to the clear outline of the distant hills. She breathed freely, as if a gravestone above her had shattered.

What dies within us only opens up deeper grounds for life. Graves become gateways.

Death! Where is thy sting! Anneliese thought silently to herself.

Turned away from the house, she did not see right away that Markus and Gitta had come. They were waving a greeting to Branhardt from the front garden, while he came their way from the veranda.

Salomo had already run on ahead. He did not even have to wait for someone to open the garden gate, for, as Gitta assured them, the constant ups and downs of the "dunes cure" had slimmed him so nicely that he could find plenty of entryways through the stonework of the wall. Gitta noted approvingly that each time the dog stayed home now had to be seen as an act of moral free will.

Ears flapping, the admired animal dashed towards his mother.

And the merry laughter of the other three at his antics made Anneliese aware of their presence.

She did not at once turn around to greet them. A tentative blush crept over her face — a last fear of being seen the way she was — no longer master of her "exuberance."

One arm slightly raised, apparently to shield her from the sun's glare, amidst thinning trees that had borne fruit and now, with a late, useless beauty, framed her in color: thus was Anneliese seen by Branhardt — and yet not seen.

Only the sun looked fully into her glowing face. And the grotesque dog, making everyone laugh, stood faithfully and guarded her emotions.

NOTES

(Works referenced in these endnotes are listed in the
"Works Cited" section at the end of the "Introduction")

Chapter I

page 1 — "The house"
The Branhardts' hillside home is based on the house into which
Andreas-Salomé and her husband moved in October 1903, after his
appointment to a professorship at the University of Göttingen in Lower
Saxony. A market- and university town about 160 miles southwest of
Berlin, Göttingen then had a population of about 30,000. The house
was located to the east of town, at 101 Herzberger Landstraße, on the
edge of a small forest called the Hainberg Woods. It was replaced by a
modern structure in the 1970s, but earlier photographs show a three-
story structure much like the one described in the novel (see Welsch
and Pfeiffer). The month after the move to Göttingen, the author wrote
to Rainer Maria Rilke: "Ever since the 'Loufried' of Wolfratshausen [the
house in Bavaria that she and Rilke shared with Frieda von Bülow during the summer of 1897], I have been wandering step by step toward
the new one . . . And now it stands here. In a spacious landscape with
beech tree forests and long stretches of hills, somewhere behind which
the Harz Mountains rise. At our feet, in the valley below, the city. And
around us orchards, gardens full of old trees, and vegetable fields. We
even have a chicken yard! Here I have become a peasant woman and my
husband a professor" (Rilke and Andreas-Salomé, 90).

pages 1-2: "But by far the most remarkable thing about the little monster was the fact that its name was Salomo." The female dog is the namesake of the biblical King Solomon, Salomo being the form of the name used in Luther's translation of the Bible (see I Könige 11 and II Chronik 1). The translation of the novel holds to the original's practice, after this paragraph, of referring to the dog only as masculine, with no further mention of its being, in fact, female.

The novel contains several allusions to passages in the Bible, some quite arcane; each is explained in the notes. They likely reflect Andreas-Salomé's studies with Hendrik Gillot, the Dutch pastor in St. Petersburg who was her tutor when she was seventeen. Her notebooks from that time show that she was engaged in a wide-ranging exploration of theological topics, including a comparison of Christianity with Buddhism, Hinduism, and Islam (Peters, 53–54).

After adolescence Andreas-Salomé did not participate in any organized religion, although she did ask Gillot to officiate at her marriage in 1887. However, her first novel was entitled *Im Kampf um Gott* (In the Fight for God; see page xiv), and she wrote numerous pieces about religion over a period of three decades; these include the 1896 article, "Jesus der Jude" (Jesus the Jew), which first attracted Rainer Maria Rilke to her writing (see page xix). All these were written against a backdrop of great interest, especially in Germany, in tracing the historical roots of Christianity, including the efforts of David Strauss (1808–74) and Albert Schweitzer (1875–1965). Andreas-Salomé was still thinking about these issues when she wrote her memoirs, in the last years of her life. The first chapter, entitled "The God Experience," concludes with: "Illogical as it may be, I must confess that any type of belief, even the most absurd, would be preferable to seeing Mankind lose its sense of reverence [*Ehrfurcht*] entirely" (*Looking Back,* 11). Andreas-Salomé's pieces on religion have been collected by Schwab (Andreas-Salomé, *Von der Bestie bis zum Gott*), and Livingstone provides a good account of the evolution of the author's religious ideas throughout her life (74–86).

page 3 — "Lieselieb"

While Branhardt's nickname for his wife could be translated as "Liesedear" or even "Lieselove," the original has been retained throughout, as it is based on her first name and because translation would result in the loss of the alliterative "l," which pairs so poetically with the rhyming "ie" in the first and last syllables (pronounced both times as a long "e"). Note also: the full name "Anneliese" consists of four syllables, the first and final "e's" rendered as an English short "e."

page 4 — "Marlitt-type dashing heroes with gold-blond beards"
Branhardt is referring to E. Marlitt, the pseudonym of (Friederike Henriette Christiane) Eugenie John (1825–87), whose first full-length novel, *Goldelse* (1866, translated in 1868 as *Gold Elsie*), initiated her career as an enduringly popular and widely translated German author of short and novel-length romances and domestic fiction. Her stories— many of them appearing in the family literary journal *Die Gartenlaube* (The Garden Arbor)—were widely, and perhaps unfairly, seen as mere Cinderella-like tales of "young, strong-willed heroines who confront adversity and overcome hardships while falling in love with a worthy man with whom she will settle down to raise a happy family"—thus "tales of suffering and love in which modern Cinderellas find their Prince Charmings" (Kontje, 409). The hero of a subsequent major success, *Reichsgräfin Gisela* (translated in 1869 as *Countess Gisela*), is indeed described as a "tall noble figure with a magnificent blonde [sic] beard" (Marlitt, *Countess Gisela*, 172).

This explicit evocation of the famous, near-contemporary Marlitt is echoed elsewhere in the novel. The heroine of *Gold Elsie*, not unlike Anneliese, early on pursues a career as concert pianist and music teacher, and the title heroine of *Countess Gisela* is, like Anneliese, a blonde woman of striking stature. While the banter between Gitta and Markus in chapter XI, referring to the Bluebeard legend (103), appears *not* to involve a reference to Marlitt's own 1866 novella bearing that title, the novel's concluding chapter is another matter. Erhart (314) notes that the ending of Andreas-Salomé's novel resembles those of some of Marlitt's popular "*Gartenlauben*-Romane" (he cites the 1876 bestseller *Im Hause des Kommerzienrates*; translated in 1876 by A. L. Wister as *At the Councillor's; or, A Nameless History*), while intimating that the "happy endings" of such narratives are belied by the multi-perspectival complexity of their ever-evolving family relationships.

In addition, the closing chapter's constellation of Balduin as hero-ically battling warrior poet and Anneliese confined to her house's gar-den seems to evoke parodically the terms that, as Katja Mellmann has shown, emerged during the literary controversies of the late 1880s. Revolutionarily inclined male writers, anticipating a "jüngstdeutsch" and "consistent" realism, summoned their creative "Kampfgeist" (fighting spirit; Mellmann, 321) against the "Salat von gartenlauben Blüthen" (salad of arbor blossoms; Mellmann, 321) of a popular tradition for which "Marlitt" and "Marlittiade" became catchwords for engaging but simplistic writings reminiscent of the earlier—and similarly attacked— Heinrich Clauren (pseudonym of Carl Heun, 1771–1854). The "Gartenlaube" setting of Andreas-Salomé's last chapter might be seen to involve more homage than ridicule of her maligned literary forerunner Marlitt, signaling how such narratives' foreground impression of happy closure can be subtly countered by intimations of lingering and evolving problems — apparently final endings may, in a wider view, be portals yet to open.

page 7 — "Brixhausen"
Bischhausen, eight miles southeast of Göttingen, is likely the model for Brixhausen.

Chapter II

page 15 — "Tessin"
This is the name, in German and French, for the southernmost canton, or state, of Switzerland, more often identified by its Italian name, "Ticino." The only canton whose sole official language is Italian, Ticino is known for its lakes and forests and its mix of Alpine and Mediterranean cultures.

page 15 — "Courland"
This is the English name for one of the three Baltic governorates, or provinces, of the Russian Empire; the area is now part of Latvia. Ruled by Russia from 1795 to 1918, Courland bordered on Prussia, and by the second half of the nineteenth century nearly one-tenth of its population were German speakers. Andreas-Salomé's father, Gustav Ludwig von Salomé, was born in the Baltic governorates in 1804. His place of birth is unknown: in her memoirs, the author says only that he was of Baltic origin (*Looking Back*, 33). Thus Anneliese's lineage is, in part, like the author's own.

page 15 — "barracks"

As the nation's capital, Berlin was home to a large contingent of army barracks. Karl Baedeker's *Berlin and Its Environs* (London: Dulau, 1903) lists no fewer than seventeen barracks in the city and surrounding suburbs. For Anneliese the barracks, along with the clinics and local tram line, epitomize the difference between her first married home, on the outskirts of town, and her second, in a city apartment. The two seem based on the author's own Berlin homes, first in the leafy borough of Tempelhof and then in the more urban neighborhood of Schmargendorf.

Chapter III

page 20 — "the print of the painting *Silence in the Woods*"

Swiss painter Arnold Böcklin (1827–1901) painted *Das Schweigen des Waldes* (Silence of the Woods) in 1885. Andreas-Salomé uses the title that sometimes appeared in reproductions of the work: *Das Schweigen im Walde* (Silence in the Woods). The description of the painting in the private catalogue of Swiss collector Otto Wesendonck, who bought the original, suggests the appeal the work had for many contemporary viewers: "From a dense spruce forest in the mountain heights, a magical female figure in a shining, light-silver robe emerges from the lonely woods. She is sitting, as though in a dream, on a wild and shaggy unicorn among tall, moss-covered trees, hands folded across a knee and a wreath of blue flowers in her hair. Between the tree trunks, narrow bands of bluish light break through the darkness of the woods. Through a wider gap in the background, the view extends to a lakeside far below. The unicorn eagerly sniffs the morning air. A squirrel pauses on his climb up a tree trunk. Branches and mushrooms lie on the brown spruce needles of the forest floor" (translated by the authors; https://wesendonck.blogspot.com/2016/12/das-schweigen-des-waldes.html). Böcklin was a widely admired artist whose realistic depictions of mythological figures and dream imagery make him akin to Britain's Pre-Raphaelites. *Das Schweigen des Waldes* is at the Muzeum Narodowe in Poznan, Poland, which acquired it in 1930.

This episode's evocation of the paintings by Arnold Böcklin and Adrian Ludwig Richter (see the following note) are only one of the

instances in *Das Haus* in which Andreas-Salomé carries on her practice of the "Kunstzitat" (the referencing and description of graphic art-
works; see Eilert) in her fictional works. Holmes has commented on
the role of a Max Klinger etching in the *Ausschweifung* novella (esp.
623–25; compare also Schütz, 143, and Wernz, 138, 152), while Eilert
(179n11) notes another Klinger citation in Andreas-Salomé's 1896
novella *Aus fremder Seele: Eine Spätherbstgeschichte*. Later chapters in
Das Haus include a reference to the Sistine Chapel's "Creation of Adam"
(see below, the note on chapter IV, 31) and to the Boscoreale fresco that
Balduin describes in his letter to Anneliese in chapter XIX (190; see
the note, below). Anneliese's question in her dialogue with Renate in
chapter VI—"What are weeds?"—might also be seen to involve a veiled
allusion to a painting by Nikolai Ge that Lou and Rilke likely saw on
their trips to Russia (see below, the note on chapter VI, 48).

page 20 — "indelibly named 'Genoveva' by Frau Lüdecke"
  Frau Lüdecke may appear to be directing young Gitta's attention away
from the erotic tone of Böcklin's maiden-unicorn painting and towards
the pious, chaste, and abstemious life of St. Genoveva (also Geneviève)
of Paris, the young girl from Nanterre (born ca. 422) who devoted her
life to God and whose prayers, legend has it, saved Paris from Attila's
Huns in 451. Frau Lüdecke does not, however, indicate her "Genoveva"
to be a "saint," and she may have another Genoveva—and different popular nineteenth-century painter's work—in mind. The Böcklin painting bears compelling similarities to another Genoveva painting, namely
the 1841 *Genoveva in the Forest of Seclusion* by Adrian Ludwig Richter
(1803–84). The main figure in Richter's painting is Genoveva of Brabant,
not officially a saint, but the heroine of a thirteenth-century legend of
the loyal wife, who, falsely accused of infidelity, sentenced to death, and
spared by the executioner, lived for six years, with her young son, in a
cave in the Ardennes, nourished by a roe deer. Richter's painting, like
Böcklin's, centers on a luminously bright constellation of a woman with
a deerlike animal in a dark sylvan setting. Richter's Genoveva, of course,
is accompanied by her young boy, and her ungulate companion lacks
the lone erect appendage of Böcklin's unicorn—hence, perhaps, her
appeal to a Frau Lüdecke bent on guiding Gitta's thoughts away from
fantastic erotic adventure and towards the proper fidelity of marriage
and motherhood. The original of Richter's painting is located in the

Kunsthalle in Hamburg. The Genoveva of Brabant legend was popularized by Friedrich Hebbel's 1840 drama, *Genoveva*, which was the basis for Robert Schumann's only opera, composed a decade later.

page 20 — "Holding his pruning shears on his way out to trim the hedges"
The original begins with "*Trotz* der Baumschere" ("*Despite* the pruning shears, . . ."; emphasis added) and goes on to the comparison to a banker about to do some gardening. But the "despite" ("trotz") is misleading. It is *because* Lüdecke, with his usual reserved bearing and gold-rimmed spectacles, is carrying the shears that he looks like a garden-bound banker. The translation departs from the original in order to avoid this error.

page 23 — "Now he banged his fist on the table, making the dishes jump."
Branhardt's paternal anger on behalf of his fellow doctor seems to have a strong impact on his daughter. Later, however, when he reacts similarly to the way she has treated his male colleagues—first Helmold, then Markus—Gitta is unable to recall the cause of his anger on the first occasion, described here. Cormican (*Women on the Works*, 149–50) notes this subtle indication of how the reader's faith in Branhardt's authority is undermined.

Chapter IV

page 30 — "about which she . . . did not give a *pfifferling*."
The "pfifferling" is German for the chanterelle, *Cantharellus cibarius*, a popular edible mushroom. The German phrase "keinen Pfifferling geben auf etwas" (literally: to not give a chanterelle about/for something) is a close equivalent to the English phrase "to not give a fig about/for something."

page 31 — "gymnasium"
This is the term used in German-speaking and Scandinavian countries for the secondary school that prepares pupils for university entrance.

page 31 — "nearby Hasling"

There appears to be no community by that name near Göttingen. The lone "Hasling" in Germany today is in Bavaria, approximately twelve miles west of Passau.

page 31 — "Early the next morning"

The original begins this episode of Gitta's early morning with "Einmal . . ." ("once," or "one time"), which misleadingly suggests that those morning events were a one-time, past occurrence. In fact, this early morning immediately follows the events of the day described from the opening of the chapter, with Balduin expected to arrive the following day (27) and Branhardt away overnight (28). The episode introduced with the "Einmal . . ." (31) depicts Gitta waking early the next morning, believing she hears her father arriving home but then finding that it was Balduin, not Branhardt, whose cab she has heard (31). The translation deviates from the original in order to prevent misconceptions of these chronologies.

page 31 — "the outstretched finger of the Lord God on the ceiling of the Sistine Chapel."

Michelangelo completed the frescoes and ceiling paintings of the Vatican's Sistine Chapel (built 1477–80) between 1508 and 1512. Central to the ceiling's nine scenes from the book of Genesis is "The Creation of Adam."

page 34 — "smitten with sore boils"

Gitta's comment on Balduin in the original as "mit Schwären bedeckt" evokes the Bible's Job 2:7, which describes its title figure as having been smitten "mit bösen Geschwüren von der Fußsohle an bis auf seinen Scheitel." The King James version states that Satan "smote Job with sore boils from the sole of his foot unto his crown."

Chapter V

page 39 — "If I rest, I rust!"

Frau Hutscher is repeating a well-known German proverb, "Rast' ich, so rost' ich!," often attributed to Martin Luther.

page 40 — "the wages of sin is death"

Frau Hutscher is quoting The Epistle to the Romans 6:23, in the New Testament, translated here according to the King James version. The Luther Bible version reads: "Denn der Tod ist der Sünde Sold."

page 40 — "What is accomplished comes from God!"

With her "Das Vollbringen gibt Gott!" here, Frau Hutscher offers an abbreviated paraphrase of The Epistle to the Philippians 2:13, which in the Luther Bible reads: "Denn Gott ist's, der in euch wirkt beides, das Wollen und das Vollbringen, nach seinem Wohlgefallen." The King James version reads: "For it is God which worketh in you both to will and to do of his good pleasure." Frau Hutscher's appropriations of the Bible are occasionally exact, occasionally "loose," and sometimes wrong.

page 40 — "Come unto me, all ye that labor and are heavy laden!"

Here Frau Hutscher offers an exact quotation of another New Testament passage: the Luther Bible's version of Matthew 11:28, which reads: "Kommt her zu mir alle, die ihr mühselig und beladen seid. . . ." The King James version is used here.

page 40 — "well begun is half done!"

Here Frau Hutscher repeats a well-known maxim of the Roman poet Horace, from his *Epistles* 1.2, 40: "Dimidium facti qui coepit habet," usually rendered in German as "Frisch gewagt ist halb gewonnen!" (literally "Freshly dared is half won"), and in English as "well begun [or 'boldly ventured'] is half won [or 'done']."

Chapter VI

page 45 — "Just as she had been able, even as a young woman, to sustain a charitable society on the international stage"

Renate is partly modeled on Andreas-Salomé's friend, Frieda von Bülow (1857–1909). The daughter of two old German families, the Münchhausens and the Bülows, Bülow spent part of her childhood in Smyrna, in what is now Turkey, where her father served as a diplomat. She and her younger sister Margarethe were educated in Thüringen and

England. Margarete, a talented writer, died at the age of twenty-four while trying to rescue a child who had fallen through the ice. Her sister's death was a severe blow to Bülow, who went to German East Africa in 1885, in an effort to start a new life. The newly established colony, three times the size of modern Germany and home to more than seven million people, comprised what is now Burundi, Rwanda, mainland Tanzania, and part of Mozambique. There Bülow helped her brother Albrecht establish a coconut farm and founded the Women's Society for Nursing in the Colonies (*Frauenverein für Krankenpflege in den Kolonien*). She also entered into a relationship with Carl Peters, a colonial administrator, that became abusive. (Peters was infamous among the Africans for his ruthlessness.) After her brother's death in 1892, Bülow returned to Germany and wrote a series of novels that, for the first time, gave readers a detailed view of life in Africa under German rule. It was a system whose paternalistic attitudes, rooted in racism, were used to justify economic exploitation and oppression. Kerstin Decker has published a biography of Bülow: *Meine Farm in Afrika*.

By basing her Renate figure on Frieda von Bülow, Andreas-Salomé appears to be "returning a favor." Her friend paid literary tribute to her in the portrayal of Helga von S in the 1897 novella "Zwei Menschen." As Kerstin Decker, in her 2010 biography, *Lou Andreas-Salomé: Der bittersüße Funke Ich*, has proposed, the fictive Helga's traveling companion is based on Friedrich Pineles, and Dr. Siegfried Rosenfeld, the "little Jew from Breslau," who becomes the object of Helga's fascination and desire, is based on literary editor Paul Goldmann. Austrian writers Richard Beer-Hofmann and Arthur Schnitzler (whose 1926 *Traumnovelle* — "Dream Story"—was the basis for Stanley Kubrick's last film, *Eyes Wide Shut*) served as models for Goldmann's two friends (182–83). Regarding Paul Goldmann, including the relationship of his 1894 "affair" with Andreas-Salomé in Paris to Bülow's so-called "Goldmanniade" (Decker, 182) and his role as a model for figures in various Andreas-Salomé stories, see, in addition to Decker's biography (182–87), Binion (182, 200), Streiter ("Nachwort," in Bülow, *Die schönsten Novellen*), and Andreas-Salomé's April 1894 letter to Misulka Clementz in the Eberhard Koestler auction catalogue, *Inniger Schmatz*, 4.

Like her real-life model, Helga is a lone daughter with several brothers in whose lessons she partook as a girl, and she too now bedazzles men as an enchanting personality able to hold her own with male "comrades"—not suitors—in intellectual discussions. Helga's attraction to Rosenfeld is a recasting of Andreas-Salomé's adventurous interaction with Goldmann and seems to be mirrored, in turn, in the portrayal of Gitta—with her "Orientalizing" of the Jewish Dr. Markus Mandelstein as an Arab. Also echoed in *Das Haus* are passages in "Zwei Menschen" in which Helga speaks about women's attraction to subjugation in love—especially evident in the Renate-Anneliese dialogue later in this chapter, starting on page 46 (see below).

page 46 — "the *Appassionata*"
Anneliese plays Beethoven's Piano Sonata no. 23 in F minor, op. 57. Written in 1804–5, just as the thirty-four-year-old composer was beginning his Fifth Symphony, it is a highly dramatic work, with two turbulent outer movements and a quieter middle one based on a series of variations. The sonata's title, which means "passionate" in Italian, was added after the composer's death. The British composer Hubert Parry (1848–1918) famously said of the work, "There the human soul asked mighty questions of its God, and had its reply."

page 47 — "this insane attraction to subordination"
This conversation on "subordination" echoes passages in Frieda von Bülow's 1897 novella "Zwei Menschen," whose female protagonist, based on Andreas-Salomé, comments more extensively on this "desire." Helga claims at one point: "I do not desire victory, but rather defeat. In love, defeat and subjugation are a thousand times more beautiful than victory" (49; translated by the authors). Her comments in a later conversation run as follows: "But, dear doctor, . . . I wish nothing better than to be suppressed. You have no idea how we women simply yearn for that!" (52). And she goes on to think to herself: "Now he looks as if he would like to strike me dead! . . . If only he would beat me! I think I'd fall at his feet in gratitude" (52–53). These assertions seem to be a projection of Bülow's own thinking, rather than reflecting that of Andreas-Salomé, who did not consummate her marriage of more than three decades because she did not wish to have sexual relations with a man to whom she felt subordinate, due to the conventions of German marriage at the time. Andreas-Salomé's Bülow-based Renate comments further on her desire for subjugation in chapter XIV, page 142.

page 48 — "a few weeds amid your tidy rows of grain?"
The dialogue beginning here involves references to two passages in the Bible. Renate's question evokes the parable related in Matthew 13:24–30 about the man who sows his crop but awakens to learn that his enemy has sown "tares" (the King James version's rendition of "weeds," "Unkraut," as here and also in the Luther Bible) amongst his wheat.

page 48 — "What are weeds?"
Anneliese's response to Renate's question extends the weeds/wheat evocation of Matthew 13:24–30 and ends with a veiled reference to Pilate's interaction with Jesus as related in John 18:29–40, specifically to verse 38, in which Anneliese alters Pilate's question "What is truth?" to "What are weeds?" Anneliese has just defended the beneficial potential of "weeds" against the traditionally negative implication of their name (i.e., the "Un-" in "Unkraut") and thus appears to be provocatively altering "truth" to "weeds" so as to invite critical reflection on the validity of unequivocal claims to truth or value.

This veiled citation of "What is truth?" may have been inspired by the 1890 painting *"What is truth?" Christ and Pilate* by Nikolai Ge (1831–94). Initially exhibited in St. Petersburg at the eighteenth annual show of the Society for Traveling Art Exhibitions on February 11, 1890, it elicited alarmed objections, with its disturbingly dark and unsympathetic portrayal of Christ, and was removed from the exhibition and banned from being publicly shown in Russia. On the advice of Ge's friend Leo Tolstoy, it was sent to Hamburg, Berlin, and Hannover in April of 1890 and, three years after the artist's death, acquired by the Pavel Tretyakov gallery (Tatiana Karpova and Svetlana Kapyrina, "Nikolai Ge: A Chronicle of the Artist's Life and Work").

In 1903 the canvas was included in exhibits of Ge's works in Paris and Genoa, but Andreas-Salomé and Rilke may have seen it at Moscow's Tretyakov Gallery, which they visited on their trips to Russia in 1899 and 1900 (Michaud's footnote in Andreas-Salomé, *Russland mit Rainer*, 45n32).

Ge's painting might be seen to allude parodically to the Pilate-Christ constellation in the 1871 painting *Ecce Homo* by the Swiss-Italian Antonio Ciseri (1821–91). Pilate's pose in Ge's painting resembles that in Ciseri's but is reversed: he gestures with his right hand rather than his left, and now with his head slightly turned to reveal a sneering, arrogant smile. The Christ figures differ even more radically. Ciseri's heroically posed Christ to Pilate's left is radiantly lit, his bare torso bright in the sunlight above the red robes covering his hips and legs; though surrounded by courtiers in the foreground, he dominates the painting's center as he looks out over a multitude gathered below and in the background. He is the center of attention, presented by a faceless Pilate. Ge's painting omits all figures other than Pilate and Christ, who confront each other, rather than being together before a gathered crowd; only Pilate faces the sunlight, his back to the observer and casting a long shadow; with his assured, superior smile, he gestures now with his right arm to a Christ who stands, his back to a wall and deep in its gloomy shadow, sullen and downcast, a disarmingly reduced, unheroic figure—a presentation that offended contemporary viewers in St. Petersburg as "vulgar realism" (see arthive.com for Anna Yesterday's account of the work's genesis and reception). Some contemporary readers of the novel likely knew of Ge's notorious painting and pondered its role in sharpening the revisionist subtext of the Anneliese-Renate dialogue here.

page 52 — "who guides his children's hearts 'as he does the rivers of water.'"

Renate is evoking Proverbs 21:1, which, in the King James version, states that the "king's heart is in the hand of the Lord, as the rivers of water: he turneth it whithersoever he will." The version in the Luther Bible reads: "Des Königs Herz ist in der Hand des HERRN wie Wasserbäche; er lenkt es, wohin er will."

Chapter VII

page 60 — "that had seduced Balduin into casting her in Ophelia's wreath of straw."

The reference to Ophelia concerns her entrance in act 4 of Shakespeare's *Hamlet*, scene 5 (in some versions and translations broken up to have Ophelia's entrance begin scene 7). Ophelia was early on depicted making her entrance at this point with "straw," a tradition likely established by the stage directions in Nicholas Rowe's 1709 edition ("Enter Ophelia, fantastically drest with Straws and Flowers") and followed in David Garrick's productions later in the eighteenth century, which had her carrying a bundle of straw (see Rosenberg, 800). The Schlegel-Tieck translation, in Andreas-Salomé's day the standard

German version, makes no reference to "Stroh" (straw), "Kranz" (wreath), or "Strohkranz" (wreath of straw) at this point. However, Christoph Martin Wieland's 1766 translation, which influenced German productions and translations of the play through the late eighteenth century, appears to have adopted and translated Rowe's stage direction for act 4, scene 7 (quoted above): "Ophelia, auf eine phantastische Art mit Stroh und Blumen geschmükt, tritt auf."

page 60 — "platform ticket"
Beginning in 1893, many German railways required persons who wished to accompany a passenger to or from a train to buy a "platform ticket," which granted access to the station platform but not to the train. The last remaining German system using "Bahnsteigkarten" is the municipal transit service in Hamburg.

page 63 — "Ah, in times past, long since lived out, you were my *sister* or my wife."
Branhardt is quoting lines (27–28; translated by the authors, emphasis on "sister" added in the novel) from a poem by Johann Wolfgang von Goethe (1749–1832), untitled but often referred to as "An Charlotte von Stein" (the poem having been sent to her in a letter from Goethe of April 14, 1776) or by its first line, "Warum gabst du uns die tiefen Blicke" ("Why didst thou give us this deep vision?"—the opening question addressed to destiny or fate). H. F. Peters's biography of Andreas-Salomé evokes the same poem with its title, *My Sister, My Wife.*

page 65 — "it was the son of man."
With "des Menschen Sohn," Renate is using a phrase that recurs in the Luther Bible in Christ's references to himself (Matthew 18:11; 24:44; 25:31; Mark 9:31; Luke 12:40 and 19:10). In the King James version it is "the Son of man."

Chapter VIII

page 76 — "Ark of the Covenant"
As told in the Bible's Book of Exodus, this was a gold-covered, wooden chest that held the two stone tablets on which the Ten Com-

mandments were engraved. The Israelites are said to have carried it with them through the centuries until it was enshrined at King Solomon's Temple in Jerusalem. The Babylonians destroyed the temple in the sixth century BCE, and the fate of the Ark is unknown. The "covenant" of its name refers to the Jewish belief that an agreement exists between the people of Israel and their god, Elohim, whereby they will worship only him and obey his commandments and he, in turn, will protect and help them.

Chapter IX

page 82 — "It portrayed a child's face"

The child in the chalk sketch is not explicitly identified. Woodford's claim that it is a portrait of Gitta as a young girl ("Pregnancy and Ambivalence," 115) seems unlikely. It is much more likely a portrait of the deceased Lotti. Markus appears never to have seen this face before. He notes the "lovely, lovely eyes" and the face's "poignant beauty," but he has to "guess" who it is. A childhood portrait of his Gitta, still quite a young woman at this point, he would surely have recognized at once. Finally, with a child generally expected to bear a resemblance to its mother, Markus's wish that their offspring might resemble the child in the portrait would be unnecessary if the portrait is of Gitta.

page 83 — "taking on the role of chaperone—or 'propriety elephant'"

The original states Balduin to be accompanying Markus and Gitta as "Schicklichkeits-Elefant," its literal translation included here along with "chaperone." The picturesque phrase appears to originate with the author.

Chapter X

page 88 — "courting Leah for seven years, before Rachel gave herself to him"

Markus is making a passing—and confused—reference to the story of Jacob's complicated marriages in Genesis 29–31. Jacob labors seven years in hope of marrying Rachel, but her father, Laban, then insists that he first accept her older sister, Leah, as his wife, whereupon he gives Rachel to Jacob as a second wife. Jacob at first only has to spend seven nights with Leah, not "courting" her but as her husband. In return, Rachel becomes his wife, and he works for Laban for another seven years. Furthermore, Rachel does not "give herself to him"; Laban *gives her* to Jacob. The author seems to have misremembered the tale. Nonetheless, her meaning is clear: accepting an incomplete love can be a way of winning a complete one later.

page 88 — "they still were not using the informal address with each other"

As early modern English once did (with informal "thou" and formal "you") and as French, Russian, and other languages still do, German has informal ("du," used to address children, close friends, or family members) and formal ("Sie") forms of the second-person address. Around 1900, as today, it would have been unusual to hear an engaged couple address each other with the formal "Sie." In any dialogue, a speaker's shift from one form to the other signals a significant change—or attempt to change—the relationship to the other figure, as happens on page 90 (see the note, below).

page 89 — "he also thought using 'du' between them would at once turn the painful, embarrassing barriers—all of them—into mere chalk lines."

With his comments on barriers reduced to chalk lines, Markus echoes Andreas-Salomé's much-quoted statement in her letter of March 26, 1882, to her mentor Hendrik Gillot: "Let us see whether the vast majority of the so-called 'insurmountable barriers' that the world draws are not harmless chalk lines!" (trans. by the authors). The original is "Wir wollen doch sehn, ob nicht die allermeisten sogenannten 'unübersteiglichen Schranken,' die die Welt zieht, sich als harmlose Kreidestriche herausstellen!" See Andreas-Salomé, *Lebensrückblick*, 78 or Andreas-Salomé, *Looking Back*, 45–46 for the entire letter.

page 90 — "To be *your* wife!"

The original ("'Deine Frau sein!' — Das Wort kam ihr atemlos, an seinem Hals") would more literally be translated as "'To be your wife!' The word came to her breathlessly, there at his neck." However, that would have lost sight of the fact that Gitta, by using "deine Frau" instead of "Ihre Frau," has shifted from the formal form of address, which she and Markus have used up to this point, to the informal form, which is normally used only for children, close friends, or family members. That detail is immediately apparent to readers of the original, highlighted by the rules of German word order, which place the infinitive phrase, "to be," at the end of an infinitive clause and thus have Gitta's statement begin with the revealing "Deine Frau." The narrative has previously referred to the couple's unusually formal way of addressing each other (see endnote to page 89, above). By italicizing Gitta's "your" and adding a comment on the shift to the informal form, the translation attempts to retain that otherwise lost signal. A similar play with the "du" versus "Sie" forms of "you" occurs in the story "A Reunion" (see Andreas-Salomé, *The Human Family*, 97–98; Whitinger, "Introduction," xiii).

page 90 — "On the morning of Saint Sylvester's Day"
    Saint Sylvester's Day, often known simply as "Silvester," as in the original German here, is December 31, commemorating the death of Pope Sylvester I, who served as the thirty-third pope, from 314 to 335. In German-speaking countries, New Year's and New Year's Eve celebrations are generally referred to as "Silvester."

page 91 — "and then her mama would carry on like the princess"
    Gitta is evoking the fairytale "Les fées" ("The Fairies") by Charles Perrault (1628–1703). While the older and unkinder of two sisters is punished for her abusive behavior by having toads and snakes tumble from her mouth when she speaks, the younger sister's kind behavior is rewarded by having either a jewel, a precious metal, or a pretty flower fall from her mouth whenever she speaks.

page 94 — "Frau Lüdecke had been . . . floating nutshells in dishes of water and pouring the Saint Sylvester's Day lead."
    Frau Lüdecke is involved in two New Year's Eve customs. The first is a party activity in which slips of paper bearing the guests' name are rolled up in nut shells, which are then set afloat in a pan of water. When two nutshells float close together, it means that the two individuals will wed within the coming year. The second, "Bleigießen" (lead pouring), is another oracular game, in which participants melt a small chunk of lead in a spoon over a flame and then immerse the molten droplet of

lead in a pan of cold water. The hardened chunks can then be "read," like tea leaves or coffee grounds, to discern shapes that foretell events in the New Year.

Chapter XI

page 99 — "Don't toss your rifle into the barley, son!"
Branhardt uses a German idiomatic phrase for giving up an impossible struggle ("die Flinte ins Korn werfen"). It originates in the military sphere, where soldiers in a hopeless battle might opt to throw their rifles into the field and give up, rather than die for the cause. The phrase is most often translated into contemporary English as "don't throw in the towel" or "don't throw in the sponge," both of which originate in the context of boxing, the thrown towel or sponge indicating one fighter's decision not to continue the match. Those two options, however, have a closer German equivalent in the phrase "das Handtuch werfen" (throw the towel), which also originates in the sphere of prize-fighting, and, in any case, that context of competitive pugilism seemed at odds with the Branhardts' world. Accordingly, a near literal translation of the German phrase seemed best suited both to capturing Branhardt's picturesque speech and to retaining an aspect of the novel's "foreignness" for English readers.

page 103 — "he added that for the empty room he would have a golden key made, as Bluebeard had done"
Markus is evoking the folktale of the wife-murdering Bluebeard, most famously remembered in the 1697 version by Charles Perrault (1628–1703). The Perrault version does not refer explicitly to a riddle, although riddles are mentioned in other versions of the tale. Nor does the 1866 novella *Blaubart* by Eugenie Marlitt (see the endnote to chapter I, above) involve those elements.

page 106 — "*equus morbus*"
Markus is being playful, using the custom of German doctors of the time to name a disease in Latin by combining the word "morbus," which means "disease," with the name of the first person to identify it,

e.g., "Morbus Hodgkin" for Hodgkin lymphoma. In this case, "*equus morbus*" is Latin for "horse disease."

Chapter XII

page 114 — "but the features of the father were present as in a picture-puzzle"
The term "picture-puzzle" is the translation of the German "Kippbild," which, unfortunately, has no concise equivalent in English. A "Kippbild" (literally "flip image," also translated as "reversible figure") is a graphic image involving an optical illusion, initially appearing as one thing to one observer (one well-known example: a white vase against a black background), while another observer might see it as something quite different (in that case, two human silhouettes in black, facing each other and separated by a white background). The term's usage here intimates that what Anneliese "sees" in Balduin's poetry might not be "seen" by another reader.

page 117 — "the violation of one person by another"
The term "violation" is the translation of the German "Vergewaltigung." Cormican aptly points out that Anneliese's term "Vergewaltigung" is also commonly used in the context of sexual assault and rape, thus affirming Anneliese's sympathy, as a woman, with any oppressed victim of patriarchy (*Women in the Works*, 53–54). She suggests that Anneliese's word choice "indicates the violation of real women in a patriarchal structure" and at the same time, given the non-gendered context of her statement, "suggests the feminization of everything that patriarchy, represented by Branhardt's exclusive authority, violates or attempts to suppress" (54).

Chapter XIII

page 121 — "before he left for the Dutch congress for natural scientists"
Markus is most likely attending the Dutch Congress for Science and Medicine. The *Nederlandsch Natuur- en Geneeskundig Congres* first met in Amsterdam in 1887 and was held every two years during the

Easter vacation, in various cities in the Netherlands. This makes more specific the indication of the novel's subtitle that the events are set at the end of the nineteenth century ("vom Ende vorigen Jahrhunderts"), although the novel's events at this point seem to be occurring some weeks past Easter.

page 124 — "which can happen to any poor Grete."
    Renate's use of the name "Grete" might be seen as a veiled and oblique allusion to the "Gretchen tragedy" of Goethe's *Faust. Part One*. Faust's ardently courted but doomed beloved is Margarete. She is also referred to in the play as "Gretchen," "Gretel," "Gretelchen," and "Margaretlein," but never as "Grete" or "Greta," although the latter two were and remain common short forms of the name "Margarete." Renate uses the name here to refer to any young woman (Grete, Margarete) who, like Goethe's Margarete/Gretchen, takes up with a man who causes her hardship and ruin. The allusion might also be seen to anticipate Renate's assumption, suggested later in this chapter (see note to page 125, below), that Gitta is pregnant.

page 124 — "You just said I've suffered. No, Liese, I've *enjoyed*"
    While Frieda von Bülow's "Zwei Menschen" (see notes to chapter VI, page 47, above) had depicted its Andreas-Salomé-based protagonist, Helga von S, extolling suffering and subjugation, Andreas-Salomé again portrays its Bülow-based Renate voicing similar thoughts.

page 125 — "Renate smiled knowingly"
    Woodford proposes that at this point "the narrator implies strongly" (115, "Pregnancy and Ambivalence") that Gitta is pregnant, her drowsiness and absentmindedness being "tropes conveniently employed in realist fiction to intimate pregnancy" (115). While Woodford astutely grasps essentials of Gitta's emancipatory moves against parental authority and expectations, her inference of a pregnancy and (later in chapter XIII, page 126) of a miscarriage on Gitta's part finds only tenuous support here and none whatever elsewhere in the text (see below, the notes on page 126 of chapter XIII and on page 144 of chapter XIV). Renate assumes a condition that Anneliese, from what she has heard from Gitta about the honeymoon, might rightly suspect not to exist. Anneliese's

tactful silence forestalls embarrassing open discussion of the—for Gitta rather anti-climactic—details of the Mandelstein couple's honeymoon.

page 126 — "something peculiar happened"
With this episode, the alleged pregnancy that Woodford dubiously finds "strongly implied" earlier in this chapter (see note to page 125, above) is declared a certainty: Gitta's thoughts here "point to only one thing" (Woodford, "Pregnancy and Ambivalence," 116), namely that "the pregnancy, which had seemed so certain and final, has vanished" (116). However, nothing in this episode or any previous episode speaks for a spontaneous abortion, and the support for such a reading that Woodford finds in chapter XIV is based on a misreading of the text (see below, note to page 144 of chapter XIV).

Chapter XIV

page 141 — "In your hour of need — when you simply can't go on without it — then do so."
Anneliese's words to Balduin echo a message that Andreas-Salomé scribbled on the reverse of Rilke's milk bill when they broke up in February 1901: "If one day much later you feel yourself in dire straits, there is a home here with us for the worst hour" (according to an unnumbered footnote in the Snow/Winkler translation of the letters, Rilke and Andreas-Salomé, 42). She refers to that note at the end of her letter to Rilke of February 26, 1901, where she says: "That is why I was so moved when as we parted I wrote down the last words on a scrap of your paper, *because I couldn't make myself say them to you out loud. I meant every one of those words*" (Rilke and Andreas-Salomé, 41–42; emphasis in the original).

page 141 — "blond hair and Junker features"
The "Junker features" is the translation of the original's "junkerliche Kopf" (literally: Junker-ly head), that is: he has the features of a "Junker," a member of the Prussian landed nobility, the term deriving from Middle High German "juncherre" (young nobleman), designating a young or lesser nobleman.

page 143 — "they danced on, caught up in gay abandon, to an old waltz melody Anneliese sang"

In the passage that follows, we learn that the melody that Anneliese and Branhardt dance to is from Anneliese's childhood, presumably in the 1850s or thereabouts. Thus, it is probably not one of the famous waltzes of Johann Strauss II. (His most popular work, "The Blue Danube," was not performed until 1867.) Perhaps the author had in mind the dances of Schubert, such as those collected as *Sentimentales* or *Valses Nobles*; earlier generations often used them for at-home music making. These are simpler pieces, still linked to the folk dances from which the waltz evolved. As British musicologist Arthur Hutchings notes: "They come from street, suburb, private party and public festival and have more direct jollity in them than the more languishing waltzes of Strauss's Vienna, which had moved further towards decadence; here is the true Viennese *Gemütlichkeit* [coziness] with the flavour of beer, rather than the more heady wine of the later waltz, so alluring, so suggestive of private romance and personal languishment. Allurement of a kind there is in Schubert's dances, but subjective romantic emotions take subsidiary place in a general come-all-ye" (148–49).

page 144 — "she came upon some papers"

Woodford takes Gitta's finding here to be "some medical papers that seem to refer to the pregnancy" ("Pregnancy and Ambivalence," 117) and that thus make her pregnancy (and her alleged miscarriage in chapter XIII, page 126) "so certain from a rational viewpoint" (118). In fact, these "densely written papers on a doctor's stationery" are the writings that Gitta herself undertook in chapter XIII, in her conviction that writing was the way to capture the happiness that otherwise only "visits" her. These begin with her attempt to "ghostwrite" a more romantic letter from Markus to her and that day's subsequent writings on the medical stationery at hand in Markus's empty waiting room (chapter XIII, 130). She carries these papers with her on her flight to the heath and on to the Danish coast (chapter XVII, 167). They constitute the "storytelling" that Anneliese, in her conversation with Markus in chapter XVIII, is initially inclined to disparage (179). In this context, Gitta relates to the writing women whose presence Woodford (in "Female Desire") has noted in Andreas-Salomé's *Eine Ausschweifung* and other contemporary works by women: she might be seen to represent an emerging state between that earlier novella's articulately self-conscious letter-writer, Adine, and the younger sister of Gabriele, Mutchen, who is captured at one moment creating mysterious jottings on the misted windowpane (see *Fenitschka and Deviations*, 68).

Chapter XV

page 150 — "you can't drive out the Devil with Beelzebub."
Renate is evoking here the opening clause of Matthew 12:27. Both the Luther Bible and King James version have plural "devils." The Luther Bible version reads: "So ich aber die Teufel durch Beelzebub austreibe, durch wen treiben sie eure Kinder aus? Darum werden sie eure Richter sein." The King James version reads: "And if I by Beelzebub cast out devils, by whom do your children cast them out? therefore they shall be your judges."

page 152 — "It seemed to her that her father had only once before given her such a scolding."
Readers, however, as Cormican points out (*Women in the Works*, 50), can recall that such a confrontation occurred in the episode regarding Helmold's alarm clock (chapter III, 22–23). Cormican proposes that this reveals how Gitta "unwittingly" undermines her father's authority.

Chapter XVI

page 162 — "When she says 'Balder' it's as if she means 'Baldur'"
Norse mythology's "Baldur" (also Baldr, Balder) is the son of Odin and Frigg and brother of Hodr, and usually depicted as the god of beauty, purity, love, righteousness and peace, and summer sunshine. He perishes when Höd, the blind god, hurls mistletoe at him, the only plant that can do him harm.

Chapter XVIII

page 180 — "that earliest homeland of mother and father"
These reflections on the "homeland" (*Heimat*) of childhood, determined by one's mother and father, and "house" (*Haus*), as a metaphor for a developing personality, are stated with a challenging grammatical

complexity and poetic intensity. They are taken up in Anneliese's ensuing thoughts on constructing the "house" of a marriage that, perhaps
too daringly, dispenses with the confining "walls" ("Mauern") a par-
ent might see as necessary to the structure of an adult's successful life.
They also call to mind ideas that Renate formulated when she and
Anneliese discussed the hopes and challenges of parenting. There, she
saw a mother's impulse to guide with godlike sovereignty (chapter VI,
52) as running the danger of reducing her complex daughter to "only a
girl" (53). Later, she reflected on how children, as "mere continuations"
of their parents, "might become mere imitations and dilutions," never
breaking break free of that confining circle to know the other "swirling"
prospects and possibilities of life (chapter VII, 64), so that the "delightful house" of the childhood home becomes a confining "cage" (64).

For Markus, too, the early personality molded and guided by parents is a homeland ("Heimat") from which he must emerge to construct
the "house" of his mature development—one with windows and perhaps without confining walls. That need not mean cutting oneself off
from one's origins: earlier Markus saw his father's acceptance of Gitta,
which he hoped for, as giving him back his "homeland" (chapter X, 88).
He makes a similar reference later in this chapter, 186.

These various views of personal development throughout the novel
build on the metaphor in its opening lines, which see the windows and
bays of the Branhardt home as "extensions of original rooms that had
been found too confining" (chapter I, page 1).

page 183 — "Herr Doktor"
Literally "Mister Doctor"; in the late nineteenth century, as today,
Germans typically addressed a physician as "Herr Doktor," with or
without the person's surname.

Chapter XIX

pages 190 — Balduin's letter
The letter is based on one Rilke wrote to Andreas-Salomé on January
15, 1904, from the studio on Viale Madama Leitizia in Rome, where he
and his wife, the sculptor Clara Westhoff, were spending the winter. The
author adapted it for use here with Rilke's permission (*Looking Back*,

108). In his letter, Rilke told Andreas-Salomé about a Roman fresco he had seen the previous spring in Paris, one of a group of paintings removed in 1900 from a recently excavated Roman villa at Boscoreale, about a mile north of Pompeii. The frescoes were soon recognized as among the finest Roman paintings ever found, the work of highly accomplished artists, powerfully expressive and, for the most part, well preserved. Archeologists determined that the villa had been the home of the family of Publius Fannius Synistor and that the frescoes had been painted in the first century BCE; the villa was buried by the eruption of Vesuvius in 79 CE. The fresco described in Rilke's letter depicts a man and a woman seated side by side. The man leans on a staff; his face is so abraded that his expression is no longer visible. The woman stares pensively into the distance.

The man's staff prompted Rilke to interpret him as a traveler who had gone a long distance to reach the woman, and he compared the two figures to himself and Andreas-Salomé, saying that his life was still a journey towards her and concluding that ". . . it will only *be* when I can tell it to you, and will be as you hear it!" (Rilke and Andreas-Salomé, 94–95; emphasis in the original). Pechota Vuilleumier has compared Rilke's letter with the one in the novel, line-by-line, showing how the author adapted the original for the purposes of her narrative (164–75). Soon after Rilke saw the frescoes, they were sold at auction and divided among four museums in Europe and the Metropolitan Museum of Art in New York. The one mentioned in Rilke's letter is on display in New York (accession number 03.14.6) and can be seen on the museum's website: www.metmuseum.org.

page 190 — "the Prize of Rome"

The "Rompreis" in the original could refer to one of several prizes for achievement in the arts, in this case likely the one by the "Preußische Akademie der Künste" (The Prussian Academy of the Arts). There may be a wordplay involved, based on the fact that the German "Preis" can be translated as "prize" or "price." The sentence also refers to the fact that Branhardt is Balduin's main financial support, and readers might thus be invited to reflect further on the "price" or "cost" of Balduin's progress with regard both to the father-son relationship and to the marriage of Frank and Anneliese.

page 192 — "child of poor folk"
Anneliese is recalling her reflections in chapter XVIII (178) on the early years of her own children.

page 192 — "Commit thy way unto the Lord"
Frau Hutscher quotes Psalm 37:5, translated here according to the King James version. The version in the Luther Bible reads: "Befiehl dem Herrn deine Wege."

page 192 — "For it is written: expect the unexpected"
In fact, Frau Hutscher is repeating a "saying" (thus, not quoting a "written" text) common since the seventeenth century, "Unverhofft kommt oft" (literally: "the unexpected often comes/occurs"). The phrase has a variety of possible translations, the one offered here deemed a close equivalent to the rhyming German phrase ("hofft"/"oft") by dint of its repetition of "expect."

page 193 — "And mortality touched her with the sting of death."
The "sting of death" here anticipates Anneliese's later full quotation of I Corinthians 15:55 on page 199.

page 195 — "Had she stopped opening her piano at all — spreading her wings"
The original ("Öffnete sie denn ihren Flügel — ihre Flügel — überhaupt nicht mehr") would translate literally as "Did she no longer open her wing — her wings — at all any more." Branhardt's question involves a wordplay on the use of the German word "Flügel" (wing) both for a grand (or baby grand) piano, deriving from the instrument's shape, and for the figurative, musical "wings" that Anneliese "spread" or "opened" when she played for him, as in chapter II, page 11, where the instrument is referred to as a "Stutzflügel" (baby grand piano).

page 199 — "Death! Where is thy sting! Anneliese thought silently to herself."
Anneliese's thought alters only the punctuation of I Corinthians 15:55. Having just experienced a sense of death's being "extinguished" by love (198), Anneliese is recalling a famous declaration of faith from the New Testament. Beginning at I Corinthians 15:51, the King James

version includes these words: "We shall not all sleep, but we shall all be changed. In a moment, in the twinkling of an eye, at the last trump; for the trumpet shall sound, and the dead shall be raised incorruptible, and we shall be changed . . . Then shall be brought to pass the saying that is written, Death is swallowed up in victory. O death, where is thy sting? O grave, where is thy victory?"

6/21